BLOOD and IRON

ALSO BY JON SPRUNK

Shadow's Son

Shadow's Lure

Shadow's Master

JON SPRUNK

BLOOD and IRON

THE BOOK OF THE BLACK EARTH
—— PART ONE ——

an imprint of Prometheus Books
Amherst, NY

Published 2014 by Pyr®, an imprint of Prometheus Books

Cover image © Jason Chan
Cover design by Grace M. Conti-Zilsberger
Map by Rhys Davies

Inquiries should be addressed to
Pyr
59 John Glenn Drive
Amherst, New York 14228
VOICE: 716–691–0133
FAX: 716–691–0137
WWW.PYRSF.COM

18 17 16 15 14   5 4 3 2 1

Library of Congress Cataloging-in-Publication Data

Sprunk, Jon, 1970
    Blood and iron / Jon Sprunk
        pages cm — (The book of the black earth ; part 1)
    ISBN 978-1-61614-893-5 (pbk.)
    ISBN 978-1-61614-894-2 (ebook)
    1. Imaginary wars and battles. I. Title.

PS3619.P78B56 2014
813'.6—dc23
                                                2013037702

Printed in the United States of America

This novel is dedicated to Jenny, my love and inspiration.
Thank you for accompanying me on this crazy dream called life.
And to our son, Logan:

My son, ask for thyself another kingdom,
For that which I leave is too small for thee.

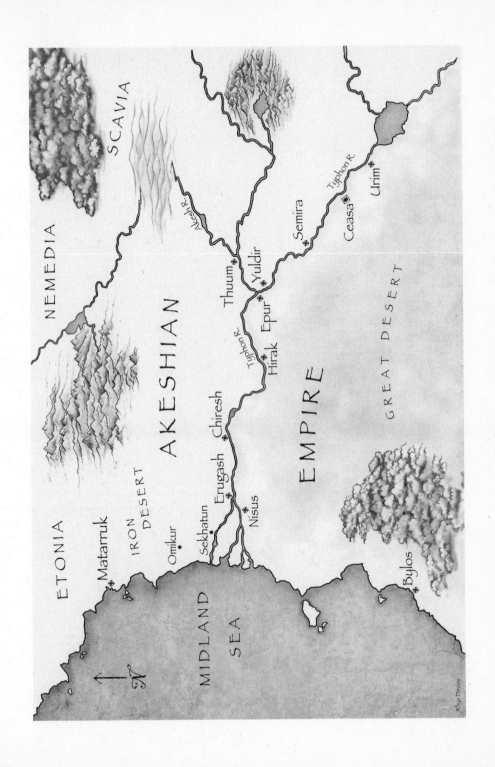

Never forget that the tiger in the cage is still a killer, for the tiger has not.

—Akeshian proverb

CHAPTER ONE

Lightning split the night sky above the masts of the *Bantu Ray*. Thunder boomed amid the driving wind, shaking the carrack's timbers, and then darkness returned to smother everything.

Horace Delrosa braced himself against the bulkhead of the staircase as the ship heaved portside. As the ship righted, he hauled himself up the last steps to the hatchway. Mountains of black water surged around the ship and poured over the gunwales to wash across the deck. Sailors clung to their posts, with two brave souls aloft in the rigging trying to secure a loose topsail. Up on the sterncastle, Captain Petras shouted commands into the winds.

Horace had signed on with the *Ray* as her master carpenter three months ago. Joining the war effort had seemed like an ideal way to flee from the ruins of his old life and start anew, but it hadn't worked out that way.

He flinched as a large hand clamped on his shoulder. Andrega, the bosun's mate, was bare-chested and soaked to the bone. "How do you like the squall, landsman?" he asked. His broad smile revealed orange-stained teeth and gums.

Horace shoved the bosun's hand away and shouted over the wind. "I've got every hand below on a bilge pump, but Belais says we have trouble."

"Trouble, aye. We picked up an admirer."

He followed Andrega's pointing finger with his eyes but couldn't see anything following them, although he knew other ships were out there. The *Ray* was part of a six-vessel flotilla transporting soldiers from Avice to the crusader state of Etonia, from there to take the fight to the unholy heathens of the East. They had risked a late passage across the Midland Sea to join the Great Crusade before winter.

They both jumped as another fork of lightning sizzled across the sky and a huge shape materialized a hundred fathoms behind the carrack.

What in the name of the Hell . . . ?

The unfamiliar vessel was at least twice the size of the *Bantu Ray* and rigged for battle. Dark faces framed in ruddy lantern light peered down from her forecastle amid points of gleaming steel.

Andrega chuckled. "Aye, you see. We're running with the wind now, but soon we'll be fighting for our lives. Best make sure you're ready."

Horace looked again to the *Ray's* rigging. Several of her sails were torn away, flapping like angry wings as the crew worked to take them in. A tall wave crashed against the hull, and the carrack listed onto her side, every board groaning with the strain. Lightning flashed, and a burning sensation rippled down the center of his chest. Horace sagged against the open hatch as the afterimage of dancing lights faded from his vision. That last flash of lightning had been a ghastly green shade. He'd never seen anything like it. He rubbed his chest as the sudden urge to hit something came over him.

"All hands!"

The captain's cry lifted Horace to his feet. He ducked back through the hatch and stumbled down the steps. A sickening odor assaulted him as he reached the main hold, which the crusaders had converted into a barracks. His gaze went immediately to the seams, checking for leaks. A gray-haired sergeant sat on a footlocker near the front of the long deck, drawing a whetstone across the edge of his infantry sword. He glanced up as Horace entered. "How's it look topside?"

"Not good. There's an enemy ship closing on us. The captain wants everyone on deck."

"Can we outrun it?"

"Maybe on a calm sea if the ship was in top condition. But we've been taking a drubbing from the storm, and I'd say we're barely making four knots."

The sergeant spat on the floor where his sputum joined the mélange of bilge water, vomit, and urine covering the planked deck. "Most of these men can't even stand up without loosing their bowels, much less fight."

Horace looked through the forest of swinging hammocks where men tried to sleep amid the groaning wind. Many soldiers clutched wooden buckets as the ship heaved and rolled. A young priest stood in their midst, chanting a prayer in Old Nimean.

"Those are some scars for a carpenter." The sergeant pointed at Horace's hands with his whetstone. "They might make it hard to hold onto a blade when the sweat and blood start running. You'll want to find some gloves before the fighting begins. If it comes to that."

Horace looked down at the masses of scar tissue across both his palms and up the undersides of his fingers. They were a constant reminder of a day he wished he could forget, of a life he would never get back. "Not for me. I'll be below, keeping us afloat."

A sick feeling fluttered in Horace's stomach as he said that. He'd spent a lifetime living on and beside the water, but this was the first time he'd ever felt like he might die at sea.

"You believe all those things they say about 'Keshian warlocks?" the sergeant asked as he went back to sharpening with a brisk *whisk whisk* of stone across steel. "'Bout how they're all eunuchs and the first thing they do when they capture a man is shear off his marbles? I'll tell you one thing. They won't take me alive. Not a chance."

Horace thought of the green lightning flashing across the sky and the hulk of the enemy ship closing in. He had to get these men topside if they were going to survive. "Get them moving, Sergeant. We don't have much ti—"

The deck bucked under their feet. The sergeant stumbled, and Horace caught him by the arm. "Much obliged, son. Tell the captain I'll gather the men, but he needs to buy us more time."

"Just hurry."

Horace started back up the staircase. The upper hatch swung open before he got halfway up, and a river of water sluiced down the steps, drenching him to the waist and getting into his boots. Cursing, he barely managed to hold onto the railing without getting swept away. The hatchway above him was a black hole without starlight or a lantern's gleam to guide him. Then Horace's stomach dropped through the floor as the stairs tilted under his feet. The carrack was tipping backward like a fish balancing on its tail. His arms were almost yanked from their sockets as he held onto the railing with a death-grip. Hand over hand, he pulled himself up to the hatch.

The waist deck was empty except for two sailors huddled against the starboard capstan. The captain and both mates stood at the helm, staring into the storm. Horace looked past them to the great black leviathan rising behind them. The enemy ship was close enough to exchange arrow fire, though none was offered. Any minute it would be close enough to board.

Another bolt of ghoulish green lightning slashed across the sky. Flames rose fifty yards off the port side as another ship in the flotilla caught fire. Its sails went up like paper, billowing black smoke. Horace couldn't make out the name on the side, but he thought it might be the *Albatross*. Then something snapped above his head with a violent crack. Horace turned as the smell of burning cloth engulfed him. Then an explosion of light and sound hurled him off his feet. Pain burst inside his head like a thousand knives carving into his skull. He tried to yell, but a fist of water slammed into his face. The tide lifted him up and plunged him down into a bath of icy blackness.

Stunned, he tried to swim to the surface, but he had no idea which way was up, and his limbs were slow to respond. He kicked until something hard rammed into his back. His mouth popped open, and seawater rushed in. As he fought against the darkness that threatened to descend over him, memories flashed before his eyes. Images of fire and blood twisted his insides into painful knots as the faces of his wife and son floated before him.

Sari! Josef!

Horace reached out to them as a quiet calm washed over him. The pain was soothing. The storm raged somewhere beyond his senses, but it couldn't touch him anymore. As he sank down in the darkness, the pain in his head dwindled to a dull ache that flowed down to encompass his entire body. He heard a distant sound like the words of a prayer echoing in his mind.

His last sensation was the current pulling him along, just another piece of jetsam in the cold of the deep.

Horace dreamed he was back in his old home in Tines. He was lying in the bedroom he shared with his wife on the second floor of the narrow townhouse.

If he was lucky, Josef would sleep late and allow him some time alone with Sari. Horace reached out beside him with a smile. Reality seized him as his fingers encountered only hard-packed earth and not the warm body he'd expected. He sat up, heart hammering in his chest, as the memories came crashing back—the storm, the enemy ship, and then washing overboard.

But I'm alive.

Sweat soaked him under a thin white sheet, which was the only thing concealing his nakedness. He sat on a pallet on the floor in a small room about the same size as a ship's galley. The walls and ceiling were dried mud. There was a door near his feet and a slatted window over his head through which entered a balmy sea breeze and the faint rumble of crashing waves. His clothes were folded beside him—the navy-blue shirt and black breeches of his uniform. His boots had been cleaned of salt and spray.

He wanted to stand but didn't think he had the strength. He was wrung out like he'd gone ninety rounds with Iron-Belly Friedmon. He couldn't remember anything after the storm. Where was he? Etonia?

Smells of food rose from a tray beside his bed. He lifted the cloth cover to find a small loaf of brown bread and a clay cup. Horace lifted the cup and sniffed. The amber liquid inside had an earthy smell. Too thirsty to care what it was, he drank, spilling some down his chin. The taste was bitter and malty, almost like ale but heavier. He drained the cup in two long swallows.

He was wolfing down the bread when the door opened and an old woman entered. She was so thin and bent over that he almost took her for a child at first. She picked up the tray and carried it away without a glance at him. He was reaching for his shirt when she returned a few moments later with a broom which she used to sweep the narrow space of floor with brisk motions.

"Pardon me," Horace said. "Can you tell me where . . . ?"

But the old woman left again without looking at him and closed the door behind her.

Horace pulled on his breeches. He was starting to suspect he wasn't in Etonia but somewhere south along the Akeshian shore, and that meant he was in trouble. He didn't need to recall the chilling tales of the soldiers onboard the *Bantu Ray* to know he couldn't expect to live long in enemy custody. His hands shook as he slipped on his boots. He had been a fool to join the crusade, even as a ship's crewman. He knew nothing of fighting. His life before had been filled with books and building plans. Yet even as hopelessness threatened to overwhelm him, he felt the old familiar pain—the loss of his family— enclosing his heart like steel armor. He clung to the grief like a lifeline because it was the only thing he had left.

Steeling himself, Horace tried to stand up. First he climbed to one knee and then slowly straightened up. His stomach clenched a little, but the discomfort went away once he was fully upright. He expected the door to be locked or otherwise secured, but it opened at his touch.

In the larger room beyond, three people glanced up from seats around a low table. Like the cell where he had awakened, this room also had mud walls and ceiling, but the floor was covered in overlapping carpets woven in beautiful designs and colors, including a rich indigo purple that was difficult to obtain and highly prized in Arnos. To see these works of art used to cover the floor of such a mean home was jarring. The people around the table included a man about Horace's age, a woman who might have been his wife, and a boy about eight or nine years old. All three had the same dusky complexion and curly black hair. The woman and boy wore undyed homespun clothing. The man was bare-chested, showing off a lean, wiry frame. He had an imposing black beard and deep-set eyes.

Horace stood there looking at the people, and they stared back at him. Then a curtain of beads parted, and the old woman came into the room. She carried a large clay bowl from which came an appetizing aroma both sweet and spicy. She stopped when she saw Horace, and the man stood up. "*Sar alakti*," he said and beckoned with a curt sweep of his hand. He wore a white linen skirt.

The old woman shuffled to the table. As she sat down, the man motioned for Horace to come as well. Horace hesitated. The suspicion that this was an elaborate setup lurked in the back of his mind. There was another door to his left, made of dark wood and inset with a shuttered peephole. It could be a way out, though he had no idea what he would do if he got free. In his weakened condition, he didn't think he could outrun even the old woman. The smells coming from the bowl convinced him to stay, at least for now.

The table was lower than he was used to and surrounded by plush cushions instead of chairs, but once he was settled, he found it quite comfortable. The boy said something to his mother that sounded like a question. She shushed him as she uncovered the serving bowl and began ladling out portions. The man was served first, and the next bowl was set before Horace. He leaned down to inhale the steam rising from a soupy yellow concoction. He could identify rice and chunks of white meat, possibly some kind of fowl, but the spices didn't smell like anything he'd ever encountered. He looked around for a fork, but there was nothing in front of him. The others held the bowls to their mouths and used their right hands like spoons. After watching them for a few seconds, Horace fell in with gusto.

His tongue exploded with the first bite. It tasted like a combination of savory and hot spices much stronger than the usual cumin or cloves found in Arnossi food. He wanted to take the time to savor it but found himself eating as fast as he could shovel it in, devouring the entire bowl in moments. He licked his fingers before noticing the others were staring at him. Embarrassed, he put down the bowl and wiped his hand on his shirt. He watched them eat, trying to learn as much as he could about them. They spoke little during the meal, and, of course, he couldn't understand a word of it. Their language was completely unlike Arnossi or Nimean, or the smattering of Altaian he spoke.

Everything about this experience—sitting with this family, eating their food—felt odd. Was it possible they were just trying to make him feel welcome? Why should they? He was a stranger. No, there was some deception at play.

After a few minutes, Horace stood up. Every eye at the table followed him as he went to the door, but no one tried to stop him. Horace pulled on the wrought iron latch, and the door swung inward with a long squeal. He blinked as bright sunlight poured through the doorway. He started to step outside when two men appeared in his way. Both wore their hair cropped down to the scalp, leaving a short mat of black fuzz. They wore simple smocks and skirts, but each man also held a spear and a small, round shield of animal hide stretched over a wooden frame.

"*Sekanu ina'bitum!*" one of them shouted as he raised his spear.

BLOOD AND IRON

Horace retreated behind the threshold. Beyond the armed men he saw a village of wooden huts, reminding him of any number of fishing hamlets along the coastline of Arnos, except for the bronze-skinned people walking past. He glimpsed a hill on the far side of the village, topped by a house that was larger than the others. Constructed of brown brick, it appeared to be all one-story with a flat roof and arched windows. One of the guards pulled the door closed.

"Isu ka annu."

Horace looked down at the old woman standing beside him, holding out a clay cup. The rest of the family watched from the table. Suddenly concerned by what these people must think of him, he took the cup with a nod. The drink was cool and mild-tasting. He was touched by her kind gesture, but he could not help wondering what these people had in mind for him.

Horace followed the old woman back to the table. The wife refilled his bowl and placed it before him. The father continued to watch him with an intense gaze. Horace was reaching for the bowl when a staccato of hard knocks shook the front door. Someone shouted from outside. Horace's stomach sank as the husband leapt to answer it. Four men wearing burnished steel breastplates and conical helmets tramped into the house and took up positions around the room. Short swords hung from their broad leather belts. Horace started to get up, until the one of the soldiers put a hand on his sword hilt and glowered at him.

The young boy looked at Horace with fearful eyes and shook his head. Horace settled back onto the cushion. He was getting agitated, but there didn't seem to be much he could do about it. He still felt as weak as a child, and a dull pain had taken up residence behind his forehead.

Then another man entered the house. He wore a leather cuirass chased with silver accents. The pommel and guard of the curved sword at his side were silver, too, which must have cost a fortune, but Horace didn't think it could be very practical. By the deference shown to him, the new arrival was obviously in charge. The family all bowed to him, the father going down on one knee.

The father and the man in command exchanged a few words. Horace sat, frustrated, while they talked and cast meaningful glances in his direction.

At one point, the old woman made a loud sigh and looked down at her half-empty bowl.

Horace finished his drink and made as if to stand up, but stopped as the soldiers drew their swords. The wife gasped and pulled her son close.

Horace raised his hands, careful not to make any threatening movements. "I can't understand a word you're saying. I'm just a sailor shipwrecked on your shore. Do you know what happened to my—?"

The commander drew his sword. The women gasped as he laid the blade alongside the father's neck. Looking at Horace, he shouted, "*Asar ulukur, pur maleb!*"

"I don't know what you want!" Horace yelled back.

The commander grunted and sheathed his weapon. Then he and his soldiers left the dwelling. The two peasant guards peeked inside with wide eyes before closing the door behind them. Murmuring something, the father walked out through another beaded curtain, leaving Horace alone with the women and child. The old woman whispered to the boy and gestured to his food, while the wife stared at the table without making a sound.

With a sigh, Horace got to his feet. He wasn't hungry anymore. No one paid him any attention as he went back to his small cell. He slammed the door a bit harder than he intended, but the loud thump soothed his temper. He sat down on the thin mat and tried to envision a way out of this place, but after a few minutes the heat and his fatigue lulled him into lying down. Soon he fell asleep.

CHAPTER TWO

Jirom reeled back with blood pouring into his right eye. He blinked it away as he retreated. He blocked a hard jab and grimaced as the iron spikes protruding from his opponent's gloves gouged long furrows down his forearm.

Boos rained down from the stands where workaday freemen of the empire stomped and swilled from clay mugs. Their betters sat in shaded wooden boxes along the top of the tiny arena, fanned by slaves and served wine from silver chalices. Jirom would've killed for a flagon of beer right now.

A blow to the ribs knocked the air from his lungs and left stinging gashes along his side. Jirom covered up and circled away, and the crowd continued to make its displeasure known. His opponent was called the Lion. He was ferocious, young, and as strong as his namesake. With his light complexion and proud, hawkish nose, he could have passed for a member of the upper caste except for his iron collar and the sigil—three diamonds joined in a triangular pattern—branded on the right side of his face that marked him as a permanent slave, unable to ever regain his freedom again. It was possible his family had sold him into slavery as a child, or he'd insulted the wrong person. There were many ways to end up a slave in Akeshia, as Jirom well knew. Most gladiator bouts—whether fought with sword, spear, or bare-handed—didn't last long because the fighters were criminals or slaves who had sinned against their masters. They usually died their first time out, fed to the more experienced gladiators. But the Lion was a different breed. Jirom didn't know his story, save that he'd been brought down from Chiresh for these games. That meant money had been invested in him—a lot of it.

Jirom blocked a right hook that would have caved in his head, and more blood poured down his arms. As he stepped back from a straight-armed jab, his shoulders hit the rough boards of the arena's eight-foot-high partition. A hard punch to the gut nearly forced him to drop his guard, but he saw the follow-up to the head and slipped away. Something wet and sticky struck his back. Rotten pomegranates and oranges landed around him, making pulpy divots in the sand. Jirom looked into the stands. In one of the private boxes, a portly, middle-aged man with deep brown skin was talking to an equally portly, slightly older patrician. The first man was Jirom's owner, Thraxes, so engrossed in conversation that he wasn't even watching the bout.

A grunt warned Jirom in time to cover up before a powerful clout smashed against his temple. He staggered, his vision fading into black-and-white spots, before righting himself. Through the speckled haze, he saw the Lion drawing back for another blow. Jirom slipped past a punch aimed at his chin and pushed off to make some space between them. More jeers rocked the arena.

"Come on, you dog!" someone in the stands taunted. "Fight!"

Jirom slapped away another punch and continued his slow retreat around the pit. The familiar twinge in his lower back from an old injury climbed up his spine, making every movement that much more painful. He glanced up to the private boxes at the wrong moment, and his opponent charged with a hoarse bellow. Jirom covered his face as he backpedaled, but a couple punches got through, drawing more blood. His feet got tangled up, and he fell hard on his backside. A kick to the back as he rolled over sent jangling shocks of pain down his legs. His opponent stood over him with arms raised to the crowd, and the onlookers showered him with adoration. Thraxes was still engrossed in his discussion.

Jirom crawled to his knees as the Lion paraded around the arena. His opponent didn't give him time to fully recover before charging at him again. Jirom circled away to his left, always the left, and more boos came down from the stands. The people wanted to see death.

His or mine, it doesn't matter whose.

Another hard blow almost knocked Jirom down again, but he kept his footing. The Lion came after him, relentless and seemingly inexhaustible. If anything, his attacks were getting stronger and more confident. Jirom glanced up. Thraxes was now standing in front of his seat. With a bored expression, the slave owner yawned and scratched his ample belly. That was the signal.

About time, you fat bastard.

The Lion unleashed another straight punch with a growl. His eyes widened as Jirom caught the fist with an open hand. Air exploded from the Lion's mouth as Jirom drove his other fist into the younger man's ribs. A punch to the back of the ear dropped the Lion to his knees, and the next one laid him out flat with blood trickling down his branded cheek.

Jirom felt the rage churning inside him. Breathing through his mouth because his nose was clogged with blood, he knelt down and wrapped both arms around the Lion's neck. With a heave, he twisted until he heard the spine snap with a sharp pop. The crowd roared with approval.

Cheers and a few copper coins fell from the audience as Jirom walked to the gate, but he ignored them. As he traveled down the dark tunnel to the slave cells, scores of feet pounded on the boards above his head.

The sweltering chamber at the bottom of the tunnel was filled with men, some standing, others sitting on benches. Most wore little more than a loincloth and a layer of sweat. Moldy sawdust covered the floor. The veteran gladiators called this area the Temple for all the prayers these walls had heard.

Jirom sat down and peeled off his gloves. His arms were lacerated by dozens of cuts and punctures. More injuries crisscrossed his torso, but none of them looked serious. A comely slave boy approached with a basket of bandages torn from old, bloodstained clothes. Jirom leaned back as his wounds were smeared with a thick liniment and wrapped up.

A bulky Akeshian called Fat Rabok shuffled past. His tight leather breeches squeaked with every step. "You live to fight another day, Jirom. Eh?"

"So it seems."

Rabok shrugged, his thick shoulders nearly touching his neck. "That is a good thing, my friend."

Jirom chuckled, feeling the tension of the fight leave his body. "Perhaps."

The slave boy's hand crept up his thigh to tickle under his loincloth. Jirom swatted it away. He was too tired for sport . . . for now. "The gods smile on you, Rabok. And grant you a swift death when the time comes."

The hefty fighter laughed and slapped his hands together. "The gods can go bugger themselves for all I care."

As Rabok headed up the tunnel toward the arena, Jirom closed his eyes. The noise of the crowd grew as the gate opened and then died away with its slamming shut. Every inch of his body ached. His bones ached. Yet the cuts and the bruises would fade. Seven months of fighting in these small-town arenas, and before that twenty-odd years of selling his sword from the steppes of Scavia to the shores of the Western Ocean—soldiering under so many flags he couldn't remember half of them—had left him with a weariness inside that never healed. When his company was captured after a campaign along the Isuran border, every fighting man was given the choice of chains or crucifixion. Jirom chose slavery. Now he was still fighting for money, but this time with a brand on his face and an iron collar around his neck. Yet it was better than the alternative.

Hearty laughter jarred him from his thoughts. Jirom opened his eyes as his owner entered the Temple. Thraxes waded among the gladiators, talking to his fighters and those he wanted to acquire. For an owner, he was well-liked in the pits. The slave boy darted away.

"Jirom, my champion!"

Thraxes pursed his lips in an imitation of concern as he looked over Jirom's battered frame. The expression almost looked convincing, if you didn't know him. "The mighty warrior from the south wins again. Very impressive." He patted his heavy purse. "And *very* lucrative."

"And you'll be keeping my share again?"

"Ah, Jirom. You know slaves are forbidden from keeping money. Otherwise, I would be honored to share the winnings. But one day perhaps you will be free, and then you will be a rich man."

Jirom curled the bandaged fingers of his left hand into a fist. "I'd settle for killing you."

"Is that any way to treat the owner who just secured you a fight in Sekhatun?"

Jirom lowered his hand and closed his eyes again. Thraxes lied as easily as a Myrish trader. "Go away before I do something we both regret."

"I swear upon the Sun Lord himself, this is the truth. The man I was sitting beside today, do you know who he is? Mituban, chief proctor to Lord Isiratu! He was very impressed with our performance."

"With me, you mean."

"Of course! He said he would speak with His Magnificence about bringing you to the imperial gladiator circuit. Sekhatun isn't Ceasa, but it's a damn sight better than this cesspit."

Jirom opened one eye. "You're selling me?"

"Think of it as an opportunity. To fight in the imperial circuit before all the lords and ladies. You might even earn your freedom someday. Then who will you thank?"

With a grunt, Jirom settled back against the wall with the urge to throttle his owner burning in his gut. But he was too tired to move. "Bring me some beer."

Thraxes slapped him on the shoulder and laughed. "Only the best for my champion!"

As the man left to the clap of fine leather sandals over the dusty floor, Jirom considered his future. More fighting. More crowds craving blood. More pain until the day he fought someone better. Then, if he was fortunate, a quick death and a shallow grave. His breath left his lungs in a heavy rush. This wasn't the life he'd imagined. But what could he do?

If I was ten years younger, I'd break out of this place. Maybe go back south and offer my spear to another company.

Jirom climbed to his feet, feeling every day of his thirty-six years. He held up his battered hands and eyed the cuts down his arms, across his body. How much longer could he survive like this?

The roar of the crowd burst into the room as the gate opened. Fat Rabok emerged from the tunnel, covered in blood and sweat. His right hand was bare, the fighting gauntlet torn away, but he was smiling broadly enough to light up the dim chamber.

"You live," Jirom said, "to fight again."

Rabok slapped his belly with his free hand. "Aye. And tonight I will feast and fuck and wake up tomorrow to do it all again."

Jirom walked through a low doorway and down a narrow corridor toward the gladiator cells where—if Thraxes wasn't lying—a pitcher of beer waited for him. Maybe he'd send for the boy to come visit him after all, if he didn't fall asleep once his head touched the mattress.

Overhead, the ceiling's boards trembled as the crowd welcomed another pair of fighters.

CHAPTER THREE

On the third day after he awoke in the village, Horace was allowed out of the house where he'd been confined since his capture. He didn't know what had changed, but he was grateful for the reprieve. Walking along dirt pathways between the huts, he felt almost normal. His weakness had left him by the second morning, thanks to a steady diet of bread, rice, and the malty beer these people drank with every meal.

This morning he'd been given a new set of clothes in the native style, a skirt of homespun weave, a lightweight tunic, and a pair of sturdy sandals. At first he'd felt silly putting on the skirt, which ended just below his knees, without anything underneath except his loincloth. He couldn't help imagining what a stiff wind would expose, but after a little while he'd begun to feel more at ease. The material was cooler than his wool uniform, the sandals more comfortable than military boots.

The past couple days he had tried to make the best of his situation. He kept his eyes and ears open, hoping to learn about his captors. He still anticipated that he might be rescued or escape, and the information could be useful.

Seagulls cawed as he strolled about. Two peasant spearmen shadowed his footsteps. There seemed to be a rotation among the house guards, but he'd begun recognizing their faces and given them each a nickname. Today he was guarded by Potato, named for the unfortunate shape of his head, and an old man Horace had taken to calling Grandfather, who looked to be at least eighty years old and had only two front teeth, both of them brown. Horace tried to ignore them as much as possible. The beach was half a mile on the other side of the large hill that dominated the center of the village. Horace shaded his eyes and looked up to the house atop the tor. No flag flew from the rooftop. Though he was sweating under the hot midday sun, Horace decided to satisfy his curiosity and started toward the mound at a quick pace. His guards hurried to keep up. Grandfather puffed with every other step and used his spear as a walking stave.

BLOOD AND IRON

His guards stopped him before he could reach the big house, but Horace didn't mind. He'd really just wanted the view. The hill was steeper on the western side facing the ocean. Horace looked out to the water, hoping to see a set of familiar sails, but the skyline was unbroken. The sea was sapphire blue under the bright sunlight. White-capped waves slapped against the shore, empty except for several fishing boats. He didn't know exactly where he was, but he guessed it was well south of Etonia. The fleet must have swung off-course during the storm and run into Akeshian waters.

Despite the gorgeous day, he couldn't help thinking back to the night of the storm. The black clouds swirling over the ship, the wind roaring in his ears, the strange green lightning, and then the sudden shock of hitting the water. He should have drowned, but instead he'd been saved. Was that the hand of the Almighty? Notwithstanding what the priests back home said, he'd never felt the divine at work in his life before. And why him? The mere thought of redemption dredged up painful memories from his old life.

Pushing the dark thoughts away, Horace looked down on the beach where a group of fishermen hauled their boats out of the surf. One was the father of the family sheltering him. He looked much like any of the fisherman Horace had seen in his lifetime in Arnos.

Is that the face of my enemy?

Horace turned to his guards. Potato was scowling as if angry for the exercise, but Grandfather leaned against his spear like he had no better place to be. With a nod to them, Horace headed back.

A group of armored soldiers was gathered outside the home of his hosts when they arrived. When they sighted the walking party, the soldiers surrounded Horace. The door opened, and the wife slipped out with a small bundle wrapped in white cloth. She ran up to the soldiers, and they allowed her to extend the bundle to Horace. He took it. The cloth was warm to the touch. Inside was a small loaf of bread.

Horace nodded and said, *"Kanadu." Thank you.*

The wife went back inside. Her son's small face peered out the slatted window. The family had been kind to him during his brief stay. He wished them well.

The soldiers goaded Horace onward. They turned down a path that led to a large circle of bare ground outside the village. A dirt road led away to the east. Several peasant men in simple smocks and skirts stood in a ragged line beside the circle. Each carried a wicker basket strapped to his back. Horace was made to wait while the soldiers stood about, chatting to each other. He looked for a piece of shade to escape the midmorning sun, but there was nothing convenient unless he went back into the village, and it didn't seem like they would allow that. So he stood by himself and tried to be patient. The air was redolent with the odor of fish coming from the baskets.

After a bell, or half an hour, the clop of hooves sounded from the village. An older soldier in heavy armor walked ahead of a procession of oxen. The animals were piled with bundles and boxes. Behind them rode a man on horseback. Horace recognized him as the commander who had come to his hosts' dwelling three days back. He looked more regal atop his white steed, which was possibly the most elegant horse Horace had ever seen. Its limbs were slender, its lines sleek and graceful, unlike the more muscular horses he'd seen back home. A round steel shield, its face polished to a mirror shine, hung on the saddle.

The commander spoke, and the soldiers formed a square around Horace. With hand motions they urged him to start walking down the road. He gazed down its length and saw nothing but barren land stretching into the unknown east. Away from the sea and home.

He stood his ground. When he did not move, the soldiers cast glances between themselves. The peasants whispered in hushed voices.

One of the soldiers, who had two bronze slashes emblazoned on his breastplate, looked to the commander and then hurried over to Horace. He pointed down the road. *"Kanu harrani sa alaktasa!"*

Horace crossed his arms and stayed where he was. He wasn't going to follow them like a sheep to his own execution or whatever deviltry they had planned. If they wanted him to move, they'd have to carry him.

The marked soldier grabbed him by the shoulder with one hand and shoved. Horace kept on his feet by twisting around. Everyone was watching. Horace stood up straight and crossed his arms again. The officer's face bunched into a fierce expression. He drew back his shield. Horace lifted his arms to protect his face, but a shout rang out.

"*Kima parsi saalak!*"

Horace braced himself as the commander climbed down from his horse. He considered trying again to communicate but didn't have time to form any ideas before the commander walked over and struck the officer across the face with an open hand. The officer stood at strict attention without responding. Horace curled his hands into fists, feeling the tug of the scars on his palms, when the commander turned to him.

If he raises a hand to me, I'll punch him in the mouth. I don't care if it gets me killed.

But the commander merely pointed down the road and spoke a long string of unintelligible words in a calm voice. Horace lowered his arms. He could continue to resist, and probably be tied over the back of one of the oxen, or fall in line. By the time the commander climbed back into the saddle, Horace decided that going along was the wiser course. He started walking.

After a while, he calmed down and started to enjoy the sensation of moving in a specific direction. Since waking up in this strange land, he'd felt lost. He still didn't know where he was going, but he was going *somewhere*. The road was mainly packed sand. Although not as impressive as the stone highways of his homeland, relics from the days when the Nimean Empire had ruled most of the civilized world, the road was straight and level. But there were no markers that he could see, no way to tell what lay ahead.

The soldiers set an easy pace, spears resting on their shoulders. They had the look of professionals. Their gear was well-maintained, and they possessed the easy manner of men long accustomed to their duty. The officer, who stalked around the formation as they marched, actually appeared younger than the rest of the soldiers. The commander was younger, too. Horace guessed they were both in their mid-twenties, which would make them about the same age as him. Their banter reminded Horace of his time spent hanging around the crusaders. If he ignored the difference in languages, he could almost believe he was back aboard the *Bantu Ray*, listening to their war stories. To hear the soldiers tell it, there had always been hostility between the east and west, but a sudden increase in piracy on the Midland Sea a few years ago had convinced the western nations to expand their navies. When Arnossi warships inevitably encountered Akeshian vessels, the conflict turned to war. No one was sure which side attacked first, but soon afterward the fathers of the True Church preached that Akeshia was an evil realm that needed to be conquered and converted. When Prelate Benevolence II called for a holy war, the faithful responded in the tens of thousands, boarding ships to seek their salvation in a far-off land.

Sweat ran down Horace's face. The sun burned near its zenith, battering him with its rays. He'd never felt heat so intense in Arnos, not in the worst days of summer. As they traveled inland, the ground became rocky and barren. The few trees to be seen were dry, leafless things with claw-like branches. An hour past midday, even walking had become a chore, and Horace found himself swaying with every step. He didn't realize the column had stopped until he almost ran into the soldier in front of him. Horace put out a hand to steady himself, and got it slapped away with a harsh word, but he was too tired to complain. His throat felt like it was choked with dust.

A peasant walked down the line with a bucket and gave every man a drink from a ladle. Horace licked his lips until it was his turn. The warm water tasted of wood and metal, but he gulped down his share anyway and eyed the drops that fell on the ground with longing. The commander remained in the saddle and flicked his quirt at flies while a peasant watered his steed. The rest of the villagers sat on their heels at the rear of the group, weighed down by their burdens. After a couple minutes, the officer barked a phrase. The villagers jumped to their feet and got back in line. The soldiers formed up, and the company set off again.

Horace didn't know how much longer he could go on. His feet dragged. His head began to ache. Finally the sun sank behind the plains, and the commander called for a halt. Horace collapsed on the hot ground, his legs shivering and twitching. When the water-bearer came by, he barely had the will to lift his head. The water splashed off his lips, most of it going into the earth, but he was too exhausted to care. Another man handed out bread. Horace took a piece and held it to his chest as he closed his eyes.

BLOOD AND IRON

It would have been easy to fall asleep, but he didn't. He estimated they had traveled about twenty miles today. Tomorrow they would likely travel twenty more, getting farther away from the coast with every step. He couldn't let that happen if he ever wanted to see home again. He had to escape.

Footsteps crunched nearby and then faded around to the other side of the camp. Horace cracked open his eyes. The peasants had bedded down around the fire. Most of the soldiers had done the same, except for the commander, who sat apart from the rest, leaning back against his saddle on the ground. The officer spoke with the sentry pacing around the camp, and then lay down in the open space between the commander and the men. Snores whispered around the camp as people fell asleep, one by one. All except for the sentry, who marched in a wider circle with his spear propped on his shoulder.

Horace counted as the trooper performed his watch. Each circuit around the camp took him between eighty and one hundred breaths to complete. Horace lay still as the sentry came around again. When the man had passed by, Horace stole a quick glance around the camp. All heads were on the ground. This was his chance.

He crawled away from the fire on his hands and knees. Darkness enveloped him within ten paces. After another ten, he stopped and listened. There was nothing to indicate that he'd been seen leaving. No cry of alarm. He took a moment to orient himself, using the rising moon to locate due west. Then he took off.

Though his legs were tired from hiking, a renewed rush of energy coursed through him. The light of the stars and moon was enough to guide him across the uneven ground. Following the road directly was too obvious; they'd catch him for sure. His captors might expect him to head north toward Etonia, so he chose to go south for now. Horace trotted at a quick pace but did not run. He had to conserve his strength. Come morning, he wanted to be back at the coast. He would avoid settlements as he made his way westward, except for stealing what food and water he needed at night.

While he made plans for survival, his right foot caught in a hole he thought was just a shadow. Horace pressed his lips together to suppress a yell of surprise as he pitched forward. He caught himself as he landed, and something pierced the palm of his left hand. With a muffled shout, he climbed to his feet clutching that hand. He didn't feel any blood, but it hurt like hell. Massaging the injury, he started off again, this time being more careful of divots. He spent more time watching the ground than his surroundings, but the landscape was not much to look at, especially at night. A couple times he spotted the glow of yellow eyes in the distance, but they vanished before he got close. Something fluttered off to his left—perhaps a bird taking flight— but he didn't see anything move. As Horace looked back to the ground in front of his feet, loud hoofbeats pounded a dozen paces ahead of him. A bright light appeared from a shuttered lantern to reveal a rider on horseback.

Horace sprinted to his right. The commander wheeled his steed around and raced alongside him. Horace zigged around a low bristle bush and tried to put some distance between them. He was watching the commander's approach out of the corner of his eye when something hit him square in the chest. Stars burst before his eyes as he fell backward. The edges of his vision turned black like he was losing consciousness, but he was still awake when he struck the ground with enough force to rattle his teeth. A dark silhouette stood over him holding a club. Horace groaned as more soldiers appeared. They picked him up by the arms and dragged him back.

The peasants were all awake when they returned. They watched as the soldiers dumped him beside the campfire. Horace folded his legs underneath him and wondered what was going to happen next. He expected he would be tied up to keep him from running again. He'd heard rumors of things that were done to runaway slaves, including permanent maiming. He hoped they wouldn't take it that far.

The commander conferred with the officer, and then one soldier—the one who had been on sentry duty—was seized. He was stripped of his armor, and ropes were tied around each of his wrists. As two soldiers held his arms outstretched to their fullest extension, the officer produced a short, thick whip with four leather tails. Horace's stomach coiled into knots as he eyed the fearsome instrument. The punishment was swift and brutal. Horace flinched at the first strike, which tore a long furrow across the sentry's shoulders. He started to turn his head, but a soldier kneeling behind him grabbed him by the hair and forced him to face forward. Another soldier placed the point of a dagger against his throat. Horace had to watch as the whip cracked again and again, until the victim's back was a mass of oozing stripes. The sentry grunted with each strike, but did not scream.

When it was over, the victim was released. He crawled over to his pile of gear and collapsed. The soldiers holding Horace let him go. He glanced around as he rubbed his neck where the dagger had pricked him. The camp was returning to how it had been before, although this time three soldiers were put on sentry duty, two patrolling in circuits while the third stood nearby, watching over him. Horace ground his teeth together. The peasants were lying down again; some had even fallen asleep already. The commander was back in his blanket while a soldier groomed his horse. It was all orderly and neat.

Horace wanted to shout at them. He wanted to scream in their faces. However, he was too exhausted to make the effort. Weary deep down in his bones, he lay down on his side facing the fire. The flames danced, slowly turning the pile of dung biscuits into black ash. Stray thoughts stole across his mind. Memories of his family, sharp as daggers. He pulled them close as he drifted into a troubled sleep.

Horace awoke with a sense of ominous dreams, convoluted and portentous, but could remember none of them.

The ground was cool beneath him. The officer walked among the group, shouting and kicking the men awake. Water and bread were distributed. Horace accepted both this time, his thirst and hunger driving him to make the best of the situation. The commander sat apart on a small cushion, eating something from a wooden bowl. When everyone had been fed, they started off again.

A soldier remained by Horace's side all day. His feet were still sore from yesterday, but he kept up with only a slight limp as the sun climbed higher and the temperature rose. He was able to sit up and take his evening meal with the others. He listened to the peasants talk in hushed voices while they ate. Although he couldn't understand them, by watching their gestures and listening to their tones, he imagined they were complaining about having to hike in the dust behind the soldiers.

One of the peasants saw him watching them and called it to the others' attention. They stared at him until he turned away, feeling even more isolated. He sighed as he laid down. Three paces away, a soldier stood watch.

The stars shone like beads of molten silver. Many nights he'd sat on the *Ray's* deck, staring up at the sky like this. Horace imagined what his life might have been like if he hadn't taken the carpenter's post. Without something to occupy his time and his skills, he probably would have drunk himself to death by now. His mind worked backward to happier times, in Tines before the outbreak of plague, back when he was still working in the royal shipyards. Every evening he'd return home to listen to his wife tell him about her day and play toy soldiers with Josef on the rug in front of the hearth. It seemed like a lifetime ago.

The next day they sighted a river, mud-brown and wider across than a bowshot. It came up from the south and ran due east. Small boats plied its waters, some with sails and others powered by long paddles at the stern. Huge fields of gold and brown stretched from its banks for miles on both sides. Peasants in long skirts walked among the rows of wheat and barley, plucking weeds and ministering to an ingenious system of ditches and wooden dams that conducted water from one field to another. Like the peasants of the village, they seemed not so different from the serfs of his homeland. There were men and women working together, old and young, and even some children, all sharing the labor. Large, hive-like buildings with no windows were scattered among the fields.

Horace was so intent on his surroundings that he didn't notice the town they were approaching until the officer shouted an order and the column picked up the pace. Jostled along, Horace craned his neck to see. Buildings appeared a couple miles ahead of them. The settlement sat on a table-flat plain. The outer wall formed a perfect square protecting an area not quite as large as Tines, which was small as northern ports went, but many towers and narrow rooftops were nestled together inside the walls.

The company closed the distance in less than an hour. Horace was soaked in sweat by the time they reached the walls. The gate guarding the road was open, but a squad of men-at-arms in steel breastplates stood before it.

The commander reined up before the sentries and exchanged words. Horace eyed the waterskin hanging from the commander's saddle and was considering making a grab for it when the sentries finally waved the column through. Passing under the gate's shaded archway was a blessing, but a momentary one. The heat met him again on the other side as he was herded through crowded streets lined with rows of cloth awnings and recessed door-ways. Because of the closeness of the avenues and the height of the buildings around him—some rising five or six stories above the street—Horace couldn't make out much of the town beyond the jagged skyline. Most of the buildings were constructed of brick and had flat roofs. The streets were dried mud, pitted with potholes and wheel ruts, though they were cleaner than he might have guessed. Horace wondered what they did with the sewage. He had never seen so many people pressed together, not even in the markets of Avice. They streamed past him on both sides like schools of fish.

The commander led the party down several twisting streets until he stopped before a door that didn't look much different than any other. It was painted green, but the town had doors and window shutters of all colors. Horace noted a pictogram drawn above the lintel, of a black horseshoe with the open end down and a horizontal line drawn under the legs.

The commander went inside. The rest of the soldiers fanned out around the doorway, facing outward, while the peasants crouched in the shade of the building and swatted at flies. On the other side of the avenue, a team of young boys with sticks were corraling a herd of goats.

Horace leaned against a wall and wondered when the pleasantries would end. For the most part, his captors had treated him well, but he was an enemy on their soil. He expected imprisonment, quite possibly involving torture, followed by a summary execution. That was how his homeland would have handled a prisoner of war unless they had some hope of ransom. Horace studied the soldiers. Did these people assume he was a high-ranking officer? They shouldn't have, considering he had been shipwrecked in a simple seaman's uniform. It was a stretch, but possible. He could play the part of a landed aristocrat, if it would get him back to civilization.

The door opened, and three young men with short-cropped hair hurried out. Each wore a long skirt, like the men in the fields, but of bright white cloth embroidered with crimson scrollwork along the hem, and no shirts. Their smooth chests glistened in the bright sunshine like oiled clay. The young men ushered the soldiers inside with many bows and nods, and they brought Horace with them.

The door led into a roofless courtyard paved in mosaic tile. A small fountain burbled against the wall to his right, surrounded by leafy plants and young trees planted in clay pots. Oblong yellow fruit hung from their branches. Horace looked up to several balconies above, their iron handrails framing a square of azure sky.

Voices approached, and the commander entered through a wide archway on the other side of the courtyard accompanied by a heavyset man with a sagging gray mustache. The hem of his simple robe swept across the floor. The commander indicated Horace, and the older man clapped his hands. Two large men wearing cloth kilts and leather harnesses entered. Each had an iron collar around his neck and a short sword hanging from his side. At a word from the old man, they came forward and grasped Horace by his arms. He didn't have time to resist before they hauled him through a side archway and down a flight of dark steps. Not that resistance would have helped. The muscular guards handled him with ease, walking him down a hallway and down another flight of stone steps. The air was cool down here, at least. The light became scarce, but when they tossed him into a small room, he was able to see by way of a narrow window in the ceiling.

The sound of the door shutting was almost enough to break Horace, but he stood in the center of the cell and listened as the guards barred the entry from the outside. The floor and walls were hard stone blocks. The ceiling was just a couple inches over his head, which made him want to duck.

Horace inspected the window, but it was far too small to allow for any chance of escape. So he lowered himself to the floor and sat with his elbows propped on his raised knees, staring at the door. After a few minutes his gaze wandered down to his hands, drooping before him. The patches of scars glowed pale white in the ghostly light. He traced their rippled contours with his gaze as he waited.

CHAPTER FOUR

The wagon rumbled down the hard-beaten roadway. Jirom picked at the scabs on his arms as he looked out through the iron bars. The rattle of chains and the clop of hooves drowned out the breeze and the buzzing insects flying past his cage. The sun was only halfway to its zenith, but already the day was sweltering. Not so hot as the desert, yet still enough to drive a man mad.

His scalp itched, too, where the hair was growing in. He'd kept it shaved for years, but he didn't think anyone was going to give him a razor after what he'd done. Breaking the jaw of a smart-mouthed drover on the first day of the journey had been satisfying, but now they kept him in the cage night and day. He ate in the cage, slept inside it, and shit and pissed through the hole in the floor. He'd long since gone nose-deaf to his own smell.

Standing up, he met the gaze of Umgaia in the next cage. Their wagons were linked together and pulled by the same train of oxen. Umgaia smoothed her luxurious hair over her shoulder and winked at him with the single eye in the center of her forehead. "It's soon time for another show."

Beyond her wagon, the brick walls of a settlement emerged from the dusty savannah. Another village, another show. Chief Proctor Mituban was, among other things, a procurer for his master, Lord Isiratu. The wagon train held tribute from a dozen holdmasters, as well as some curiosities that Mituban had encountered during his trek around the territory. At every stop along the road to Sekhatun, the caravan displayed its oddities to the common people.

Jirom leaned against the bars of his cage as the wagon train rolled past the fields and pastures surrounding the village. The smell of manure clung to the air. He had seen hundreds of settlements like this in his soldiering days. Akeshia was said to be the world's breadbasket for good reason. Every year shipments of wheat were sent to nations near and far, and Akeshian merchants brought back a wealth of cotton, timber, and gold. It wasn't difficult to believe that someday her armies would march to the far corners of the earth. Long ago, that notion had inspired Jirom to take up a spear and seek his fortune, but a series of misadventures, and some poor choices on the part of his employers, had set him on another path.

He settled back onto the floor and rested his back against the bars. The gladiator circuit was renowned for its brutality. If he was fortunate, he'd get put against a few young bucks like the Lion with more muscles than sense, but eventually he would be pitted against someone better. It was just a matter of time.

When the caravan reached the village, a crowd had gathered. Looking out over their brown faces, Jirom remembered his childhood and the bubbling excitement he'd felt whenever someone new came to his tribe's remote corner of the world. That same excitement was reflected in the eyes watching him pass.

The wagons stopped at the village center and pulled into a semicircle. Caravan guards went around, watering and feeding the animals. The doors of the lead wagon opened, and Chief Proctor Mituban appeared, wearing a long robe of ivory-white with a crimson sash around the middle. The village elders kept their distance until Mituban beckoned them closer.

"Come and see," Mituban said for everyone to hear, "the wonders I have collected for our lord and master!"

Jirom didn't move as Mituban walked past his cage, introducing him as "the cannibal gladiator from the dark heart of Abyssia!" even though he'd never been to that land. Umgaia was billed as "the fabled cyclops of Sidon." People gawked as they passed by, pointing and laughing. Jirom suppressed the desire to reach out and strangle the first person to stray within arm's reach. Instead, he sat back and closed his eyes, and tried not to dwell on the humiliation. He had been a soldier and a warrior, but now he was an animal in a cage. Something hit him in the shoulder and rolled off. He looked down at the dry turd on the floor beside him and clenched his hands into fists.

Don't give them what they want. Just sit back and think of something else.

After a meal of hard bread and a cup of water, the menagerie packed up. The oxen were re-hitched, and the wagons rolled out past the crowd of watching villagers. Jirom chewed on his crust and simmered.

The sounds of pipes and laughter floated through the camp. The oxen murmured in their roped enclosure. Wagon drivers and guards sat around the fires, passing skins of beer back and forth.

Jirom wrapped his shirt around the lock of his cage door. Earlier in the day, while the guards grew lax under the afternoon sun, he'd grasped a fist-sized rock from the ground and hidden it under his shirt. All afternoon he had contemplated what to do. Fight his captors and likely be killed? Perhaps. Dying on his feet had long been his professed ideal, but these past few years he'd come to understand that even a life of degradation was better than death. He'd thought about escaping every day since his capture, but never with much optimism. Anyplace beyond the reach of Akeshian justice seemed too far away. And there was the matter of his brand, which wouldn't be easy to hide. He couldn't walk around with his face covered for long without raising suspicions.

He watched the sentries. When they wandered to the far side of the camp, past the chief proctor's pavilion, its white silk walls glowing in the moonlight, he slammed the rock against the lock. The muffled clang sounded loud to his ears. He hunkered down and waited, but no one came to investigate.

A desert owl hooted somewhere in the darkness.

He struck again. This time his blow glanced off, and he hit his knuckles on a bar. Hissing, he swung again and froze as a metallic snap echoed through his cage. He waited for a dozen pounding heartbeats and then pushed. The cage door swung open.

Still clutching the rock, he hopped down. The feel of solid ground under his feet was a relief. He took a step but halted as he saw Umgaia watching him. She sat near the edge of her cage, wrapped in a blanket. They looked at each other for a moment, and then she flicked her hand toward the darkness beyond the camp. *Get away.*

He went to her door instead. She watched as he tested the bars. The lock on her cage was older than his, probably because Mituban didn't think her likely to escape. Jirom hit it before he could talk himself out of it. The lock's metal face bent on the first blow and cracked open on the second. He opened the door and held out a hand, but she backed away. Jirom heard the footfalls behind him an instant before the whip slashed across his shoulders.

He turned and swung at the sentry standing behind him, not realizing he still held the stone until it collided with the guard's temple. Bone crunched, and the guardsman crumpled to the ground like an empty sack. Jirom stood over the body, weighing the stone in his hand. It suddenly felt much heavier. He tensed at a touch on his flayed shoulder.

"You must go, gladiator," Umgaia whispered.

"Come with me."

"No." She smiled and was transformed into a true beauty despite her deformity. "Out in the world I would just be a beggar, not even fit for a whore. Mituban feeds me well and his men leave me alone."

Before he could stop her, she scurried back into her wagon and closed the door.

Fool of a woman.

With a last look at her, he turned toward freedom and stiffened as several shapes emerged from the darkness. The sentries hemmed him in, their spears leveled. Jirom looked over his shoulder. Three guards brandishing stout clubs came around the corner of his wagon.

Jirom hefted the stone. A fierce heat rose in his chest. This was his moment. Fight to the death. Feel his enemies' blood on his hands. Scream out his rage and loathing as he fell beneath their spears.

Jirom opened his hand and let the rock fall to the ground. He braced himself, but the club striking the middle of his back still drove the wind from his lungs. A spear butt barely missed shattering his kneecap as it knocked him off his feet, and then he was under a pile of pummeling fists and bludgeons. When they hauled him to his feet, blood poured from his face and dripped down onto his bare chest. The guards dragged him back toward this cage, but a voice stopped them.

"Here. Let me see him."

They held Jirom up by his arms as the chief proctor came out from his pavilion. The top buttons of his robe were undone, revealing a patch of black hair. He sipped from a slender glass as he strode over to them. "What's all this?"

Two sentries hauled the body of the man Jirom had killed into the light. Mituban's gaze went from the corpse to Jirom. "How dare you raise your hand to one of my servants, slave? You are the property of Lord Isiratu!"

Jirom said nothing. Mituban stepped closer, peering into his eyes. "I can see you are nothing more than a beast, unfit for the company of men. I would have you executed, but that pleasure belongs to His Lordship. Believe me, before the end you will beg for d—"

The rage exploded inside Jirom. With a violent shudder, he threw off the men holding his arms. A red haze blurred his vision, but through the fog he could see Mituban on the ground, grasping at the large hands clutched around his neck. Jirom wrenched, and the lord's struggles ceased. His wine glass lay broken in the dirt.

A sharp crack echoed in Jirom's ears, followed by a red-hot pain at the back of his head. As he slumped forward, the last thing he saw was the chief proctor's expression of complete surprise.

CHAPTER FIVE

Horace was dreaming the familiar dream again.

"Hold on!" he shouted over his shoulder as he pushed through the crowd.

Everywhere people were jostling, shoving, and yelling as they pressed toward the gates. Men, women, and children—the entire population of the Trade Quarter—were all trying to get out at once. He squeezed Sari's hand as he looked back.

"We're going to make it out," he told her.

The terror was plain in her wide blue eyes. That same fear was reflected in every face around them as word of the plague's arrival spread throughout the port town of Tines. The crowd was edging toward a riot, and his family was stuck in the center of it.

Josef squealed in his mother's other arm. "Fes-ti-val, daddy! Go to fes-ti-val!"

Horace tried to smile, but it was difficult with the anxiety governing his thoughts. "It's not a festival, Josef. We're going on a trip."

"Trip, trip!" the boy shouted as he started to squirm. "Want to get down! I can walk!"

Sari hugged the boy tighter. "Not yet, darling. We have to get out of the city."

She looked into Horace's eyes, and he redoubled his efforts to get them through the throng. Yet after ten minutes he was forced to concede that they weren't getting anywhere. He couldn't even see the walls yet, and he was beginning to fear that the nearest gates had been closed.

They wouldn't do that. It would sentence thousands of people to die.

Horace stood up on his toes. The air was humid from the press of bodies. Some people were shoving each other. Curses and threats rose above the din of the crowd. He had to get his family out. Then his gaze strayed to the cliffs overlooking the town—the pale cliffs of Tines—and he knew where they had to go.

"Come on!" he shouted as he ducked past a bearded man struggling under a heavy sack.

"Horace!" Sari yelled, but he didn't stop to explain.

He pulled her and Josef out of the street, into the shelter of a dim alleyway. The buildings on either side crowded out the sky. Horace knew the general direction they needed to go, but they'd have to hurry. They passed an old couple helping each other down the refuse-cluttered alley. When the old man coughed into his hand, Horace held his breath and hauled Sari along faster.

He almost fell to his knees and kissed the ground when they reached the waterfront, and at the same time he wanted to slap himself. As a shipwright, escaping Tines on an outgoing vessel should have been his first thought. He scanned the many berths, and a sinking sensation pooled in his gut at the sight of so many ships that had already put out to sea, their billowing sails waving good-bye. Flames danced at several spots on the piers where other vessels had been put to the torch. He could guess why. Signs of plague onboard. While soldiers in city livery set another ship alight, clusters of sailors crowded the boardwalk, shouting and waving their fists, no doubt as terrified as he was at the idea of being stranded here.

"Horace, do you think we'll find anyone to take us on?" Sari asked.

"I think I know someone who will."

"Boats!" Josef screamed with joy. "Boats, daddy!"

"That's right, my boy. We're going to ride on a ship."

Squeezing Sari's hand, Horace led them along the quay. Fishermen were hauling their belongings aboard their shallow craft in preparation to depart. Horace kept moving with long strides, trusting his instincts. Calbert would take them, if he was still at port.

A weight lifted off Horace's chest as he sighted a familiar yellow mast at the end of the waterfront. The *Sea Spray* was still nestled in her berth. Horace had spent two weeks refitting the merchant frigate, and during that time he had gotten to know her crew. He hoped they remembered him fondly. He pulled harder on Sari's hand to urge her along while Josef continued to yell "Boats!" at the top of his lungs.

They passed a gang of sailors loading barrels onto the *Spray*. Captain Calbert stood on the ship's waist, exhorting them to work faster.

Horace raised his free hand. "Captain! Captain Calbert!"

The middle-aged sea captain squinted in their direction. He held up a finger to the marine standing beside him with a loaded crossbow. Horace stopped in his tracks and gathered Sari behind him. "Captain, it's me. Horace Delrosa."

A smile creased the captain's lips. "Shipwright! I'd ask what you're doing down here at a time like this, and with that pretty lass who must be the wife you've been telling us about, but I think mayhap I can guess."

"We need passage out of Tines."

Calbert climbed down from the ship. "Aye. I can fathom that much, but there's orders come down from his lordship saying that any ship that takes on townsfolk as passengers will be set alight."

Horace looked to the burning hulks along the waterfront, proof that it was no idle threat. Shouts arose as the two-masted schooner in the next berth was set on fire. Horace tightened his grip on Sari's hand as a melee erupted between the sailors and soldiers not more than thirty paces from where they stood. "Please, captain. They've shut the gates. I can't keep my family here. It's not safe."

The captain shook his head. "I understand what you're going through, but that don't change the weather, if you take my meaning."

"Captain," he said. "I don't have much money, but if you'll take my family to your next port, I'll serve as your ship's carpenter for a year without wages."

"I'd like to help, son, but—"

"I'm begging you, sir. If I'm serving on your ship, that makes me crew, so no laws are broken. My wife can wash and cook, too."

Calbert sighed as the flames climbed up the neighboring schooner's sleek sides. "All right. I can't leave you behind to face this unholy mess. Get on board."

Horace clapped a hand on the captain's arm before leading Sari and Josef up the gangplank. Sailors hustled across the deck carrying tackle and provisions, hauling on lines, and scrambling through the rigging. Horace pulled his wife into a spot of relative calm beside the forecastle ladder and hugged her close. Josef pulled on his hair, eager to see the goings on. All the anxiety Horace had held pent up came out in a long breath.

"We made it," Sari whispered.

"Aye. Soon we'll be underway."

"Where will we go?"

Horace turned to the railing. Distant noise echoed from the city. Above the fortified walls, the white cliffs sparkled in the afternoon light. He could see the shipyards past the breakwater. In the huge dry dock beside the warehouses and port offices sat his latest creation, a four-masted ship-of-the-line. "It doesn't matter. We're safe."

Josef wriggled free of Sari's grasp and ran across the middeck. Horace laughed as his wife chased after the little hellion and shaded his eyes for a better view of Tines. The town was in shambles. Come nightfall, those still trapped inside the walls would realize their fate, and then things would get truly ugly. He tried not to think of all the friends he was leaving behind—the men of his work crew and their families. The only saving grace was that both his and Sari's parents were already gone, so they would be spared this nightmare. His family was safe, and all he could do was pray for those left behind.

The opening door woke him.

Horace jerked upright as two soldiers entered his cell. By the light coming down the narrow window chute, he guessed it must be morning. He didn't resist when the soldiers indicated he should come with them.

They escorted him back to the open court inside the house. After spending the night underground, the sun felt wonderful on his face. They went outside to the street where the commander sat astride his steed talking to the older man. The rest of the soldiers were assembled behind their leader, but there was no sign of the villagers.

After a few moments, the commander finished his conversation, and the company got underway. Horace was famished, but his thirst was even worse. He thought about using gestures to ask one of the soldiers for a drink, but they weren't wearing their field kits. No waterskins or packs; just armor, weapons, and shields. Like they were marching into battle. That got his attention.

The streets were packed with people, mainly commoners carrying produce and driving domesticated goats and oxen. There were few horses, making the commander stick out. People moved aside for him, or perhaps it was the multitude of spears marching behind him. The company paused at an intersection of broad avenues as a pair of palanquins with gauzy silk curtains crossed in front of them. The men bearing them were naked save for breechclouts and sandals. Their oiled limbs gleamed in the morning light. Horace noticed that each bearer also wore an iron collar. He hadn't made the connection at the townhouse between the old man and his muscular bodyguards, but now it was clear.

Slaves.

Slavery wasn't unknown. The practice had been legal centuries ago under the old Nimean Empire, but many of the western nations outlawed it after they broke free of the imperial yoke. Yet slavery was evidently still alive and well here in the east. He couldn't help but imagine what it would feel like to wear a metal collar.

The company entered a large open square. The buildings facing the plaza were grander than most of the others Horace had seen so far, but the palace directly across from where he stood was by far the most ostentatious. Though not very tall—three stories at most—it sprawled across the entire length of the square with a double row of columns supporting an impressive entablature that reminded Horace of classic imperial architecture with eastern accents.

At the center of the square, hundreds of workers struggled with a rope-and-pulley crane to erect a stone statue. Horace couldn't tell what it was going to be, but based on the four massive legs rising from the base, the final product would be gigantic. A small crowd watched the construction, but most of the people seemed to be here on some kind of business. Merchants hawked their wares from tents and wooden stands to shoppers passing by. The clamor echoed off the brick and stone walls.

The company made their way through the teeming masses to face a line of soldiers guarding the entrance of the grand palace. The commander dismounted to present a small clay tablet, and the soldiers waved them through.

Beyond the arcade of columns, two tall bronze doors stood open. Stone statues flanked the entrance. The effigies were bizarre, having human heads with long, curled beards on lion bodies. They were also quite old by the look of them.

Through the doors they passed into a long atrium. Rectangular skylights open to the heavens illuminated the chamber. The walls were covered in vibrant paintings depicting a procession of people bringing various goods—sheaves of wheat, fruit baskets, even a herd of sheep—to a huge building that Horace initially took for a palace. Yet he soon realized it was a temple. There, men in yellow vestments took the spoils and placed them on a burning altar, where the smoke from the offerings was inhaled by a row of towering men and women on tall thrones. A great sun dominated the sky above the tableau.

Horace would have liked to study the drawings, but his escorts pressed onward. They climbed a broad staircase to the second floor and entered an antechamber where a group of people waited—men in crisp white shirts and kilts with necklaces of gold and lapis lazuli; the women in colorful gowns, some of them so sheer Horace had to stop himself from staring. Before he could make a fool of himself, he was ushered through another doorway into a more spacious chamber.

Chill air met him at the threshold, like he had stepped out into a frosty autumn evening in southern Arnos. Horace froze while the sweat from the day's heat cooled on his face. A high ceiling and large windows along the far wall made the room feel open, as if they had gone outside onto a shaded veranda, but the breeze was not enough to explain the sudden drop in temperature.

It has to be my mind playing tricks. Maybe I've suffered some kind of heat exhaustion.

Shivering slightly, he followed his escort farther into the chamber. The floor was pale hardwood, polished to a high sheen. Three men sat on cushioned divans, with sentries and slaves posted along the walls. The man seated in the middle had a gray mustache and beard, both trimmed and brushed neatly, but his head was completely bald. He wore a brocaded shirt with gold stitching that couldn't disguise his stocky build and a long skirt down to his ankles—all in black silk. Wide pads flared out from his round shoulders like wings. The man sitting on the left was also bald, but his gleaming scalp was stamped with several tattoos in carmine ink, the most notable being a sunburst over his forehead. His robes were golden yellow with ivory buttons down the front and tied with a white slash. The third man was the youngest of the group, perhaps fifteen or sixteen years of age, but he already had a full mustache. Of the three, he was the only one who still sported a full head of hair, pulled back in an oiled queue. The young man's eyes were a light—almost clear—shade of brown.

The commander bowed. The older man greeted him with a nod and indicated a spot on the floor beside them. A slave scurried over with a cushion, and the commander sat down with his ankles crossed. No one offered Horace a cushion. He stood while the seated men talked. From time to time they glanced in his direction. At first he ignored them. Yet, as the minutes passed, he began to resent this treatment. After the commander described, with emphatic gestures, a terrible storm with thunder and lightning, the eldest man spoke at some length to the one in yellow robes. When he was finished, the robed man turned to Horace and shocked him by speaking in fluent, if slightly stilted, Arnossi.

"What is your name?"

Horace hadn't heard his native tongue spoken since the wreck. He fumbled with a response before answering, "I'm Horace. Who is—?"

Yellow Robe spoke to the elder before Horace could get out his question. The older man replied, and then Yellow Robe said, "You are part of the Arnossi fleet sent from Ah-vice, yes?"

The man had an odd pronunciation of Avice, but Horace understood him well enough. "Yes. Where am I?"

Yellow Robe cut him off with another question. "How does your nation intend to invade the land of the black earth?"

"What's that?"

"The empire which you call Akeshia."

"Who are you? And how do you come to speak Arnossi? No one else around here seems to."

"I am Nasir et'Alamune-Amur, counselor to Lord Isiratu." He nodded to the elder man in the center seat. "I serve as a translator as well as his lordship's spiritual guide."

"So why am I here?" Horace asked. "What do you plan on doing with me?"

Nasir turned his head as the older man spoke, and then said, "Lord Isiratu requires that you draw a map of all the invader strongholds in Etonia and along the northern shore of the Great Sea from Miktonas to—"

Horace hardly listened to what the man was saying. "My ship sank off the coast five days ago. Do you know if anyone else survived?"

Nasir frowned, which pulled the bare skin of his scalp taut. "Lord Isiratu requires—"

"Damn you!" Horace stepped between the two soldiers guarding him. "Tell me if anyone else survived!"

Nasir licked his lips with a narrow tongue, and Lord Isiratu spoke rapidly. Horace noticed the younger man watching him intently with his light eyes. The youth hadn't said anything up to this point, but he must be important if he was sitting here with the lord.

"Please," Horace said to the youth. "All I want is to know if any of my countrymen survived."

The others stopped talking and looked to the young man. Then Lord Isiratu nodded with a short grunt. Nasir said, "One other foreigner was found on the beach, but he died not long after."

Horace sighed. So that was it. He was alone. Without preamble, he sat down on the floor, hunched over his folded legs. The four seated men gazed at him in astonishment. The commander, his face turning crimson, reached for his sword, but a terse word from the lord stopped him.

Nasir cleared his throat. "Lord Isiratu wishes to know why you addressed his heir." He nodded to the youth. "Lord Ubar."

"I didn't know what else to do. He just seemed . . . I don't know. Decent."

The young man spoke to his father, and then Lord Isiratu rattled off several long sentences in a gruff voice, ending with a slashing hand gesture. Nasir looked to Horace. "My lord repeats his request that you divulge the locations and strengths of your invader strongholds."

"Are you a fucking parrot?" Horace asked.

"Pardon?"

"Never mind. Tell your lord I have no information. I don't know of any strongholds in this part of the world because we never made landfall on account of the storm."

Horace frowned as Nasir translated. Lord Isiratu was staring at him, eyes narrowed, his mouth bent into an impatient frown. Horace met the intensity of the lord's gaze without blinking. "And furthermore, tell his lordship that even if I did know these things, I wouldn't tell him for all the gold in the world. Now, if you're going to kill me, just get it over with."

The commander said something, and Nasir replied, but Horace was focused on Lord Isiratu. Their gazes locked in a battle of wills. Horace squinted, digging in. He'd be damned before he stooped to cowering before this foreign satrap. Yet within moments he felt a strange pressure across his forehead, stretching from temple to temple. He started to reach up to touch it when another spot began to throb behind his left ear. Together they hurt like the worst headache he'd ever had in his life. He ground his teeth together and tried to ignore the pain, but it only increased. Then he saw a peculiar expression on Isiratu's face, as if he were looking at someplace far away in the distance even though their gazes were still entangled. It was unsettling, and a strange thought crossed Horace's mind.

He's doing this to me.

Horace was ready to discard the thought. Yet it might also explain the coolness of this chamber. Magic.

No. No. That's crazy. There's no such thing—

However, the more the pressure in his head grew, the more he began to believe it might be true. The lord was affecting him without touching him. A chill ran through Horace that had nothing to do with the temperature.

He's touching me with Light-be-damned sorcery.

He'd heard tales of eastern witchery, but experiencing it firsthand was a far different matter. It made him feel dirty inside, like he'd been cut open and soaked in a vat of festering slime. Everyone else had fallen silent. His eyes held captive, Horace couldn't see anything except Isiratu's face, rigid with effort. Horace tried to move, to break the contact, but his body didn't respond. He was trapped as the pressure in his head increased. Any moment the lord would break him, and he suspected he wouldn't enjoy what happened afterward. A growl clawed its way up Horace's throat, but then something caught his attention. A fold of skin in the corner of the lord's mouth was widening. In less time than it took to draw a breath, it split open into a raw, red crevice. A bead of blood welled from the cut. Horace watched it dribble down the lord's chin. Then something popped in the back of his head. A torrent of anger, lying just beneath the surface of his emotions, flared up inside him. He hated these people, especially this haughty aristocrat with his unholy powers. All of a sudden, Horace's arms and legs were free of the eerie paralysis. He leapt without thinking, diving toward the lord with both hands extended.

Isiratu's eyes widened, but he seemed too shocked to even raise his arms in defense. The soldiers failed to react in time to stop Horace, but something intervened as he closed his fingers around the stocky lord's throat. Cold and hard as iron, it clamped Horace around the middle like a vise and tried to pull him away, but he shook it off. Droplets of blood flew from Lord Isiratu's flabby face as Horace's first punch landed with a wet smack. The nobleman fell backward, and Horace fell onto top of him to continue his assault, swinging both fists. Then a gaggle of men piled on them, and the melee devolved into a jumble of flailing arms and legs.

Horace was hauled off Lord Isiratu and dropped on his back. His right cheek hurt from where someone had kicked him, and he was sure he had bruises down his back and sides. There was no sign of what had grabbed him, but his tunic was wet around the middle.

He started to get back up, ready to renew the fight, until a dozen spears and swords were leveled at him. A shudder wracked his body as the powerful impulse to kill receded, leaving him weak and confused. The soldiers and bodyguards looked ready to murder him out of hand. The commander was on his feet with sword drawn, his face red and angry. Nasir and Lord Isiratu looked aghast, like they had just seen the Prophet dancing naked with their daughters. But the young lordling appeared neither shocked nor upset. Instead, his expression appeared curious.

A slave brought a linen cloth for Isiratu, who wiped his face as he shouted something that Horace assumed were the orders for his execution. The soldiers closed in around Horace. He curled up to protect himself, but they merely picked him up and carried him out of the chamber.

Lord Isiratu's fierce gaze followed him out.

CHAPTER SIX

The subterranean chamber stank of feces and rot mingled with moldering straw, as if its last occupant had died within, which Horace suspected might have been the case.

His new cell was not as large as the last one, and the lack of windows left it decidedly darker. The walls were stone blocks fitted together with very thin lines of mortar. He could barely reach the ceiling on his tiptoes. He had been given an old blanket, which he used as a pallet over the cold floor stones. He tried sleeping—God knew he was tired enough to sleep for days—but every time he closed his eyes he saw the same graphic image of himself wrestling on the floor with his hands wrapped around Lord Isiratu's neck. Finally, he stood up and used the piss-bucket in the corner.

After relieving himself, he went to the door. It was heavy with rough beams bound in rusty iron. Long grooves were scratched down the wood like someone had tried to claw their way out. Horace tried not to think about what could drive a person to that. He had enough problems without adding madness.

Starting with why in the Almighty's name did I attack Isiratu? It was the worst thing I could have done. Now they're sure to cut off my marbles, followed by my head.

He could still recall the pressure that had squeezed his skull when the Akeshian lord stared into his eyes, and the incredible rage that had accompanied it. Now, hours later, he found it difficult to believe that Isiratu had been using some kind of mentalism on him. It was more likely that he'd been feeling the effects of prolonged exhaustion and thirst. But it had felt so real.

Horace pounded on the door. He listened for footsteps or voices, but nothing came through the thick beams. He kept at it, alternately punching and kicking. After several minutes, a metallic clatter announced that he had been heard, and the door swung open. Harsh yellow light from a lantern blinded him, and he retreated a few steps with his hands held over his face.

"*Minu shomana?*" a rough voice demanded.

BLOOD AND IRON

"Water! I need some Prophet-damned water!"

The turnkey, or whoever he was, shouted something else and then slammed the door. Horace resumed pounding, but the guard didn't return. He stopped when his hands became too sore to continue. Finally, frustrated and more tired than before, he sat down on his blanket. They obviously didn't intend to kill him, or they would have done it already.

Unless they're devising a public execution.

He dozed off with his back against a wall. The clatter of the door lock woke him abruptly. Instead of the jailor, a slim man entered. He wore only a simple linen kilt and leather sandals and carried a candle instead of a lamp. Still, the tiny flame seared Horace's eyes. The man set something down on the floor and took the piss-bucket with him as he left. There was a splashing sound, and then the man returned with the empty bucket.

Horace stood up.

"Can you help me?" He switched to Nimean but still got no response. Then he noticed the iron collar around the man's neck. Another slave.

The slave left without saying a word. Horace lunged for the door, but the turnkey reappeared and slammed it shut in his face. The sound of the lock turning made Horace sick to his stomach. He beat on the door and shouted until his throat ached. Then he roamed around his cell, blood pumping and fists clenched.

It was a long time before he was calm enough to inspect the bowl the man had left on the floor. Sitting on the blanket, he dipped his fingers inside and felt a cold, sticky goo. He tasted it with the tip of his tongue. The substance had a consistency like gruel but no flavor. He finished the bowl in three large finger-scoops before he remembered the cup. It held tepid water, which he gulped down. Then he sat on the floor. With nothing else to do, he drifted off again.

When he woke he couldn't tell if he had slept for minutes or hours. He'd dreamt of home. Lying on the cold blanket, he clung to the memories, replaying the better ones again and again in his mind even though they scoured his soul. He recalled the day of his son's birth, savoring every moment of that experience until at last he came to the part when the midwife placed

Josef in his arms for the first time. He rolled over and pressed his face against the stone wall as tears gathered in the corners of his eyes.

After another sleep, he relieved himself in the bucket again and tried to suck a few drops of water out of the empty cup. He licked the dried film of gruel from the bowl. Then he dozed some more.

The opening door jarred him awake. Horace sat up and blinked as a pair of soldiers entered. They grabbed him by the arms and hauled him out of the cell. He hung limp in their grasp as they shuffled him past rows of doors, from some of which issued faint groans and muttered whisperings. The guards carried him up many steps until a golden glow appeared above. Even before he could feel it on his skin, Horace knew it for sunlight. He started walking on his own, feeling the strength return to his legs. By the time they passed through the doorway and out into the light, he was standing upright.

They brought him out to a walled courtyard. The sky was glorious blue like a sheet of glass without a trace of clouds. The clay pavement was hot, but after the chill of his cell, Horace reveled in the warmth. A line of twenty or so men and women waited in the courtyard under guard, chained together by the neck. They varied in age from young adult to a couple old enough to be his grandparents. All of them appeared to be Akeshian, or easterners at any rate.

Horace was hauled to the end of the line where a squat man in a leather apron waited. The smith held up an iron collar, open on one side. Horace tried to pull back, but the guards wrestled him to the ground. He bucked and kicked as the cool metal slid around his neck, but the guards didn't relent until the collar had been hammered closed. When they finally released him, he sat up and put his hands to his neck. The collar was thicker than his thumb and heavy. A rivet sealed the opening where it fit together.

The soldiers hauled Horace to his feet and connected him to the back of the line by attaching a heavy chain to his collar. None of the other chained people bothered to look back at him.

Horace was tugging on the chain, testing its strength, when a racket of creaks and clomping hooves announced the arrival of a large wagon pulled by a team of four oxen. The wagon was painted scarlet red with brass accents and tall wheels. Two drivers sat in the front, one holding the reins, and the other an unstrung bow with a quiver of arrows between his feet. A company of soldiers marched behind the wagon in double file.

A large hand parted the gauzy curtains that covered the wagon's window, and Lord Isiratu peered out. His son and the priest sat inside with him.

Horace shaded his eyes and asked no one in particular, "What's going on?"

One of the guards wheeled around and punched him in the side of his face. Points of light flashed before Horace's eyes as he fell back on the hard ground. Glaring at his attacker, he put a hand to his throbbing cheek. He itched to respond in kind, but the surrounding guards eyed him with obvious anticipation.

Before he could stand back up, a loud bellow erupted from the doorway leading to the dungeon cells. The soldiers in the courtyard drew wooden truncheons from their belts. As they stepped toward the entrance, a large man in armor tumbled out, skidding across the ground in a clatter of metal scales. The soldiers poured into the doorway, and the sound of heavy blows echoed from inside. Horace held his breath as he listened. There was another bellow, almost like a growling animal, and then silence.

Eight soldiers marched out the doorway, wrestling a man out into the courtyard. The prisoner was huge, almost a head taller than any of his captors. Black stubble covered his shaved head. Slabs of muscle bunched under ebony skin. His face was marred by the marks of a recent branding. Blood trickled from a split lower lip.

An officer gestured, and the aproned smith released Horace from the chain. Then they shoved the giant, who was already collared, in front of Horace, and both of them were joined to the coffle line. The big man breathed loud and heavy, as if he was ready to resume the violence. Horace backed away as far as the leash would allow.

The wagon driver flicked the reins and started the vehicle moving, followed by the column of soldiers, out a wide gate to the street. The captives came last. The collar chain compelled Horace to keep up or risk being dragged along. The guards strode up and down the line, urging the captives onward with liberal use of their whips. Being at the tail end of the line, Horace had nowhere to hide. The first few blows caused him to curse, but they were no more painful than slaps, and he learned to ignore them.

Onlookers on the street bowed as the wagon rolled by and then straightened up as it passed to gawk at the rest of the procession. Horace fumed at the looks they gave him, like he was less than human. He squeezed his fists tight until his nails bit into his palms, but the pain took his mind off the humiliation.

The buildings became longer and lower until the procession finally passed under a stone archway that marked the town's limits. The road beyond was wider than the one that had brought Horace to the town, but it was still hard-packed dirt. The river ran alongside the highway, its brown waters rippled with a gentle current.

Where were they taking him? He had expected an execution, maybe with some kind of trial before a magistrate, but not another journey. And Lord Isiratu was coming with them, so it must be someplace important.

Horace studied the big man in front of him. From the powerful muscles moving under his dark skin, he looked strong enough to haul Isiratu's wagon all by himself. Long scars crisscrossed his shoulders and down his back. Many of them were old and gray, almost blending into his skin, but a few showed the stark whiteness of being new. Horace felt the dimpled surfaces of his palms. He knew the impact that scars could have. What was this man's story? He clearly wasn't Akeshian. Horace had heard of dark-skinned peoples who lived on the southern continent, but he'd always assumed they were myths.

I thought the stories about warlocks and sorcery were myths, too.

Judging by the sun's low position in the sky, shining right into his eyes, the time was approaching midmorning. They were traveling east again, the opposite direction Horace wanted to go. He longed to see the ocean. He imagined the smell of the sea air and the sound of the waves hitting the beach. And he would have welcomed an ocean breeze now. His simple clothes were lightweight, but he still sweated profusely. Every time he reached up to wipe his forehead, his hand hit the chain running from his collar and he got angry all over again.

To take his mind off of his situation, Horace tried talking to the big man. He waited until the guards were bunched up near the front of the line and pitched his voice low. "Hey. Can you understand me?"

BLOOD AND IRON

The giant didn't respond, but the pair of men chained in front of him looked back. The one on the left was about Horace's height with a long, hawkish nose; the other was short and spindly with a bald head. Horace had a hard time guessing his age, but by the lines on his face, he had to be at least forty.

The bald man started to reply, until a violent blow caught him across the side of the head. The guard drew back his arm for another whack as the little man howled and held his bleeding face. A surge of anger overcame Horace. Before he could think it through, he ran forward and pushed in front of the victim. The whip cut into his raised forearm. Horace had never been much of a fighter, even as a child, but the sharp pain drove him to lash out. His fist connected with the guard's forehead, which was—unfortunately—protected by the low visor of his helmet. Horace recoiled from the burst of new pain across his knuckles, but the guard kicked his legs out from under him and put him on his back. Horace threw his arms over his head as the short whip beat up and down his body. He tried to roll away from the blows, but the neck chain kept him from going very far.

When the beating finally ended, Horace breathed heavily through a bloody nose. His arms and legs were covered with painful welts. The guard standing over him shouted a command, and he crawled to his knees. All the furious energy had drained from his body, leaving him listless and weak. He started to get a foot under him when a large hand reached down. Horace took it and was lifted to his feet. The dark-skinned man looked even more formidable up close.

Horace extricated his hand from the big man's grasp. "Uh, thank you."

The giant turned around without speaking. The guard glowered at them both but kept his whip by his side, and the line resumed its march.

Hours rolled by as they trudged under the blazing sky. The tracts of farmland gave way to arid plains covered with dusty earth and scrub grass. A clump of low hills arose against the haze of the northern horizon. The river twisted away southward until its bends were lost from sight. The road kept running due east as far as Horace could tell, deeper into the wastes.

Lord Isiratu's procession traveled through the midday hours, despite the brutal heat, and long into the evening before a halt was called. While the soldiers made camp, the prisoners were herded together. The guards brought out wooden mallets and spiked the coffle chain to the ground. Then one sentry kept watch while the rest of the guards ate and relaxed.

Horace collapsed. The smells of cooking were intoxicating, but he couldn't even summon the energy to sit up when a servant brought their evening meal. He sucked down the two ladles of water he was allowed and ate lying on his back. It was more of the flavorless mush, but he hardly cared. He longed for the solace of sleep, for a few sweet hours when he could forget he was alive at all.

As he closed his eyes, a soft voice whispered in his ear. "I am Gaz."

Hearing the words spoken in stilted Arnossi made Horace bolt upright. Beside him sat the short, bald target of the guard's abuse, with his legs folded under him. His head gleamed in the firelight.

After a glance at the guard, who was busy eating his supper, Horace replied, "I'm Horace. You speak Arnossi?"

"Yes, a little. Good to mat you, Sire Horace."

"Huh?" Then Horace understood what the man had meant. "Oh, yes. Good to *meet* you, too. Are you Akeshian?"

The small man scratched under his armpit as he bowed from the waist. "Indeed. I am born in J'gunna. You will please tell about your land? I am very want to know."

"Ah, sure." Horace rubbed his forehead. After days without anyone to talk to, he had a hundred questions. "But first, where are they taking us?"

"We are on road to Nisus. We are. . . ." Gaz pursed his lips and looked up at the purple sky. "Gift. Yes? We are gift."

Horace didn't like the sound of that. "A gift for who?"

Gaz said a word that sounded like *amanamatturi*, but Horace didn't catch it all. "Is that another lord?" he asked.

"No, no. Is the god son." Gaz pointed up to the sky. "Son, yes?"

It took Horace a moment to understand. "The sun! The sun god."

Gaz nodded while Horace tried to put the pieces together. They were being taken to a place where they would be given to a cult of sun-worshippers. It wasn't as shocking as he might have guessed. The pagans' worship of false gods was the driving force behind the Great Crusade. He had listened to the

BLOOD AND IRON

Archpriest of Avice deliver a sermon on the front steps of the basilica the day they set sail. The words still rang in his head.

"The pagan masses of the East are beyond our Prophet's redemption. Their souls cannot be saved by the staff, and so their existence must be ended by the sword. This Great Crusade is the instrument of the Almighty. Go forth, my sons, and suffer no heathen to live."

"If you're Akeshian," Horace asked, "why are you a captive?"

"Yes, yes. I am Akeshai. I am slave."

After several attempts, Horace finally got the man to comprehend his question. "I am very poor," Gaz said. "You understand? Sell ox. Sell farm. Then nothing left to sell. Must sell self."

That made no sense at all. "Wait. You sold yourself?"

Gaz wore a dejected look as he nodded. "Yes. Master demanded it, or take my life." He touched his collar. "Better than death, yes?"

Horace wasn't sure he agreed, but he kept that to himself. He spotted a copper disc hanging from Gaz's wrist by a thin leather cord. The disc had squiggly lines drawn on its flat surface. "What's that?"

The man held up the talisman. *"Gigim'libbu.* A charm against spirits. You get one. Very good protect your *qa* from night-demons."

Night demons? "What kind of hell is this place?"

"Yes, you are man of the gods. But we Akeshai see this as the natural way. The *zoanii* rule from heights, and rest must suffer in this life. If we serve well, we be birthed again after our long resting. You understand?"

Horace didn't, but he was getting the sense that there were a great many things about this land he didn't understand. He was about to ask what a "zo-ah-nee" was when a cry echoed through the camp, followed by coarse laughter. On the far side of the slave ring, three guards were standing over a chained woman, one holding her by the hair. The nearest slaves cowered away from the spectacle as far as they could move. While the other guards watched, the woman's captor tore away her thin tunic. Her shrieks filled the air. Horace could guess what was going to come next. He started to get up.

"No!" Gaz put a hand on his arm. "You must not."

"To hell with that."

A few slaves looked up as Horace stood, but he saw no camaraderie in their eyes. Only painful acceptance. That made him angrier. He pulled on the chain attached to his collar as he took a long stride toward the disturbance. The guards took notice. The two watching the show advanced toward him, their hands going to the whips at their belts. The third guard leered as he continued to fondle the protesting woman. Horace didn't have a plan, but he wasn't going to sit by while they molested her.

The first blow caught him across the chin. He ducked under the follow-up, but the next one landed on his shoulder with enough force to make him grunt. Horace tried to lunge at the guards, hoping to knock them down, but the chain jerked him to a stop. He bent under a barrage of whip blows. When one of the guards grabbed him by the neck, Horace lunged and wrapped his arms around the man. They both tumbled to the ground, but the guard punched Horace several times. Bright spots exploded in front of his eyes as the guard lifted his whip.

A large hand closed around the guard's wrist and hurled him backward. Horace flinched as a whip cracked, but it didn't land on him. The giant had waded into the brawl, throwing punches. Whips cut into his dark skin, but the big man didn't seem to notice as he picked up a guard by the throat and a leg and threw him into the campfire. Blinking to clear his vision, Horace climbed to his knees. He barely saw the boot coming at his face in time to bring up his arms to block it. Then something hard struck him across the shoulder. The breath rushed from his lungs as he pitched forward. A few paces away, the giant bowed under the weight of several soldiers who had joined the fight. Horace covered up his face as the blows continued to fall.

They beat him savagely and kicked him dozens of times in his ribs and back. Curled up in a tight ball, Horace lost all sense of time. The blows stopped falling, and there was only pain for what felt like hours, and then . . . nothing.

CHAPTER SEVEN

"**Y**ou live!"

Horace cracked his eyelids and winced. The sun was only a couple fingers above the horizon, but already its light was blinding. He started to sit up and groaned as pain erupted all over his body. His entire back felt like one huge bruise.

"Slow! Go slow. Here."

Gaz knelt beside him holding out a cup. Horace accepted it and savored the warm water. Then he laid back and sighed. What had he been thinking last night?

I wasn't thinking. Just reacting. Again. What's gotten into me?

Reacting was all that he'd done since the shipwreck. He felt like a dinghy swept up in a hurricane, at the mercy of the winds, and he didn't like the direction they were blowing him. He needed a plan, some star to set his course by.

"Must not drag attention to self," Gaz said.

"Draw," Horace said, handing the cup back. "Don't *draw* attention to yourself."

"Yes. Hate them in your heart, but not show it. This is best."

Horace stretched his sore shoulders, feeling the skin pull taut across his back. The soldiers strode around the camp, packing up to depart. The big slave who had come to his aid last night sat a couple paces away. Several new bruises marred his skin, but otherwise he looked little worse for wear.

Then Horace turned his head. Several guards were approaching with their whips held ready. Horace braced himself for another onslaught, though he didn't know how he could survive another beating like he'd gotten the night before. When the guards yelled, the slaves rose to the jingle of rattling chains. Horace began the slow process of standing up as the coffle was dragged and shoved into a semblance of order. The soldiers lined up in formation, and then everyone waited. Horace risked a glance over his shoulder to the elaborate pavilions where Lord Isiratu and his entourage had spent the night. A manservant emerged from the largest tent, a long wooden chest in his arms, and was soon followed by his masters, Lord Isiratu and Lord Ubar, and the priest Nasir.

My masters now, too.

Horace found it difficult to accept the idea, but this was his reality. He was a slave.

While Isiratu entered the wagon, his son walked to the center of the camp. Horace watched as the young noble closed his eyes and held out both hands at waist height. It almost looked like he was praying. A dark spot appeared on the ground at Lord Ubar's feet. The spot grew wider and became a muddy puddle. Horace almost swallowed his tongue when a knee-high jet of water spurted from the wet earth. Ubar stepped away from the newly made spring, and several slaves approached with buckets, which they used to refill the caravan's water barrels.

Horace grunted as a line of pain sliced across his back. A guard growled in his ear. Horace balled his hands into fists, but he didn't move. Fortunately, another guard called down from the front of the line, and his tormentor hurried off. Horace kept his head down as the procession started moving and focused on maintaining the pace.

As he had already learned, the end position was the worst place to be. He was continually breathing in the dust kicked up by the many feet ahead of him, and if he failed to keep up, the others could simply drag him along. Yet being alone at the back also allowed him the illusion that his suffering had no witnesses, even if he was only fooling himself.

The big man glanced back every once in a while. The guards didn't notice, or perhaps they were willing to let it go as long as the giant kept moving. Horace caught one of these glances and acknowledged it with a nod. The big man did nothing in return.

He probably thinks I'm insane, and he might be right.

Horace couldn't help but admire the man, who marched with a straight back and shoulders thrust back as if he were leading a victory parade. The nearby captives gave him as much space as their chains would allow, and even the guards left him alone. Horace tried to emulate him, standing up tall as he marched along.

The sandy waste continued ahead of them for as far as he could see. This was, he comprehended with a shock, what they called a desert. He'd heard of such places. Apparently the east was rampant with them, great dry seas of sand where a man could die of thirst in hours. The sun's heat became even more oppressive as the day wore on, but Horace didn't die, though he began to feel light-headed and his mouth became so dry he couldn't summon enough saliva to swallow.

"What is this place?" he croaked.

"The Iron Desert," the big man said.

Horace blinked and tried to clear his throat. "So you speak Arnossi."

"I'm better with Nimean. Arnossi is too hard. The words have too many meanings."

Horace might have laughed if his situation weren't so dire. He held out his hand. "I'm Horace from Arnos. From Tines, specifically. What's your name?"

The big man ignored the offered hand. "Jirom, son of Khiren of the Muhabbi Clan."

"Good to meet you, Jirom. Where are you—?"

A guard walked by, brandishing his whip, and Horace closed his mouth. Jirom faced forward as if he hadn't said anything. The procession stopped for a break at midday. A man came around with the water barrel, and Horace gulped down the cup offered to him. While they rested, he shaded his eyes against the intense sunlight and tried to make out the landscape ahead, but all he could see were a few clouds in the eastern sky, highlighted in gold. And more sand. Leagues of it.

Keeping an eye on the guards, Horace leaned over to Jirom, who lay beside him, stretched out on the hot sand. "So you're obviously not Akeshian. Where are you from?"

"The Zaral, far to the south and west."

Horace had heard of such a place, supposedly a land of vast plains and mountains that touched the sky. "How did you get all the way up here? It has to be . . ." He tried to calculate the distance in his head from his recollection of seafarers' maps. ". . . at least five hundred leagues."

"Closer to a thousand. But I've been farther from my homeland than this."

BLOOD AND IRON

Jirom listed all the distant lands he'd traveled as a sellsword, some of them places Horace had never heard of before. "That's incredible," Horace said, trying to imagine all those years away from home. He gestured to the man's iron collar. "So what happened?"

"I ended up on the wrong side of the wrong war. I was given the choice between death and becoming a slave. Now I fight for our masters' pleasure."

Horace studied the man beside him. A hardness showed through past the scars and raw branding welts that marred his dark skin, until you looked into his eyes. Rather than the dull, brutish eyes Horace might have expected in a foreign mercenary-turned-gladiator, Jirom's gaze held quiet intelligence. "Do you have a wife back in the Zaral? Children?"

Horace regretted the questions as soon as he asked them. He most of all should have known better than to inquire about someone's family.

Yet Jirom answered without ire. "No. No one."

Horace was quick to change the subject. "So what lies ahead for us?"

"I've heard that the priests of Akeshia worship their gods with blood. Perhaps we go to our deaths on their altars, but I won't kneel for them like a goat. They'll have to fight if they want to feed me to their demons."

Gaz glanced at them in alarm but said nothing. Horace nodded. He liked the big man's attitude.

After a short rest, the caravan resumed its trek. The sand dunes became taller until they often blocked out the horizon like long, rippling hills. Dust devils chased each other across the desert floor. Whenever one approached the procession, some of the slaves muttered words that sounded like prayers and touched their foreheads. Each time this happened, Gaz clutched his talisman to his chest, but Horace didn't see anything menacing about the tiny whirlwinds.

Not long after high noon, the caravan was reaching the top of a dune when Horace spotted a pair of reddish-brown dots on the horizon ahead. The spots grew with each passing mile, from small pebbles to narrow boulders until they were finally revealed as towering pillars of rock. Eventually, Horace began to notice features carved into the stones. They were statues.

"Holy God," he whispered.

He tried to guess their height but stopped after his estimation surpassed two hundred feet. He couldn't imagine the technical skill required to construct such immense effigies. They must have taken an army of artisans years to finish.

The road passed between the statues, giving Horace the chance to see them up close. The colossus on the left was male, the right female. Both were carved standing up. The male statue wore only a long skirt down to his ankles and a crown of circles on his brow. The female had a long gown belted just under her high breasts. Her head was unadorned, her long hair hanging down past her shoulders. Both had expressions of peaceful serenity, or so it appeared to Horace. He wondered who they were supposed to be. Guardian totems? If so, they weren't very frightening except for their titanic proportions.

Horace was so preoccupied with the statues he didn't notice the view beyond them. Several gasps made him turn forward and look down into the canyon of deep red stone that opened before them. Lord Isiratu's wagon had already started down the road, which cut through the center of the valley, but Horace's gaze was drawn to the structures built along the steep walls on either side. They looked like stone palaces, scores of them. Most had extravagant entrances with columned arcades and statuary, surrounded by high walls. A few of the larger edifices had two or even three layers of concentric fortifications. Yet he saw no people among the buildings.

"The Valley of Souls."

Horace looked to Jirom, who had stopped a few paces in front of him. "What is it?"

The big man looked back. "A city of tombs."

Horace gazed about in awe as the caravan descended into the valley. The necropolis was about five miles long and half that across at its widest point. The road descended farther than was first apparent from above. Once they reached the floor of the gorge, the cliffs loomed several hundred feet above their heads, enclosing them in a cocoon of ruddy stone.

The caravan halted midway across the valley at a square platform beside the road. The square was made from a deep-red stone shot through with black veins. Lord Isiratu's wagon pulled up beside it while the guards spread out to make camp on the opposite side of the road. The sky turned deep lavender as the sun went down behind the canyon walls, and long shadows reached across the tombs, shrouding them in gloom. A cool breeze floated across the camp.

Lord Isiratu, his son, and Nasir emerged from the wagon. Usually when they stopped for the night, the lords retired directly to their tents to eat and bathe, but tonight they climbed onto the platform and knelt in the dust with their heads bowed. Braziers were produced and set alight at each corner. Then Nasir led the nobles in a slow chant. They repeated this ritual three times, each time turning to face a different direction. Food was brought forth and thrown into the braziers. Wine was poured onto the stone floor, making Horace lick his cracked lips. Yet even as he was haunted by his thirst, a strange feeling intruded on his thoughts. He felt warmth coming from the direction of the platform, though the braziers were more than a dozen yards away and the temperature on the valley floor was dropping. The warmth played along his skin like the touch of a furnace. Thinking it might be heat-sickness, he sat down.

After the libations for the dead, the ritual ended. By that time the tents had been erected, and the masters went inside. The guards came around with water and hard bread for the slaves.

Chains rattled as Jirom sat down beside him. "Want company?"

Horace nodded as he sipped from his cup. "Sure. I'd be glad for it."

The other slaves were eating and lying down on the ground, trying to get what little sleep they could. Horace was exhausted, too, but sleep wasn't on his mind as he gazed upon the rows of tombs and mastabas dotting the landscape and tried to imagine what would compel a people to put so much labor into their final resting places. "This is beyond belief."

Jirom grunted around the last bite of his supper. "The Akeshii bury their dead in stone mansions if they're rich enough, or in the dirt if not. They believe their souls pass down into the earth to the afterworld to be judged."

Horace shook his head. His own faith taught that only the evil descended into Hell, while those who had been saved by the Prophet's grace rose to the glory of paradise. Yet he kept that to himself, not wanting to insult Jirom in case he shared the Akeshians' beliefs. "Whatever the reason for these tombs, I never thought I'd see any place like this. It makes me feel small, like a child getting his first glimpse of the ocean. Except here, the drops of water are measured in years. Some of these temples must be centuries old."

"Older than that. These high walls protect the tombs from the winds and weather. They'll still be sitting here when the world ends."

"And here we sit before them, a couple of slaves on our way to discover our fates."

Horace chuckled at the absurdity of his life. Jirom looked over and then laughed. A handful of guards glanced up but didn't bother to quiet them. Finally, Horace took a deep breath and let it out, feeling better. "So how does a man from the southern continent find himself here?"

"It's a long tale."

Horace leaned back on his elbows and stretched out. "I'm a good listener."

The big man looked up at the deepening sky. The first stars were out, twinkling like fireflies above the valley. The wind had picked up, strong enough to make the brazier flames flutter. "I was with a mercenary unit out of Maganu, one of the few sane outfits to come out of that Death-loving country. After putting down an uprising in Bylos, we were hired by an expatriated prince of Isuran to take back his city. The enemy was a rival prince with dreams of empire. The sacking took only two days, but that's when the real trouble began. An Akeshian legion showed up on the doorstep. What we didn't know was that our royal employer had received an Akeshian envoy the previous year, and had hung him from the city walls as a testament to his independence. The Akeshii had returned to answer the insult in blood.

"Our employer, of course, demanded our protection. . . ."

As Horace listened to Jirom's tale of battle and deceit, he realized how little he knew about the world. He'd spent his entire life thinking Arnos was the center of civilization, but these past few days he had come to realize that his homeland was just a small piece of a vast puzzle connecting millions of lives. Had he not been shipwrecked, he would have never met this man sitting next to him. "So the Akeshians took the city?"

Jirom nodded as he finished his cup of water. "Aye. They had us outnumbered more than ten to one. At the end I killed our employer for betraying us, but most of my unit was dead by then. The conquerors gave me a choice: the collar or the stake. I chose to live."

I chose to live.

The words echoed in Horace's mind. Would he have made the same choice? He couldn't say for sure.

"You and I are survivors," Jirom said. "Alike in mind, I think."

"I don't know about that. You're . . . well, you're the scariest man I ever met. I'm just a sailor."

"No. I don't know much about you, but I already know you are more than that. You have a strong spirit."

The big man held out his hand. Horace took it and squeezed firmly.

"Sleep well, Horace-of-Tines."

"Good night, Jirom of the Zaral."

Jirom lay down and closed his eyes, but Horace stayed awake for some time, watching the twilight turn to true night. He thought about what Jirom had said about them both being survivors. What was the point of surviving if everyone and everything you loved was taken from you? What awaited him in the future except more of the same, the empty loneliness that corroded his every waking thought and plagued his dreams with visions of the life he'd lost? If he had learned anything from the shipwreck, it was that he no longer feared death. In its place had emerged a new fear, of being alone in this world.

He reclined on the firm ground. Exhaustion from the long day dragged on his thoughts. As he closed his eyes, he said a silent prayer of thanks for another day, and for the new friend he had made.

CHAPTER EIGHT

Dark clouds gathered in the east, like ink smudges marring the horizon. Horace shaded his eyes as he studied the storm front and prayed it wasn't a mirage.

"It feels like we're marching into the ovens of Hell."

The caravan had left the Valley of Souls before dawn, hastening up the canyon road and onto the desert plain as if in a rush to put the city of the dead behind it. Horace, for one, had been sorry to leave. The necropolis was peaceful and inspiring at the same time. Yet, as the sun pounded the caravan with its merciless rays, the misery drove away thoughts of the tranquil burial ground.

"I would suggest you pray," Jirom said, beside him. "But even the gods aren't crazy enough to visit here."

Horace smiled, but he couldn't summon the energy to laugh. He didn't know how much longer he could go on. With each passing mile, the urge to give up and lie down grew more powerful.

"Be strong," Jirom said, as if he could sense these thoughts. "Focus on the ground in front of you and don't think about the individual steps."

"You talk like you've done this before."

"Many times. You have to march to find work when you're a mercenary."

A warm breeze blew over the caravan as Jirom started a story about another desert he had crossed while soldiering. Horace studied the clouds ahead. At first, he thought it was a trick of the morning light, but now he noticed they were a strange, green hue. They grew darker and taller with the passing minutes, until Horace realized they were coming in this direction. Fast.

A cry went up from the front of the column. Horace couldn't pull his gaze away from the advancing storm. He'd spent most of his life on and around the water. He knew weather, but he'd never seen anything like this. Not since the night the *Bantu Ray* went down and he'd washed ashore here.

The soldiers hurried to surround the wagon. Some took spikes and hammers from their packs, and others retrieved coils of rope. Working quickly, they threw the ropes over the wagon and spiked both ends to the ground. The drivers rushed to cover the draft animals with tarpaulins.

The slaves dropped to the ground. Horace followed along, but he and Jirom stayed up on their knees to see while the others pressed their faces to the sand. The clouds were still approaching. Every few seconds an emerald glow would highlight their billowing masses. He heard the first thunder boom when the front was still a couple miles away. The strength of it reverberated in his chest. His hands started to shake.

Within minutes the sky was awash in roiling clouds. Sand flew in all directions as the storm smashed into the procession like a tidal wave. At the front of the caravan, the soldiers huddled around the wagon as if to protect its wooden sides with their bodies, but several of them scurried back as the wagon door opened. Lord Isiratu and Lord Ubar climbed down. Horace watched, shading his eyes with both hands, as the two noblemen walked out in front of the procession. Ubar looked nervous, grasping the folds of his long skirt as if forcing his legs to keep from bolting, but Lord Isiratu strode with confidence into the face of the storm.

The two noblemen stopped twenty yards ahead of the lead oxen. Horace's mouth fell open as Lord Isiratu raised his right hand toward the clouds. A tingling warmth suffused Horace's chest directly behind his breastbone. The sensation grew into a stabbing ache as it expanded throughout his body. At the same time, a powerful urge gnawed at the back of his mind, a yearning to lash out, to scream and rage and destroy.

What the Hell is happening to me?

Then a blast of wind slammed into him. Unprepared for its force, Horace tumbled backward in a cloud of stinging, choking sand. He tried to stop his momentum, but he couldn't find purchase in the loose ground. He yelled, knowing there was no one to help him. The urge to hurt something bled into his frustration and fear. Then the coffle chain yanked hard against his collar.

Fighting to keep from being strangled by his collar, Horace could hear chanting through the howling tumult. He managed to get to his knees, but he froze as a solid wall of sand rose from the desert floor. The wall grew into a semicircular rampart curving around Lord Isiratu and Ubar and the front of the procession. The wind abated for a moment, allowing Horace to catch his breath. Then the wall exploded, crumbling to the ground as if it had been kicked over by a malicious titan. The wind returned in a roaring rush. While his father staggered backward, Lord Ubar made clawing gestures with both hands. An inky fog billowed up from the ground around him, but the storm scattered the mist before it could accomplish anything.

Horace tried crawling back to the huddled slaves. The sand slipped away beneath him, and he felt himself sliding backward. Then a strong grip seized his wrist. Jirom pulled him back into the crowd of cowering slaves. Horace nodded in thanks. The big man smiled back.

Ahead of them, the wagon rocked from side to side and the oxen bellowed. Isiratu and Ubar stood firm against the storm's fury, their clothes fluttering in the wind. Horace gasped through his teeth as the pain in his chest returned. His vision darkened for a moment, and he felt like he was back onboard the *Bantu Ray*, battered by the wind and waves. He shook the memory away, but when his eyesight cleared, everything had changed. The storm clouds overhead had turned midnight black. Emerald bolts of light passed between them, almost too fast to see. It was beautiful and terrifying at the same time. Horace felt the urge to reach up, as if he could touch the swelling clouds. He imagined the tickle of the lightning across his skin, the smell of ozone and moisture entering his lungs with every breath.

He didn't realize he had stood up until he felt the hand tugging his arm. Jirom kept a strong hold on him, but Horace shook his head. The impulse to move—to *do* something—compelled him. He pulled free and rose to his full height. He sensed some sort of connection to the storm, as if the energy flowing through him was reflected in the clouds above, or maybe it was the other way around. He reached up with his fingers spread.

Horace gasped as a blinding light exploded in front of his eyes. Searing agony ripped through his body like he had been dropped into a vat of acid. His muscles writhed, contracting so hard he thought his sinews were going to pull free from his bones. His lungs froze in mid-breath. Yet, through it all, the alien energy continued to pour out of him. Or into him. He didn't understand what was happening. He wanted it all . . . to . . . just . . .

BLOOD AND IRON

Stop!

Thunder boomed in his ears. The wind disappeared. The wagon settled down, and the whipping sand wafted back to the ground. Horace looked around. The sky was clear once more. The sudden stillness was deafening.

Lord Isiratu was on his knees, his head bowed as if suffering under a gigantic weight. Streaks of blood ran down his face. Ubar stooped beside his father, blood staining several spots on his robe. The soldiers left the cover of the wagon to surround the nobles, helping Isiratu to his feet. Lord Ubar assisted, too, but his gaze was focused on the slave line, staring right at Horace. As the soldiers helped their masters back to the wagon, Horace sat down on the ground. The other slaves backed away from him as far as the chain allowed—even Gaz. They whispered to each other while watching him with wide eyes. Only Jirom seemed unconcerned; he had turned around to face the wagon.

Horace looked down at his hands. The vibrations were gone, the surge of energy departed, but he couldn't forget what it had felt like coursing through him. He'd never experienced anything like it before. *He* had stopped the storm with nothing more than his mind. It was insane, and yet he had no other explanation.

Horace's stomach rolled over as he saw Lord Ubar approaching with four soldiers. Their eyes were fixed on him, and there was no place to hide. He started to get up, but the soldiers raced ahead, drawing swords as they formed a line between him and the young noble.

Ubar pushed past his guardians. Trickles of blood ran down the front of his robe, but he didn't seem hurt beyond that. The young noble pointed to the now-clear sky and said, *"Minat in'azama qatiya? Kima nepalu simmu im?"*

"The storm," Jirom said. "He wants to know what you did."

Horace wanted to shout that he didn't know, but he was too tired to fight. He held out his hands, palms up. They looked normal, showing no sign of the power that had flowed through them only minutes ago. Ubar nodded, and then he motioned to one of the soldiers, who put away his weapon and brought out a set of long iron tongs and a hammer. Horace flinched when the soldiers came over to him but held still as he understood what they wanted. In a few moments, his collar came off.

Horace felt his bare neck as the soldiers stepped back. He was free again. Or was he?

Ubar spoke a few more words and gestured to the front of the procession. Then he and two of his bodyguards went back to the wagon. The other two remained with Horace. They put their swords away but otherwise gave every indication of watching over him.

"What happened?" Horace asked.

The chain jangled as Jirom stood up. "You are a free man."

"But why? What did he say?"

The other slaves were getting up, too, but they kept their distance.

Jirom shrugged his broad shoulders. "They don't know what to do with you. You're a slave and a foreigner, but you also have *zoana*, so you can't be a slave. He wants you to remain with the caravan until Lord Isiratu makes a judgment."

"What's a zoana? What kind of judgment?"

But the guards had returned, shouting and plying their whips, and the slaves started moving after the wagon again. Jirom gave him a resigned look before following the coffle.

Horace watched the caravan go, not sure what he was supposed to do. If he was truly free, he could leave. Yet he doubted the soldiers were going to let him walk away, free or not, especially with this talk of *zoana*, whatever it was.

With an eye on the horizon, he set off after the procession.

"*Zoana* is black magic."

Jirom sat across from Horace, chewing on a crust of black bread. The caravan had stopped at a small oasis of palm trees around a burbling spring. The other slaves refused to talk to him. Even Gaz wouldn't look him in the eye.

Horace squinted at Jirom. "What?"

A smile crossed the big man's chapped lips. "The power that our masters wield. They call it *zoana*."

BLOOD AND IRON

"And they think that I . . ."

The idea was so far beyond Horace's existence that he had a hard time crediting it. Magic was the stuff of legends about the elder days when terrible monsters supposedly walked the land. No one believed in such things anymore. Yet these people did, and they believed he possessed it. But he didn't feel any different than before.

No, that's not true. There's something different about me. Something changed during that sandstorm.

Horace tried to recall the storm, hoping to figure out what had happened to him, but it was difficult to see the incident in his mind. Instead, bits and pieces flashed before his eyes, which only added to his confusion.

He looked over at the pavilion erected between the tall trees. Lord Isiratu had been transferred from the wagon to the huge tent. "What made those gouges on Isiratu's face? I've seen it happen before."

"They get those wounds when they use their sorcery," Jirom replied.

"Who gets them?"

"People like you who wield the *zoana*. Sorcerers."

"I'm no god damned magician!"

Jirom leaned close enough that Horace felt his imposing presence. "We all saw what you did. You turned away the storm with your magic. That is why the lords fear you now."

Horace pondered that for a minute. If they truly feared him, he could use that.

A soldier approached from the direction of the tents. The slaves looked up with apprehension as the trooper stopped in front of Horace and held out a wooden bowl covered with a linen cloth. Horace glanced at Jirom, but the big man sat quietly without giving any clue what this might be. Clearing his throat, Horace took the covered bowl. It was cool, as if it had been kept on ice. As the soldier walked away, Horace pulled away the cloth. Inside were half a dozen small white eggs on a bed of lettuce. His mouth watered at the sight.

Horace showed Jirom. "What's this for?"

"A sign of respect. A gift to honor what you did."

Horace took an egg and put it in his mouth. The taste and the soft, crumbly texture were delicious. His stomach grumbled for more. He offered the bowl to Jirom, who took an egg and plopped it into his mouth with a smile. He also offered some to Gaz and the other slaves, but they turned away as if afraid to be seen conversing with him. Horace shrugged.

If that's the way you want it.

While he and Jirom shared the meal under the dimming sky, Horace learned how Jirom had served in several armies before he was captured by the Akeshians, and how he'd fought in the arena. Jirom wasn't so forthcoming about the circumstances that had led to him being attached to this lot of slaves, but after the big man went to sleep, Gaz shuffled over to tell Horace that the brand on Jirom's cheek marked him as a murderer. Such men, Gaz warned, couldn't be trusted, and Horace wondered what the small man said about him behind his back.

Horace watched the sky. With his collar off and the temperature starting to drop, he could almost pretend he was back home. The breeze rustling through palm leaves could be the roar of the waves. He closed his eyes and tried to conjure images of his wife and son, but his life with them felt like so long ago, like it belonged to someone else and he was watching from the outside.

Footsteps in the sand brought him back to the real world. Two soldiers came over and motioned for Horace to accompany them. He complied, but slowly, stretching his arms above his head before he followed them. They led him through the camp to a smaller tent staked out beside Lord Isiratu's pavilion. Horace frowned as they indicated he should enter. This tent had been erected for Lord Ubar and was guarded by a cordon of bodyguards. What did the noble's son want with him? Had the judgment been rendered already? Not wanting to be forced, Horace ducked inside.

Two lamps sat on the tent's floor, which was covered in thick carpet from wall to wall. Stepping on the rugs with his dirty sandals felt felonious, but there was no other option. Horace tried not to track too much sand onto the fine weaves. Lord Ubar sat on a broad cushion. He wore a clean purple coat brocaded with silver thread. His hair had been brushed and oiled. Horace ran a hand across his head and grimaced when his fingers came away covered in a film of sweat and grit.

Nasir sat beside Lord Ubar, wearing a crimson stole over his robe. A pattern of golden sunbursts was stitched into the silk. Ubar gestured to the floor. "Please. Sit."

He had a thick accent, but Horace could understand him fine.

A slave girl—quite fetching with her black hair held back with jade pins—rushed forward to place a cushion in front of Horace. With a nod to her, he sat down and tried not to notice the cloud of dust that settled around him. "Thank you for the extra food. And for my freedom."

Nasir translated this to Ubar, who nodded. Horace caught a few of the words that passed between them as Nasir related the young noble's reply. "It is the law that *zoanii* cannot be enslaved. Please forgive me, *Inganaz*, but you are an outlander and possibly a spy."

"Inga—?" Horace glanced at Nasir. "What did he say?"

"*Inganaz*. It means 'He who does not bleed.' I believe it refers to your lack of immaculata after the storm."

"Yes," Horace said. "About the immaculata, what are—?"

Lord Ubar resumed talking through the translator. "My father is still recovering from the storm-of-chaos. But when he is well, he will decide your final status. Until then, you will remain free, but under guard."

Horace didn't like the sound of "final status," but he didn't have a chance to inquire further as Lord Ubar launched into a flurry of questions. "Who are the most powerful *zoanii* in your country? Do they all support the invasion of our land? Is the *zoana* common in your country? Where were you trained?"

Horace held up his hand. "Hold on. I don't understand most of what you just asked me."

"Please tell us which questions you did not understand."

"You can start by explaining the *zoanii* and *zoana*. One of the slaves said it meant sorcery. Is that what you think I am?"

"*Zoanii* are the rulers of the empire. *Zoana* is . . . the closest word in Arnossi would be 'magic.' However, it also has a divine connotation. *Zoana* comes from the celestial realm where the gods dwell in perfection, and the *zoanii* are their instruments in this world."

Horace tried to make sense of the words. "So, are you and Lord Ubar are both *zoanii*?"

Nasir indicated the noble's son. "His Highness, Lord Ubar, is *zoanii* like his noble father. I am not. Now, if you please, Lord Ubar has many questions regarding your homeland and its customs. And also about yourself."

Horace's first instinct was to tell them both to go to hell, but he reminded himself that he was in their power. And, for what it was worth, Ubar had shown him a measure of . . . well, compassion, if not kindness. "Tell him that I honestly don't know anything about this *zoana*. Like I told his father, I'm just a simple craftsman. I build and repair ships."

Nasir took some time relating this to Lord Ubar, and Horace started getting anxious. This was his chance to influence his own destiny. Ubar obviously had his father's ear. If he could convince the son that letting him go was the best option . . .

He cleared his throat. "May I ask a question, my lords?"

Ubar and Nasir halted their conversation. Ubar nodded. "Yes."

"The other prisoners say you're taking us to a place called Nisus. Is that right?"

After a short discussion, Nasir answered, "Yes. Lord Isiratu has honored the temple of Amur with a gift."

Amur must be their pagan sun god.

"And will we—the captives—be killed?"

Nasir's lips turned down in a disdainful frown. "That is the talk of foolish peasants. Most of them will live their remaining years serving in the temple or tending the olive groves."

That didn't sound so bad, but Horace had noted something. "You say most. But not all? Me, for example. Why send a—" He was going to say a *prisoner of war*, but changed his mind. "—a foreigner to this temple?"

Nasir closed his mouth. It didn't appear as if he was going to reply. Then Lord Ubar, who had been watching the exchange, interjected. Nasir nodded twice and then said, "Lord Ubar says that is his father's prerogative. Once you landed on his father's domain, you became his property. Yet things may have changed. He asked you here tonight for another purpose."

"Please," Ubar said in his own voice. "With all humility, I ask. May I examine you?"

BLOOD AND IRON

Horace's mouth dried up as those words sank in. Examine him? He didn't think the noble's son had a medical examination in mind. He meant sorcery. Black magic. An image came to mind, of his wife Sari kneeling beside Josef's crib, praying for the Prophet to protect their son from the Evil One and his infernal host of demons. The very idea of submitting to magical "examination" was repugnant, but part of him wanted to know more about what had happened during the storm, and these people were the only ones who might have the answers.

"I suppose that would be—" Horace started to say when the tent flap opened and two soldiers appeared.

They addressed Lord Ubar. Horace heard something about a captive—which he assumed meant him—and Lord Isiratu. Ubar and Nasir put their heads together. Horace leaned forward. "Is something wrong?"

Nasir broke off their conversation with a gesture from Ubar. "You have been summoned by Lord Isiratu. You are to go at once."

"But what about—?"

The soldiers didn't give him time to protest as they hooked him under the arms and dragged him to his feet. Lord Ubar and Nasir followed them out. Twilight had slipped into night while they were talking. The moon hung low in the eastern sky.

"All right," Horace said as they pulled him out of the tent. He struggled to walk under his own power. "I said all right!"

The soldiers let him go. Then, with as much dignity as he could muster, Horace accompanied them to the pavilion. The door flaps were held open by soldiers wearing deep indigo tabards over fine-mesh chain mail. Horace saw more soldiers in the same livery on the other side of the oasis setting up tents against the cool white of the moonlit dunes. A score of horses were being fed and watered inside a new, roped-off paddock.

Inside the pavilion, Lord Isiratu reclined on a bed of cushions. Both of the nobleman's arms were wrapped in bandages. A long gash, stitched closed, ran from his left temple down to the corner of his mouth. Lord Ubar and Nasir bowed as they entered and took seats to the left of Isiratu. To the noble's right was an old man who sat with a hunch as if his spine couldn't support his slender frame. The stranger wore a long robe of purple so dark it looked almost black. Thick gold bracelets adorned his wrists that, if real, must have weighed half a stone each. His head was shaved bald like Isiratu's.

No cushion was provided for Horace, so he stood while Isiratu talked with the new arrival. Ubar and Nasir sat attentively but said nothing. Purple Robe's voice was deep but breathy, as if he had trouble speaking more than a few words at a time. After several minutes of standing and listening to their jabbering, Horace began to get irritated. He was about to demand that Nasir tell him what was being said when the conversation stopped. The old man stood up with assistance from one of his soldiers. As he turned to the exit, Horace saw a huge scar of twisting brown and gray lines dominating the right side of his face. Horace was so disturbed by the sight he didn't notice the old man's limp until he was out the door.

"Who was that?" Horace couldn't help from asking.

Nasir replied, "That was Lord Mulcibar, High Vizier of Erugash."

"What is Erugash?"

But Nasir wasn't paying attention. Instead, he watched as Lord Isiratu leaned over to his son and began a long speech punctuated by violent hand gestures, most of them directed out the pavilion door. Horace asked what they were saying, but Nasir waved him away like an annoying insect. Eventually Isiratu ended his harangue. Nasir hesitated, a stunned expression on his face. Then he bowed his head. "Lord Isiratu has decided that we shall go to Erugash instead of Nisus."

Horace could tell that none of the three men were happy about this development. Even Ubar appeared perturbed—a faint sheen of sweat had formed on his forehead. "So Erugash is a place?" Horace asked.

Nasir smoothed his silken stole. "Erugash is the city of Queen Byleth. In your society, she would be Lord Isiratu's liege lord."

"Why the sudden change of plans? Is it because of the new lord? What was his name?"

"Lord Mulcibar," Nasir said, "shall accompany us on the journey."

Isiratu clapped, and a pair of soldiers escorted Horace out of the pavilion. As he departed, it occurred to Horace that no one had thanked him for saving their lives.

CHAPTER NINE

Oxen bleated as they were fed and watered by sleepy drovers. The sentries on duty stretched and rubbed their eyes while their brethren crawled out of their blankets looking for something to eat. Soon, the smells of beer and cooking wheat cakes floated through the camp.

Horace sat cross-legged on the sand, watching people move around as he broke his fast with water and unleavened bread. The sun climbed a clear azure vault. A faint breeze rustled the sand around him, but otherwise there was no weather to speak of. Not a single cloud to mar the heavens.

Another morning on the march. By evening we'll be ten leagues farther from the coast. Farther from any chance of getting home.

He still hoped to find some way to Etonia, and from there back to Arnos, but that hope grew fainter each day. Part of him was desperate to get back, but another part—the side of him that loved the wild capriciousness of the sea—was intrigued by this new land. He had already seen things beyond his most daring dreams. What else would he discover on this journey?

Lord Mulcibar was the first noble out of his tent. After a quick look around, he hobbled to his wagon and climbed inside. Lord Ubar was next, scratching his chest while he ate a pastry, berry filling dripping down his chin. Evidently, Lord Isiratu was feeling better because he was able to walk unassisted from the pavilion to his wagon. Neither he nor his son so much as looked at Horace as the caravan prepared to depart.

Lord Mulcibar's wagon—a behemoth on six wheels—preceded Isiratu's smaller vehicle. Horace also noticed that Mulcibar's soldiers outnumbered Isiratu's entourage by two to one.

The wagons set a swift pace from the start, much faster than the caravan had traveled before. The guards used their lashes more freely today to keep the slaves moving. Each blow made Horace's jaws clench in sympathy. He remained at the tail of procession, still with his personal guards. The sand kicked up by the vehicles and people in front of him soon had him squinting and coughing, but the heat was worse. By midmorning it felt like his brain was baking. He took off his shirt and wrapped it around his head. That helped a little with the flying sand, too. When the caravan halted for the midday rest, his shoulders were red and sore to the touch. He gulped down his ration of water and gestured for more. The water-slave started to turn away, but one of Horace's guards said something in a harsh tone, and the slave stayed in place, allowing Horace a second cup. After he took another swallow, Horace offered the cup to his guards, but they refused with short bows that made him uncomfortable.

He was starting to pick up their language here and there, but it was slow going because the words didn't sound anything like Arnossi. The soldiers watching over him didn't talk much beyond what he was pretty sure were complaints about the march and the heat, although from time to time they were clearly talking about him. The slave guards were freer with their speech, but it usually boiled down to invectives hurtled at their captives.

The nobles remained inside their wagons during the rest. Horace imagined it had to be sweltering inside. Perhaps Isiratu still felt weak. Horace didn't understand how the nobleman had received his wounds, though he got that it had to do with sorcery. Jirom had made it sound like it was something that happened to anyone who used such powers, but the big man also insisted that Horace was one of those *zoanii*, and he didn't have any wounds like that.

He tried to recall exactly what had happened during the sandstorm. He remembered the fear, the feeling that he might die. There had been an instant of pain, both warm and cool at the same time, centered inside his chest. That's where his memory of the incident ended. Horace concentrated on that fire-and-ice feeling that had enveloped his insides. If he truly had this power, it might be the weapon he needed to escape this situation. He tried to envision the burst of pain and re-create it. Minutes passed and beads of sweat rolled down his face, but nothing else happened.

Soon the caravan started off again. This time Jirom fell back to walk beside him. The soldiers guarding Horace didn't appear to care, so he risked some conversation. "What do you think about our new destination?"

Jirom shrugged. He was covered in sweat and sand but otherwise appeared unaffected by the heat. "It makes little difference to me. I have wanted to see Erugash, though I always imagined it would be at the head of a conquering army."

Horace laughed. The big man had an easy way of talking that cut through their differences. "Will it be the executioner's block for us then?"

"I don't think you need worry," Jirom said. "If they wanted you dead, you would not be here."

Horace supposed that was true, but it didn't give him much hope. From what he could infer, Lord Isiratu had been willing to give him over to the priests, for whatever purpose. Now they were going to Erugash, but Horace still had no idea why, or what they expected from him. "What about the rest of you? Has Isiratu changed his plans about giving you away?"

"What will happen, will happen."

Horace nodded as they walked together. Neither of them had much control over their immediate future. The caravan started up a long rise. The road was rockier here, which made for uncertain footing. Horace shaded his eyes to see to the top and then wished he hadn't. A cluster of poles crowned the low hilltop. No, not poles. Stakes, more than a dozen of them. A body hung from each. As the caravan approached the gruesome display, a cold grip of dread tightened inside Horace's chest. Most of the corpses were men, but he saw a couple women, too—all of them stripped nude and impaled through the back so that the pointed end of the stake protruded from their stomachs. Long, bloody tracks covered the bodies where they had been scourged before being impaled. Flies swarmed around the torn flesh. Several of the captives in the coffle muttered to each other and touched their foreheads.

"Who are they?" Horace asked.

"Slaves," Jirom answered. "Likely they tried to escape or stole from their masters."

Horace forced himself to look away from the bodies. No matter what their crimes, no one deserved this. Jirom ignored the impalements the way he disregarded the heat and the lashes of the guards. Horace wished he could be as implacable.

"Why haven't you tried to escape?"

Jirom kept walking as if he hadn't heard. After a couple minutes, he said,

BLOOD AND IRON

"Where would I go? I have been running a long time, but everywhere is much like what I left behind, or worse. I've begun to wonder if the gods are testing me. Perhaps if I stay this time and let my path unfold, they will reward me."

"With what? Freedom?"

"One way or the other, we will all be free in the end."

They passed beyond the impaled bodies. On the other side of the hill, the bleached sands gave way to a lush countryside. The earth was dark and rich, tilled into neat squares of gold, russet, and green. The road extended for miles through these fields, as straight as a carpenter's rule, until it reached a great city on the horizon. Its walls gleamed like beaten copper in the sun. Even from this distance, Horace could tell the city was much larger than Avice back home. His elevated vantage allowed him to see a maze of white, flat rooftops and golden spires, but none of the buildings compared to the mammoth construction that rose from the center, grander than anything he had ever seen before. It was shaped like a pyramid with several tiers, rising high above the metropolis. A shimmering ribbon of green water cut through the city in a channel that fed a large lake north of the pyramid. The waterway joined to a mighty river running along the southern wall.

The leagues between the tor and the city passed quickly. There was so much to see that Horace lost track of time, and the sun was heading toward its nocturnal home when the caravan neared the walls. Unlike in the west, this city had no burg, no surrounding buffer of structures outside its walls. The fields ran up to within a bowshot of the ramparts and stopped, leaving a barren track of ground in between where nothing grew.

The lead wagon halted before a massive pair of bronze gates like the valves of a cathedral. Up close, Horace could see that the city's gleaming walls were made of brick coated with some sort of glaze. Two huge statues of lions flanked the entrance, their mouths opened in eternal roars. Battlements loomed above the gatehouse, topped with triangular merlons. Archers stood watch on the ramparts, their pointed helmets shining in the fading light.

While Horace watched from the rear of the procession, gate wardens approached Lord Mulcibar's wagon. The troopers wore bright-yellow tabards over their armor. One soldier, with a scarlet corona stitched over his breast, knocked on the door. Lord Mulcibar emerged and spoke with the soldier for several minutes, passing various scrolls back and forth. The soldier read these documents, sometimes going back over the same scroll twice or even three times, before finally giving them back and waving the wagon through. Lord Mulcibar paused a moment, as if waiting for something, but then he climbed back into his vehicle and closed the door.

Lord Isiratu's wagon went through the same procedure, except that Lord Ubar and Nasir stood outside and handed documents to the soldier while their liege remained inside. Horace's personal guards closed in on either side of him, hands on the hilts of their swords. He looked around, feeling the tension rise. The gate wardens appeared touchy about their duty, but he didn't see any reason for Isiratu's guards to take it personally. After a quarter of an hour, the warden in charge finally rolled up the papyrus scrolls and handed them back. Ubar and the priest returned to the wagon as the signal was given for the caravan to enter.

Horace studied the wardens as he walked past. Their steel mail shone bright against their bronze skin. The soldier with the corona stitching stood in the doorway of a small shack beside the gates, speaking to someone inside. Horace turned his head as he passed and caught a glimpse of deep-red fabric, but nothing else.

The caravan entered a long tunnel that passed under the walls and into a huge walled square where they were stopped for another checkpoint. After a lengthy inspection of both wagons—which forced even Lord Isiratu to make an appearance—and the persons of the caravan, they were allowed to pass through. When the soldier in charge moved to give the documents back to Lord Ubar, Isiratu snatched them from the man's hand and stomped back to his wagon, slamming the door behind him, leaving his son and the counselor to walk alongside the wagon as it passed through another pair of gates. By this time, Lord Mulcibar's wagon was gone from view.

Inside, the city awaited. Within a few steps, Horace was lost in an eruption of sights, sounds, and smells. The caravan trundled along a broad avenue paved in hard clay, wide enough to allow three, or even four, wagons to drive side by side if not for all the people that streamed along in both directions.

BLOOD AND IRON

The city dwellers wore garments of dyed linen like schools of multicolored fish. Many of the men went bare-chested, wearing only long wraps around their waists and sandals. The women wore sleeveless shirts and tunics, but their skirts were often shorter than those of the men, rising above their knees. Horace was more shocked by the number of iron collars in the crowd. It seemed to him as if half the passersby were slaves. Many had the same bronze complexion as their Akeshian masters, but he spotted slaves of lighter and darker browns, too. Both men and women wore collars, and even a few children, which shouldn't have surprised him, but it did.

Most of the buildings were made of the same brick as the outer walls, though without the coppery glaze. Horace was struck by how ancient many of the structures appeared. By their design and crumbling masonry, they had to be centuries old. Some of them might have been built before the Nimeans founded their empire in the west. It was a sobering thought.

Many doors were sunken into the street, some fully hidden so that they could only be accessed by sheer flights of steps. The building facades gave off waves of heat even as the sun sank out of sight, and the clay underfoot was warm through the soles of his sandals. How did people survive in this blistering country?

The procession passed a stone obelisk rising at least eighty feet from the street. Craftsmen on wooden scaffolds were carving pictures into the square column, but Horace couldn't make out if they depicted a language or were just decorations.

A woman in a sack-like garment stood in the mouth of an alley behind the obelisk with her hands extended to the people passing by. She couldn't have been older than twenty. Someone threw a coin into the dust at her feet. When she dropped down to snatch it, Horace saw another person huddled behind her, a young child. A girl perhaps, though she was so dirty it was difficult to tell. The child's round stomach protruded from her scrawny frame. Once the mother had the coin in hand, she hurried away, leaving her child behind to watch the crowds. The little girl's deep brown eyes remained in Horace's thoughts long after he passed the alley.

The caravan halted in the middle of the avenue. Horace wiped at the sweat dripping down his face as he peered ahead, trying to see why they had stopped. He caught a glimpse of white garments passing in front of Lord Isiratu's wagon. It appeared to be a parade of some sort. With a glance at his handlers, Horace took a chance on his supposed "freedom" to move up for a closer look. No one tried to stop him as he passed Jirom and the rest of the slaves. From beside the wagon's rear wheel, he watched as a parade of men marched past to the slow beat of a drum. They varied in age from fresh-faced youths to old men with long beards. Every one of them was bald and wore a crisp white robe. They chanted in Akeshian, something that sounded like a hymn. In fact, the entire demonstration had the tone of a religious rite.

After the last man in white had passed through the intersection, Isiratu's driver cracked the reins, and the wagon lumbered off. Two blocks farther, the caravan entered into a vast square. Tall windows stared down from the surrounding buildings. Horace's gaze followed the arching lines and intricate scrollwork of the architecture. It was so different than the staid style of his homeland, and on such a grand scale.

The procession stopped before a broad building with a beautiful facing of marble columns, each carved to resemble a woman with her arms lifted above her head to hold up the portico roof. The guards moved the slaves against the wall as the wagon door opened and Lord Isiratu emerged. Ubar and Nasir awaited him, but the nobleman brushed past and entered the building before them. The soldiers fell in behind. Horace anticipated they would be taken inside, too, perhaps by a different entrance—the homes of the highborn in Avice often had separate doors for their servants. Yet the slaves were made to stand against the side of the building for more than an hour. Horace's guards complained until a slave woman emerged with a tray of cups. The slaves had to watch while their captors drank in front of them. Horace's tongue pressed against his lips, wanting to seize a cup from their hands and gulp it down, but the sudden crack of a whip snatched his attention way. A party of men had approached. Five wore bronze breastplates, polished to a brilliant shine, and had swords at their sides. Two were older men in robes.

The two elders walked down the line of slaves, speaking back and forth as they examined each man and woman. They paused a moment when they got to

Jirom, pointing to the mark on his face, but when they got to Horace at the end
they hardly glanced at him before retreating a few paces to confer. After a brief
conversation, the caravan guards unhooked the majority of the slaves, including
Gaz. The small man walked behind the soldiers with his head bent low, the
perfect model of obedience. For some reason, the attitude bothered Horace.

Hold up your head! Don't just follow at their heels like a dog.

The soldiers herded the chosen slaves toward the northern end of the
square where several large wooden platforms stood. Auction blocks, Horace
guessed. Jirom and five other male slaves were left behind. Horace tried to
understand what was happening. Why were they being separated? He swallowed his mounting anxiety as the old men talked back and forth, pointing
to each of the remaining slaves in turn. They didn't look in his direction as if
he was invisible, but somehow he didn't think they had forgotten about him.

"What are they doing?" he asked.

Jirom was looking east across the plaza where two covered wagons stood
along the far side. A crowd of people stood around the wagons, listening to
a man in a red uniform reading from a scroll. Jirom scratched his neck under
his collar. "Culling."

"What's that?"

"When an animal gets sick, it must be separated from the rest. Or if it is
unfit to breed, it is taken away."

"So which are we? The sick or the unfit?"

"I think we'll soon find out."

As if summoned by his words, the guards came for Jirom and the last
slaves. Horace started to go with them, but the guards held out their hands.
He stayed.

Jirom grasped his shoulder and bent down to meet his eyes. "Be strong."

Horace nodded. "You, too. Maybe we'll meet again someday."

"Perhaps."

As Jirom and the last slaves were taken to the tall wagons, Horace expected
to learn his fate. However, the old men turned and departed, leaving him
alone with his guards. Horace glanced around. The soldiers weren't paying
much attention to him. He could have slipped away and vanished into the

crowd. But where would he go? He was a foreigner and an enemy, and he didn't even know enough of their tongue to ask for directions.

Stay calm. Use your eyes. What are you missing?

Murmurs drew his attention as the crowd made way for a white palanquin carried by a team of eight burly men. Opaque curtains hid the occupants from view, but Horace's guards drew themselves up straight, arms by their sides, eyes forward. A trickle of sweat ran down his back as the sedan chair drew up in front of him. The bearers stopped in unison, their muscular limbs gleaming with an oily sheen.

A guard opened the door and stood aside. Horace looked at him, and the guard nodded. The interior was vacant, just two empty bench seats. Horace glanced back at the building with all its windows and the carved columns. Then, without any idea where he was being taken, he climbed inside the chair.

CHAPTER TEN

Alyra hugged the satchel to her chest as she closed the door to the armory. She had just enough time before the second bell to get to her secret cache and back before she was expected in the queen's chambers. She dared not be late again for Hetta's sake.

She stole down the empty corridor in the direction of the slaves' quarters, where there was an exit near her hiding spot. The main level of the palace was empty this time of day except for slaves assigned to cleaning duties, which was why she'd picked now to visit the armory. By midmorning, these halls would be overflowing with diplomats and petitioners, with nobles and their prodigious entourages. The audiences and meetings would continue well into evening when formal matters of state gave way to frolics and feasting and other entertainments. After three years as a chamber-slave, Alyra had ceased to think of the palace as just the home of the queen; it was more like a carnival for the lascivious and the disturbed that never ended.

Marble squares of black and vermillion covered the hallway's floor. Artful decorations in bronze and iron hung on the stone walls. While the outer chambers were rich in natural light from many windows and skylights, Alyra was glad that these interior corridors were dim. Officially, she wasn't supposed to be in this part of the palace, but as one of the queen's handmaidens, she had more access than most of the other slaves. But she didn't wish to rely upon that flimsy protection if she got caught, especially because she was more than just a household servant. She had been sent by the neighboring nation of Nemedia to root out signs of Akeshian aggression against that country. Three years was a long time to live among one's enemies, serving them, suffering under their heel, but she believed in her mission with all her heart. Her father had been the governor of an Arnossi colony on the island of Thym when the Akeshians attacked. He'd died giving Alyra and her mother a chance to escape. After the Nemedian secret police took them in, she gladly joined their network to fight the empire that had destroyed her family.

BLOOD AND IRON

She approached an intersection between two large drawing rooms and froze as heavy footsteps echoed down the corridor. Her first thought was that she had been caught during the changing of the guard, but the chime hadn't rung yet. Then she realized the sounds were coming from behind her.

She threw herself into a shallow niche and hid behind the marble bust of King Ubinhezzard. She held her breath and pressed herself deeper into the niche as someone passed by. She waited for several frantic heartbeats before peeking out. A black cloak fluttered behind a tall man as he strode down the corridor. It was Lord Astaptah, one of the queen's chief viziers. As he disappeared around a corner, Alyra knew she should turn around and head in the opposite direction, but instead she kicked off her slippers. Holding the satchel with care to keep its contents from clanking together, she stole after the vizier on quiet footsteps.

This is crazy. This is crazy. This is . . .

The words ran through her head as she peeked around the corner. This *was* crazy. She didn't want to even think about the ramifications if she was discovered, but this was also a golden opportunity. Lord Astaptah was the most mysterious man in the city. No one knew where he came from, although rumors were rife, but within a few months of his arrival he had risen to the top of the social ladder to become the queen's highest servant. Rarely seen at court functions, he dwelled in the catacombs beneath the palace. Alyra had long wondered what he did down there and why the queen favored him, but opportunities to find out were so rare that when faced with one—like now—she had to take it.

Alyra hurried down the corridor, deeper into the interior of the palace. Small lamps glowed high up on the walls. She avoided their pools of light as best she could while following Lord Astaptah into a part of the palace she had never seen before. They were far from the slave quarters and ever farther from the kitchens. If she were caught here, she'd have very few excuses as to why she had wandered so far from her assigned duties. Biting her bottom lip, she pressed on.

The vizier turned down a dark corridor. After a dozen steps Alyra lost sight of him. She kept close to the left-hand wall, trailing her fingers along its stones to keep her sense of direction as she followed Lord Astaptah's heavy strides. Then the strides drifted off to her right, and Alyra barely stopped in time to keep from walking face-first into a wall. She felt the corner and turned with it. A thought struck her as she trailed after the footsteps. How was Lord Astaptah finding his way without a light?

He must have the route memorized.

But why not carry a candle? Why the secrecy? That's what she wanted to find out. So she continued onward through the dark. The satchel was getting heavy, but leaving it behind was out of the question. Lost in her thoughts, Alyra halted in mid-stride as a cold shiver ran through her body. The footsteps had stopped.

She held her breath, straining to hear the slightest sounds, but there was nothing louder than her own heartbeat pounding in her ears. Where was he? Had she been discovered? She cursed herself for not paying more attention. Then a sound traveled down the corridor, like two boulders grinding together. Vibrations ran up through Alyra's bare soles. She remained perfectly still, afraid to move.

The grinding noise stopped. Footsteps echoed somewhere in front of her or perhaps to the left. She was becoming disoriented. Then the noise began again. Not sure what she was doing, she inched forward with one hand extended in front of her, and barely stifled a yelp of surprise as her fingers touched a moving surface. It was stone and very large. Running her hands up and down, she determined that it was a door, and it was closing before her. She hurried to reach the opening, but it was narrow and shutting quickly. She had only a moment to decide. Should she wait for another time when she was better prepared? What if there wasn't another time?

The grating noise stopped as the door settled into its frame. She had missed it.

Alyra rested her forehead against the stone. What had she done? As she berated herself, she noticed that the surface was warm. She put down her satchel and ran both hands across the door's smooth face. It was definitely warmer than the surrounding stone. Almost hot, in fact. What was behind it? There was no handle or latch in the expected place. Alyra was searching for an opening mechanism when footsteps echoed behind her.

An icy dread filled her chest as she heard voices. Alyra started to dart back up the corridor to the last intersection but then remembered her satchel and ran back to it, searching along the floor until her hands bumped into the coarse burlap. Clutching the bag, she sprinted down the corridor, her feet slapping on the marble. She stopped at the intersection and listened above her own breathing. Yes, there was no doubt. She had run into Xantu and Gilgar. The twin brothers were two of the most notorious members of the court. Many referred to them in private as the Queen's Hounds. They served as Her Majesty's enforcers, and their penchant for cruelty was legendary. There was a saying in Erugash: better to risk the fire than let the Hounds sink their fangs into you. It sounded like they were coming from her right, but she couldn't be sure. If she guessed wrong, she would run directly into them, and that was trouble she didn't need. She slipped into the left-hand corridor, ran a few steps, and then pressed her back against a wall. A spot of orange light appeared in the darkness. It bobbed like a hot coal on the end of a fishing line but showed enough for her to see their approaching faces.

Alyra retreated deeper into the darkness. There was nowhere to hide and no way that she could escape from magicians of their caliber if she was discovered. She let out a soft sigh of relief as the twins turned the corner in another direction. Now she could go back to searching for a way to open the stone door. She hurried back toward the intersection, but she hadn't gotten halfway there when a deep, rolling chime rang above her head.

I'm late!

She turned and ran, cursing herself the entire way. The second bell faded away before she got back to the lighted corridors. The appearance of daylight ahead made her breathe easier. She passed by a trio of slaves scrubbing the floor and had to tread carefully for a few yards to avoid spilling onto her backside. Following a corridor reserved for slaves, she almost stepped into the Grand Atrium before she realized she was still holding the satchel. It was too late to get it to her hiding spot. Looking around, she found a service closet and tucked it onto the highest shelf behind a pair of buckets. With a prayer that the sack and its contents would remain hidden until she could return to fetch them, she smoothed her hair and brushed the front of her tunic for stray dust, doing the best she could without a mirror. Then she went out to face the consequences of her tardiness.

Head bowed, she crossed the atrium's golden flagstones at a quick walk. The chamber was a marvel of engineering. Twelve pillars—each so thick that five men could not reach around them with their hands linked—held up a ceiling seventy paces above the floor. Brilliant sunlight poured through the round crystal windows in the ceiling. Gigantic frescoes covered the walls, depicting the history of Erugash from its humble origin as a trading village to the sprawling city-state it had become.

She took a side door and started up the long series of zigzagging staircases. It was several minutes more before she arrived at the queen's residence on the top tier of the palace. The royal suite had its own foyer, bedecked with fine furniture and a collection of erotic sculpture. A squad of brawny bodyguards stood at attention, their tulwars held in perpetual readiness. Alyra slipped through the inner doorway, hoping—praying!—that she would arrive unnoticed. A strong contralto voice dashed her hopes.

"Ah, my errant handmaiden arrives at last."

Alyra froze on the threshold of the main parlor. The voice came from the doorway to her right, accompanied by a slosh of water.

How does she always know?

Alyra curled her fingers into tight fists at her sides. Of course the queen knew. She was *zoanii*, descended from an ancient line of powerful sorcerers.

"Alyra, come. I'm getting a chill."

She obeyed at once. The queen's bathing chamber was as large as the house Alyra and her mother had shared in Nemedia. Every surface was faced in pink marble, including the floor and arched ceiling. The bathing tub set into the floor could have held a dozen people, and Alyra had seen it filled to capacity on more than one occasion. Her Majesty's parties were notorious affairs throughout the empire.

The queen stood at the edge of the tub. Rivulets of soapy water ran down her exquisite body. Tall with long, firm legs and a thin waist, she looked like a dancer. Her long, black hair hung in wet ropes about her slim shoulders. Alyra kept her head down as she took a towel from a nearby bench and attended the queen, drying her gently before wrapping the towel around Her Majesty's body. She used a smaller towel to cover the royal hair.

"Thank you, child," the queen said. "Now come."

Alyra followed her through the sitting room and into one of the suite's three lounge chambers. This one was decorated in shades of red and pink with white accents. Plush couches piled with pillows were arranged around the room. This was where the queen often entertained her male guests. Alyra stopped short when she saw who was chained against the far wall. "Hetta," she whispered.

"I don't know how many times I've told you, Alyra."

The queen walked up to Hetta. The girl was only ten years old, and as skinny as an alley cat, but beautiful with her olive skin. The queen believed in surrounding herself with lovely things. Alyra's stomach twisted into knots.

The queen ran her fingers down the girl's bare back. "You must be on time when I have my morning bath."

Alyra rushed forward and fell to her knees. "Yes, Majesty. Please forgive me. The blame is all mine. Please! Do not—"

"Shhhh." The queen patted Alyra's head like she was a lapdog. "You know that I must punish you. How else will you learn?"

"Yes, Majesty! Please let Hetta go and punish me. I take full responsibility for my lateness."

The queen laughed. It was such a lovely sound, but it filled Alyra with dread. "Silly child." Her hand caressed Alyra's face and then dipped down across the upper slope of her chest. "This is how you learn."

A tiny shudder ran through Alyra as the clipped staccato of high-heeled boots entered the room. Hetta whimpered, and Alyra didn't need to look to see who it was. The queen's personal torturer brought a case of whips and canes that she set at Her Majesty's feet.

"The red one," the queen said as she pulled Alyra over to the nearest couch. "To begin with."

As the blows began to fall, and Hetta's cries resounded through the room, the queen held Alyra close and forced her to watch the spectacle. With each crack of the switch, Alyra focused on the importance of her mission, even as a woeful refrain ran through her mind.

I'm so sorry. So sorry. So sorry.

CHAPTER ELEVEN

Horace lounged in the tub with his eyes closed, enjoying the warm water as it lapped against his chest and leached the aches from his tired muscles.

This is surely heaven. And if it's not, let me die now.

After climbing aboard the mysterious sedan, he had been carried out of the plaza and down a broad avenue where he got a better view of the city. Everything was built in tiers, the buildings and ramps rising like stone hills all around him. There were green spots, too, with gardens growing on rooftops and balconied terraces. Many of the buildings were painted, the most popular shades being ochre red and a pale orange that reminded Horace of a summer sunset. The avenue crossed several bridges under which flowed narrow channels of water. After about a quarter of a mile, the sedan turned into a courtyard surrounded by high walls that blocked out most of the sky. A squad of soldiers in indigo uniforms met Horace as he stepped out and ushered him inside a huge manor house. He had flashbacks of his cell in Lord Isiratu's town, but the soldiers took him upward instead, climbing several flights of steps and one long spiral staircase to a well-appointed room. They left him there.

Exploring this cell hadn't taken him long—the room was a circle. Two windows showed views of the city below. Several larger buildings stood out, many of them topped with broad domes. He'd stood at those windows as the twilight deepened, watching the moon rise to take its place among the stars. Finally, too tired to stand any longer, he collapsed into the bed.

Waking up on the fluffy mattress instead of a hard space of ground had been so luxurious that he didn't rush to get up, even as dawn's rays stretched across the floor. He might have stayed in bed all day but for the clatter of the door being unbarred and the entrance of four serving men. Their collars advertised them as slaves, but they wore clothing of fine linen and supple leather sandals like men of means. Though they did not speak his language, they made their wishes clear, and within an hour Horace had been shaved, barbered, and set to soak in a copper bathtub. He had no idea what it all meant—the slave coffle, the culling, the sedan chair, and now this treatment. It was all so confusing. He almost wished his captors would just cut off his head and be done with it.

Careful what you wish for. There are worse things than being confined in a nice room with a bed and bath.

The door opened again, but instead of slaves, three soldiers stepped inside. Each man held a sword with a curved blade, like a scimitar but with a more pronounced arc. Their blades looked sharp enough to shave with. Horace sat up, dropping one hand to cover his privates and feeling quite defenseless. A moment later the slaves reentered. They laid out an outfit on the bed as a stooped figure appeared in the doorway.

Lord Mulcibar looked older in the light of day. His skin was jaundiced with a crinkled texture like ancient parchment. A mass of scar tissue like melted candle wax covered the right side of his face. His limp was more pronounced as he entered.

Horace didn't know what to do. The tub, which had seemed like a haven only moments ago, was now his prison. Standing and bowing from his current position wouldn't be wise, and waving seemed too flippant, so he remained in place. Then Lord Mulcibar surprised him by speaking in passable Nimean. "I wanted to formally make your acquaintance."

Horace shifted, sloshing some water on the floor. "Uh. That's very nice of you, my lord."

"I am Mulcibar Pharitoun et'Alulu."

"Horace Delrosa at your service."

"Have you been made comfortable?"

"Yes, sir. Thank you for your hospitality. It's a far cry from running across the desert."

"I suppose it must be. I would ask your indulgence for Lord Isiratu, but I am of the opinion that the man is a slug."

That took Horace aback. In Arnos, it wasn't often that one aristocrat was heard criticizing another. Perhaps things were different here.

What am I thinking? Everything is different here.

"So this is your house?" Horace asked.

"Yes. It was originally the royal palace of Erugash, but it was bequeathed to my grandfather."

"Does that make you royalty?"

"Yes. Although some have said that the bloodline has thinned in recent generations."

Horace had no idea how to respond to that. Thankfully, Lord Mulcibar filled the silence.

"Please put on this attire. I will send for you within the hour."

As the nobleman turned to leave, Horace raised a hand to forestall him. The soldiers shifted to place themselves more firmly between him and old man. "Send for me for what, my lord?" Horace asked. "Are we going somewhere?"

"Yes. You have been summoned to the palace. The queen wishes to examine you."

Horace slumped back in the tub. The cooling bathwater sloshed about him.

The chains clinked as Horace lifted a hand to scratch his nose. Each wrist was encircled by a wide cuff of silvery metal, joined together by a twelve-inch chain of the same material.

Well, at least they're pretty.

He rode in the palanquin, this time sitting across from Lord Mulcibar. The hunched nobleman looked like he was about to be swallowed by the cushioned seat. Before they left his mansion, Lord Mulcibar had apologized while his soldiers placed the manacles on Horace, explaining that it had to be done. The metal was too heavy to be silver, weighing his arms down like lead. He'd asked his captor about the chains as they climbed into the litter.

"They're made from *zoahadin*," Lord Mulcibar said. "It translates to 'star metal.'"

When Mulcibar explained that the metal was very rare, coming from stones that fell from the sky, Horace had asked, "Why use it for chains?"

BLOOD AND IRON

"*Zoahadin* restricts the flow of ethereal energies."

Horace looked at the shackles. They didn't seem very special, except for their bright gleam. Yet, now that the old man mentioned it, he felt a little different. Rundown, of course, but that was expected after the long march to the city.

No, there's something else. Like a piece of me is missing inside. Odd that I never even knew that part existed until now.

"All rogue magicians are chained thus when they are brought before a tribunal," Lord Mulcibar said. "Or, in this case, the queen's court."

Though Horace didn't like being called a "rogue magician," he accepted that he was completely in the power of his captors.

Besides the chains, he wore a fine suit of dark gray linen, softer than anything he'd ever worn before. The embroidery stitched into the collar of the short jacket and down the sides of the calf-length skirt in a pattern of interconnecting squares looked like real gold thread. In an odd turn, the sandals he'd worn since the fishing village had been replaced with a pair of black leather boots. They were a little small for him but were polished and goodlooking. Wearing them almost made him feel normal. Except for the chains and the rolling motion of the sedan chair. He didn't like knowing that underneath him were people being used as beasts of burden.

"So what's she like?"

Lord Mulcibar looked up. He had been gazing into the floor for the last several minutes. "Pardon?"

"The queen. What is she like in person?"

The nobleman cleared his throat. "She is a goddess in the flesh. Without peer. Flawless."

Horace hadn't expected such a fervent response, but he'd heard that the heathens of this land worshipped many things. Why not their rulers? "Is there a king, too?"

"Queen Byleth inherited the throne from her father and has not yet married. She is betrothed, however."

"Byleth. That's a pretty name."

Lord Mulcibar gave a raspy chuckle. "Pray you don't say as much to Her Exalted Highness in court."

Horace smiled. Despite the shackles, he liked this man, who didn't treat him like an animal. But this summons had him worried. He'd never been in the presence of royalty before, although his father had once had the honor of presenting a new ship-of-the-line to King Fervold. Horace had been only four years old at the time, but he still remembered the blustery autumn day and how his mother had cried. Tears of pride, she'd said afterward.

An idea occurred to Horace. "Can you teach me to say hello in your tongue?"

"You would say *sobhe'etu*, which means 'the evening is well.'"

Horace whispered the phrase to himself until he had it memorized. He was hoping that being able to speak a little of their language would make these people see him in a more favorable light. And their tongue was, he had to admit, quite interesting, nothing at all like any of the languages of the western realms.

The sedan stopped, and a sharp knock rapped against the door. Lord Mulcibar got up, his face contorting into a mask of pain as he stood. The door was opened by a young footman in purple livery. Mulcibar went to exit but paused before leaving the car. "One piece of advice. Be honest. Many have tried to dissemble with Her Majesty, and they all paid for it."

Horace mulled those words as he followed the nobleman out. A dozen guardsmen surrounded them as they exited. The soldiers appeared ill at ease, as if expecting trouble, but Horace couldn't imagine what danger he might pose while shackled. He followed Lord Mulcibar's slow footsteps across the courtyard of red bricks, which was bounded by walls at least thirty feet high. A wide set of stairs at the end of the courtyard rose to the base of the breathtaking pyramid he had seen from outside the city. Horace didn't know whether it was a palace or a temple, as it had the features of both, consisting of several immense square tiers stacked on top of each other, narrowing in size as they rose toward the sky. Made entirely of polished white stone, the edifice gleamed like the blade of a knife under the hot sun. The roof of the top tier was sheathed in gold.

"It's unbelievable," he said, but neither Lord Mulcibar nor the soldiers escorting them acted as if they'd heard.

BLOOD AND IRON

They ascended the outer stairs and walked along the flat top of the lowest tier, eventually arriving at a set of tall doors. They were bronze, dark with age, their coffered panels cast with images of animals and people in minute detail. Some of the faces were only as big as his thumbnails, but they were rendered with such skill that Horace could make out their expressions perfectly. Most of the figures were depicted venerating larger, more beautiful people, though whether these giants were meant to be gods or rulers Horace could not say. Considering what Lord Mulcibar had told him about the queen, he supposed they could be both. Huge columns flanked the doors; the stone pillars were painted deep blue like the ocean.

More soldiers opened the door and stood at strict attention while the entourage filed inside. There was no sign of the yellow tabards Horace had seen at the city gates, and he wondered if the colors designated different branches of soldiery.

The chamber beyond was monumental on a scale Horace had never seen before. The ceiling was so high it felt like stepping into another open-air court-yard. He half-expected to see clouds drifting above him. More pillars, these painted light blue, supported the titanic span. The center of the chamber was dominated by a garden of vibrant flowers and small trees. Intoxicating per-fumes wafted in the air. Huge pictures were carved into the walls in bas-relief, portraying enormous people—mostly men—with long, curly beards and open wings. Were they supposed to be angels? If so, they bore little resemblance to the celestial beings Horace had seen in the cathedrals and churches of his homeland. These figures were more imperious in their stance, not cherubic in the least. One panel showed a line of chariots rolling over an army of smaller figures. Another showed scenes of daily life—farmers planting and harvesting, ranchers herding cattle, miners digging.

Horace tried to take it all in as the soldiers and Lord Mulcibar led him through the chamber. There were some people milling around in small clus-ters, men mainly. They turned to watch as he was paraded past. Some of their expressions were not kind.

That's right. Gawk at the evil foreigner.

They passed through a wide corridor. Full-body portraits were painted on the walls and outlined in vibrant mosaics. By their golden regalia, he took them for kings and queens. Some of the paintings looked quite old. The light from the grand chamber was lost behind them and was replaced by burning flambeaux set in bronze cressets on the walls. He also spotted small holes, like narrow windows, near the ceiling. He wasn't sure what they were for—arrow loops for hidden archers?—until he noticed that the smoke from the torches was sucked out through the holes in some kind of ventilation system. It took him by surprise. He'd come to believe, through tales told to him by others and what he'd read in public bills, that the Akeshians were a backward people whose recent conquests were the result of mindless ferocity and a lack of respect for human life. Yet some of the things he'd seen already in his short time here were quite innovative.

The procession halted before another pair of immense doors. Horace had trouble swallowing when he saw the tall valves reflecting in the torchlight. Like the top of this building, they appeared to be made from gold. He tried estimating how much they must weigh and what each of them would be worth just based on their material alone, but the numbers staggered his imagination.

Two men stood in front of the doors with their arms crossed. They were perhaps in their midtwenties and so alike in appearance—the same style of tight-fitting robe across their muscled shoulders and chests, long skirts, and black as squid ink from collar to hem—that he thought they must be related. Then he looked closer. They had to be twins. One had short, dark hair, spiked in the front, while the other wore his hair long and shaggy.

Lord Mulcibar spoke with the men. Horace couldn't hear what was said, but the two brothers turned and made pushing motions with their hands. The hairs on the back of Horace's neck stood up as the huge doors opened. No one stood behind the doors, no straining slaves or apparatus that he could see. It looked as if the men had opened them with a mere gesture.

More sorcery.

Horace's manacles clinked as the procession started moving again. Beyond the doors was another chamber. He had thought the entry chamber was huge, but the one before him dwarfed it in every aspect. He stood on what looked like an acre of white marble. Rows of colossal pillars festooned with golden scrollwork marched down the sides of the hall. Sunlight poured down from dozens of skylights to illuminate a raised platform at the far end of the chamber. The platform, like the palace itself, had several tiers. A squad of soldiers stood along the bottom, their features hidden behind full helmets. Above them sat twelve old men in somber scarlet robes. A magnificent ivory-and-gold throne rested on the highest tier. The seat was vacant. Behind it, a purple curtain spanned the entire back wall.

A crowd waited in the chamber, all bedecked in splendid apparel and jewels. The men favored elaborate tunics with short capes. The women were garbed in long, flowing dresses that, despite being sheer where the fabric wasn't gathered, were almost plain in comparison with the men's attire. The women also wore pigments around their eyes in a variety of shades. Everyone moved out of the way as the twins entered at the head of the procession. Horace didn't flinch from the glances cast in his direction as he was marched into the hall. A cool draft circulated through the chamber, such as he had experienced at Lord Isiratu's palace. He sighed as the sweat dried off him.

By the Almighty, what a blessing! I know the True Church doesn't truck with sorcery, but it might make an exception for this.

As Horace swallowed the tiny blasphemy of his thoughts, he noticed a familiar face. Lord Isiratu stood at the foot of the platform, flanked by his son Ubar and Nasir. Ubar wore the same quizzical expression he'd shown often during the trek to Erugash. Yet both Lord Isiratu and Nasir stood stone-faced like first-day recruits being reviewed by the High Marshal of the King's Army.

The robed twins ascended to the step just below the empty throne and turned to face the throng. As they looked down from this height, Horace felt an uncomfortable stirring in his gut. Tingles ran across his scalp and down the back of his neck, and all of a sudden the chain binding his wrists felt ten times heavier, as if the manacles were pulling him down to the floor. He strained, breathing through gritted teeth, to remain upright.

The heaviness vanished as the curtain parted and two people emerged, a man and a woman walking arm in arm. The man was draped in a white silk tunic, open at the chest to reveal a large golden amulet in the shape of a blazing sun. Yet it was the woman who drew Horace's attention. A purple silk gown covered her from the neck down. The sheer fabric clung to her body so that even the mere act of walking was transformed into a thing of beauty. Tearing his gaze away from her outfit, Horace looked to her face and was enthralled all over again. Her features were narrow, refined in a way he'd only seen in paintings, but her eyes were wide and dark, outlined in black kohl. Her rich, midnight hair was braided and piled in a tower atop her head, the plaits interwoven with slender gold chains in a look both stunning and demure at the same time. This could be no one other than the queen of Erugash. The entire crowd fell to its knees, lords and ladies alike, as she took her place on the throne. The man sat on a smaller chair beside her.

Horace didn't have time to decide whether or not he should kneel. The nearest soldiers seized his arms and shoved him down on the floor. His face pressed to the stone, he held himself rigid in anger, until clothing rustled and people began to rise. Horace tried to push himself from the floor, but the soldiers continued to hold him down. He struggled in their grasp, but they were too strong, and he was hampered by the chains.

He ceased fighting when the queen spoke in a cool, clear voice. Then the soldiers pulled Horace to his feet. He yanked his arms from their grasp. Everyone was watching him again, staring like he was an oddity at a village faire.

"Master Horace," Lord Mulcibar said, "the queen wishes to know how you came to this land and under what intentions."

Horace gazed up at her again. His embarrassment fell away, and the only thing he could think about was her. He answered at once. "*Sobhe'etu . . .*"

He hesitated, realizing he had forgotten to ask the proper way to address a queen in this land. So he uttered the first thing that came to mind. ". . . Your Excellence. I was a crewman aboard a ship out of Arnos. We were hit by a storm and driven south. Then the ship went under, and I washed up on your shore."

"What was your vessel's mission?"

"We were carrying soldiers to Etonia to fight the heath—"

Lord Mulcibar spoke in Akeshian, but every eye was on Horace. "Yes," the nobleman said when he had finished translating. "To fight whom?"

"Your people, my lord." Horace braced himself. He had decided to be honest with these people. If they were magicians, they might know he was lying and hold it against him. If he was going to hang, he would go to the gallows telling the truth.

No one seemed surprised when Mulcibar translated his answer. The queen spoke at some length. Meanwhile, the man sitting beside her reclined in his seat, looking uninterested, and drank from a golden cup.

Lord Mulcibar turned back to Horace. "Her Radiant Majesty asks if you know where Lord Isiratu was taking you before I arrived. Be aware that the other slaves have already been interrogated, and any lie will be punished most harshly."

Horace tried to recall the name of the town where he'd heard they were going, but it escaped him. "I think it was Nissa or something like that."

"Do you mean Nisus?" Lord Mulcibar asked.

"Yes, that's it."

As the nobleman interpreted, soft murmurs rippled through the crowd. Lord Isiratu burst out in a barrage of angry words. The queen lifted a finger, and Isiratu shut his mouth, his face purple and shining with sweat. The queen's expression remained neutral, though still lovely. Horace noticed how the black jewels in her golden necklace complemented her eyes.

"Are you quite sure?" Lord Mulcibar asked. "Lord Isiratu was taking you to the city of Nisus?"

Horace shifted his weight, and the chains clinked. "That's what I was told. Something about giving us to a temple."

Lord Mulcibar spoke to the queen at some length. Horace couldn't make out enough to give him a gist of what was being discussed. Yet, by their expressions, and the heated look on Isiratu's face, it was something bad. Finally, the queen stood up and spoke to the hall. Her words carried a heavy finality that leaked through despite the language barrier. When she was done, two soldiers came forth and flanked Lord Isiratu. The nobleman bowed to the queen and then walked away with the soldiers. His son and Nasir followed behind. As he was escorted out, Lord Isiratu shot a hard glance at Horace. Ubar nodded to him as if nothing had happened. Nasir ignored him completely.

Horace sidled a few steps closer to Mulcibar. "What just happened?"

"Lord Isiratu has been found guilty of disloyalty to the crown. He is stripped of lands and title, and will henceforth be demoted to the *hekatatum* caste."

Horace looked back over his shoulder where Lord Isiratu and his retinue were leaving the chamber. "What are heka—whatever you said?"

"They are the warrior society of Akeshia. It is not a dishonorable path for those of common birth, but for a *zoanii* such as Isiratu . . ."

It's a fall from grace, and a hard one. "What will happen to his family?"

"Most will accompany him in his lesser station. His heir, Lord Ubar, may be taken in by another *zoanii* family as a ward. With time and patience, he may yet achieve a dignified rank."

The atmosphere in the hall had turned taciturn with the ejection of Isiratu, but the queen behaved as if nothing had happened. She asked a question, and Mulcibar translated, "Her Glorious Radiance wishes to hear your account of the storm that struck Lord Isiratu's caravan."

A cold sweat formed on Horace's forehead and under his clothes. He'd been avoiding those memories in his own mind because he didn't understand what had happened, and part of him didn't ever want to know. He considered lying or faking forgetfulness but then recalled Lord Mulcibar's advice. *Be honest. Many have tried to dissemble with Her Majesty, and they all paid for it.*

So he told the story as best as he was able to remember, until he got to the part where Isiratu fell. "With all honesty," he said, "I can't explain what happened after that. I felt a surge of energy like my heart was going to burst. Then the next thing I knew, the storm was gone."

As Lord Mulcibar interpreted, the queen watched Horace with a fierce intensity that made him uncomfortable. He'd never been timid with the fairer sex, but this woman radiated power. Once Mulcibar was done, the old men seated on the platform's middle tier spoke among themselves, and conversation broke out among those in the hall. Horace itched to know what they were saying about him. It was maddening to be surrounded by chatter and not be able to understand it. But he did catch two words being passed around: *zoanii* and *amenakru*, the latter of which may have meant "enemy," but he wasn't sure.

The queen appeared about to say something, but a loud voice rang out from the crowd. People parted, making way for a tall man in a silver breastplate over a purple silk chiton. His complexion was darker than many in the crowd, almost coppery. His hair and eyebrows were jet black. He wore a sword at his side; the pommel gleamed with a ruby the size of a knucklebone. The tall man continued to speak, throwing his words at the throne even as he stared in Horace's direction.

Before Horace could ask what was happening, Lord Mulcibar said, "That is Prince Zazil, brother to the queen and commander of the royal legions. He has asked why the savage foreigner—you—has been allowed into this hallowed hall. And Her Majesty replied that she wished to see you in person."

Horace rubbed his wrists where the manacles were chafing. "I take it he doesn't like my people much."

"Considering that His Highness has spent the last several years fighting on the frontier, I surmise you would be correct. Tread carefully, Master Horace. The prince is not one to cross."

Not that I have much choice, chained up and surrounded.

While the prince continued his tirade, Horace noticed something. It was subtle, but Lord Mulcibar inched forward, placing himself between Horace and the prince.

The queen spoke, and the prince fell quiet, though he cast a menacing glare at Horace. Lord Mulcibar bowed before translating. "The prince, has expressed a wish to test the foreign devil—ah, you again—in a duel. But the queen is more interested in hearing your story. Her Majesty asks how she can be sure you are not a spy. Your arrival on our shores, the lone survivor of your ship, is very convenient. Not to mention your abilities."

Horace considered his words. The prince was still glaring at him with one hand resting on the hilt of his sword as if he was waiting for any excuse to pull it out and chop off Horace's head.

The bastard looks like he might enjoy that.

"Please tell Her Majesty that I am only a shipwright. If there's something special about me, I did not know it before I arrived in your land. And I would happily depart back to my own country if she would permit it."

He winced inside at the smartness of his last words but clamped his mouth shut before he could retract them. The nobleman raised an eyebrow, but he translated without any trace of ire that Horace could detect. While Horace waited to hear the queen's reply, he glanced around the chamber. The platform and the main exit were surrounded, but he noted several other doors that appeared unguarded, at least from this side. His hands were shackled, but not his legs. If he had to flee, he could try to squeeze through the crowd and get to one of those side exits—

The queen's laughter interrupted his thoughts, the melodic notes forcing him to look up. For a moment, Horace could understand why people might worship her. She was too beautiful to be real. Through her mirth, she talked to Lord Mulcibar and then gestured to Horace.

"The queen," Mulcibar said with a small smile, "says she will take your request under . . . ah, advisement. In the meantime, she wishes to further discuss your role in the quelling of the storm. When you say that the power surged—"

A loud voice resounded through the hall. Lord Mulcibar stopped talked and looked back toward the main doors where a group of bald men stood on the threshold. By their body language—straightened shoulders, lifted chins, mouths pinched into firm lines—they appeared like they were about to plunge into battle. The man in front of the group had wide shoulders and a powerful chest contained within a pale gold robe that contrasted with his bronze skin. Vivid red and indigo tattoos covered his scalp. He held a wooden staff topped by a golden orb—a sun, by its look, complete with a corona of sharp rays. The ornate headpiece reminded Horace of the scepter held by the Archpriest at St. Ephrates' Basilica when he blessed the crusaders before they boarded the ships—the golden suns were almost exactly the same.

The men standing behind him were clad in deep-red robes like those Horace had seen elsewhere in the city. Then it struck him. They were priests. Horace looked to Nasir with his bald, tattooed head and realized he was a priest, too. He'd thought the man was just a translator.

And they were taking me to his temple for an "interrogation."

Horace surveyed the party of new arrivals with a fresh perspective. The hall was quiet as they approached the throne. The robust priest in front stopped just a few feet from the bottom step and rapped the butt of his staff on the floor. The queen's face had lost its earlier animation, becoming as still as the marble statues lining the walls. While her gaze rested on the priests, she spoke to Lord Mulcibar. The nobleman bowed and turned, limping from the hall. The guards closed in around Horace and indicated he should follow. He did so. Looking over his shoulder, he watched as the tattooed man addressed the queen while she sat rigid on her throne like she was confronting a snake.

"What's happened?" he asked.

Lord Mulcibar remained silent as they left the hall. The huge doors closed behind them with a heavy thump, and the nobleman started walking down the corridor leading away from the grand hall. Horace made to follow, but the soldiers surrounded him, cutting off his avenues of escape. With their spears, they gestured toward a branching passage.

Horace called after the nobleman. "My lord?"

But Mulcibar kept walking, leaving him alone with the soldiers.

CHAPTER TWELVE

The *zoana* coursed through her blood, hot and raw. Her connection to the Imuvar dominion pulsed within her breast like a cobra ready to strike. Byleth pictured the envoy's bald head exploding in a mess of red and gray all over the pristine floor and almost laughed in spite of herself.

". . . sent here at the behest of His Grand Holiness, the Primarch, to discuss this matter in person, Your Majesty," Rimesh said.

The light gleamed off the priest's forehead in a most annoying way when he spoke, or perhaps it was his tone, which was a bothersome cross between a lecturing pedant and a true zealot.

She wanted this meeting over as quickly as possible, but she would not give this envoy the satisfaction of knowing how much he irritated her. She would have preferred to continue her audience with the foreign crusader, who was nothing like she had imagined. He was tall and rugged in an exotic way. And bold, as well. The way he looked at her bordered on insolence. "Menarch Rimesh, I do not concern myself with the intricacies of the city treasury. If there is a discrepancy in the latest tribute payment to the capital, I would advise you to consult with the royal treasury. But I will remind you that Erugash shoulders the burden of defending the empire against the western invaders while suffering under this blood debt—"

"This 'blood debt,' as you call it," he said, his voice becoming deeper and louder, "was the price you agreed upon when your father died on the fields beneath these storied walls and the armies of ten great cities were at your gates."

Byleth had been just a girl when the Sun Temple defeated the other cults of the empire in the years-long struggle that came to be known as the Godswar. In the aftermath, her father had refused to bow to the new order and had raised his banners in opposition to the idea that a single priesthood should govern the spiritual lives of all Akeshians. It had ended in tragedy and would have spelled the end of her house if she hadn't hammered out a peace agreement that allowed her to inherit her father's tarnished throne, at least in title.

BLOOD AND IRON

Now the Sun Temple ruled Erugash in everything but name while she sat in state within the palace, a toy queen presiding over a neutered court. She had learned to endure in the face of these hardships, for she believed that someday she would be free of the scheming priests, free to rule her city in truth.

"Nine," she said.

"Pardon, Majesty?"

Byleth cleared her throat. "The armies of *nine* cities were camped outside our gates, Menarch. The army of Erugash, the tenth city, was manning those walls."

"As I recall, Majesty, the army of Erugash lay scattered across the black earth, returning their life blood to the soil."

Hunzuu, First Sword of her Queen's Guard, took a step toward the delegation with murder written across his face, but he halted when she shook her head. Then she smiled down at the envoy. If things were different and she wasn't a virtual prisoner inside her own palace, she would show this priest what it meant to insult a queen of Erugash to her face.

"But that is immaterial," Rimesh continued, folding his hands across his flat stomach. He was in surprisingly good physical shape for a temple official, standing as tall as her brother Zazil and almost as broad across the shoulders. "You signed the armistice, Majesty, and so the empire demands that you abide by its strictures. Eight hundred *mana* of gold are past due. The amount must be delivered to Ceasa by the next moon."

"Or what?"

The statement garnered sharp looks from the menarch's entourage and a few whispers from her court. Byleth snapped her teeth shut, half-wishing she had held her tongue.

Rimesh reached inside his left sleeve. Xantu and Gilgar descended a step, their *zoana* peaking so hot Byleth could almost see it shimmering around them. Yet the priest merely drew out a thin scroll, tied with a gold ribbon. "The temple has heard disturbing rumors, Majesty. The local priests say—"

"Yes. What *do* they say?" Byleth struggled to keep from grinding her teeth. The temples and their priests had long been an irritation, since even before her father's time as king. Always grasping for more power, always presuming to judge. Astaptah was right in his mistrust of them. How she wished she could eradicate the Sun Cult from her city once and all.

Rimesh made a show of looking around the hall. "They say they are no longer welcome in Your Majesty's court."

She gestured to the doors. "Walk through the palace, Menarch. You won't be able to go a dozen paces without running into a soothsayer or astrologer. For five pieces of silver they will tell your future."

"They say that you dismissed your temple-appointed vizier without sanction."

"I need no sanction within the boundaries of this city, Menarch. The armistice be damned. I choose my own counsel."

"There are other whispers, too. More dire rumors about secret meetings and forbidden places within the palace."

"You speak much, priest, but say little. What are these rumors? Reveal them to the court, I bid you."

"Very well. To put a blunt point on it, there is a suspicion that a prohibited cult operates somewhere inside Erugash."

A chill ran through Byleth, but she kept her face perfectly calm. "A prohibited cult? Your temple makes so many decrees, night and day, it's a wonder if anyone could keep up with today's dogma. I daresay there are heretics in every city in the empire."

"I am not speaking of an ignorant layman mixing the wrong kind of wine with his sheep's blood."

The priest was flushed, and a thin line of sweat had formed above his upper lip. Byleth leaned forward. She enjoyed making him wriggle. "Go on."

"I am not—" Rimesh cleared his throat again. "—prepared to make accusations at this time. I have been sent to observe and report back to the Primarch, and so I shall."

She said nothing, staring at him as the silence stretched out over several heartbeats. "Very well."

She thought that would be the end of it, but the priest did not move from his spot. "Was there something else?" she asked.

"Yes. The subject of your betrothal."

BLOOD AND IRON

Byleth looked across to the chair beside her throne where Prince Tatannu lounged against the padded rest, one boot propped on the cushion and the other splayed beneath him in repose as he sipped from a golden cup. The prince of Nisus, her betrothed. His house claimed to be descended from Amur, the Sun God, but she didn't sense much divinity in him. Saddling her with a fiancé was merely the latest in a string of indignities perpetrated by the cult. She forced herself to smile. "What of it?"

"The temple is concerned. You have postponed the date of your nuptials four times, Majesty." The priest tapped the scroll against the palm of his hand as if it were a stick with which he intended to chastise her. "The last time, just a month ago, with no new date set."

"That's correct, Menarch. With our people suffering so horribly and the threat of invasion from the west, we cannot possibly consider marrying at this time. Perhaps next spring, when the lotus are in bloom."

"On the contrary, a royal wedding might be the thing to lift the city's spirits."

"That's what I told her," Prince Tatannu said, sitting up and dribbling wine down his tunic. "Why the wait? I am eager to sample the pleasures of our marital bliss."

Byleth dug her fingernails into the armrests as her *zoana* bubbled close to the surface. "I have consulted the oracles, and they say that the time is not auspicious."

"Allow me," Rimesh said, "to perform a new augury for you. The planets will be in perfect harmony this evening."

"No." She forced herself to add, "Thank you. We will not trouble the gods over such petty problems."

The priest sighed. It was such a dramatic exhalation, Byleth wondered if he had practiced it beforehand. "In that case, Majesty, I have been instructed to give you this."

He extended the scroll. A ludicrous gesture, since he stood a dozen paces away from her.

Does he expect me to get up and take it from his oily hand?

"What is it?" she asked.

Rimesh untied the ribbon, letting it fall to the floor in another dramatic flourish, and unrolled the scroll. "This is a petition, signed by every ruler of the *nine* cities of Akeshia. It states that unless you, Byleth et'Urdrammor, . . ."

Byleth braced herself as his stentorian voice rang throughout the hall.

". . . do wed Prince Tatannu of the House Murannash at the festival of *Tammuris* before the turning of the new moon, you shall be deposed from the throne of Erugash, and a new ruler for the city shall be chosen by your brethren monarchs."

Tatannu grunted as if amused by the pronouncement. Whispers arose from the court. Byleth pried her fingers from the throne's arms and clasped both hands in her lap. The rite of *Tammuris* was less than three weeks away.

Too soon. My plans are not ready yet.

She drew in a deep breath to calm herself. She was angry enough to bring down the entire palace but refused to show it. "That is out of the question."

Rimesh had the good sense to bow his head, if only for a moment. "You have my abject apologies, Your Majesty. But this petition will be carried out if the terms are not met."

"You are dismissed, Menarch."

Byleth waited, but the priests did not move. The red-robed dogs of the temple's Order of the Crimson Flame, she knew, would not budge until their master instructed them to leave, but she was shocked at the menarch's brazenness. To defy her here in her own palace.

"Just one last matter, Majesty."

Byleth considered the ramifications if she unleashed her own wolf-hounds on these curs. It would be a bloodbath. The temple would call for sanctions against her, but what else could they take? She was already a puppet, and everyone knew it. Her word hardly extended beyond the palace gates. She lifted a finger, pointing to the priest. "Yes?"

"The war, Majesty."

"I already have a High General, Menarch." Byleth glanced over at Prince Zazil. Throughout this entire exchange, her younger brother had stood idly by without once coming to her aid. It was so like him to do nothing while she shouldered the burdens of the realm. "But if you would like to apply for the post . . ."

BLOOD AND IRON

A few titters raced through the crowd. Byleth smiled to show them she approved of their mocking laughter.

"I wouldn't presume, Majesty." Rimesh bowed to Prince Zazil, who nodded in reply.

My, aren't they cozy with each other . . .

"But I bring word from His Imperial Divinity," the priest continued. "Erugash's new levies have been late in arriving."

"They are not late, Menarch. They are not coming."

Rimesh frowned. "But Majesty—"

She stood up. At once, everyone fell to one knee, save for the priests. They stood at ease as if she were nothing more than a commoner.

"Erugash has bled more than her fair share," she said. "Sending her soldiers to defend the empire's far-flung interests. But now invaders threaten our shores while the heartland grows fat and prosperous. Until the emperor's council sees fit to answer our requests for a suspension of the land tax, Ceasa will receive no more of our fighting men."

This time, Rimesh did not press her but simply nodded. "I shall inform the capital of your answer, Majesty."

Byleth's fingernails bit into her palms as she realized the trap she had stepped into. For a moment, she almost allowed herself to lash out.

Yes, you will inform them, won't you, priest. And with glee, no doubt.

"This audience is ended," she said.

The court nuncio cleared the hall as Byleth strode to the door behind the throne. Xantu and Gilgar accompanied her into the corridors beyond. Sometimes she would banter with the brothers as they walked. She had known them for most of her life. They had played together as children, their families sharing a close bond that she had inherited from her father. But today she stalked the passages in silence, walking so fast they had to hurry to keep up. Ascending a flight of spiral stairs leading to the private entrance to her chambers, she passed inside and went to her dressing chamber while the soldiers took posts outside. Her slaves hopped up from where they had been lounging and rushed over.

"Majesty!" Aisa said. "We didn't expect you to return so soon."

Byleth did not allow her displeasure from the audience to appear on her face. "Hetta, instruct the First Sword to summon Lord Astaptah at once. Alyra, I've had enough of bright colors today. Bring me the magenta gown."

While her slaves hurried to obey, Byleth sat at her dressing table. She hated the image glaring back at her from the huge mirror. She hated her tiny nose with its upturned tip. She hated the ugly splotches that formed under her eyes when she got angry. She hated her hair—so drab and dark. "I wish I had your golden hair, Alyra. It's so striking."

"Your hair is the envy of every lady in Erugash, Majesty," Alyra said as she laid out the gown.

As Byleth tried to imagine herself with blonde hair, she replayed the conversation with Rimesh in her head. Unless she devised a way out of their trap, she would remain at the mercy of the Sun Cult for the rest of her life, however long or short that was. She had few allies, even within the city. The aristocracy of Erugash consisted of over a dozen noble houses, of which her family was one of the oldest. In her father's time, they had all flocked to the court to seek royal favor, but in the years following his death the Sun Cult had wooed many *zoanii* away from her with promises of power and influence. If she defied the cult, how many of those houses would support her? Some families owed her favors, and Lord Mulcibar might be able to sway a couple others to her cause, but she had to tread carefully.

When she finished dressing, Byleth stepped out into the suite's central chamber. A lean man stood near the outer door. Gazing down at the floor with his hands clasped behind his back, he gave the initial impression of a scholar. Perhaps he was studying the plush white carpet under his feet. Sometimes Byleth forgot the riches that surrounded her—the marble stonework, the gold and silver decorations, the jeweled mosaics on the walls, the hardwood furniture imported from distant Oshan. Situated at the top of the palace, which had been begun by her father early in his reign and finished by her just five years ago, her chambers were literally the pinnacle of the civilized world. The windows of the western exposure gave way to a terraced veranda that provided an unparalleled view of her city. At night, the lights below glowed like a carpet of fireflies beneath her.

BLOOD AND IRON

"Lord Astaptah, I have just returned from an unpleasant visit with the Sun Cult."

Astaptah's amber eyes glowed with an inner fire, twin stars set in deep sockets, as they focused on her. The hood of his robe concealed his head except for a long, sallow face. An odor like stale incense lingered around him.

"Menarch Rimesh from Ceasa," he said. His voice was calm, as always. Since the day she first met him, bedraggled and half-dead at the foot of her palace, Byleth had never seen Astaptah in an excited state, neither in glee nor rage. His voice never changed its even tone. "I observed him leaving the palace."

"Did he see you?"

"No. But he did not appear pleased."

She took several steps toward the windows and then walked back. "That little worm. He stood there in front of my court and requested—no, he demanded!—that I wed that slob from Nisus. They can all rot for as much as I care about their plans and their threats. Do they think I don't know the law? The moment I am wed, my husband assumes the throne of Erugash, and I become nothing but a vessel to bear his royal brats."

"Perhaps the menarch could meet with an unfortunate fate. The streets of Erugash are not as safe as they once were."

She glared at him out of the corner of her eye. "If that is an example of your wit, my lord, I am not amused."

"The longer you can postpone your matrimony, the better our chances for success."

"How long can I hold out while they hound me day after day? I trusted you. I trusted what you told me, that I could be rid of these priests and the noose around my neck! Why? Because of you and your poisonous advice."

He tilted his head slightly to one side. "If my presence is no longer desired—"

Byleth waved the back of her hand at him as she continued to pace. She wasn't oblivious to the connection between Astaptah's presence and the amount of tension in her life, yet he gave her something she'd never had before. A chance at true power. "I need what you promised me. I need the weapon."

"And you shall have it, but these things cannot be rushed. The storm engine is not ready to be unveiled yet."

She stopped pacing to face him. "But it works, Astaptah. Tell me that it works."

"It will do everything I promised. Soon. The other cities have come to depend on the gold and soldiers Erugash provides. Denying them has made those rulers uneasy. Pressured by their people and the cults, their crowns rest upon the edge of a knife."

I will put the priests in their place and cleanse my city of their taint.

"My work," Astaptah continued, "will strengthen your position and put pressure on the Cult of Amur. Is that not what you wished?"

It *was* what she wished. It's what she had wanted since she was old enough to realize that she would someday rule this city but saw how the priests constrained her father's power at every turn. She had larger dreams for her reign, perhaps even the beginning of a new imperial dynasty with her as its founder. "We have no complaint of your service, Lord Astaptah. But everything rides on this gambit. The Sun Cult has only grown more powerful since the Godswar. If our plans are discovered, it will mean the end of everything. For both of us."

"I need better test subjects."

"I've been sending you all that I can. It's not so easy to make people disappear, even in a city as large as this."

"The vagabonds and drunkards I receive are next to useless," he said. "I need quality subjects to take my research to the next level."

Alyra entered carrying a silver ewer. The queen gestured, and the girl poured two cups. "What would you have me do? Kidnap members of the court?"

Astaptah waved away the wine. "Power is the key. Once the machine is in full operation, neither the priesthood nor the other cities will pose any threat."

Byleth took a long drink and shook out her hair. "Fine. I will do what I can, but you must move quickly now. We don't have much time."

The sweetness of the fortified wine took some of the heat out of her temper. She thought of Mulcibar's captive, the western spy. A *zoanii*, if Isiratu could be believed. His face and limbs were pleasing enough to the eye, but she had sensed no power to him. She made up her mind to interview him again.

BLOOD AND IRON

She deserved a diversion from this tedious politicking. "So how will we handle Menarch Rimesh?"

"I will monitor the menarch's efforts with care."

"See that you do. Now leave me."

He started to depart, but Byleth stopped him. "Wait. Why did you insist that we give Isiratu's lands to Xantu and Gilgar?"

Her question appeared to catch him off guard. He paused a long moment before answering. "The sons of Ekuzakir et'Mamaunothos are powerful and amoral, a combination which makes them useful."

"Yes. Useful as long as they remain loyal."

"The gift of additional lands and wealth will go far to ensure their continued faithfulness."

Astaptah was nothing if not logical, but his ideas frightened her as much as they excited her. "And what do you require, my lord, to ensure your continued devotion?"

For a moment, his eyelids widened and gave her another glimpse of the furnaces burning within. "Only to serve you."

"That's the same answer you gave me on the day I rescued you from starvation and thirst, as I recall."

"My aims have not wavered since that day."

Satisfied, she dismissed him and reclined on a padded lounge beside the open windows. A breeze played across her skin. The setting sun inked the heavens in swaths of gold and orange.

She lifted her hand for another cup of wine while she pondered how she would handle the new envoy of the Sun Cult.

CHAPTER THIRTEEN

The steel crescent sliced through the air in an elegant arc. Blood spurted onto the ground behind the rolling head. Two hundred men stood as silent witnesses, watching the execution of one of their own.

Jirom had seen beheadings before. Most had been messier. He'd never forget the deserter in Gallean. It had taken the headsman six cuts with his axe to finally chop through the ex-soldier's thick neck. Later, he'd heard that someone had bribed the executioner to use a dull blade. Today was a different story. The camp commander, *Kapikul* Hazael, had kept his blade sharp. Jirom admired the sword—a two-handed *assurana* blade with a long, almost delicate, curve. *Assurana* swords were rare. Passed down from father to son in the oldest Akeshii families, they were said to be unbreakable.

A slave ran forward to wipe the blade, but even after it had been cleaned, it held a scarlet tint Jirom had never seen in steel, as if the metal had absorbed the victim's blood. When the *kapikul* slid it back into its sheath, it was like watching poetry.

But not for that grunt.

The corpse strapped across the chopping block had been one of them, a new slave recruit training in the queen's army. A dog-soldier, they were called. The lowest rung of the Akeshian military machine. The dead man's crime was being caught stealing food from the officers' dining hall. In some of the armies Jirom had served with, that meant a few lashes. Here it meant death in front of your comrades. A whistle sounded, and the company fell out. A few soldiers were assigned to untying the corpse and dragging it to the caves to be buried, while the rest, including Jirom, were sent to the Hill as their part of the punishment. Apparently, execution wasn't considered enough of a deterrent to theft.

As he ran across the dusty parade ground, Jirom hoped for a breeze to lessen the brutal heat, but there was none to be found. He ran a hand over the smooth curve of his scalp. At least he'd been able to shave his head when he arrived, but that was about the only good thing. When he first learned of his reassignment to the army, Jirom had welcomed it. He'd served in enough military camps to be confident in his chances for escape. He had started planning how he could get inside the city and find Horace. The younger man had made an impression on him. All during the long trek through the desert, Horace had refused to submit to their captors, no matter how much they tormented him. And what had happened during the storm . . . Jirom had never seen such courage. Akeshian storms could break the strongest of men, but Horace had faced it on his feet. Not only that, he had defeated it. At that moment Jirom had known this was a special man, what his people called an *askari'muhagin*. Chosen of the gods.

If a man like that could walk in chains, unbroken, then Jirom, son of the Muhabbi Clan, could do no less. And it had nothing to do with the fact that Horace's light eyes, the color of tropical seas, often visited him in his dreams. He'd spent his entire life running from his feelings about men, but this was something more than physical attraction.

Yet Jirom's plans to find Horace and escape together into the wilds of the desert crumbled when he had arrived at the camp. It was built at the bottom of a round canyon about a mile from the walls of Erugash. Hundred-foot cliffs surrounded the complex. Sentries peered down from the towers built atop the bluffs. It hadn't taken Jirom long to realize the camp wasn't a training facility; it was a death sentence. He'd seen more men die on his first day than in a week fighting in the arena. They died from beatings by the guards, from the brutal regimen of combat exercises that lasted for hours without rest or water breaks, and from each other. There had been six stabbings in his company barracks last night. Jirom had slept sitting up with his back to a wall.

He peered over his shoulder to the execution block. The *kapikul* was striding away with his retinue of slaves and personal bodyguards, probably back to the cool shelter of his quarters. Jirom glanced at the body being carried away. A sorrowful end to a pitiful life.

Why do you care? You didn't even know his name.

They arrived at the Hill, a steep mound of stones ranging in size from fist-size chunks to boulders as large as draft horses. The guards shoved them into a line along the foot of the Hill. As always, a couple men balked and were beaten down under a crowd of batons. Jirom never tried to resist. Life in the camp was hard enough without calling attention to yourself, but that wasn't always easy. As one of the biggest men in his company, he was a natural target. Most of the other dog-soldiers stayed clear of him, but he saw them watching him, waiting for him to make a mistake.

The whistle cried out again, and the company began to climb. Jirom leapt up the incline. Sharp points of rock stabbed through the soles of his sandals as he scrambled higher. Every day they were forced to climb the Hill. This was the second time today, and the muscles in his thighs and lower back started cramping before he got halfway up, but he kept churning his legs.

He was the first one to the top. As he balanced on the craggy summit, Jirom looked down at the men climbing toward him. The first to reach him was a pale-skinned northerner with a shaggy brown beard. He grabbed for Jirom's left foot and earned a kick in the face. The northerner flailed for balance, but the rocks shifted under his feet and sent him spilling down the slope in a shower of stones. Jirom winced as he heard the crack of a snapping bone, and watched the northerner clutch his leg as he slid down the rest of the way to the bottom.

The point of the Hill was simple. Whoever stayed on the top the longest was the winner, and only he was guaranteed to eat that night. The rest would have to fight over the slops and scraps from the guards' dinner. Jirom needed that food. Food was life, and as long as he was alive there was a chance for freedom.

Not every man made it to the top. The Hill was treacherous, and many fell down its slopes with broken bones and gashed flesh. Others got involved in scuffles on the way up as they pushed and grappled to get higher. Those who got to the last few steps found Jirom ready to defend his perch. He threw them back down again, though he tried not to be too rough. These men were trapped in the same circumstance as he was, forced to work and grovel under constant threat of death. The worst part was, he didn't see the logic in it. A training camp was supposed to be a place where new recruits were conditioned for battle by building up their bodies and learning how to fight as a unit. Here everything was backward, and the men were lucky just to survive.

BLOOD AND IRON

Was that the point? To winnow out everyone but the very strongest, the most brutal? How could an army exist under those conditions?

Jirom fought for what seemed like hours. Many of the dog-soldiers were little more than boys, which was the case with most of the armies he'd served in. Throwing them off the mound made Jirom feel sick, but he did it anyway. Finally, the whistle blew again. The men remaining on the Hill started back down. Jirom sat at the top, his chest heaving, his arms and legs throbbing. His back was a solid mass of knots. He might barely be able to walk tomorrow, and yet he would be forced to run and climb and fight, or else he'd join the bodies sealed up in the caves. The cries of the dying reached up to him as the guards put the injured out of their misery—there was no infirmary in the camp. A squad of raw recruits dragged away the dead.

Finally, a guard on killing duty noticed Jirom and pointed a bloody dirk at him. Jirom's knees crackled as he lumbered to his feet and began the long slide down. The same guard made as if to reach for the baton swinging from his belt, but turned away instead. Not wanting to press his luck, Jirom jogged to the parade ground. Most of the company had already disappeared inside the mess tent, but a few still struggled to cross the distance because of their injuries. Jirom could see the panic in their eyes as they glanced back at the guards killing the wounded. A young man, no more than eighteen or nineteen summers judging by the wisps of fuzz on his chin, hobbled on a bad foot. Against his better judgment, Jirom slipped his arm under the youth's shoulder. Acts of kindness were discouraged by the guards, who often singled out the do-gooder for an especially cruel beating, so most of the dog-soldiers kept to themselves.

"Thank you," the young man whispered as they reached the open entrance of the tent. He had the coppery complexion and straight, dark hair of an Akeshii, but his accent hinted at something more eastern. Perhaps Moldray or one of the Jade Kingdoms. He had beautiful eyes, deep black like cheetah spots.

Jirom slipped his arm out of the embrace. "It was nothing. Can you make it from here?"

"I'll be fine."

The young man limped inside. The men in Jirom's company found places to sit at the long tables. There they would wait until the officers and guards had eaten. Jirom went to the lone table at the head of the tent. If there was a drawback to winning on the Hill, it was that he had to enjoy his prize in front of the others. While they watched with hungry eyes, a cook brought over a platter and dropped it in front of Jirom. The smell of roasted meat filled his head like nectar, reminding him that he hadn't eaten since breakfast.

"To the victor!" the cook said with a laugh and then tromped off.

The cut of meat wasn't the best, probably a slice off the rump, but it looked like a feast to Jirom, pinkish-brown and oozing juices. He dug right in, using both hands to hold the roast while he tore off chunks with his teeth. The first time he'd won the Hill, he had felt odd eating in front of so many hungry men, but today he devoured it without pause. None of the others would think twice if they'd won.

He was so enjoying the meal he didn't notice someone walking up to him. All Jirom saw was a body. Then a huge hand snatched the meat out of his grasp. The giant of a man standing before his table was nearly seven feet tall and had to weigh at least thirty stone. His small, greedy eyes stared at Jirom as he bit off half the meat haunch in a single bite and started chewing. Jirom had seen this man around the camp. He was in a different company, but he seemed to be allowed to wander about as he wished, and the other dog-soldiers cowered wherever he went. This was the first time Jirom had seen him up close, and he had to admit it was an impressive sight. But that was his food the giant was eating. His food and his respect.

"Put it down," he whispered. "And walk away."

The huge man smiled with brown juice running down his chin. "This is my camp, runt. First I'm gonna eat your dinner. And then I'm gonna take you out back and fuck y—"

Jirom shoved hard against the table with both hands and drove the wooden edge into the giant's belly. As the big man staggered back, Jirom leapt to his feet and lashed out with his right fist. His knuckles cracked against the underside of the man's jaw, rocking his head back. The giant wobbled a moment before righting himself. It was like watching a water buffalo try to maneuver—huge and ungainly and liable to crush anything in its path. With a growl, the giant swung a roundhouse punch. Jirom covered his head, but the buffet knocked him to the floor anyway. Ears ringing, he shook his head.

All conversation in the mess tent had ceased. The giant grinned and took another bite of the victory meal. Jirom considered letting it go.

No, to the hells with that.

He kicked out, and his heel made a satisfying crunch as it connected with a kneecap. The giant grunted and tipped sideways. Jirom shot to his feet, ignoring the pain tearing down his lower back, and landed two solid punches before his assailant could react. The giant looked stunned but not seriously hurt. Then his eyes narrowed to thin slits and his massive shoulders hunched. Huge hands gripped Jirom by the neck and squeezed. Jirom pounded on trunk-like forearms to loosen their grip, but without any success. He kicked at the injured knee, only to have his boot bounce off without eliciting a response.

Unable to breathe, Jirom heaved with his entire body. He managed to stand the giant up a little taller, but he didn't have the leverage to lift the bigger man. Feeling consciousness slipping away, he summoned all his strength in a last-ditch effort. Instead of trying to outmuscle the giant, Jirom stepped back with his right foot and twisted in that direction. The sudden change in momentum caused the other man to stumble forward and fall to the floor with a resounding crash. Jirom followed up by dropping all his weight on top of his fallen rival. He was grinding his elbow into the man's throat when the assembly horn sounded. Everyone jumped up and hustled out to the yard. Everyone except Jirom and his foe.

Jirom glanced at the man beneath him, his blood coursing with the rush of violence. The feeling took him back to his days in the arena. He looked over and spotted the dust-covered remains of his meal on the floor. He could still taste the juices on his tongue.

I'll just have to win another one tomorrow.

He rolled off the giant and went to the doorway, feeling every ache in his body. He took his place in the fourth row of the formation. The positions were based on seniority, how long you had survived in the camp, but the guards evidently had some discretion because they moved men around daily.

The benefits were tangible: the top squad was treated the best and were often allowed to skip grueling exercises like the Hill. Even better in his eyes, every sennight the first squad of each company graduated from the camp to join the queen's legions.

Jirom stood still as the guards checked the columns, which took almost half an hour. Anyone who grumbled received a baton to the back of the head. The entire camp was assembling on the parade ground. Full-camp reviews such as this were done every morning at first light and every night before the men turned in. This was a change in the routine. Was it another execution?

"Hey," the man next to Jirom whispered. He was short but thick-chested and covered in rust-red hair. "You better watch yourself."

Jirom clenched his right hand into a fist. "Why is that?"

The man jerked his chin back toward the mess tent. "What you did in there. Algo has friends among the guards. You better sleep with your eyes open."

"If he has so many friends, why hasn't he been picked to leave yet?"

The man leaned closer and dropped his voice. "'Cause he *likes* it here. And the guards hold him back."

"Why do you care what happens to me?"

The man shrugged. "Who says I do? Look, I saw you help that kid with the busted foot. Not too many people would do that here. So maybe I'm helping you with some advice."

"All right. I'll be careful."

A baton smashed into Jirom's shoulder.

"Shut your mouth, you black dog!" a guard shouted in his ear. "You don't talk in formation or I'll have your tongue!"

Jirom swallowed his ire until the guard marched away to harass someone else. A hush fell over the ranks as *Kapikul* Hazael arrived, followed by the slave who carried his sheathed sword. Hazael stopped in front of Jirom's company and eyed the troops of the first rank, hands clasped behind his back.

"Form up!" an officer shouted.

Boots stamped on the ground as dozens of camp guards rushed to surround the company. Every guard was armored in hardened leather from head to boot; each carried a bared sword. An itch tickled the back of Jirom's scalp.

BLOOD AND IRON

This was new. His hands clenched and unclenched as his heart beat a little faster.

"Every sixth man!" the company commander yelled.

Jirom glanced down the line as a crew of guards rushed past. They seized the short man beside him, who happened to be standing in the sixth position of his row. Along with the other unfortunates, he was rushed to the front of the company. Jirom anticipated what would happen next as the chosen men, all thirty-some of them, were forced to their knees before the *kapikul*. The short man wrestled with his holders and managed to throw one of them off, but four guards jumped in and pinned him to the ground. Jirom's feet shifted as the instinct for survival warred with his sense of honor.

Their commander addressed the assembly. "This company has been deemed unsatisfactory. By order of our Great Leader, an example will be set so that every man will know the price of failure."

The entire camp watched in silence as the *kapikul* drew his sword from its ornate scabbard. The last rays of the sun reflected in the polished *assurana* blade in glimmers of orange and gold. Jirom took a step. He knew he couldn't make a difference against the dozens of guards surrounding the company.

But if I set an example, the rest might rise up.

No one else moved as *Kapikul* Hazael went down the line with quiet efficiency. The kneeling soldiers were forced to bend forward. One by one, their heads were lopped off. Blood glittered in the air each time the *assurana* blade rose up. After the first couple executions, those farther down the line started to struggle, and extra guards came up to hold them. Some of the men yelled; others begged. A few broke down and cried as their turn approached. Jirom saw Horace in his mind, facing the desert storm, defying its power. Before he knew it, he was pushing through the ranks. His first targets were the guards holding down the short man, who continued to scrap and kick and bite. If he could free that one, maybe a few others would see it and make a stand for their lives. He didn't have a plan beyond that. He knew it was suicide, but he'd rather die fighting than live in fear.

Jirom grabbed the nearest guard by the back of his jerkin and heaved him away. He kicked another in his stomach. The other guards holding the short man raised their swords, and Jirom rushed at them. They all crashed to the ground together. Jirom slammed one guard's head against the ground and punched him in the teeth for good measure, and then head-butted the other in the face. That guard rolled over, clutching his nose. His sword landed at Jirom's feet.

Jirom glanced down at the fallen weapon. If he picked it up, he might kill a few of the guards, but he would surely be killed in the end. Then again, this might be his last, best chance to die on his feet with a weapon in his hand. To die like a warrior.

Just as he started to reach down, something struck the back of his head. Points of light burst in front of his eyes, and an intense feeling of nausea stirred in his stomach as his legs gave way. Another blow rocked his skull to the side, and the ground rushed up to collide with his face.

Sweat dribbled down Jirom's face and neck, dripping onto his thighs as he sat in the tight space.

He had been locked inside one of six iron boxes positioned atop of the canyon's southern wall, exposed to the sky. Large enough for a man to sit inside, but not to stand or lie down, each was its own encapsulated hell. It had been only a couple hours, judging by the angle of the sunlight filtering through the rectangular slot in the box's door, but already his legs were cramping. Yet the heat was worse. There was no escaping the feeling of being inside an oven. Even his lungs burned from breathing in the sweltering air.

This is where I'll die. Cooked like a hen.

His head still throbbed from the blows that had knocked him out. He tried not to touch the tender spots, but every time his head tilted back against the side of the box, a sick feeling roiled in his stomach. While he suffered, his mind wandered. He relived the events of his life, seeing his family again in their small home on the edge of the great plain. He recalled the day he had left, and his first battle. Faces passed through his mind, the faces of the men he'd killed during those wild, bloody days, and the faces of the men who had marched by his side. He saw cities burning and the violence that followed as the victors took out their pain and fear on the survivors. He smelled the stench of death and knew that this time it had come for him.

A scratch at the door of the box stirred his senses. Shifting like a drunkard, he hunched forward. A face appeared at the screen covering the slot. Jirom might have expected a guard, or even the *kapikul*, come to taunt him, not the scraggly man peering at him through the wire mesh. He was dark-skinned for an Akeshii, and not unhandsome in a dangerous sort of way. Black whiskers covered his chin. His eyes were a peculiar color. At first glance they looked black, but a closer look revealed the deepest green Jirom had ever seen. They stared into the box without a trace of compassion.

"What's your name?" asked a voice as hard as those piercing black-green eyes.

Jirom stared back. Talking required energy, and he had little to spare.

"Here." The man held the mouth of a small bladder to the screen.

Jirom smelled the water as he leaned forward and pressed his lips to the screen. The tepid drink tasted better than wine. When it was gone, he sat back with a sigh. "Thank you."

"That was quite a show," the man said. "I can't decide if it was the bravest thing I've ever seen, or the dumbest."

Jirom rapped his knuckles against the top of the box. "Judge by the result."

"Aye. You got a powerful desire to die?"

"Not particularly."

"But you've soldiered before."

Jirom nodded. His past didn't matter anymore. Nothing mattered but getting out of here and being free again.

"You know what they're preparing us for? War." The man smiled. "War against the infidels, they say. But I think they mean to use us elsewhere."

Elsewhere? What did that mean? Into the southern continent? Akeshia had tried that before and gotten its imperial nose bloodied. The ragtag slaves he'd seen below in the camp weren't going to accomplish any grand conquest. No, it had to be something else. What would the queen of Erugash want? He thought of Ceasa, the seat of the empire. Was Queen Byleth preparing to make a play for the Chalcedony Throne? It was insane. But what if she succeeded?

The man nodded as if reading his thoughts. "Listen. I've been watching you. You know how to fight and you're not stupid, despite that stunt today. Tell me, are you willing to fight those bastards again if it meant a chance to get out of here?"

"Open this door and you'll get your answer."

"Anxious, eh? Can't say that I blame you, but you'll have to stew in there a little longer. But don't fret. They'll let you out in the morning. Maybe give you a little thrashing and then back into the ranks you'll go."

"I'm not to be executed?"

The man grinned, making him look somewhat like a jackal. He was missing his upper left canine tooth. "No. I imagine they'll be promoting you. They like fighters here. The nastier, the better."

"So when do I get to fight our captors?"

"Soon. I got myself an outfit with one thing in common: we all hate the empire enough to risk our lives fighting it. There are a lot of slaves who feel the same way. That sound like something you want to be a part of?"

"Maybe, but I have a request."

"The slave in the box has a request? What is it?"

"The *kapikul*. I want him for myself."

"You go for the throat, don't you? All right. That's a deal—when the time is right. And I say when it's right. Agreed?"

It was Jirom's turn to smile. "Agreed."

As the man started to move away, Jirom had a thought. "Wait!"

The black-green eyes returned to the screen. "Quiet down! You trying to get me tossed in there with you?"

"What about the slaves taken into the city? I know a man inside. He's a friend."

"Is this friend as tough as you?"

"Tougher," Jirom said.

"Do you know where he is?"

"The palace."

"The queen's palace? Then mourn for him and be done with it. The palace is locked up tighter than a royal virgin's cunny. I can't waste lives on a doomed rescue mission."

Jirom backed away from the door. "Then leave me. I'll get to him myself."

"Listen. It will be hard enough to get away ourselves. I don't like leaving good men to die, but it's not possible."

"Give me one chance," Jirom said. "He's . . . special."

The man hissed in a language Jirom didn't know, which was surprising. He thought he'd heard every profanity that existed. "All right. You'll get your chance, but you need to be patient."

"I have your word?"

The man pressed his hand to the mesh. "On the honor of my name and the names of my forefathers."

Jirom reached out to the screen. "Then I will follow you, for good or ill."

"Good for us, and ill for our enemies. I'll see you tomorrow when they let you out of this cage. We'll talk more then, and maybe work up a plan to get your friend out when the time comes."

"It is agreed. My name is Jirom, son of Khiren."

The man touched his forehead. "I'm Emanon."

The face vanished from the screen. A distant voice called out, but no one answered.

As Jirom settled back in the box, thunder rumbled overhead. It shook the box with tiny vibrations. Outside the slot, the daylight was finally waning. A storm was coming, and though he was locked inside this box he felt exposed to the elements. As he prepared for a long night, plans turned around in his mind. Plans of how to escape this camp and find the man who had given him hope.

CHAPTER FOURTEEN

*H*e held tight to Sari's hand as the people closed in around them. They tried to run, but the crowd was too thick. Everywhere Horace turned, townsfolk stood with their backs to him. He could hear Josef talking behind him, but his son's words were nonsense. Baby-talk, even though Josef was seven . . .

No, he just turned three years old last . . . last. . . .

He tried to pull Sari closer, but something was holding her back. He was afraid to turn around, afraid of what he might see. Her hand was hot in his grip, blistering his palm. She was speaking to him, too, but her words were carried away on the wind. Somewhere in the distance, a woman screamed.

Horace bolted upright. His heart thumped in his chest like it wanted to break free. He saw it again so vividly, that last day in Tines. He held onto that moment, savoring the pain because it was better than feeling nothing, until the images faded. A sigh rattled in his chest as he opened his eyes.

The cell had no lamp and no window, but enough light filtered under the door for him to make out its narrow confines. The floor was cold stone beneath him. There was no bed to lie on, no benches or chairs. Nothing except a noisome hole in the corner. The only way in or out was through the door, and that was locked and barred from the outside.

They had left him in fetters. The metal gleamed bright in the dark cell. Horace had tried pounding the chains against the floor, tried scraping them against the walls, but he couldn't so much as scratch them.

It was difficult to say how long he'd been confined here. He guessed four or five days, long enough for the cold of the floor and walls to seep into his bones. He'd tried some simple calisthenics on the first day to keep his blood moving, but not much since then. He didn't see the point. So he spent more and more time thinking about the past, reliving the best moments of his life. Childhood recollections like holidays and namedays, the day his father had been recognized with a formal commendation signed by the king, the day his first ship was launched, his wedding day, Josef's birth. Tears gathered in his eyes as those powerful remembrances took hold of him. But eventually the fear crept back into his mind. What were they going to do to him?

The door creaked, and Horace scuttled closer. A bottom panel swung open, and bright light streamed through, burning his eyes. Blinking through the protection of his fingers, he saw a copper plate shoved through the opening, followed by a small pot.

"Hey!" Horace's voice echoed off the walls. "When are you—?"

The panel slammed shut before he could finish his question.

He sat back as the footsteps tromped away from his door. He was alone again. He leaned down to the plate and found a cold glob of pasty substance that smelled like curdled porridge. The water in the pot had a metallic taste, but he drained it anyway. As soon as he set down the vessel, he regretted drinking it all. He'd be thirsty again soon, and no amount of beating on the door would get him more. Every time they served him, Horace tried to talk to his jailors, but they never responded.

Sometimes he heard noises through the walls, like people talking, too low to make out the words. Other times he thought he heard laughing. At some point he started talking to himself to pass the time, playing out conversations he'd had in the past. He imagined there were two Horaces. One was optimistic he would eventually be freed and returned to Arnos, but the other constantly berated him for such romantic gibberish. He would never see his home again. He was going to die in this cell. The two sides bickered in his head, and sometimes he would stop, frozen in terror, as he realized he was muttering both sides of the argument out loud.

After finishing the mush, he licked the water pot to be sure he hadn't missed a drop. Then he stretched out on the floor with his hands folded across his stomach. The chains clinked as they settled around his middle. He slowed his breathing and focused on staying perfectly still, imagining that if he didn't move a muscle maybe he would die in this pose. He wondered what the jailors would say.

Such a dignified corpse. Why can't the other prisoners die so quietly as this one?

His eyes grew heavy as he imagined himself gliding through the sky on a cushion of clouds. Minute by minute, the tension drained from his body. This was freedom. Whether he lived or died, his captors couldn't claim his spirit. An odd sensation formed behind his breastbone, a feeling of lightness as if he were actually about to float off the floor. A kernel of cool heat penetrated his chest, flaring up briefly each time he took a breath. Horace focused on the tiny seed of sensation. Was this the *zoana* that Gaz and Jirom had been telling him about?

The knot of icy warmth vanished as the door opened and a party of soldiers in full armor entered his cell. Horace stood up, blinking against the light of several torches. Without a word, they escorted him out into the corridor where waited a short man with deep wrinkles on his face and a gray beard down to his chest. He wore pale-green robes and a square-brimmed hat. With a sniff, the robed man headed off down the passage, and the soldiers escorted Horace after him.

Horace didn't remember much from when he was first brought down to these dungeons under the palace, but he paid better attention this time. The hallways were arched and dressed in smooth stone. They passed through three doors, including a big iron door at the end, before climbing a long flight of stairs. Horace was winded by the time they reached the top, but he felt good. Calm, like nothing could disturb him. He could face anything.

Even death?

A note of doubt skittered across the surface of his mind as they passed through a series of halls and lavish chambers. Horace walked as tall as he was able, though his legs shook a little. His captors took him up another set of staircases. Arched windows let in light and gave Horace a spectacular view of the city as they rose higher and higher.

When they reached the top Horace guessed they had to be a dozen floors or more above the ground. He was taken through more doors, all made from fine-grained wood with bright brass hinges and pulls. Artwork in metal and fired clay adorned the walls of the hallways. The floor was flagged in cardinal-red stone, the walls and ceiling in sand-colored blocks with flecks of black and gold. Despite the opulent surroundings, or perhaps because of them, Horace began to sweat. Where were they taking him? He looked around every turn expecting to be startled by something horrible. By the time they stopped at a door at the end of a hall, his hands were shaking. He tried to recapture that feeling of calm, to accept whatever happened, but his nerves refused to obey.

The robed man opened the door and went inside. Horace waited with the silent soldiers. The doorway led to some kind of antechamber tiled in cream-colored stone. One soldier produced a key and unlocked Horace's shackles. He almost wept with relief as the metal cuffs came off. His wrists were red and raw. While he massaged them, the soldiers took position on either side of the doorway, but none of them moved. With a deep breath, Horace entered.

The door closed behind him. The robed man disappeared through another archway, leaving Horace in the antechamber. The ceiling was domed and painted to resemble the sky. People in bright garb sat on clouds, laughing and cavorting while tiny children played pipes and other instruments. In the very center was the sun in yellow, its shining rays emblazoned with gold leaf. It was quite striking.

A throat cleared.

Horace almost jumped when he saw the woman, standing in the archway the robed man had taken. She was . . .

Better-looking than the painting.

The thought popped into his head before he could squash it. But she *was* good-looking. Her face, with its perfect cheekbones, could have graced a masterpiece. She looked younger than him by a few years, with startling blue eyes and long, golden-blonde hair that tumbled past her shoulders. Her tunic matched her eyes, short-skirted and belted with a white cord, but his gaze was drawn to the gold collar around her neck. It was slender, almost like a choker necklace, but there was no denying that it was a slave's collar.

"Please," she said. "Come in."

"You speak Arnossi?" It made sense. She *looked* Arnossi.

He followed her into the next chamber, which was circular and set up like a sitting room with three large, cushioned divans and a pair of chairs. Everything looked like it was of the finest quality, from the furniture to the pastel frescoes painted on the curved walls. Three other doorways radiated out from the room, two of them closed. A nice breeze entered the room through a tall, open window.

The robed man spoke, and the young woman translated. "Sire, Chancellor

Unagon says these rooms have been provided to you by the queen. You are instructed to remain here until Her Majesty calls for you, but you are her guest. Anything you require, you need only ask."

"All right," Horace replied. "Tell him I'm honored and I will call on him personally if I need anything. And thank him for me."

He listened closely as the young woman interpreted his words. Chancellor Unagon nodded and walked out to the swish of his robes, but the young woman remained behind. Horace looked to her, not sure what he was supposed to do.

"I am Alyra," she said. "I'll be your servant while you stay in the palace."

"I don't want a . . ." He gestured to her collar.

"I have been commanded to serve you. Please. I have drawn a bath. You must want to refresh yourself."

Horace looked down at himself. He was filthy, and the sumptuousness of the room only made him feel more out of place. He followed her through the open doorway into the largest bath chamber he had ever seen. It was almost as big as the townhouse he and Sari had rented right after they were married. A huge copper tub stood in the center of the floor, filled with steaming, soapy water. A mosaic of four nymphs cavorting in a stream decorated the far wall.

Instead of leaving, the young woman untied the cord around her waist and set it on a wooden bench beside the tub. Sudden warmth suffused Horace's face as she stripped out of her tunic. He held his breath without intending to, unable to take his gaze off her, even as she turned back to face him.

"Shall I help you remove your clothes?" she asked.

Exhaling slowly, Horace shook his head and undressed himself. When he got down to his small clothes, he whisked them off and stepped into the tub. Only after he was submerged in the hot water did he chide himself. Why should he be embarrassed? She was a servant of the palace, certainly accustomed to seeing people without their clothes. But then she leaned over the tub holding a sponge, and the nearness of her nudity was impossible to ignore. The women of his homeland did not parade around stark-naked. At least, not outside houses of ill repute.

To take his mind off the situation, Horace asked her, "Where did you learn to speak Arnossi so well? Your accent is almost nonexistent."

"My parents were Arnossi, sire."

He turned around in the water, sending waves across the tub. "They were? Then how did you become a . . . ?"

"A slave? We lived at the colony of Marico on the island of Thym when the Akeshians attacked. My father died in the fighting, but my mother and I were taken as slaves."

"I'm sorry. That's horrible. How old were you?"

"Ten, sire."

He leaned back against the side of the tub. "May I ask, what became of your mother?"

"I don't know. We were separated a couple years after our capture and sold to different owners. I haven't seen her since."

The knot in his chest returned as he imagined how a child might feel to be enslaved by the people who had killed her father, and then to be separated from the only other connection to her old life. He could understand what that would be like. "I'm . . . that's . . . I'm sorry."

The talk of slaves reminded Horace of Jirom. "Alyra, I have a friend. We came to the city in the same caravan, but he was taken somewhere else. Sold, presumably. Is there any way I can find him?"

He described Jirom and what had happened at the slave market.

"I'm not sure," she said. "But my guess is that he was shipped out to the mines. Or maybe sent to the army training camp north of the city."

"Can you try to find out, please?"

"I'm afraid there isn't much I can do, sire. Please forgive me."

Finished with his arms and chest, Alyra poured a fragrant white liquid into his hair and rubbed it in, then rinsed him with fresh water from a copper pail. Afterward he felt better. His eyes drifted shut for a moment, but they snapped open as something warm and slimy attached to his face. Horace bolted upright, reaching for his chin. His fingers came away covered in a warm, brown sludge. "What are you doing to me?"

Alyra stood beside the tub, holding a cup. Inside was more of the odd-looking substance. "Shaving you, sire. Please sit back."

Horace put his fingers to his nose. The stuff had a minty smell, which was rather pleasant, actually. He returned to his former position and leaned back, allowing her to finish applying the salve. "What is it?"

"An extract of honeymint and the bark of the *sarbatu* tree. It will nourish your skin and make the shaving easier."

It occurred to Horace, as she stood over him with a steel razor, that his life was literally in her hands. He held still as the blade ran across his neck, but breathed easier after a few strokes. She had a sure hand, and within a short time he was relaxed enough to enjoy the sensation of being shaved, surrendering to the hot water and the bubbles and the slick whisk of the razor across his skin.

"May I ask you something?" she asked.

Horace let his eyes droop half-closed. "Sure."

"I've heard rumors among the palace servants. They say a storm struck your entourage on its way across the desert. They also say that you saved everyone. Is that true?"

He recalled the sensations he'd experienced in the cell, the feeling of lightness and the seed of hot and cold in his chest, and suddenly he felt empty. "I suppose it is."

He told her what he remembered of the storm, but just like when he'd told the queen, he didn't have any way to explain his actions or the results. "Nothing like that has ever happened to me before. It was unbelievable."

"It's amazing," she said.

"I don't know. Lord Isiratu didn't seem pleased."

"You shamed him, sire." Alyra wiped his face with a wet towel. "You succeeded where he and Lord Ubar had failed. According to the law, you had the right to take his life, had you so wished."

"That's crazy. I didn't even know what I was doing."

"All the more impressive, my lord."

Horace reached up to find his chin smooth and tingling. "Do all *zoanii* have this power of sorcery?"

"Yes, sire. It is what makes them *zoanii*."

"And they are the ruling class of this land."

"That's right."

"Are all children of the *zoanii* also sorcerers?"

"Often that is the case, especially with the older bloodlines. Or so I've been told. Yet sometimes there are children born without the *zoana*, which is why producing a true-born heir is so important. Such is the case of Lord Isiratu. Lord Ubar is his sixth son, by a third wife, but the first among his children to possess the power. Very sad."

"What happens to the children without it?"

"It is not spoken about," she said, "but some are killed by their families to rid them of the shame. Many are sent to the temples to become priests and priestesses."

Horace imagined all those unwanted children, consigned to lives of prayer. "I've seen some of these Akeshian priests. Why do some wear yellow robes and others red?"

"The clergy of the pantheon wear many different-color robes, sire. Among the Sun Cult, the ministers wear gold, while the members of the Order wear red."

"The order?"

"The Order of the Crimson Flame. They are responsible for enforcing the temple's edicts."

"Like a private army?"

"Somewhat, sire. The Order's members are chosen at a very young age and train for many years."

That sounded like a secret society. Arnos had them, too, although they were mainly political movements. "How are they chosen?"

"They all possess *zoana*."

She said it as a matter of simple fact, but a chill ran down Horace's back. More sorcery. It seemed like it was everywhere in this forsaken country. "Wait. So they are sorcerers, but not *zoanii*?"

"Yes, sire. Once accepted into the Order, they disavow all former ties, including the bonds of family and rank, to serve the Sun Temple."

"Why would someone do that?"

"There are many reasons, sire. Some members of the Order were orphans raised by the temple. Others committed an offense against their family or liege. Please, excuse me."

Alyra left the chamber, and Horace took the opportunity to hop out of the tub. His legs wobbled a little as he stepped onto the floor. He started to reach for his clothes and then realized they were gone.

She probably took them to burn, and I can't blame her.

Dripping wet, Horace looked around for something to put on. He opened a cabinet but found only more sponges and a row of small bottles. He was just closing the door when Alyra reappeared. Horace covered his groin with his hands as he stood there, dripping water on the tile floor. She offered him a robe. As soon as the fabric touched his skin, Horace looked down in wonder. He had never worn silk before. The robe was a rich burgundy color with a black border and wide cuffs at the wrists. Alyra tied the sash around his waist in an intricate knot that resembled a flower blossom. While he was admiring the garment, she held out a swath of material that looked like a tiny hammock of black silk. It took Horace a moment to realize it was some form of undergarment. His face heating up again, he took it from her and bent away as he slipped it on. The garment felt strange, riding up between his legs and into the crack of his behind. As he moved his hips from side to side, trying to get the thing to sit right without adjusting himself in front of her, Alyra assisted him in putting on a pair of sandals. He felt a little odd as she knelt to help him, but the sandals fit so well, the soft leather molding to his feet like they had been made specifically for him, that he forgot his qualms.

"Does everyone dress this way here?" he asked.

She stood up and began to put on her clothes. "This is the customary garb for a *zoanii* man of the *do'jun*, the tenth rank, sire. You must look presentable for your private audience with the queen."

Horace was about to tell her that he wasn't *zoanii*, that this was all a big mistake, but her mention of a private audience stole his attention. "I'm going to see the queen again?"

"Yes. Right now, in fact."

A loud knock echoed from the front room.

"Excuse me," Alyra said, and she hurried away to answer it.

He followed, dreading the upcoming interview. The queen's presence had been powerful and alluring when he saw her in the great chamber. He wasn't comfortable with the idea of meeting her in a private setting. He couldn't help wondering if this was all just a hoax, some cruel torture designed by his captors to lull him into complacency before they tossed him back into a cell.

Alyra opened the door, and two soldiers in scale armor entered. They both stopped in the atrium and placed a fist over their hearts.

"They are here to escort you, sire," Alyra said.

Horace tried to swallow, but his mouth had gone dry. "All right. I suppose this is it."

"May the blessing of Sippa be upon you," she said, bowing to him.

Not sure how to respond, Horace nodded as he left the suite. He impressed himself by not stumbling, even though his legs were still shaky and his stomach flipped somersaults. More soldiers waited in the hallway outside the apartment. They fell in around him.

As Horace followed them through the confusing corridors of the palace, he considered his options. He supposedly possessed some great power. What if he lashed out with it? Would it be enough to subdue these men and let him escape? But then he considered that he was alone, a stranger in a strange city with many leagues between him and the shore. Even if he made it back to the beach, what then? It wasn't like he could spread his arms and fly home. No, he was well and truly trapped. His best option was to keep his head on straight and try to come up with a reasonable plan. So he watched everything, trying to memorize the route they took, the chambers they passed.

The soldiers led him up a flight of pristine white marble steps to a door made of a lustrous red wood. Horace took a deep breath as they pulled it open and stood aside. If he thought the apartment he was staying in was lavish, he had no words for what he saw before him. The atrium at the front of the suite was large enough to hold a feast, its floor inlaid with a beautiful mosaic of cut glass in swirling patterns of sky-blue, turquoise, and white. The walls were covered in golden plaster upon which rows of colorful figures had been painted. Horace felt like he was walking through an art gallery, the lifelike eyes following his every step. On the left was a battle scene involving two armies of easterners. The details were exquisite down to the links of mail in their armor. The painting on the right was a landscape showing a great city on the banks of a green river. He knew it at once for this city, Erugash, though in the picture the mighty palace was only half-built with tiny scaffolds clinging to its sloped sides.

Two soldiers—freakishly big men in mail armor—stood at attention flanking the door on the far side of the chamber. Large, curved swords rested against their shoulders.

Horace took a few steps into the chamber and stopped, clasping his hands before him. Then a young woman walked out between the soldiers. She couldn't have been older than eleven or twelve and wore a sheer tunic, unbelted so it billowed around her slim figure. Horace smiled at her until he noticed the gold collar around her neck. He had to remind himself this was a heathen land, and *he* was the outsider.

The girl motioned for him to follow, so he did, passing between the huge guards and into an even larger chamber. The interior room had a high ceiling, and the far wall was open to the sky. The side walls were limned with colorful frescoes that reminded Horace of the paintings in the cathedral of St. Ephrates. The men in the pictures wore long, square-cut beards and bright garb. They had such haughty expressions that he thought they might be kings, and the women queens, perhaps. Then he noticed the clouds under their feet and the stars twinkling around them.

Not kings. Gods.

He studied the paintings as the girl left him alone. He didn't hear anyone else enter until a contralto voice made him turn quickly. "Welcome, Horace of Arnos."

The queen stood behind him. Her hair was down, the inky-black tresses cascading almost down to her waist. A dress of white silk clung to her curves, and a jade amulet the size of a chicken egg hung around her neck. Two servant girls, both wearing delicate gold collars, entered behind the queen. Smiling, they sat on a cushioned divan in a corner of the room and took up a game that involved rolling clay dice and moving wooden pegs across a marble tile.

Horace made an awkward bow to the queen, not sure if he was supposed to kneel or kiss anything. "No chains this time, Your Excellence?"

"I don't think we'll need them, do you?" Queen Byleth smiled as she sauntered toward him, as elegant as a leopardess prowling through the jungle.

BLOOD AND IRON

"Ah, no, Your Excellence. I, er . . ."

Stop staring at her, idiot!

Horace cleared his throat. "If I may say, you speak flawless Arnossi."

"I had very good tutors." She stopped before him, one hand placed on her hip. "As a girl, I wished that I would someday visit the countries of the West."

"That would be . . . something." He grasped for something witty to say and failed. Instead, he tried to steer the conversation toward the thing nearest his heart: going home. "Perhaps that day will come when our nations can meet in friendship. I would like that very much."

"Would you?" The queen looked to the painting again. "I see you were admiring the murals. Are you a lover of art?"

"Ah, not exactly. I mean, it's very beautiful."

"It's called *Nura'in Anunnaka*. The Lights of Heaven. At the top is the god Endu, lord of the sky, with Enkath the Earth-lord and Temmu the Water-lady at his sides. They are the elder gods of Akeshia."

"And the smaller people around them?" he asked.

"They are the children of the elder gods. That one with the golden eyes is Amur, the lord of the sun. His twin sister there is Sippa, the moon."

As the queen named each of the divinities and the part of the natural world they embodied, Horace couldn't believe he was actually talking to royalty. Her beauty was bewitching, making it difficult to concentrate on the conversation. "Do you know what I like most about this mural, Master Horace?" she asked.

"No." He added a hasty, "Your Excellence."

"The violence."

Horace looked at the painting again. It was certainly a beautiful masterpiece, but he didn't see any hint of violence. "I don't understand."

The queen pointed to the god of storms. "See Harutuk and the way he is turned away from Kishar, his earth-bound bride? Why does he hold his hand behind his back so? What is he hiding from her? In the legends, Harutuk poisons his wife before regretting it and questing to the depths of the underworld to find her. So is he hiding more poison, ready to repeat his crime? Or is that the antidote, held ready in case she should try to get even with him?"

She indicated a small woman sitting in the corner by herself. "And here is Erimu, the mother of the gods."

Horace leaned over to get a better look at the small figure and by doing so placed himself closer to the queen. The scent of her perfume filled his head, sweet like a blend of flower blossoms and lemon. "If she's their mother, why is she alone in the corner?"

"See the cut across her neck and the chains around her ankles? She was killed by her own children and entombed under the earth. But she has a secret. Look in her sleeve."

Horace saw what she meant. A thin, serpentine tail curled around the goddess's wrist and disappeared into her clothing. Near the neckline, a reptilian head emerged, sprouting sharp fangs. Another head peeked from under the hem of her gown.

"She has other children as well," the queen said. "And they wait for the day when they can avenge their mother."

Horace stepped back from the mural. He never would have seen those details if they hadn't been pointed out. The queen regarded him. "Akeshia's politics are not unlike her myths. Polite and cultured on the surface, but teeming with danger underneath."

He had no idea why she was telling him this, but he nodded. "I will keep that in mind, Your Excellence."

"That is a curious title," she said. "Is that how the royalty of your homeland are addressed?"

"I apologize, Your . . . well, I don't think so. We usually refer to our king as 'Majesty' or 'Highness,' but I was unsure how it was done here, so I just said what came to mind. I'm very sorry if I offended."

"Not at all. I actually enjoy it. Please, continue to use it."

Horace bowed his head. "As you wish, Your Excellence."

He noticed there were no guards in the chamber with them. That struck him as odd. He had always envisioned royalty as being surrounded at all times with underlings and courtiers and minstrels. "Pardon me, Your Excellence, but why am I here?"

"I wanted to measure you for myself."

There was a look in her eyes that made him want to step back, but he held his ground. "Measure me?"

"Yes. To evaluate you without all the prying eyes of the court. I want to know what kind of man you are, to wield such power. And yet so meek, to allow yourself to be taken as a slave."

He gestured around the room. "Aren't you concerned to be alone with me?"

She showed her teeth, which were straight and white against the fullness of her red lips. "There are many in this realm, Master Horace, who would tremble to be alone with *me*."

Oh, I believe it.

"I can't tell you much more than I did before. I don't know what happened during the storm. I don't know if I really affected it, or it just ended on its own. I'm no magician or wizard, or whatever you call it. Just a simple man."

The queen strolled over to a sumptuous divan and sat down. Her perfume hung in the air, beckoning him to follow. Horace had to force himself not to let his gaze linger too long on her curves.

"Whatever you are, Master Horace, I'm convinced that 'simple' is not part of the description. I believe what you say, that you have no knowledge of what you did. It is not a common occurrence in Akeshia for someone to possess the *zoana* unknowingly, for we test our children at an early age and cultivate those who show the signs. But it may be different in your country."

"I've never heard of any such tests, Your Excellence. And we have no *zoanii* among us. At least, we aren't ruled by witches and sorcerers." He winced at that last statement.

Good work. Call the woman who decides whether you live or die a witch.

"Pardon my ill manners, Excellence," he added quickly. "I have little experience with talking to mighty persons like yourself. I meant to say that our king is just an ordinary man. Well, not ordinary, exactly. He's royalty after all, but . . ."

The queen leaned back and turned in such a way that her breasts pressed against the fabric of her dress. "I've heard that some people in your country don't believe in the *zoana*. But you know differently now, don't you? You've seen it. Felt it flowing through you."

"With all respect, Excellence, I don't know what I felt."

He braced himself. What would come next? Torture? The rack and red-hot pincers? Castration? He'd heard the horror stories about these people. He swore to himself that he would face it bravely, without begging or sniveling, no matter what they did to him.

"Will you let me examine you?" she asked.

Horace knew what she meant. The same thing Lord Isiratu had done to him, entering his mind with sorcery. He gazed into the queen's jet-black eyes. He wanted to trust her. "All right. What do I do?"

She patted the seat next to her. "Come here."

As he sat down, the queen lifted her hands. She had delicate fingers, the nails painted deep crimson. She wore two rings, a huge diamond-bedecked circlet on her left middle finger and a band of plain white gold on her right forefinger. She laid her hands against the sides of his face. Horace took a deep breath. "What do you want me to d—?"

His question was strangled as a rush of pressure clamped around his head. His lungs seized up as she stared into his eyes. Horace wanted to pull away from the vise squeezing his skull, but he couldn't move. Her eyes held him tight, and he felt himself drawn into their black depths. Pictures flashed in his head, distracting him. He stood on the deck of the *Bantu Ray* again as the carrack pulled out to sea, Avice dwindling in the background. Then the sky darkened and the sea turned into a boiling cauldron as the ship bucked beneath his feet. Ghostly-green lightning flashed through the storm clouds, and a sharp pain pierced Horace's chest. Suddenly, the ship vanished and he was drowning in the frothy sea. His vision grew murky. After some time, light appeared in small spots that wheeled about each other. Slowly—ever so slowly—they resolved into an image. It was Sari, his wife. She stood in the tiny yard outside their home, smiling over her shoulder as she hung their laundry on the line. Josef played at her feet with a stick. Sorrow, sharp as a razor and tinged with sweetness, sliced through Horace as he relived that memory. The day had been blustery. He could feel the cold through the oversized seaman's coat he had inherited from his father, felt the wind scuffing his face. As always, his wife and son never seemed to mind the cold. He started to turn, to walk back inside the warm house.

BLOOD AND IRON

Go back! Look at them one last time, just for a moment. Just a moment longer. Please!

The image was replaced by an older memory. Horace saw his father, with a stylus behind his ear, bending over the old drafting table he kept in his workroom behind the house. The windows were dark, the room lit by a rusty oil lamp hanging from a nail. Horace stood in the doorway, afraid to disturb him while he was working. But then his father looked up and smiled through his thin gray beard and beckoned for Horace to come closer. Horace took a step, but then he remembered that this was just a dream of the past. His father was dead and buried.

Horace felt the queen's magic sifting through his memories. He had understood that she would do something like this, but he hadn't expected it to be so intrusive. He pushed back, unwilling to let her dig deeper. The pain in his head expanded, seizing him and shaking him like a mouse caught in the jaws of a wolfhound. He pushed back harder, getting angry, and this time the pressure diminished. The parade of memories in his head stopped, catapulting Horace back into the queen's chambers. She frowned as her eyes bore into him. Horace tried to tell her to stop, that he wanted this to end, but he couldn't utter a sound. He summoned all his strength, backed by the resentment that had been building these past couple weeks. The deaths of his countrymen. His enslavement. The imprisonments. All of these humiliations welled up inside him on a tide of rage. He would have screamed if he was able. Instead, everything channeled into one great mental push.

The queen flew back against the divan, knocking two cushions to the floor. She held up her hands as if they had been burned, though nothing marred the smooth palms. Panic gripped Horace as he looked at her face. For a moment her features were stretched tight in indignation, nothing like the beautiful seductress she had been a moment ago. She looked so wild he almost expected her to attack him. Then the moment passed, and her face smoothed once again. But Horace couldn't forget what he had seen. It still lurked behind her fathomless eyes, a lethal spider waiting under its trapdoor to spring.

Horace took a deep breath. He felt wrung out. If not for the queen's presence, he would have collapsed against the remaining pillows, but he was afraid now more than ever. He had seen the ferocity that hid behind her stately facade and felt its response within himself. He didn't know which scared him more.

"I'm very sorry," he mumbled as he stood up, hoping his legs were stable enough to hold him.

But the queen reclined, wearing a lazy smile as if nothing had happened. "There is no reason for apologies, Master Horace. Your mind is quite . . . interesting. And now I believe you more than ever. There is no sign of esoteric teaching in your thought patterns."

"So you're done with me then?"

"There is so much more to you than meets the eye. Your strength is quite phenomenal. I would like you to remain."

"Here?" Horace struggled to calm his breathing. "In your—?"

"In the palace," she finished for him. "As our guest. You represent a new factor in the growing conflict between our two nations. We would like to learn more about you. And perhaps we can show you some new things, as well. A cultural exchange. Will you do this for us?"

Horace nodded even as he found himself taking a step backward. "All right. I suppose, if it would help matters between our countries."

Do I have a choice?

"Tomorrow night there will be a small gathering here at the palace. You will accompany me." The queen clapped her hands. "Good day, Master Horace."

Horace struggled to find his voice. "Of course. It would be my honor. Good day, Your Excellence."

The two guards from the atrium entered. After bowing to the queen, they escorted Horace out of the chamber. He looked back, but the queen was departing through an archway with her slaves. He had the impression that he had escaped the tiger's den.

That thought followed him all the way back to his room.

CHAPTER FIFTEEN

The moonlit fields outside Erugash rippled in the cool breeze coming off the plains, except for a barren strip of dark earth surrounding the city walls. The northern winds carried the scent of cactus blooms laden with the dry traces of ancient sands. Alyra pulled the hood of her cloak down low over her face as she slipped across the killing ground. Thankfully, there was no sign of a storm.

Those hellish tempests were her greatest fear whenever she left the city. She couldn't imagine facing one out here where there was no protection. The chaos storms had been little known when she was a child, and her searches of the palace histories revealed they were an infrequent phenomenon, but that was changing. Each year they struck more often and with greater power. The largest had leveled towns and flattened buildings, leaving behind nothing but devastation. Even the *zoanii* were powerless to stop them.

And yet Horace had dispelled one by himself.

When she had first heard that this enigmatic foreign captive was being brought to Erugash, Alyra called in every favor she'd earned over the last three years to contrive her way into his service. The hardest part had been convincing the queen to release one of her handmaidens, but in the end a certain royal chamberlain had made the right appeal on her behalf. It also didn't hurt that she spoke the stranger's native tongue. Alyra had the sneaking suspicion that Her Majesty secretly approved of the move, perhaps hoping to ensnare the foreigner with something familiar. Alyra had been given as a gift to more men than she could easily count, and to no few ladies as well. It was the most repulsive part of her mission. Yet, even during the worst of these encounters, she held fast to her purpose and it got her through.

As for Horace, she wasn't sure what to make of him. The queen's court was convinced he had to be a spy, but he didn't act like any operative she'd ever met. He wasn't coy or mysterious. He was . . . confused, was the best way she could put it. She almost believed his tale of being shipwrecked, but she had long ago given up trusting in coincidence. Part of Alyra was glad the queen had conscripted Horace into her entourage because it made it easier for her to spy on them both. Yet she couldn't help feeling bad for Horace. He was out of his depth.

Alyra hurried past a divot of suspicious sand—watchful for trapdoor spiders, which could grow as large as housecats out here—and slipped into the shadow of a tall boulder. The rendezvous was just over the next rise. She couldn't take the road from the city for fear of being seen; getting caught outside the walls alone at this hour would raise too many questions she didn't want to answer. Her mission made it necessary for her to associate with all walks of life, from the street-cleaners who reported to her the daily activities of certain *zoanii*, to the temple prostitutes who revealed their clients' secrets in exchange for Nemedian gold. Last year she made contact with a group of rebellious slaves operating from the queen's training camp outside the city. They were natural allies to her cause. Fearless and fanatical, and their goal—to disrupt the plans of the Akeshian ruling class—suited her. Their leader had impressive resources for a slave. She hoped tonight's meeting would bring her important news, especially considering the risk she was taking.

Alyra hefted the satchel hung over her shoulder. Her back was tired from lugging the load all this way, but she comforted herself with the knowledge that she was almost at her destination. With silent footsteps, she stole down a weathered footpath. She bent down as she climbed a long mound, not wanting to make a conspicuous silhouette in the moonlight. Three hundred paces away, a guard tower watched over the city's northern approach. Alyra had come this way enough times to know what to look for as she scanned the tower's catwalk. It was empty at the moment, but she didn't move. Fifty heartbeats later, light bloomed and a dark figure appeared. The sentry walked a circuit around the tower's battlements before disappearing again. Alyra scrambled down the hill. She had five minutes, on average, before the guard made another round.

She ran past. If there were any sentries patrolling the area between the towers, things could go bad for her. However, she got to the edge of the canyon without attracting attention.

The site of the camp was a stroke of malevolent genius. Nestled at the bottom of an old stone quarry just north of the city, it was hidden from prying eyes. Yet Alyra suspected the real reason for its placement was to keep its inmates inside. The crucible where Queen Byleth's armies were forged was more like a prison than a training ground. Its denizens struggled just to survive. However, the troops who *did* survive were among the most feared in the empire, able to endure conditions that could cripple other soldiers, even hardened veterans.

The canyon walls dropped more than a hundred yards below her. Climbing it would have taken her half the night, assuming she didn't misstep and get herself killed. Fortunately, she didn't have to.

Alyra put two fingers in her mouth and gave a whistle that mimicked the cry of a milk-hawk. Not two heartbeats later, the cry returned to her as several forms rose from the sand dunes. She breathed easier when she saw a familiar face. Emanon had clipped his hair short in the military fashion. She was accustomed to seeing him with longer, almost curly brown locks. He smiled when she handed him the satchel. Then he beckoned for her to follow to the lip of the canyon where a rope had been fixed around the trunk of a sturdy cactus tree. One by one, the men went over the side and down the rope. Emanon motioned for Alyra to go before him. She took the rope and shimmied down. It was only twenty feet or so to the mouth of a narrow cave.

As Alyra's feet touched down on solid stone, she released the breath she'd been holding. The cave was deeper than it appeared. Emanon lowered a blanket over the cave entrance as he ducked inside after her, blocking out the moonlight and plunging the cave into total darkness. Stone scratched against steel, and a spark bloomed. A small lamp ignited in the hands of a slave-soldier. Most of the men waited at the cave entrance. Each carried a crude weapon—daggers made from tools, spikes, an iron mallet.

"It is good to see you, Lady Alyra," Jerkul said with a shy smile. Every time they met, he never failed to be courteous.

She placed a hand on his corded forearm. "Have you had any word from your family?"

"Erma wrote me. Says my son is growing fast. He's almost up to her hips."

"I'll be glad for the day when you can return to them," Alyra said.

BLOOD AND IRON

Taking the lamp, Emanon said, "Come."

Alyra followed the rebel leader to the back of the cave, which widened into a small chamber about thirty paces into the canyon wall. She stopped short as she sighted an unfamiliar man waiting for them. He had been standing there in the dark, completely still. Her first reaction was awe. The stranger was huge, easily half a foot taller than Emanon, who was no small man. Veins bulged under his dark-brown skin. Her second reaction was terror, fear that the man might be an agent of the queen waiting for the conspirators to assemble. But Emanon approached him without pause. "This is the woman I told you about. Alyra, this is Jirom, one of my new recruits."

Alyra controlled her expression as she greeted the newcomer. This was the man Horace had mentioned. She was surprised, to say the least, to find him here. Emanon usually wasn't the trusting type. Yet he opened her satchel in front of Jirom and spilled out its contents. Six large ingots of bright metal clattered to the floor. Though she had seen it often enough at the palace, Alyra's eyes were drawn to the *zoahadin*. Just this small amount was worth a fortune. The means of its production was tightly controlled, and if the queen ever discovered this theft, Alyra could look forward to a slow, painful death.

Emanon lifted a silvery ingot. "Just six? Enough for a few sword blades, at most."

"I brought what I could," she answered, angered that he would question her effort. "I'll try to get more next time, but there are dangers."

"No. Forgive me, Alyra. I'm grateful for the risks you take. Don't mind my grumbling."

Jirom picked up an ingot. "This is the stuff you said was going to set us free, Emanon?"

"Aye. At least, that's my hope. You want to enlighten our new friend, Alyra?"

"*Zoahadin* is antithetical to sorcery," she said. "We don't know exactly how it works, but armor forged from *zoahadin* is impervious to their magic."

"And weapons made from it," Emanon said, "will cut through their defenses like they were regular people."

Jirom put down the metal. "I've seen the effects of their magic firsthand on the battlefield. We'll need more than a couple swords, unless you've got an army hidden somewhere."

Emanon clapped him on the shoulder. "We'll get more. Oh, Alyra. Jirom has a friend who might be inside the city. A westerner. His name is—"

"Horace," she answered. "Yes, sorry. He mentioned you, Jirom. I wasn't sure how much Emanon wanted to divulge about our operation inside the city."

Jirom's large brown eyes focused on her. "You've seen him?"

She wanted to retreat, but she held her ground. "Yes. I'm one of the palace handmaidens, and I've been assigned to be his servant for the time being."

"He's in the palace?" Emanon asked.

But Jirom overrode him by asking, "Is he all right?"

"He's fine," Alyra answered. "The queen is holding him captive, but he has been treated well for the most part. He's being kept in one of the suites reserved for visiting dignitaries. He's not in danger. Well, not any more than anyone else who dwells in the palace. My new position puts me in a good position to follow his activities. And I can get a message to him, if you wish."

Emanon chuckled. "How do you like that, Jirom? Your friend's living it up while you're stuck in this hellhole with us."

Jirom leaned closer to Alyra. In a lowered voice, he asked, "Has he done anything . . . strange while he's been there?"

She knew what he meant. After a moment's pause, she answered, "The queen knows that he's *zoanii*."

"What?" Emanon looked to Jirom. "You didn't tell me he was one of them."

"He just found out recently," Jirom said. "For the first half of our journey to Erugash, he was collared and chained like the rest of us. Then a storm swept over us, and he stopped it."

As Jirom explained about the chaos storm in the desert, Alyra detected a few differences from Horace's version of the tale. The one that disturbed her the most was how Horace hadn't suffered any immaculata after defeating the storm. That was unheard of. She wasn't sure how the court would react to such news. Not well, she guessed.

Jirom finished with, "I need to free him."

BLOOD AND IRON

"The palace is a fortress," Emanon said. "And the queen has her own army, not to mention any number of sorcerers on hand. We'd never get close to this man, much less get back out alive."

Jirom towered over the rebel leader. "I won't leave him to—"

"Excuse me," Alyra said.

"And I won't sacrifice my entire command for one person," Emanon barked back, stepping up to the big man. "I don't care who he—"

"What about the party?" Alyra shouted, and winced as her voice echoed through the cave.

Both men stared at her. Alyra swallowed as a knot formed in her throat. She was taking an awful risk.

"What party?" Jirom asked.

"The queen is hosting a celebration at the palace tomorrow night," Emanon said. "The entire court will be there. We were planning a mission inside the city while it was going on."

"What kind of mission?"

"An attack on a couple key locations. It's more of an exercise for the new recruits, really, as well as a chance to bloody Her Mightiness's nose."

"That would make a good diversion," Jirom said. "While the queen's soldiers respond to the attack, I enter the palace and find Horace."

"Maybe," Emanon said. "But security will be tight. That means more guards at all the gates, and more *zoanii* walking around. You can't just charge in like a crazed wildebeest."

"There's another problem," Alyra said. "Horace will be escorting the queen to the fete."

Emanon threw his hands in the air. "Well, that does it. There's no way we'll be able to sneak him away from under her nose."

"I'll go alone, if I have to."

Alyra noticed something odd in the way the two men looked at each other as they spoke, a familiarity as if they had known each other for years. Like brothers in a way, but there was a note of tenderness to it, too. Then she realized what she was seeing. They were attracted to each other.

Oh, my heavens. How is this going to affect the rebellion?

Emanon held up a hand. "Listen, Jirom. I understand you want to help your friend, but that's insane. We can try to free him, but only after the operation is done. You must trust me on this. I will make every effort to get to him—this Horace—but I won't waste the lives of other men to do it. Agreed?"

With a growling affirmative, Jirom strode out of the cavern. Alyra watched him go.

"He'll be fine," Emanon said. "Let's finalize our plans for tomorrow. Will your people be able to secure the Mummer's Gate?"

They walked through the plan again. She knew her role. She just hoped Emanon would be able to pull off his end of the arrangement. Once the details were ironed out, she asked him, "Are you sure about tomorrow night? We could still call it off."

He smiled, showing his missing incisor. "What? And miss a chance to tweak Her Dreadness's nose? No, we'll go through with it. And we'll rescue this friend of Jirom's if we can. What do you think of him?"

Alyra had been thinking of Horace. "Hmm? Who?"

He nodded toward the dark passage behind her. "Jirom."

"I'm not sure what to think," she replied, choosing her words carefully. "Have you ever been to Haran?"

"No. Why?"

"They have a tradition there called the *hudda* where men try to jump on the back of a captured lion and ride it like a horse. I hope you know what you're doing with this one."

Emanon chuckled as he loaded the ingots back into the satchel. "Jirom might be as strong as a lion, but I'm not stupid enough to try riding on his back. We're allies united against a common enemy."

"I hope so. Emanon . . ."

"Yeah?"

Alyra hesitated. She was tempted to tell him about the queen's conversation with Lord Astaptah. She wanted another person's perspective and maybe some advice about how she should handle this information. She'd already reported it to her handlers in the network, but so far no new orders had come down. She started to say something but then changed her mind.

BLOOD AND IRON

He has enough to deal with, and I don't want him doing anything foolish.

"Nothing," she said. "Just good luck tomorrow."

"Don't worry. We know what we're doing."

Alyra followed Emanon back down the narrow cave tunnel. She was dreading the trip back to the city. But even worse, she dreaded what might happen tomorrow night. She had never wavered in her duty, but now so many doubts lingered in her mind. Was the prize worth the cost? She would have to find out.

CHAPTER SIXTEEN

The afternoon heat formed a gray haze over the city. Sunlight glinted off the murky green waters of the inner harbor far below, and small boats moved along the waterfront where busy pedestrians hurried through the maze of twisting clay streets. Rimesh sipped from the glass of iced lime juice in his hand as he gazed out the window of the temple's receiving chamber. His eyes strayed to the heart of the city where, in flagrant defiance of tradition, the royal palace rose higher than the temple by a good thirty cubits. He turned away from the window. "Tell me again about the storm."

The younger priest rubbed his hands together in a washing motion. "As I said, Menarch, we were crossing the desert when a chaos storm arrived. Lords Isiratu and Ubar exited the carriage to confront the storm. Then—"

Rimesh held up his pointer finger. "A moment, Brother Nasir."

No matter how many times he heard accounts of *zoanii*, he was always struck by their natural arrogance. The other thing that struck him was the danger of allowing persons of such power to roam free. At the Order academy, initiates who could not obey without hesitation were terminated from the program and sent into the next world on pyres of burning prayers. "When you say they went out to confront the storm, what exactly do you mean?"

"They both got out and faced the storm on foot. They didn't do anything that I could see, nor did I expect to. I have no talent for the Sight, Menarch. I was passed over by the Order while still a novice and placed in a small temple in Gahem—"

"Carry on with your account, Brother."

"Ah, yes. Forgive me. As I said, they stood there facing the storm, but the winds kept getting stronger. Lord Isiratu staggered as if he had been struck a blow, and Lord Ubar turned to help him. There was so much sand flying that I could not see them well, but it appeared as if Lord Isiratu had given up."

Rimesh stepped onto the soft woven carpet that covered the center of the floor and set his glass down on a lacquered table. "What happened next?"

BLOOD AND IRON

"There was a shout from the slaves at the rear of the caravan. It was quite horrible, even in the midst of the storm. Then the winds just died away."

"The storm left?"

"Yes, Menarch. The clouds vanished and the holy light of heaven shone down on us again."

A cough echoed through the chamber as the high priest of the Sun Cult in Erugash leaned forward in his chair. Kadamun et'Hittsura-Amur was quite old but was still a man of vitality and keen intellect. He cleared his throat. "Who was responsible, my son?"

"The savage," Nasir said. "A westerner captured by one of Lord Isiratu's vassals. He reported being shipwrecked on the—"

"An outlander?" Rimesh had to fight to keep his tone even.

"Yes, Menarch. It was a miracle."

"A miracle? I view it as quite the opposite. The power of the Gods in the hands of a savage is surely the work of the evil ones."

Of course. This new information fit the reports he'd received before coming to Erugash. Temple soldiers found dead at their posts with no apparent wounds. Two priests of Amur disappeared. Rumors of clandestine meetings. And now the arrival of this outlander. It all pointed to a foul corruption infecting this city.

Nasir bowed and placed a hand over his heart. "Of course. I spoke without thinking."

"Quite understandable under the circumstances," High Priest Kadamun said with a smile.

Rimesh frowned at this interruption and tried to get the young priest to focus. "What did Lord Isiratu say to this savage after the storm?"

"Very little. Only that we were going to Erugash following Lord Mulcibar's arrival."

The high priest muttered something that sounded like "meddling relic," but Rimesh ignored it. "Anything else?"

"No, Menarch." Nasir took to dry-washing his hands again. "I believe Lord Isiratu would have preferred to just be rid of the savage, yet he had no choice but to answer the queen's summons."

"I see. Thank you. You have been very helpful."

"Thank you. Thank you very much, Menarch! And may I say it's been an honor meeting you. I've heard so much about your early days at—"

Rimesh gestured and a pair of guards entered. "May the light of Amur shine upon you, Brother."

Nasir took a step toward the door. "And you as well." He bowed twice, once to Rimesh and once to the high priest. "Ah, Menarch?"

Rimesh allowed his eyebrows to rise to show his dwindling patience. "Yes?"

"The savage, sir. He did not bleed."

"Explain yourself."

"He did not display any signs of the immaculata after dispelling the chaos storm. Not a single cut or bruise. Lord Ubar took to calling him . . ." Nasir cleared his throat. "*Inganaz.*"

"Thank you, Brother."

Nasir bowed again and left with the guards. Rimesh held his smile until the door closed. Then he sat in the vacant chair opposite his superior. "I recommend that the brother be sent to a silent cloister for a year, Your Luminance. The sooner, the better."

The high priest's brows came together in a bushy line of ivory-white hair. "Brother Nasir understands the virtue of discretion. He'll be returning to Sekhatun with Lord Ubar. And please call me Kadamun. It is rare to have such a distinguished guest from the capital."

Rimesh leaned back in his chair with a sigh. He could feel the excess energy coiled inside him, wanting release. Back in the capital, he trained daily with sword and shield, a holdover from his formal education, but since arriving in Erugash he hadn't found the time for a workout. "I am but a humble servant of the Light, Brother Kadamun. And I will trust you regarding Brother Nasir's . . . discretion. I would not wish my confidence betrayed by a wayward whisper in the wrong ear."

The high priest gestured to the window and the spire of the palace that marred their view of the heavens. "Byleth is impulsive and flagrantly disobedient, but she is no fool. She'll soon know you talked to Nasir, if she doesn't already."

Rimesh tilted his head slightly.

BLOOD AND IRON

Kadamun chuckled. "Erugash may be far from the bright center of the empire, but you'll soon learn that this city's politics are every bit as sharp as the games played in Ceasa. What do you make of this 'he who does not bleed' tale?"

Rimesh flicked an invisible speck of lint from his sleeve. "Further evidence that this savage is a servant of darkness. And Queen Byleth has taken him to her bosom, in clear defiance of temple law."

Kadamun just sat there, looking off into the distance, until Rimesh cleared his throat. "Your Luminance?"

The high priest shook as if rousing himself from a bad dream. "I've led this temple for nearly thirty years, and in that time I've seen many changes. Famine, plague, epidemics of rats. You know, for a time during the old king's reign I thought we would be cast out of the city. Yet those days seem calm compared to what we face now. Byleth is not like her father. King Rathammon was headstrong and difficult to control even before his rebellion, but his daughter is as unpredictable as a serpent, and ten times deadlier than her father."

"So what will she do?"

"Much of that depends on the advice she receives from Lord Mulcibar. As I said, she is unpredictable. Yet the High Vizier was a staunch supporter of her father and he has the queen's ear. If he counsels her to break ties with the temple, it may be the excuse she's been seeking."

"But by the terms of the armistice—"

Kadamun waved the liver-spotted fingers of his right hand like he was batting away an annoying insect. "The armistice is only as powerful as the will to enforce it, and Ceasa is far away with its eyes cast to the East. What? You think we don't hear the rumors? The empire dreams of new conquests, but it risks ignoring the two asps under its foot."

"Two asps? Does Her Majesty have a twin?"

"The slaves, Menarch. They are uneasy."

"Slaves are always uneasy."

The high priest held up a finger as if lecturing a novice. "When the servant is discontented, the master sleeps lightly."

Rimesh let out a deep breath through his nostrils, already tired of this man. "If there are agitators, the Order knows how to handle them."

"Yes, I suppose it does. But with vital resources spent securing our colonies and staving off foreign incursions, domestic matters have gone unattended. I send instructions to the Order Chapter House, but they are ignored. Inquiries are answered with silence. I took your arrival as a sign that my complaints have been heard."

"I wish it were that simple, but I have been sent here to investigate certain rumors of heresy. Not to bring some rebel slaves in line."

The high priest worked his mouth like he was chewing his gums. "You are, I presume, referring to a—"

"A forbidden cult operating within the city, with the queen's compliance if not her outright collaboration. *That* is what I am referring to."

"Well, I never gave much credit to the rumors, personally."

Rimesh studied the high priest's eyes, which were rheumy and jaundiced within the sagging folds of his face. "Why is that?"

"Because it is preposterous. For that to be true, I would have to be a fool or . . ." His eyes narrowed to mere slits. "Or complicit. Is that what you're driving at, Menarch? Have you been sent to investigate heresy, or to replace a doddering old man?"

Rimesh reached into the pocket sewn into the lining of his robe and pulled out a silver tube. Its ends were sealed with golden wax and impressed with the Primarch's personal sigil. He extended it to Kadamun, who took it with a shaking hand. Rimesh waited as the high priest opened the tube and spilled out the rolled papyrus inside.

Kadamun's lips moved as he read the message. When he lowered it, his face was pinched with anger. "This gives you authority over all temple matters in Erugash. Is this how the Primarch replaces me? With a fiat delivered by the hands of my successor? Will you see me killed, too, or shall I be carted off to some abbey in the desert to live out my last years?"

"There's no call for dramatics, Your Luminance. I am not here to replace you." He put his fingers together in a steeple. "But I will use every ounce of that sanction to root out this evil. And I will crush any obstacle that gets in my way. I trust I am making myself clear."

"Quite. Yet there is little I can tell you on the matter. Yes, there are rumors, but I served in the temples at Yuldir and Epur in my younger days, and there are *always* rumors of one kind or another. As high priest, I have endeavored to rein in Her Majesty's more unbecoming vices, and been moderately successful, if I may say so. But a cult to the Old Ones here in Erugash? No, I cannot conceive of it."

Rimesh stood up. "That is why the Primarch sent me. You will make all of your staff available to me. You will also pass along that my instructions are not to be countermanded by anyone, under any circumstances, save by the direct order of His Primacy."

The high priest rose slowly to his feet. "Is there anything else?"

"Yes. This savage in the queen's possession."

"What of him?"

"I want you to issue a decree declaring him a blasphemer and an enemy of the empire. He is to be remanded to the temple at once for investigation."

The high priest's eyebrows climbed his forehead. "That will cause some problems, Menarch. The foreigner—"

"He's an abomination before the eyes of Amur and all of heaven!" Rimesh took a breath to calm himself. "Forgive me, Your Luminance. I know that you revere the sacred *zoana* as much as I do. Its divinity cannot be permitted to exist within a savage such as this. It is an affront to both our lord and our empire."

"Of course. Yet Byleth is still queen of Erugash, regardless of the armistice. Unless you intend to seize the palace by force, issuing such a decree will do no good."

Rimesh scratched his chin to give the slightest impression that he was considering just such a course of action. "In that case, I withdraw my suggestion."

The relief that passed across the old priest's face would have been comical if it wasn't so pathetic. Yet he bowed with grace. "As you wish."

When the high priest exited the room, Rimesh went back to the window. The day was getting hotter. The sun's rays struck the palace, reflecting off its golden summit. He had prepared his entire adult life for this assignment, groomed with years of schooling and then sent into the field as a chaplain in the imperial legions. All for this moment. If he could tie Queen Byleth to the worship of the Dark Ones, the people would rise up and he could reverse four hundred years of temple abuse at the hands of the *zoanii*.

He looked down to the people in the streets, so far below they looked like insects crawling through a warren of tunnels.

I do this for all of us, so that we may be free.

CHAPTER SEVENTEEN

The suit was black silk, so smooth and glossy it looked like it had been spun by faeryland spiders. The sleeves and legs were puffy like cavalry breeches, but the fabric gathered tight at his wrists with black leather bracers and around his waist with a matching belt. Gold studs—real gold, not fake or plated steel—accented the bracers and belt. A long, black cape and knee-high boots completed the ensemble.

Horace held out his arms, feeling like a prince while a servant brushed his shoulders.

Or a man impersonating a prince.

"*Tidru hisi kapparantu, belum?*" the chief tailor asked as he held up a plate-sized mirror.

Horace nodded, still not believing what he saw in its wavy depths. "It's extraordinary, if that's what you're asking."

The tailor snapped his fingers, and his assistants gathered up their implements and left. Horace stood alone in his apartment, afraid to sit down or brush against anything for fear of marring his suit. Tonight was the queen's party, which he would soon be attending. He had hoped Alyra would be here to attend to him. She had a talent for calming him, something he could really use right now, but she had been called away. Horace played with his collar, trying to get more air. This entire affair was surreal. His country was at war with Akeshia, yet in a few minutes he was going to a fancy gala on the arm of its queen.

He started to look for a drink—preferably something with a lot of alcohol—when the front door opened. He hurried to the foyer hoping it was Alyra, but instead a short, stooped man with a cane limped through the door.

"Lord Mulcibar," Horace said. "It's good to see you again."

"Good evening, Master Horace. I trust you are well?"

Horace held out his arms. "What do you think?"

Lord Mulcibar leaned on his cane as he examined Horace's attire. "I think you have a come a long way from being a slave. May we sit a moment?"

BLOOD AND IRON

Horace ushered the nobleman into the parlor, and they reclined on the soft divans. "Can I offer you anything, my lord? A drink?"

"No, thank you. We don't have much time. The Queen's Guard will be here momentarily to escort you, but I wanted a chance to speak with you first."

"Of course. I hoped I'd see you as well. Can you shed some light on what's happening? I feel like a carpenter's apprentice handling his first hammer."

"Master Horace, I'm afraid you are in extreme danger."

Horace's stomach flipped over. He had feared that something was wrong, that he was being set up for a big fall. "How so?"

"Erugash balances on the edge of a precipice. On one side there is the queen—may she live forever—and arrayed against her are a variety of forces. The royal court is a pit of vipers, all vying to be Her Majesty's favorite. It's a never-ending game of deception, shifting alliances, and betrayal. Then there is the temple of the Sun God, never satisfied no matter how deep its tentacles have sunk into this city's affairs. And you are caught in the middle of it."

Horace rubbed his palms together. "I didn't ask to be."

"Of course not. You were simply unaware, and it's no wonder. *Zoanii* who have played this game all their lives can fall prey to their competitors at any moment. What should concern you is a plot that, I believe, is aimed at supplanting the queen herself."

Horace started to pace the floor. "How does this involve me? I don't know anyone at court, except for you and the queen."

"I don't know. I have been chasing down this particular scheme for a long time, but I'm afraid I know little except that they want to use your arrival in Erugash to their advantage."

"What do they want?"

"As far as I can tell, they want the queen dispatched."

Horace stopped pacing and faced Mulcibar. "You mean they aim to kill her."

"Assassination attempts are not uncommon. And oftentimes those caught in the line of fire are the first to die."

Horace thought of Alyra and was suddenly worried about her prolonged absence. "So what should I do?"

"Conduct yourself as normal. However, if there is an attempt on Her Majesty's life, it will be sudden and lethal. I advise that you defend yourself with any and all means."

Horace frowned as he walked around the divan. He knew where this was going. "I don't know how to control the power. Even if I did, this isn't my concern. No offense, Lord Mulcibar, but I was a captive yesterday, and a slave not long before that."

A loud knock sounded from the foyer.

Lord Mulcibar stood up. "That is all true. I won't try to convince you that the queen is one of your saints, but we are involved in an internal war, Master Horace. You may not have asked to be set down in the middle of it, but that's where you find yourself. As I see it, you have two choices. You can run, and likely find yourself back in a dungeon cell, if not executed."

Horace's hands, which had been dry only a minute ago, were now damp with sweat. He fought the urge to wipe them on his fine pants. "What's my other option?"

"Pick a side, Master Horace, and hold on tight."

The door opened, and the two officers of the Queen's Guard entered. Lord Mulcibar paused on his way out and leaned close to the elder soldier. Some words were exchanged, and the soldier nodded. Horace followed them out.

The soldiers remained at a respectful distance as they escorted him down the broad corridor toward a flight of stairs. In his few forays through the palace, Horace had come to glimpse how mammoth it was and could only imagine the amount of effort it must have taken to build.

They arrived at a chamber that was every bit as large as the audience hall, if not larger. Hundreds of tiny lights illuminated the high walls and the graceful curves of the vaulted ceiling. At first Horace thought the lights were candles, but he passed by a cluster at the doorway and saw that the lights were wavering tongues of energy without wick or taper, just hovering against the stonework like a cloud of fireflies. He was whisked into the grand chamber before he could study them, and then the new sights inside drew his attention.

Lit by the spectral lights, the entire room had a magical atmosphere. Gold accents glittered on every decoration. The walls were painted with frescos in bright tones of purple, salmon, and yellow. The sounds of harps and lyres floated in the air to the soft beat of a drum.

Lord Mulcibar excused himself and disappeared into the crowd. The hall was filled with people draped in silk and jewelry. The men walked with their backs stiff and their shoulders thrown back, strutting like gamecocks, while the women glided past as serene as swans on a still lake.

I don't belong here. I'm nothing but a prisoner in borrowed clothing.

The soldiers watched but otherwise left him alone as he made a casual circuit around the chamber. He was looking at a wall painting when a sultry voice called his name.

"Master Horace!"

He almost swallowed his tongue as the crowd parted. Queen Byleth sauntered toward him in an outfit he couldn't quite believe. The smoky silk gown left her arms and the upper slopes of her breasts bare, but she might as well have been nude since the material was virtually transparent. Gold baubles hung around her neck, from her ears and around both wrists, and a layer of gold powder sparkled on her face and arms, but he was mesmerized by the lush flesh moving under the veil of silk. Somehow it was more erotic than seeing her naked. In Arnos, such a dress would have been too scandalous for even a dockside whore, but the queen appeared perfectly at ease.

Her twin bodyguards stood behind her. They wore black robes again but tailored in different styles. Xantu wore a tight, straight robe of rough cloth with a crimson sash belt as his only accessory. Gilgar's robe was shimmering silk, cut to expose his muscular arms. A bracelet of gold links flashed on his right wrist.

"There you are," the queen said as she closed in on him. "We've been waiting for you."

Horace mustered his best courtly bow. When he straightened, the queen was by his side. "I hope I'm not late," he said. "You look, well, amazing, Your Excellence."

He nodded to the twin sorcerers, but they stared through him, not deigning to acknowledge his presence.

The queen latched onto his arm, seeming not to care as she smeared gold dust on his sleeve. "And you look good enough to devour. Come, there are people I want you to meet."

Horace forced himself to smile as she pulled him through the crowd. He felt like he was caught in the jaws of a shark and was being dragged out to deep waters. He tried not to think about the hard-eyed sorcerers walking behind them. Everyone inclined their heads, not for him, of course, but it was a heady experience to be in the queen's company while surrounded by such aristocracy. Every time she introduced him, Horace gave a firm nod and said hello. He tried to relax, reminding himself that he could still be rotting in a prison cell instead of here among the cream of society. As Queen Byleth guided him through the crowd, he asked, "What is this party for?"

She nodded across the hall to a group of men in white and gold military uniforms with colorful badges on their chests. "We're welcoming the new emissary of Thuum. Each city of the empire sends a representative to Erugash to sit on the governing council for a term of seven years."

"I confess, Excellence. Your country's system of government confuses me."

She leaned closer and whispered, "You're not alone. Sometimes I think the bureaucrats create new laws and protocols just to keep the rest of us ignorant of what they're up to. But it's a product of the armistice."

Horace looked down at her and felt his pulse beating faster. She was beyond beautiful, and here she was on his arm, talking to him while a hundred lords strolled by. "Uh, I'm not familiar with that."

"About twenty years ago," she said, "there was a war between the priestly factions. We called it the Godswar. It wasn't a war between armies, although there were occasional skirmishes in the streets. It was more of a political battle. The Sun Cult emerged victorious, with some assistance from the imperial family, and embarked on a campaign to spread its power throughout the empire as the preeminent priesthood.

"My father, King Rathammon, did not agree with this. Our family had long supported the faith of the Moon Goddess, who is our city's patroness. So we rose up in rebellion. My father did not seek conquest, but he knew that no city would be safe from the tightening leash of the Sun Cult unless something was done."

"But things didn't go so well?"

"The other nine cities, coerced by the priests of the Sun Lord, banded together against Erugash. My father died within sight of the walls. I had just turned eleven."

Horace started to murmur his condolences when a servant woman came forward with a tray of brown squares set on tiny pieces of paper. He blinked when he noticed the servant was Alyra, wearing a sheer topaz-blue tunic that came down to the tops of her thighs and nothing else. Her face had been made up with rouge and kohl, but Horace could still see the hints of a blush reddening her cheeks. Her eyes were downcast.

Byleth took two pieces from the tray and offered one to Horace. "Try this. You'll love it."

He considered the brown substance as he watched Alyra out of the corner of his eye.

"I hope you don't mind that I borrowed my favorite handmaiden back," the queen said as she inserted the strange food into Horace's mouth. "But there's no one else I would trust to attend me at an event like this. This one has such skillful hands, as perhaps you are already aware."

"Of course not," Horace mumbled around the stuff in his mouth, which was actually quite good. It was soft and melted into sweet goo on his tongue.

The queen led him away. Each time he turned his head as they walked, Horace couldn't help from glancing back at Alyra, following behind them. The makeup made her eyes seem larger and darker, like they could swallow him whole.

"So why am I—?" he started to ask the queen when a loud voice cut in.

"*Il shari azratum!*"

Horace turned to face a huge man. He was half a head taller than Horace and corpulent in the extreme. His pristine white uniform looked large enough to shelter an entire family. Byleth and the man, whom she called Lord Baphetor, spoke back and forth in rapid Akeshian. The heavyset nobleman winked several times as he laughed with gusto, which made Horace a little uncomfortable. While they exchanged banter, Horace watched Alyra. She was looking around as if studying the faces in the crowd.

"This is Master Horace Delrosa," the queen said, placing a hand on Horace's chest. "A traveler from the land of Arnos."

Horace bowed his head. But as he looked up, he saw a frown crease the envoy's plump lips. *"Simtum'nu libriuti, sarratum,"* the lord said with a low rumble.

The queen started to lead Horace away, but the envoy said something else. Horace caught the word *Tammuris*, but he had no idea what it meant. Byleth nodded and smiled but kept walking away. Horace caught the envoy's dark look in their direction before the crowd obscured him. "That didn't sound very friendly."

The queen ignored the greetings from a pair of older ladies in floor-length gowns as she pulled Horace away. "Lord Baphetor never passes an opportunity to remind me of my fallen stature. He can barely light a candle with his *zoana*, but his family is wealthy and has powerful alliances, so I must pretend to enjoy his company."

"What is *Tammuris*?"

She guided him to a corner of the hall and stopped before a large fresco. It showed a slender woman rising from the earth. She was quite beautiful and garbed only in a white cloth about her loins. "This is Tammuz," the queen said. "She is the goddess of seasons and also the cycle of life and death that all things experience. Here she is shown by herself, but oftentimes she is shown as four women. The child, the mother, and the crone."

"That's only three."

"The fourth is Death."

He tried to keep his voice neutral, though he felt foolish discussing heathen myths. "And the *Tammuris* has something to do with this goddess?"

"It is name of a high holy day when we celebrate the celestial marriage between Tammuz and the lord of the underworld."

Horace peered into his empty glass. Somehow he had drunk it all without realizing it. He frowned as Alyra put another glass of wine in his hand. "Why did that lord—Baphetor?—bring it up?"

The queen sidestepped a trio of gentlemen who seemed like they wanted a word. There was a strange look in her eyes. "You are a rare man, Horace of

Tines. There are few even in my inner court who would question me as you do. Are all your countrymen so familiar in the presence of royalty?"

"If I offended, Your Excellence, I apol—"

"There," she said, looking away. "Now you sound like every other courtier. Tell me. What do you think of these murals? I find them quite amusing."

Horace returned his gaze to the paintings. "Amusing?"

"Yes, when my father started construction on this palace, he couldn't find any artists willing to adorn the interior. The priesthoods, you see, had secured every painter in the city with long-term commissions in protest because they believed it was unholy for a king to build a palace taller than their temples."

She stood back and cocked her head to the side as if trying to find deeper meaning in the artwork. For a moment, she seemed profoundly unhappy. "My father was forced to hire artists from elsewhere at great expense. It amuses me how the priests perceive everything in life as revolving around them. Even kings and queens must come to bow before their altars."

"It's not much different in Arnos. The king rules, but the True Church guides him and everyone else as well. We're taught that service to the Almighty is the highest good a man can do."

"Our priesthoods think much the same," she said. "But my father taught me something quite different before he died."

"What do you serve, Excellence?"

Horace realized his mistake with one look at her face. The alluring demeanor had been replaced with a stern visage that would have been at home on the walls of a cathedral. "Pardon me," he stammered. "I'm not thinking straight tonight."

"I will forgive you, Master Horace, if you tell me more about your country. Courtship customs, for instance. What does an Arnossi woman do when she admires a man?"

"Ah, well, it's been quite some time since I . . . uh, dabbled in such things, Your Excellence. But I believe the custom is for the man to approach her parents with his intentions."

"And the woman has no say in the matter?"

Horace smiled, remembering his first encounter with his then-future wife. He had spotted her at a garden party, but had been too timid to approach her. One of her friends had introduced them, and they ended up talking all evening under the stars. They married less than a year later. "Well, perhaps not in the eyes of society, but I seem to recall that most of the women I knew had a great deal of say in the matter."

The queen smiled back at him. "I see."

A group of nobles greeted Byleth, and she stepped forward to meet them, all smiles and soft words. Horace looked back at Alyra. He wanted to ask if she was all right, but she hurried after the queen before he could say anything. An invisible band closed around his chest. Had he done something to make her angry? He couldn't think of anything, but he didn't know her that well. With so much going on, he didn't feel like himself either.

I have to talk to her after the party.

Gilgar smiled as if reading Horace's mind, but then his brother elbowed him and they strode after the queen. Horace caught up as Byleth left the nobles. He was about to ask her permission to leave, but she beat him to the punch.

"I'm sorry," she said, "about comparing you to my other courtiers. You are nothing like them."

"You don't need to apologize, Excellence."

"I know." She leaned closer. "That's what makes it so stimulating."

Horace saw Alyra over the queen's shoulder, studiously looking away as if she wasn't paying them any mind.

"I'll be leaving the hall soon," Byleth continued as she took his arm. Her touch burned through the thin sleeve of silk. "And I want to see you afterward in my chambers."

Horace wasn't sure how to respond. How did one refuse a queen? She was incredibly beautiful, but her manner was too aggressive. It reminded him acutely of the precariousness of his position. He was saved from the need to respond by a polite cough. Three priests in cloth-of-gold robes waited a few steps away, their bald heads shining in the mystical light. The priest at the head of the small procession was old—very old—his scalp covered in faded tattoos and brown age spots. His robe hung on him like a sack, too big for his frame. The golden medallion suspended from a chain looked heavy enough to snap his skinny neck. "*Sobhe'etu, sarratum,*" he said in a gentle voice.

"I greet you, Holy Father of the Sun," the queen replied, with more deference than Horace expected.

Horace studied the luminaries walk by while the old priest spoke at some length. The room buzzed with a hundred private conversations above the strains of music.

The queen tugged on his arm. "Horace, this is High Priest Kadamun of the Temple of Amur."

Not sure if he should nod or bow, or even kneel, Horace put his hand over his chest and bent from the waist. "I am honored to meet Your, um, . . . Eminence."

The high priest said something, and the queen translated, "He is curious about your impressions of our realm."

What does he want me to say? You have very nice prison cells?

Horace looked to Byleth, and she nodded with a small smile. His gaze settled on the glass in his hand. "You make excellent wine."

Byleth's smile became a trifle strained as she passed his answer along to the holy men. The high priest smirked as he replied. "He says you have a cultured palate," the queen said. "And perhaps one day you will allow him the honor of showing you the temple's wine cellars."

Horace smiled to mask his discomfort. "I would enjoy that."

More pleasantries were exchanged, and then the delegation shuffled away through the crowd at the old priest's pace. Most of the nobles stood back as they passed as if the priests were leprous.

"The high priest seemed like a nice chap," Horace said.

"Yes," Byleth replied. "I especially enjoyed the way he threatened to imprison you."

Horace turned to face her. "He did what?"

The queen pulled him onward. "That bit about inviting you to his wine cellars. That's what people call the dungeons beneath the temple where they keep the heretics awaiting execution."

"In that case, I take back what I said."

"Now you're learning, Master Horace." She gestured around them. "The court is a jungle filled with carnivores. The strong prey upon the weak, and the weak plot to overthrow the strong."

So which do you think I am? "I'll try to remember that."

"I hope so. I'd like to see you survive a little longer. Oh, *peshka*."

A man in an extravagant outfit of emerald-green silk strode toward them. Horace remembered him from his first audience with the queen. The man had been sitting beside her throne. His short, black hair was oiled and coiffed to perfection, yet his handsome features were marred by an angry scowl. Horace flinched at the touch of the queen's hand on his arm and thought back to the familiar way they'd been circling the hall together.

This must be her betrothed. And he thinks that she and I are . . .

The queen did nothing, but the twins strode forward to intercept the man. They did not touch him, but each held up an open hand, and the royal fiancé halted as if he'd run into a brick wall. Yet that didn't stop him from shouting and gesticulating wildly. Horace only caught a couple words. One was "savage."

Byleth pulled Horace away from the ruckus. "What were we discussing?" she asked.

Horace looked over his shoulder and tensed when the man leveled a finger straight at him. "He seems quite upset."

"Ignore him. It's nothing."

"In that case I was wondering if there was any chance Your Excellence would consid—"

The queen's face blanched as she stopped mid-step. Before Horace could ask what was wrong, a dagger-sharp pain tore through his head. Glass shattered in the background as he reached up, expecting to feel a river of blood pouring from the back of his scalp, but there was only dry hair. Yet the intense pain persisted. Distant shouts reached his ears. The entire chamber was in disarray, with many nobles clutching their heads. Then the pain was gone, as swiftly as it had come, leaving behind a buzzing itch that traveled down his spine.

"What was that?" he said. His voice sounded harsh in his ears. Was this the attempt that Lord Mulcibar had warned him about?

BLOOD AND IRON

The queen snapped her fingers at her bodyguards, who straightened up as if pulled by invisible strings. With narrowed eyes, the twins cleared a path through the hall. Byleth grabbed Horace's arm and dragged him after them. Alyra followed close behind, her wide eyes latched onto him. She was clearly terrified, and he wasn't far from it himself.

What's happened? he mouthed, but she only shook her head.

Then Lord Mulcibar was there. The queen stopped as he whispered in her ear. Horace tried to eavesdrop and watch for trouble at the same time. If someone was going to try to kill the queen, this was a spectacular opportunity. But he didn't see anyone making threatening gestures.

Although if they used sorcery, how would I know until they struck?

With that sobering thought, Horace found himself wanting to help the queen, perhaps because she was one of the few people in this land to show him kindness. He studied the faces around them, attempting to discern from which direction an attack might come. Yet everyone wore the same look of shock and fear. Before Horace could form a strategy, the ground bucked under him. He grabbed hold of Alyra, and they clung together as the palace quaked. Priests and nobles crashed into one another. The queen staggered toward Horace, but the twins both reached out and kept her upright.

The tremor only lasted a couple heartbeats, but it felt like minutes. When it was over, Horace remained still. Alyra's breathing was loud in his ear. It had been a long time since he'd held a woman. He'd forgotten how good it felt. The softness of her skin, the citrus fragrance in her hair.

A loud boom exploded outside the chamber, followed by a flash of light through the tall chamber windows. Green lightning. Horace swallowed painfully as a strong wind laden with ozone blew in through the windows. What had Alyra called it? A chaos storm?

The queen extricated herself from her bodyguards. She glanced once at Horace and Alyra, raised an eyebrow, and began shouting at people around her. The soldiers who were converging on her position turned and ran for the door. Nobles squawked as they were pushed aside, but none tried to resist. The twins retook their positions behind the queen as she followed the soldiers.

Horace's legs were still a little shaky, but he released his grip on Alyra.

"Are you all right?" he asked.

She headed toward the windows. Horace was about to join her when Lord Mulcibar emerged from the crowd, hobbling on his cane.

"Is everything all right?" Horace asked.

"We must go," the nobleman said. "Now."

"Where?"

"Follow the queen. I fear she will need every ally she can find."

The nobleman gave Horace a penetrating glance and then started in the direction the queen had taken. Most of the other nobles were leaving as well, pressing through other doors and archways. They reminded Horace of rats fleeing a sinking ship. He started after Mulcibar when Alyra grabbed his arm. "Come with me," she said under her breath.

"What? The queen—"

"I'm getting you out of here," she whispered as she steered him toward a side door.

"Now? I don't think it's a good time to be outside with the storm—"

"Listen! I have friends in the city. They'll help you escape, if we can get outside the palace . . . what is it?"

Horace was looking up at the ceiling. He could feel the power of the storm overhead, churning with a dark hunger as it lashed out. With every lightning strike, a shudder raced through his body. He remembered how Lord Isiratu had collapsed trying to dispel the sandstorm. Then he thought about Byleth attempting to do the same.

"I have to go."

Alyra pulled on his arm. "That's right. We can get you out a postern on the south side—"

"No. I have to go help the queen."

"Horace! This is your chance to get away."

"I'm sorry." He extricated himself from her grasp. "Find a safe place until the storm passes."

"But—!"

He turned away and hurried after Lord Mulcibar. He caught up with the nobleman in the grand hallway as another tremor shook the palace. Horace's legs almost collapsed as the pain returned, constricting his chest. He leaned against the archway for support, feeling like he was going to pass out. Then Alyra was there. With an exasperated glare, she propped her shoulder under his arm. She was saying something, but another barrage of thunder blocked his ears.

"—the stairs," she shouted in his ear.

"What?" he asked. His voice sounded odd. Distant.

Lord Mulcibar was hunched against the other wall, bracing himself upright with his cane. Horace stumbled over to the nobleman. Together, he and Alyra half-walked, half-dragged Mulcibar down the corridor. The sound of tromping boots echoed behind them, but they faded away into the distance. Horace focused on staying on his feet. This new bout of pain had hurt worse than the first. It was subsiding now, but he had a sneaking suspicion it would return.

Next time I'm just going to pass out and save myself the trouble.

They followed Lord Mulcibar's directions, and after a few dozen steps the nobleman regained enough strength to walk under his own power. He took them up through the central stairways of the palace, making Horace uncomfortable.

"Do these storms occur here often?" he asked.

Alyra's eyes answered him. She was holding it together, but he could tell she was frightened. "No," she whispered.

"There," Lord Mulcibar said as he climbed onto a landing and pointed his cane at a sturdy teakwood door.

Horace opened it, and a howling wail filled the stairwell. The wind whipped Horace's clothes and filled his head with a horrible stench. Through the door was a short corridor where the queen and her retinue stood by another doorway, which was open to the outside. Bright green light illuminated the corridor, and thunder shook the walls. Fresh agony ripped through his chest. It was several seconds before he could even breathe again. By that time, Lord Mulcibar had joined the queen's gathering.

Horace pulled Alyra aside. "Listen. I don't think you should be here. If these people are set on confronting the Almighty, I don't know if I can—"

"Horace!" Byleth shouted.

The queen stood by the outer door, reaching out a hand toward him. With a grimace, he left Alyra's side. The people gathered in the passageway were, he noticed, all nobles.

All sorcerers, too, I'll wager.

A few of the aristocrats frowned as Horace entered their circle, but they made room for him. The queen led them in some kind of chant, but Lord Mulcibar moved beside Horace.

"Are you all right?"

"I'm scared out of my wits. How about you?"

Mulcibar made a tight smile. "We shall find out very soon."

Horace glanced out the open door. A portico extended into the night. Driving rain beat the gray pavestones. The tickling sensation along the back of his neck itched like an army of ants was marching up his spine. The queen took a step toward the doorway. Her voice floated above the thunder and the thrashing wind. A bolt of jagged green lightning crossed the sky, outlining her form in an emerald nimbus.

"It's time," Mulcibar said.

Horace tensed as a loud boom echoed overhead. For a moment, he was back in the desert again, looking up at the violent storm as it threatened to carry him away. He couldn't suppress a shudder. He wanted to shout that he couldn't help them. Yet, watching the nobles march out through the door behind the queen, Horace couldn't let them face it alone because the truth was that he had come to admire these people. Some of them, at least. He looked over his shoulder. Alyra stood in the shadow of the hallway. She looked smaller in the dim lighting. Her hair flowed behind her in the wind, revealing her gold collar. He nodded to her and then walked out.

As he stepped over the threshold, his stomach turned upside down. The nobles stood in the center of a broad terrace, huddled close together in their soaked apparel. The sky was a sheet of black iron spitting blood-warm rain and bolts of eerie lightning. A sullen howl roared in his ears as the wind whipped past him. He looked up. "Holy Father in Heaven . . ."

The storm raged over the city, larger and more fearsome than any tempest he'd ever seen. Its sheer malevolence crashed over the city with every thunderous boom. Despite his misgivings, Horace was drawn to the play of light and shadow across the stormy heavens. Watching the sporadic barrage of levin bolts, he sensed a pattern in their movements, like a puzzle he might unlock if he stared long enough. He took a step toward the marble balustrade bordering the terrace.

"Horace!"

Tearing his gaze away from the sky, Horace saw Lord Mulcibar beckoning to him. The ache in his chest was fierce, but he hurried over to the nobles. He said nothing as he joined their circle, unsure of what he was supposed to do. The queen was giving instructions to the group. Horace tried to listen for words he might recognize, but half of what she said was lost in the clamor. With each cracking stroke of lightning, her face lit up, pale and green, her eyes open wide.

Lord Mulcibar turned to him. "We are going to try to deflect the storm in a southerly direction away from the city."

"What do I do?" Horace shouted back.

"The ritual is in Akeshian, but you don't need to know the words. The queen will lead us. Just focus on your *qa*."

"My what?"

The nobleman placed a hand over his stomach. "The seat of your energy. Feel it moving and try to lend it to the group. Don't worry. Once you feel your *zoana* rise, the ritual will take over."

Byleth shouted, her face lifted to the ebon sky. The nobles repeated her words. They didn't hold hands or light candles, or do anything Horace attributed to a ritual. Yet, as their voices joined the queen's, he felt the stirring in his chest that he had come to think of as his *zoana*. He tried humming along with the Akeshian phrases, which had fallen into a rhythm that reminded him of a church hymn. The humming seemed to amplify the sensation moving inside him, but he had no idea what to do next. How could he "lend" his power to anyone?

Nothing seemed to be happening. The storm continued to lash at them. A harsh crackle split the night as more lightning struck near the palace. Down in the city, he saw fires glowing like embers beneath the rising smoke, and it brought back memories of his flight from Tines. The flames and smoke were etched in his mind, along with the cries of frightened people, and deep back in his memories echoed a mournful scream that never ended.

A burst of yellow-orange flame brought Horace back to the present. Streams of fire, flowing like liquid, rose from some of the *zoanii* in the circle. They were joined by sluices of splashing water and vertical rockslides, all flying up into the sky inside a funnel of spinning air. Horace felt a tugging in his chest like his heart was trying to escape from his rib cage.

Wounds appeared on the *zoanii*, deep gashes across their faces and bodies that widened with every passing heartbeat. Two nobles fell to the wet tiles and did not move. Their blood mixed with the rain to run in pink streams down their expensive clothing. Lord Mulcibar and the rest kept up the chant, their voices drifting away on the winds. Byleth looked up to the sky as if searching for answers. Horace felt useless, doubly so because he could sense the others watching him. Waiting, he knew, for some miracle, but nothing happened. He just stood there, pelted by the warm rain, and tried to imagine himself anywhere else. Another noble collapsed, her eyes closed in agony as she curled up at their feet. Then the queen staggered. The twin sorcerers grabbed her by the arms before she could fall. A long cut ran down the side of her neck.

Horace started to cross the circle to her when a bolt of green lightning lanced out of the sky to strike the top of the palace. As the thunder exploded in his ears, a shock ran through Horace from head to heels. His insides contorted in every direction; he couldn't tell if he was going to be sick or pass out first. All his muscles went rigid as a wave of energy poured into him, filling him up. Terrible heat seared his lungs, but at the same time he felt like he was flying free, a sensation he'd only felt on the prow of a ship running before a gale. He could feel the storm's presence overhead, trying to batter him down. Then the heat inside him was too much. Horace opened his mouth to shout, and a torrent of energy burst out of him. His eyes were squeezed shut tight, but in his mind he imagined a jet of white-hot fire shooting into the sky.

He returned to his senses on the terrace floor, the pavestones pressing against the wet material of his jacket. The rain splattered into his eyes. He blinked it away. The queen and her nobles were also on the ground, several of them thrashing limply while a few remained still. Byleth was trying to lift her head. Blood trickled from her left nostril. That's when Horace noticed the silence.

The wind was gone, its sudden absence deafening in his ears. The rain was dying down, too, slowing to a fine mist. The sky, when he looked up, was still dark, but the violent thunderclouds had vanished to reveal a web of constellations. It was like the storm had never happened, except for the destruction it left behind. He crawled to the queen on his hands and knees, not trusting his legs to hold him. Her eyes were opened wide and unblinking. A stream of blood ran down her chest from the cut on her throat.

"Your Excellence?"

She put a hand to her head as if she expected to find something horrible. "I'm . . . I think I'm all right. What happened?"

Horace stifled a nervous laugh as he took off his jacket and pressed a sodden sleeve against her injury. "I was about to ask you the same thing."

She reached out to touch his face. "Not even a mark . . ."

Soldiers rushed over. Xantu and Gilgar were there as well, both of them bleeding around the eyes. Xantu pressed his hand to the queen's neck wound while his brother stood watch over them. A moment later, Xantu removed his hand, and the queen's injury was closed with only a long scab remaining. The twin sorcerers helped her to her feet.

Horace straightened up slowly, feeling like he'd been sewn up in a sack and beaten with a club. Then Alyra was there, holding him up again. He was too weak to resist as she steered him back toward the door. She was whispering something under her breath, but his ears were still ringing. "What?"

"I can't believe what just happened," she said.

"I'm afraid I missed most of it. You'll have to give me the details later."

As they filed back inside, several *zoanii* leaned against the walls of the corridor. Their eyes followed him and Alyra with flinty expressions. Then someone whispered a word.

"*Belzama.*"

Alyra halted, pulling Horace to a sudden stop that sent trickles of agony coursing through his body. "What?" he asked.

Others nobles whispered the word, too, looking back and forth at each other and at him.

"Storm lord," she said under her breath. "That's what they're calling you."

"Is that good?"

"I don't know."

A soldier in the queen's livery rushed into the passage. He dropped to his knees before Byleth and began talking in quick bursts.

"Something's wrong," Horace whispered.

"There's been an attack on the royal barracks," Alyra said. "Many were killed."

"An attack?"

But she shushed him. After another minute of listening, she said, "The granaries have also been set on fire."

The queen swung her hand, and the messenger flew against the wall hard enough to break bones. Everyone else scrambled out of her way as she strode past, followed by Lord Mulcibar and those nobles who had recovered enough to walk. The twins brought up the rear of the rain-soaked procession, both scowling as they bent their heads together in private conversation.

Horace looked back out the doorway to the fiery glow along the skyline. He had so many questions about the storm and the ritual, but no one to ask.

"Are you ready to go?" Alyra asked. "It looks like you could use a bath and a long sleep."

"That sounds wonderful." Horace sighed as he turned away from the city. "I could sleep for a month."

He tried not to look at the dead messenger lying against the wall as he walked past.

CHAPTER EIGHTEEN

Armed men ran through the city streets. Thick, acrid smoke filled the air. Jirom coughed as he put his back against the wall of the potter's shop. He looked up to the haze obscuring the night sky.

At least Emanon delivered his message.

Blood ran thick in Erugash this night. The point of Jirom's spear was stained red. It had been a long time since he'd been in battle. He didn't mourn the soldiers he'd slain today, but some part of him wondered if this was all worth it. It had been a good raid. He estimated his band had killed seventy or eighty soldiers. If the other team was as successful, then the rebellion had struck a stinging blow. Yet he'd fought in enough wars to know that not much changed for the people at the bottom after the dust cleared. Or if it did, it was usually for the worse.

Jirom glanced around the corner onto the main avenue that sliced through the city center. At the far end rose a towering edifice that could only be the fabled palace of Queen Byleth. Flaming braziers and torches illuminated the many tiers and balconies climbing to the sky. A city within a city, it had been built to inspire awe in everyone who saw it. Its grandeur recalled to Jirom the true power of the empire, its unwavering faith that it *deserved* to rule the world. Following the pattern of lights to the summit high above the street level, he could almost believe it, too. He had entered Erugash with thirty-six rebel dog-soldiers through a little-used gate on the north side, courtesy of Emanon's contacts. Once inside, they made their way to the government ward at the city center and divided forces. Emanon took half the rebels east to hit the granaries while Jirom and the other half attacked the militia barracks. Jirom understood the value of the targets. Deprive the enemy of a supply line and strike terror into his heart—these were the pillars of practical warfare—but the risk involved staggered his mind. Yet he had kept his reservations to himself. Emanon's insurgent slaves were a misfit band, but there was something appealing about their camaraderie. And Emanon's leadership, too. Jirom was content to follow, for now.

BLOOD AND IRON

However, the assault on the barracks had almost ended in disaster. An alarm sounded while Jirom's squad dealt with the off-duty soldiers, and reinforcements arrived before they could disengage. Jirom had ordered his fighters to scatter and meet back at the rendezvous point, but somewhere in the chaos he found himself wandering through the city's back alleys alone. He kept hoping he would run into a familiar face, but now he was almost to the meeting place and he was still alone, easy prey for the first patrol to discover him.

Jirom took another glance at the palace, wondering what Horace was doing at this moment. The slave woman, Alyra, had been convinced he was in no danger, that the queen had taken Horace under her wing, in fact. But Horace knew nothing about Akeshian politics. He was in serious danger, whether he knew it or not. Jirom understood the odds of getting to his friend were low. Apart from its architectural splendor, the royal palace was as secure as a fortress. The stone wall surrounding the grounds was twice the height of a man, all lit up with torches and guarded at every point. The main gates were bronze and heavy enough to stand up to anything short of a battering ram. Still, he wanted to chance it. He *needed* to try.

Jirom was about to venture out again to look for the others when the ground rocked beneath his feet. He grabbed hold of the wall as he struggled to keep his balance. Darkness fell over the city, swift and impenetrable, just heartbeats before a sheet of rain drenched him. Then he smelled it, the combined odors of lightning and sorcery that he'd never forget. He didn't even flinch when the first emerald-green bolt forked down from the heavens.

Of all the nights for a storm to hit, it had to be this one?

Cursing to half a dozen gods from a handful of nations, Jirom sprinted down an alleyway. He darted through the back streets searching for his missing squad members, but the darkness and the rain, not to mention the insanely tall structures blocking his view, conspired against him. He crossed another boulevard, which was blessedly empty of people. As he paused beside a bronze statue of an armored man on horseback, a gust of wind swept in behind him and tried to shove him along. Jirom dug his sandals into the clay street and held his ground. Where in the hells was Emanon?

Jirom headed in what he hoped was a northerly direction. He thought he saw some people at the mouth of a side street and quickened his pace. He was unprepared as two soldiers burst out of a doorway to his left. Jirom had a split-second to decide whether to run or fight. He turned and swung his spear. The butt end cracked against the side of the nearer soldier's head. The shaft split against the man's helmet, but he dropped like a sack of rocks. The second soldier reached for the sword sheathed at his side, but Jirom reacted first, slashing with the point of his spear. The soldier jumped back, but his heels met empty air as he stumbled down the well of a cellar window. Jirom dropped his broken spear and snatched the fallen soldier's sword out of its scabbard, and he took off into the night. A small voice in the back of his head insisted he go back to finish the soldiers; this was war, after all. But he'd had enough killing for one night.

Rain poured down his face as he ran down one nameless street after another. Occasional bolts of lightning illuminated the city. Jirom turned a blind corner and nearly collided with a group of rebel fighters. Their leader, Jerkul, was one of Emanon's lieutenants. The bronze head of his long-handled adze was smeared with blood. Silfar and Partha were from the east. Silfar didn't talk much, and Partha never shut up. Other than that, they were inseparable, and Jirom wondered privately if they were more than just comrades. Czachur was the youngest of the group. Tall and well-built, he was an orphan; his shopkeeper parents had been caught in a fight between rival street gangs and killed.

The rebels stood over a trio of corpses in the yellow uniforms of priestly soldiers.

"Has anyone seen Emanon?" Jirom asked.

"Not since we split up to hit the granaries," Jerkul said. "He might have been cut off and had to change his route."

"Are we attacking the palace next?" Czachur asked. His smooth chin jutted out like a knife blade when he spoke.

"Fuck that!" Partha muttered.

Jirom glanced around. The buildings were shuttered up tight. "Stay with me. We're heading to the backup meeting place."

"But Emanon said—"

"He's right," Jerkul said. "We'll be picked up if we stay here."

BLOOD AND IRON

Jirom gestured toward what he thought was the right direction. The rebels headed off with Jerkul leading the way and Czachur looking back over his shoulder. Jirom fell in behind them. The storm was getting worse. There could have been a battle raging on the next block and they wouldn't have heard it over the din. He could only hope his squad made it out all right.

As the rebels approached a small plaza on the edge of a hard-bitten neighborhood called The Dredge, a figure ran out of an adjacent alleyway. Jirom bent his knees and pivoted, his borrowed sword pulled back to thrust, but he stayed his hand when a voice called out to him.

"Jirom?"

Emanon's black-green eyes glowed like dusky jewels. He had let his whiskers grow for the past couple days. The dark stubble made his lower face difficult to discern in the dark, and it also gave him a roguish appearance.

Jirom lowered his weapon. "Where have you been?"

"Just having a bit of fun with Her Majesty's toy soldiers."

Jirom restrained himself from punching the man in his rugged chin. Then he saw the clump of rebel fighters behind Emanon. A weight lifted off his chest when he saw some familiar faces. "Is this all we have left?"

"No. I sent a party back to hold the gate."

Jirom scowled in the darkness. The rain was beating harder, making it difficult to hear. "We'll need every sword to get inside the palace."

Emanon looked to the others, signaling Jerkul to stay alert, and then pulled Jirom to a deep doorway on the other side of the plaza. It was nice to get out of the rain, even if only for a few moments. Emanon wiped his face with a bloodstained hand. "Listen, Jirom. I know what I said, but we can't risk it tonight. We need to leave the city now, before this storm gets worse."

"The rain isn't going to stop me," Jirom replied. "We could be in and out before anyone discovers us."

"I went to check out the palace after the last granary went up. There's no chance of getting inside tonight, not if we had twice as many men. I told you, Jirom. I'm not going to risk lives on a suicide mission. We'll try it another time."

"So that's it? We just abandon him?"

"We wouldn't be doing your friend any favors getting ourselves killed. There'll be other opportunities."

"But we're already here in the city!" Jirom clenched his hands around the hilt of his borrowed sword. "Damn you, Emanon. You knew this was important to me."

Emanon started to walk away, but Jirom caught him by the shoulder. The rebel captain shrugged off the hand. Although several inches shorter than Jirom, he was stronger than he appeared. Emanon leaned forward until they almost bumped noses. "And you swore to follow my orders. So what's it gonna be?"

Jirom ground his teeth together but controlled himself. "Fine."

"We'll get him. Just trust me. Okay?"

"So you want to tell me what we accomplished on this mission? And don't give me any nonsense about a training exercise. You risked the lives of these men. Why?"

Emanon sighed and leaned back against the wall of the doorway. "I was spreading evidence."

"Of what?"

"The empire is under attack by crusaders from Etonia. My informants tell me that the queen is concerned about their recent advances into her territory, but so far she's held back her legions. So I left some western-style weapons and scraps of foreign uniforms with the bodies of her dead soldiers."

Jirom squinted in the gloom, trying to read the rebel captain's expression. He couldn't tell if the man was lying, but he understood the implications. "You want Erugash to launch an attack on these invaders. Let them destroy each other, and then we remain to pick up the pieces. Is that your master plan?"

"Part of it."

Jirom considered what this would mean to Horace. He was one of those "foreign invaders" that Emanon was implicating with his false proof. Would the queen punish Horace for this? Jirom looked back in the direction of the palace. It was so close, and yet it felt a thousand leagues away.

Emanon gave the order to retreat, and the rebels hurried through the city streets. No one tried to stop them, possibly because most of the available hands were busy fighting fires, and they soon arrived back at the Mummer's

BLOOD AND IRON

Gate in the northwestern corner of the city. The sentries were nowhere to be seen, thanks to prior arrangements. Emanon whistled as they approached. Two crossbowmen eased out of hiding, one on either side of the gateway.

"Is everyone back?" Emanon asked.

One of the men nodded. "Aye. You're the last."

Emanon shepherded the fighters through the gate and closed it behind them. Jirom could feel his muscles contracting and releasing as they passed through the long, dark tunnel under the city walls. The tunnel's cloying smell of moist earth reminded him of a grave. They emerged on the flat plain outside the walls. Emanon was the last one out. Without a word, he led the rebels across the dark plains, back to the army camp.

Emanon had secured their temporary escape from the camp with, Jirom assumed, hefty bribes to the guards. "Getting out isn't the hard part," Emanon had said during the mission briefing. "It's being in the right place at the right time."

Jirom now knew the meaning behind those cryptic words—or, at least, he thought he did—but his doubts returned as they neared the first watchtower. A torch burned at the top of the tower, giving just enough light for them to see the lone sentry pacing along the catwalk. They waited until the watchman had turned away and then hurried past. The second and third watchtowers were empty. The advance squad was waiting in the shadow of the third. Everyone huddled around Emanon as the rain continued to pound them.

"Xon and Czachur will take point," he said. "Once they sound the all-clear, I want you all over the side. If there's a cry and we're discovered . . . well, you know what to do. The secondary meeting point is Jaggar's Rock. Any questions?"

Jirom was still angry that they hadn't tried to rescue Horace, but he understood. Emanon had almost twoscore men to worry about. A good commander tried to avoid casualties when he could. He glanced over and found the rebel captain watching him. They understood each other, perhaps too well.

No, he just thinks I'm touched in the head. But he doesn't understand what I've been through, the life I've had to lead. None of them do.

An old memory floated to the surface, something he hadn't thought about in a long time. He was back in the Zaral in the village where he'd been born, a young man bigger than the rest of the boys his age, but with a powerful secret. A young man popular with the girls of his village, yet who found himself drawn to the strong features and lean bodies of other men. And when his secret was discovered, he was cast out of his clan and threatened with death if he should ever return.

The familiar shame came over him, as powerful today as it had been more than twenty years ago when it happened, forcing him to reexamine everything in his life, making him second-guess every decision. Why had he joined this rebellion? For revenge against the Akeshians, or was it the handsome face behind the offer? He looked over at Emanon and had to admit, it was a little of both. But his stint in the iron box had given him time to reflect. Horace's example in the desert had inspired him to keep living, but inspiration was useless without a *reason* to see it through. He was done with running away from himself.

The call came. Jirom followed the rebels across the rocky plain. The storm had swallowed the moon and stars, and he didn't see the lip until he'd nearly gone over the edge. He found one of the ropes they had left and crouched beside it while the others slid down one at a time. "Go slow," he told each fighter. "The rain will make the line slick."

Finally, it was just him and Emanon atop the canyon wall. The towers were quiet, the sentries no doubt huddled inside out of the weather. Jirom looked over the cliff. "So if you're making this up as you go along, what's our next move?"

Emanon put his sword away. "That depends on what our lords and masters do. After tonight, things are going to get rough. For all of us. But I'm hoping the queen will call up her reserves and send a message to the crusaders."

"You're risking a lot on that decision. With only a handful of fighters, we don't have any room for mistakes."

Emanon grabbed two handfuls of mud and rubbed them together. "I've been fighting in this land for most of my life, first as a soldier in the imperial legions, now as a slave. But it's all the same. Blood and meat, life and death. Those of us who survive are just as dead as those we put in the ground. Most just don't know it yet. But what we're doing—resisting the empire—is a worthy thing, I think. Maybe worth dying for."

Jirom watched Emanon's eyes. They were pitch-black in the dark and as mysterious as the new moon. "So now we go to war?"

Emanon smiled as the mud dripped from his fingers. "Aye. To war."

The rebel captain took the rope and disappeared over the edge. Jirom didn't know what to think. If they were marching to war, that meant he might lose his chance to rescue Horace. But, as much as it galled him, he had sworn to follow Emanon. He'd broken oaths before, but he didn't want to break this one. Horace was smart, and the Akeshians obviously placed some value on his life or else they would have killed him already.

Keep telling yourself that. Maybe it will soothe your conscience.

Jirom dug out the anchors holding the ropes and pushed them over the sides. Then he swung his legs over the canyon wall. He was about to begin the long climb down when the tremor struck. For a moment it was all he could do to hold onto the rock lip. His feet dangled over empty space for what seemed like an hour. Then a burst of light exploded in the sky over the city. It blinded Jirom with its intensity. A crash like a hundred thunderbolts reverberated through the sky.

When he could see and hear again, the earthquake had stopped. Jirom looked up into a clear night sky. The storm was gone. A few spots of red glowed over the city skyline where stubborn fires continued to burn despite the downpour, but otherwise all was quiet. It reminded him of that day in the desert with . . .

Horace. It had to be him.

With a deep breath, Jirom found his footing and clambered down the rock wall. Below him, the camp was buzzing with shouts and blurting horns calling review formations. Yet Jirom was unconcerned. Whatever happened, he still lived to fight another day. And so did Horace.

CHAPTER NINETEEN

Byleth wrinkled her nose as she opened the stone door and smelled the noxious wind coming from the other side. She could count on one finger the number of times she had come down here into the nadir of her palace, and she wouldn't have done it tonight except that she was too angry to wait for him to come to her.

Leaving her soldiers outside, she led Xantu and Gilgar down the long, winding tunnel into the earth. The walls were rounded and almost smooth with a faint reflective sheen. Despite the glowing red runes inscribed on the tunnel ceiling every twenty paces to stifle the intense heat that flowed up from the depths of the earth, the walls and floor were still hot enough to burn bare skin. She held onto a trickle of *zoana* to maintain a halo of coolness around herself, and not a hint of perspiration dampened the sheer silk of her dress.

Three men bowed as she passed them at an intersection of two tunnels. Lord Astaptah's minions were uniformly thin to the point of emaciation, and they all wore the same ash-gray robe that matched their complexions. They never spoke within her hearing, and it occurred to Byleth that she didn't know much about what went on down here. When Lord Astaptah had first come to her with his ideas, she needed a place to keep him close but out of sight. These lava tubes under the palace had seemed like the perfect solution.

She entered the main chamber and nearly choked at the powerful stench of brimstone that billowed around her. Air currents rising from the moat of red-hot magma below played with her hair. Seven figures stared down from the shadows obscuring the chamber's ceiling—seven massive statues carved from the basalt walls. Their visages were hidden within deep stone cowls, but Byleth could swear their invisible eyes followed her. She had always been skeptical of the existence of the gods and their effect on her daily life, despite the religious training that had been drilled into her head as a child. Yet she recalled being nervous when Astaptah built this hidden shrine to the seven demon-lords of the underworld. She had stood in this chamber right after its construction, with Lord Astaptah standing before her holding a red candle and a copper dagger, lifting the implements to the statues as he chanted in his native tongue. Looking back now, Byleth wondered why she had participated in the ritual. Astaptah had said it was necessary to seal their pact. She also remembered being desperate for a means to escape her fate.

Not much has changed since then.

A drop of sweat ran down Byleth's left cheek, despite her enchantment.

Comforted by the presence of Xantu and Gilgar behind her, she descended the metal catwalks. The tall chamber didn't have a floor. Instead, a pool of magma bubbled and churned around an island of rock rising from its center. Lord Astaptah stood on the isle, working on the machine occupying most of its area. A glittering stone hovered over his shoulder. Looking like a sliver of onyx, it radiated a fierce blue light.

Stepping across the narrow stone bridge, Byleth called out to him, "You had better have a good explanation."

Astaptah turned around, holding a long metal rod. Its tip glowed cherry red. "I am busy. If this can wait—"

She strode up and slapped the rod out of his hand. "This will *not* wait. Do you realize that I was almost killed tonight?"

He drew himself up to his full height, looming over her. A powerful odor of acerbic chemicals flooded Byleth's lungs. Her bodyguards came up to flank her.

"I have been preoccupied," Astaptah said. The floating onyx stone hung in the air between them, rotating slowly.

Byleth gestured to the metal construction above them. The storm engine was displeasing to the eye, all girders and connecting struts, lacking the graceful lines that she demanded from all things in her presence. Thick cables ran from the apparatus to the chamber walls, disappearing into the stone. She remembered the day when Lord Astaptah, not long after his near-fatal journey across the southern desert, had come to her with a proposal, that she give him the means to build this metal monstrosity. Through it, he had promised, she would become the most powerful ruler in Akeshia. For the daughter of a king who had failed in his own bid to win the Chalcedony Throne, the chance to do what her father had not was irresistible.

"You told me your contraption would protect Erugash from these storms," she said.

"It did better than that," he said. "The engine achieved terminal charge fifty-eight minutes before true midnight."

Byleth bit off a bitter retort as his words penetrated her wrath. That time corresponded with the appearance of the chaos storm over the city. "Are you saying that *you* created the storm?"

Astaptah's eyebrows came together in an ugly frown. "Not precisely. A storm front was moving through the area when the engine became active. The atmospheric activity presumably aided in the—"

"Don't babble," she said. "Just tell me. Did your machine create that storm or not?"

"In a sense . . . yes."

The ember of hope she had long sheltered in her heart burst to new life, eclipsing the anger she'd felt just moments ago. "What went wrong?"

"When the surge struck, the etheric distributor went into a systemic feedback loop that . . ."

Byleth tried to follow his torturous explanation of the night's events, but all she was able to glean was that the chaos storm had broken Astaptah's machine, and he was endeavoring to repair it. She lifted a hand. "Spare me any more details. You say you can fix it?"

"Of course, though it will take time. Time better spent than talking with you—"

"Watch your tongue," Xantu said in a low whisper.

"Or you might lose it," Gilgar added with a mocking smile.

Astaptah glanced at them with an expression devoid of any emotion, like they were a pair of insects who had just crawled up his arm, and Byleth almost reached for her *zoana*. As it was, she felt the twins seething with the desire for violent release. She stilled them with a wave of her hand.

The vizier turned once again to face his creation. "I also told you that this is not a precise science. However, I, too, am puzzled. The engine should have been insulated from any harm. It's almost as if . . ."

She edged closer. She needed to know if this was truly the breakthrough she had been waiting for, the key to the gambit that might save her life and her crown. "As if what?"

Astaptah picked up the rod from the floor. Its tip had cooled to an orange glow. "It's as if a stronger force had overridden the power of the storm. But it is difficult to countenance. It would have had to be more power than a dozen *zoanii* of the first rank bound together in a single stroke."

Byleth bit her bottom lip. "I may have your explanation. When the storm struck, I took all the *zoanii* I could lay hands upon and tried to deflect the storm away from the city. I had no idea what you were doing down here. If I'd known, I would have . . ."

What? Let my city be destroyed so that Astaptah could demonstrate his toy?

"And you were successful?" he asked.

"Actually, yes. Against all odds, we dispelled the storm entirely. It was quite amazing. I don't know if another cabal in recent times could have done it."

Astaptah was studying her with his deep, amber eyes. She didn't like feeling them upon her for any extended period, especially down here in his sanctum.

"A bold maneuver," he said.

Was that sarcasm in his voice? She longed to rake out his eyes with her fingernails. Then she thought back to the storm. She could still feel the rain driving into her body, hear the wind drowning out her thoughts, and the incredible power of the cabal flowing through her. Yet the storm had defied them. She'd been on the verge of giving up before the effort killed her when a sudden explosion of power shattered her concentration. She saw Horace in her mind, his head thrown back in an imitation of agony or ecstasy. And then the storm was gone.

"He saved us."

"Majesty?"

Byleth frowned. Astaptah never referred to her royal status unless he wanted something. "The savage," she said.

His eyes came alight as if he had been dozing up until this point and was only now coming fully awake. "The foreigner? What did he do?"

"I'm not entirely sure." Byleth wasn't sure how much to tell him. She'd never fully trusted Astaptah and saw no reason to change that now. "His *zoana* is exceptionally strong, but he has no control over it. It leaps and jumps about like the Typhon in flood season, overflowing its channel and washing away everything in its path."

"Interesting," Astaptah murmured, but he no longer seemed to be listening.

"What are you going to do about it?"

The vizier turned back to his work. The end of the rod flared to life with a yellow gleam. "The foreigner is your concern."

That was most certainly true. She could not deny his allure. She'd had lovers aplenty, but there was something different about Horace. He was exotic, of course, and there was the added element of his power. Normally, she would just send for him and have her way, but she hadn't done that with this foreign shipbuilder-turned-*zoanii*, and the reason why escaped her. Her father had always encouraged her to take whatever she wanted in life. *A true king, or queen*, he'd said, *does not ask for anything. He takes it, or he lives without it. Asking is for lesser mortals.*

Yet some part of her was afraid that if she sent for Horace, he would deny her. Oh, he could not hide his obvious attraction to her, but there was also something else in his gaze when he looked at her, a touch of reservation she had never encountered before. She was a queen. Men would lay down their lives at her whim, but this savage with the sea-green eyes was different. If she wanted him, she would have to offer more than just her favors. But a queen did not bargain, and thus she was caught in an achingly delicious trap. And then there was the matter of the foreign attack on her city. Horace couldn't be involved, could he?

"Forget him," she said, unable to keep a slight growl from her voice. "You promised to deliver the empire to me."

"And so I shall."

"When?"

"In due time. This is no simple task. We will have only one chance for success. It needs to be timed with perfection."

She stepped toward him, her hands clenched at her sides. "My enemies are moving against me. I can feel them breathing on the back of my neck, and Ceasa seems farther away now than on the day I saved you."

"I am not the weakling you found on your doorstep," he said, not bothering to look back at her. "I serve you of my own free will and for my own purposes."

"But you *do* serve me, Astaptah. Never forget that."

"I would never dream of it."

She glanced up at the machine, its silver bars gleaming dully in the gloom. "I want it ready in three days, Astaptah. Or I'll come back to take your head as recompense. Do you understand?"

"I do."

"Good. Now I wish to see him."

Astaptah set down the rod on a metal box. "As you wish."

Followed by the floating stone, he led her back across the bridge and through a wide tunnel. It sloped downward, taking them deeper underground as it twisted in a slow curve. Byleth was glad she'd decided to bring the twins. She had never feared for her own safety before—her training and strength in the Imuvar dominion was unequalled in the city—but there was something about these catacombs that unnerved her.

Byleth gestured for the twins to remain outside as Astaptah ushered her into a chamber carved from the living stone. The only furnishing was an upright slab of gray stone positioned against the far wall under an array of wires and cables that extended up into the ceiling, leading—she knew—to the storm engine. By the stark light of the onyx stone, Byleth observed the man on the slab. His muscular body and limbs were bound in wide bands of *zoahadin*. His eyes were bruised purple and black around his closed lids. Dried blood stuck to a circular cut on his forehead.

It was funny. She'd known him all her life, and yet she had never understood him as well as she did now. "Zazil, can you hear me?"

Her brother opened his eyes. He tried to speak, but only a groan issued from his lips, which had been sewn together. His arms and legs twitched within their *zoahadin* binders, but that was the limit of his movement.

"So how does this work?" she asked.

Astaptah came over to stand on the other side of the table. "It is, in essence, a *zoana* pump."

For years Astaptah had been demanding proper subjects for his work. She had heard his accounts of trying to use livestock, but people produced the best results. Criminals, dissidents, and the undesirables of society had all been assigned to her chief vizier's less-than-tender mercies, but it wasn't until he chanced upon a victim—a young leper girl, if she recalled correctly—with latent magical talent that his experiments took a turn for the better.

While Astaptah explained how the machine would slowly drain her brother of his *zoana*, Byleth studied Zazil's face. This was her flesh, her blood. She could read the question in his gaze. Could she really let him die this way? She leaned down so she could look into his eyes.

"Of course I can, brother." She ran her hand across his bare stomach. "There is a price for betrayal."

Zazil shook his head violently, and Byleth placed a finger over his sewn lips to still him. "Don't bother denying it. I know all about your dealings with the Temple of Amur. You've been jealous of my birthright since we were children. I hoped you had outgrown it, but it seems you have given me no choice."

Astaptah hunched over a panel of metal levers against the wall. Each lever was marked with an unfamiliar icon, possibly derived from his native alphabet. He took a long metallic hose from a hook on the wall. Its open end was surrounded by sharp prongs like teeth, which he placed upon Zazil's forehead. An ominous hum emanated from the cable, and her brother arched up from the slab like a puppet pulled by its strings. An animalistic growl emanated from his sealed mouth. Byleth could feel the presence of *zoana* above her like an invisible sun, bathing her in its radiance. "How long will he last?"

"The prince is young and strong," Astaptah replied. "It may take days to drain him completely."

Watching her brother's contortions, she tried to imagine living in such agony for hours and days on end. "Yes. He was always strong. How did you manage to take him alive? Poison? Treachery?"

"I enjoyed a stroke of good fortune, Majesty." Astaptah reached over to adjust a lever. "And proper timing."

BLOOD AND IRON

Byleth watched the way her brother's eyes strained in their sockets. It wasn't just the torment he was suffering; Zazil was terrified of her vizier. She stored that information away. "I have delivered my end of the bargain, my lord. You have your 'perfect specimen.' You have three days to deliver on your promise."

Astaptah turned to her, his face perfectly smooth. "Once I have calibrated the engine to accept the new levels of power, I believe we shall be ready."

Byleth stepped closer to her vizier, even as her intuition cried out for caution. "And I'll be able to direct the storms however I wish? At any time?"

"Yes. However and whenever. Their power will be yours to command."

No army will be able to stand against me. Every city in the empire will open its gates to me.

"Don't disappoint me, Astaptah. My patience is coming to an end."

The door of the chamber opened, and one of the vizier's robed minions entered on silent footsteps. The wizened man stole over to Astaptah's side and whispered something. Byleth frowned. She didn't like people whispering in her presence. After a few seconds, the servant departed.

"What is it?" Byleth asked.

"Omikur has fallen to the crusaders."

Byleth fought the urge to smash something. The air whipped around her in a tiny whirlwind until she regained control. Omikur was a major trading hub and one of the most important towns in the western desert. She could not afford to let it go without a fight, for her brother kings would view it as a sign of weakness.

A ragged howl rang out through the chamber. Byleth frowned, her thoughts disturbed. Zazil had burst his lip sutures and was wailing like a starving infant.

"I need your engine to work," she said. "Now."

Astaptah's eyes glared from beneath their heavy lids as he nodded. "As you wish. The risk will be yours."

With a glare at him, she headed out the door to find out what had happened and how she might remedy the situation. The twins fell in behind her without a word.

As she strode out of the sweltering chamber, Byleth mused that this disaster couldn't have come at a worse time. Her court would need reassurance that she was in command of events. Then there was the question of Horace. How should she handle him? Part of her recognized the danger of allowing him to live. Like any weapon, he could be turned against her. Yet what if he had been sent to her by the gods? Could she risk eliminating a possible chance at victory?

Followed by the wails of her brother, she ascended back to the world above.

CHAPTER TWENTY

"*Ni.*"

"Ni," he repeated.

"*Fa.*"

"Fe."

"No," she said. "*Fa.*"

"Fa," he said.

"*Ti.*"

Horace leaned back on the divan and ran his fingers through his hair. "Can we take a break?"

Alyra set down the papyrus, upon which were drawn the letters of the Akeshian alphabet. For the last three hours she had been trying to teach Horace how to read, and his head felt like it was going to burst from all the foreign sounds and phrases running through it. She held up a stylus. "What is this called?"

Horace struggled against the urge to use the word for "shit," which she'd inadvertently taught him, and instead played the part of a grateful student. "*Kamei.*"

"Good." She pointed to the lamp. "And that?"

"I could really use a—"

"What is it called?"

"*Nuru,*" he mumbled.

"*Nuru* is 'light,'" she said. "'Lamp' is *immaru.*"

He tugged on the ends of his hair until they hurt. "Enough! I can't learn the entire damned language in a day!"

She moved back, putting space between them. "You won't learn it at all if you're going to act like a spoiled child."

Alyra picked up another scroll from the table in the center of the sitting room and unrolled the heavy papyrus. "Let's return to translating. You were doing well."

BLOOD AND IRON

Horace pushed the pile of scrolls away with his foot. "Later. I've had enough stories about pagan gods and talking animals. Between you and Lord Mulcibar, all I've been doing is studying."

"Well, you have a lot to learn."

"You think I don't know that?!" He glared at her but then sighed as he rubbed his forehead. "I'm sorry. It's not you."

Alyra sat back in the divan. "I know. So why don't you tell me what is really bothering you?"

"It's too much to absorb all at once. And I haven't been sleeping very well since . . ."

"The storm," she said for him.

"Yes."

Horace rubbed his eyes. He'd hardly slept the past two nights. Every time he tried, the events on the palace roof came crashing back. He felt the power all the time now, stirring inside his chest like a coiled serpent ready to strike, both thrilling and dangerous. Last night he'd found himself on his knees beside his bed, trying to pray for deliverance from this cursed power, but no words came.

"Everything is so mixed up," he said. "Why am I here? What does it all mean?"

"What if it means nothing?"

"I think that scares me the most. I'd like to know what the queen wants with me."

"You're valuable, Horace. The queen recognizes that, so she keeps you near."

"Valuable?" He laughed. "I'm a foreigner. I don't speak the language very well. And I'm not even worth ransoming."

"You're a sorcerer of power. In every city of Akeshia, the ruling houses bind the *zoanii* to them. By marriage, by title, even with blackmail. Because whoever controls the most power—*zoana*—controls the empire. The queen will seek to use you or, barring that, to make sure that no one else can use you against her."

Alyra was leaning close to him. So close that Horace could smell the scent of the soap she used and the faint oils in her hair. The urge to touch her came over him. Fast on its heels, though, were a host of self-recriminations.

She's a slave. She has no free will to deny you. And what of Sari? Have you forgotten her so soon?

Guilt eating at his insides, Horace picked up the papyrus and tried to commit the symbols to memory. "Anyway, Lord Mulcibar is coming by today."

Alyra shot to her feet. "He's coming here?"

"That's what he said."

Alyra all but ran to her small room. She came back out and hurried past, a short cloak wrapped about her shoulders. "I must attend . . . the queen," she said. "I forgot until now. I'll return this evening and we'll work on your penmanship."

She stopped at the door and looked back. "Horace, be careful around Lord Mulcibar."

"Why do you say that? He's been decent to me since I got here. More decent than anyone else except for you."

"I know. But he's a member of the queen's court and a—"

Alyra jumped as someone knocked on the door. She answered it, bowing from the waist as Lord Mulcibar entered. "Please be welcome, my lord."

The nobleman limped inside with a polite nod. "I trust I am not too early?"

Horace stood up. "Not at all. Come in."

Alyra dipped out the door and closed it behind her. Horace smiled to cover his unease and tried not to stare at the nobleman's scarred face. "Uh, can I take your cloak?"

Lord Mulcibar waved him away. "No, no. At my age, you live in perpetual fear of a sudden chill."

In this heat? He's got to be joking.

Horace glanced around his suite. "Very well. Where shall we . . . er, I mean is there any special place where we should go for . . . ?"

"How about the courtyard? It's a lovely day."

"All right." In addition to a grand view of the city, Horace's apartment had access to a private terrace with a garden.

BLOOD AND IRON

On the way out, Mulcibar stopped beside the table and picked up the sheet of papyrus. "I'm trying to learn," Horace said, "but Akeshian isn't the easiest language to pick up. And the writing is just a mess of scribbles to me."

"In a way, you are correct." Lord Mulcibar pointed to the first letter. "*Ska* is derived from the phrase *ska'vin sin'telluras a idadne*."

"Shit," Horace muttered. "And I thought *ska* was hard enough to memorize."

"It means 'the dawn of the first day of the world.' And it was originally written like this." Mulcibar picked up the stylus, dipped it into the inkwell, and drew an elaborate set of lines and curves. Horace craned his neck. "I see. It looks like the sun coming up over the horizon. And there's a bird flying above it."

"The bird is *He'idadne*. The first creature made by Endu, the lord of the sky. But you can see how this pictogram eventually became the first letter, *ska*."

"I guess so. It seems a lot more complicated than Arnossi."

"Keep working at it."

They went outside and down a winding set of steps to the walled terrace. Tall shrubs lined the walls amid flowerbeds with blossoms in more colors than Horace could name, lending the space a park-like atmosphere. Lord Mulcibar gazed up at the clear sky. He seemed to be looking for something, but Horace couldn't see anything except the sun riding past its zenith, its rays beating down on them.

"You have heard about the attack in the city," Mulcibar said.

A nervous feeling uncoiled in Horace's stomach. "Yes. Some soldiers were killed, and there's a rumor that foreigners were involved."

"Yes, that seems to be the case."

"I don't know what to say. I'm actually surprised that I haven't been clapped in irons again as a suspect."

The nobleman turned to him with a pleasant smile. "If I didn't know exactly where you were at the time and in the hours leading up to the attack, you might be. But Her Majesty knows you had no part in it."

"That's good."

"Yes. Now, shall we begin?"

Mulcibar walked to the far side of the courtyard, a distance of about twenty paces, and turned around. Horace stood facing him. "What do you want me to—?"

Mulcibar held up a hand. "Please, do not talk. Just listen."

Horace waited for a minute, thinking the nobleman would explain further, but Mulcibar merely watched him. "What am I supposed to be listening to?" Horace asked.

"To the wind blowing. To the stirring of the branches and the flower petals. To your own heartbeat. When you listen to these things in stillness, you are listening through your *qa*."

"I don't understand."

"Don't talk. Listen."

Horace swallowed his questions. He could suffer a little peace and quiet, especially if it meant Mulcibar was going to teach him how to use this force inside him. Yet, as the minutes passed by, his mind began to wander. Where had Alyra gone in such a hurry? He didn't believe her excuse about serving the queen. There was something suspicious going on. Perhaps she had a lover. The thought made Horace uncomfortable, and the discomfort irritated him. He had no rights to her. She belonged to the queen. And yet he felt like they had shared some intimate moments these past couple days. Certainly bathing had taken on a whole new meaning to him. She was beautiful. Perfect. In Arnos, she could have been the wife of a rich man with a family and a fine estate, but here she was just a slave. Horace felt his temperature rising as thoughts of her condition made him angry. If he wasn't careful, he would start sweating through his silk robe. A breeze tickled the nape of his neck.

"There," Lord Mulcibar said, finally breaking the silence. "Do you feel it? Moving inside you like a river of heat."

No, I don't feel anything except—

Then Horace realized he *was* feeling something. The now-familiar stirring in his chest, warm but also cold. It had come with the anger, so he hadn't recognized it, but now that he was paying attention he could differentiate between the two sensations. The anger was raw and red in his mind's eye. The other feeling was smoother and deeper. He followed it like a cord inside his

chest, down into his stomach where it blossomed into a host of strange percep-
tions. He tried to understand what he felt, but it was impossible to put into
words. It was like a second heartbeat, but somehow deeper inside him.

"You feel it," Mulcibar said. His eyes were closed, his arms loose by his
sides. For once, he didn't stoop over or lean on his cane. He looked stronger
than before, and younger, too.

"I don't know," Horace replied. "When it happened before, it was like a
fountain of white-hot steel exploding out of me. But now I see . . .".

"Yes?"

Horace described the hot-and-cold sensation and the second heartbeat,
and Mulcibar smiled. "My teacher called it the Gate of Heaven. It is your *qa*,
the source of your power. Through it, you will access the *zoana*. We spend
years discovering how to tap into this power and bend it to our will."

Horace squeezed his eyes shut as he tried to observe the mystical second-
heart. It pulsed in a strange rhythm, sluggish one moment and then faster the
next. "I don't know. When I did whatever I did to the storm, I didn't call on
any special source. It just happened."

"You did without realizing it. That is very rare and also quite dangerous.
That's why the queen asked me to instruct you. If you cannot control the
zoana, it could be unleashed at any time, but especially when you are feeling
angry or afraid."

That pretty much sums up every waking moment since I landed on your shores.

"All right. So how do we proceed?"

"Be still and listen."

Horace groaned under his breath, but he did as the nobleman instructed.

"Breathe naturally and try to focus on the gateway inside you. There
are four dominions of the *zoana*, corresponding to the elements of nature.
Kishargal for the earth. It represents solidity and physical strength. Girru is
the dominion of flame, for energy and aggression. Imuvar is the wind, seat of
understanding and emotional awareness. And the last is Mordab."

Mulcibar lifted a hand, and a ball of clear liquid appeared in the air
before him. "Water is the element of fluidity and flexibility. It is my primary
dominion. I also have some skill with Imuvar."

Horace frowned at the watery ball passing back and forth between Mulcibar's hands. "Unless you're thirsty, it doesn't sound very intimidat—"

Horace didn't have time to duck as the ball flew toward his face, turning white as it crystalized into a globe of ice. A feeling welled up inside him like all the nerves in his body came alive at once. For a moment he saw a burst of light. Then a shower of cool mist rained over him. He had closed his eyes during the explosion of sensations. When he opened them, Lord Mulcibar stood a couple feet farther away from him. The nobleman's gaze was focused to the side at the garden. Horace swore as he spotted the smoking bush, its branches blackened, the leaves gone. Behind the ruined flora was a fist-sized gouge in the garden wall.

"I only meant to test your reflexes," Mulcibar said, his tone subdued. "I've never seen anything approximating your response."

"I'm sorry. I didn't mean to . . ."

"No, it is I who must apologize, Horace. I've never had a student who could apply the *zoana* so naturally. It usually takes months to learn the proper techniques for summoning and harnessing the power."

It felt strange to be praised by the old sorcerer for almost killing him. "So what dominion was that?" Horace asked.

"I'm . . . not sure. But don't worry. With time and experimentation, it will reveal itself to you."

"But where does the magic come from?"

Lord Mulcibar walked over to one of the garden benches and sat down with his cane between his knees. "To answer that, I will have to ask your forbearance while I tell you a story. A very long time ago, when the first men came to this land, they fished in the waters of the Typhon and learned to grow wheat on its silted plains. It was during that era, according to our oldest records, that the Wanderers came down from the heavens."

"The Wanderers? Like angels?"

"They were called the children of the stars," Mulcibar replied. "The sons and daughters of the elder gods, come to teach mankind the gifts of civilization, including the use of *zoana*. Under their supervision, the great cities were built, and an age of peace and knowledge was born."

BLOOD AND IRON

Horace didn't like where this talk of pagan superstitions was going, but he wanted to know about this power inside him badly enough to play along. "So what happened to these gods?"

"They returned to the immortal world. Yet they left behind their gifts. The first magicians were priests as well as *zoanii*, but over time they separated from the people and set themselves up as the rulers."

"Hard to argue with someone who can incinerate you with a thought."

"Precisely. But it's important to remember that the *zoana* did not cause the problem. Many *zoanii* feel the power is merely a tool, but it is a manifestation of the worlds, above and below."

"But I've never had these powers before."

"I think they must have been there all the time since you were born, but they had no outlet. Not until something triggered them to come to the surface."

Horace searched his memories and came up with the answer right away. "The storm in the desert."

"Just so. The energy of the chaos storm called to your *zoana* and brought it forth."

"What are the storms? You call them chaos, but what does that mean?"

The old nobleman tapped the end of his cane on the dusty pavestones. "That is more difficult to answer. All things in the cosmos came from chaos. It is the force of creation, as well as destruction."

Horace looked down at the scars across his palms. "Each time I've seen one of these chaos storms, I get a peculiar feeling. It's raw and powerful, almost angry. It makes me want to break something. Or worse."

"Some of our seers claim that the storms are the embodiment of the gods' wrath, sent down as punishment for our failure to follow their divine ways. Others believe they are a trial to cleanse the empire of weakness and to fortify us for some great destiny."

"You don't sound like you believe either of those theories."

"My beliefs are a discussion for another day. I don't know why you feel such things, Horace, but I've been thinking about your lack of immaculata. Perhaps if I could perform some tests . . ."

Horace shifted away. "I don't like the sound of that."

"Forgive me. I was a student of mathematics and science when I was a young man, and some traces of that investigative mindset still reside with me. Yet I cannot help but suspect that the two—your tremendous power and the fact that you do not bleed while invoking it—are somehow related. Every *zoanii* sheds the sacred blood while embracing the *zoana*, even Her Majesty."

"But what causes it?"

Mulcibar placed his fingers together in a steeple. "The priesthoods teach that the immaculata are the price levied by the gods for the gift of *zoana*. Blood feeds the power, and the power nourishes the universe."

"Do you think that's why I don't get the wounds?" Horace asked. "Because I don't follow your ways?"

"It does not seem reasonable to me, but I am no theologian."

"What does the scientist in you say?"

Mulcibar smiled. "That some tests are in order."

They laughed, and Horace felt the weight he'd been carrying around inside his chest ease. Mulcibar stood up with a wince. "But for now," he said, "I would like to try something that may give you better control over your power."

"Yes, sir. That would be most welcome."

"Very good. Now relax and stand normally. Breathe in through your nose and let it out. Now repeat after me."

Mulcibar made a noise that sounded like a bullfrog croaking. Horace almost laughed, but the nobleman's face was serious. "All right," he said, taking a relaxed pose.

Horace tried to reproduce the sound. It took him several tries, but eventually he got close enough. Then Mulcibar instructed him to fold his hands together with the forefingers extended and pressed together. After a couple minutes of croaking and holding his hands in the rigid position, Horace asked, "So why am I doing this?"

"The sound is designed to focus the mind and body. And the hand positioning aligns your *qa* to your purpose."

"Which is what?"

BLOOD AND IRON

This time when Mulcibar formed a ball of ice and threw it, Horace was more cognizant of the power that welled up inside him. Like a rising wave, it flowed up from his body and ran along his arms to his fingers. He could feel it wanting to burst forth, but he remembered the hole in the garden wall and fought to pull it back. The icy sphere exploded just inches away from his face. Splinters of ice flew in every direction, striking the pavestones at his feet and the leaves of the tree beside him, but not a single shard touched him. Horace exhaled. His whole body was humming.

Lord Mulcibar led him to the bench. Horace sat quietly until the tremors subsided. It felt like a flood of energy had rushed through his body, and was now slowly leaving.

"That was," he said, "incredible. It didn't feel like what happened during the storms at all. It was more controlled."

"The *zoana* is a wild force. Easily provoked. That was quite good, but you must learn to have precise control of the power at all times, or you will be a danger to everyone around you."

Horace nodded and stood up. His legs were a little shaky, but he managed to stay upright. "All right. Let's get back to work then."

"Very good, Master Horace."

CHAPTER TWENTY-ONE

The afternoon waned as Horace spent two hours chanting with his hands locked into bizarre configurations while he tried to take control of his *qa*. By the end of the session, he was wrung out like he'd hiked twenty miles, and his head was killing him.

When Lord Mulcibar departed, Horace sat in the courtyard alone. The lesson played over and over in his mind, but rather than enjoying his limited successes, he dwelled on the failures. Control of the power seemed to slip through his grasp time and time again, leaving him frustrated and more than a little alarmed. He wished Alyra was there to talk to about it, and missing her added to his angst.

Someone knocked at his front door.

He hurried back inside his suite and answered it. Chancellor Unagon stood in the hallway with a pair of manservants.

"Yes?"

Unagon bowed and placed his right hand over his heart. Horace was getting better at understanding Akeshian, but the chancellor spoke too fast for him to follow. "I'm sorry. I didn't understand any of that."

Chancellor Unagon frowned and then indicated that they wished to come inside. Horace backed up to give them room, and Unagon strode toward the bedchamber with his servants in tow. Horace hurried after them. "Hey! Excuse me!"

The chancellor opened the wardrobe and picked out a long magenta tunic with a silver starburst design on the chest, a matching skirt, and a pair of black sandals. Then he gestured to the servants and said something about helping Horace.

He held up his hands. "Wait a minute. Help me with what?"

Chancellor Unagon spoke slowly. "Dress you, sire. You are to meet the queen."

Horace lowered his hands, and the servants went into motion. Soon Horace was wearing the selected outfit, with his face and hands washed and his hair combed. Chancellor Unagon fussed over him for about half an hour and then waved him toward the door. Horace obeyed. Outside, a squadron of the queen's bodyguard stood at attention. They saluted him in unison and then fell in around him.

What am I walking into now?

The soldiers took him a different way than before. As they started up a series of switchback staircases, a tremor of anxiety stirred in Horace. Visions of his last visit to the queen's boudoir flashed across his mind. He had to force some lurid thoughts out of his head.

Perhaps she's invited me to dinner on the roof?

The stairs opened into a hallway, a bit narrower than most of the palace passageways he'd seen. The soldiers opened a door, and ruddy sunlight poured in along with a strong breeze that rustled Horace's clothes. Stepping through, he entered onto a wide terrace at the top of the world. The patio was bedecked with so many plants—from flowers and shrubs to waving trees thirty feet tall—that it looked like a forest. Through the verdant décor, he spotted a marble balustrade along the edge overlooking a breathtaking view of the city below.

As the guards took up positions by the door, Horace looked around. The place was a paradise in the sky. He had leaned down to smell a large, yellow flower shaped like a water pitcher when the queen arrived through another door. She was accompanied by a squadron of bodyguards and one of the wizard twins, the one called Gilgar. The sorcerer glared at Horace from three steps behind the queen, and a little tickle traveled up the back of his neck. Horace was ready to pass it off as a product of his anxiety, but then he realized he'd felt it before—the exact same tickle on his neck—when he was practicing with Lord Mulcibar. In fact, he'd felt it several times since his arrival in Akeshia.

It must be tied to the zoana. *Their presence, or the queen's, triggered it.*

Horace made a formal bow. The queen returned a slight curtsey. This evening she wore a diaphanous gown of white silk, belted high on the waist. Curving designs were stitched into the gown in silver thread. She smiled at him. "I'm so glad you accepted my invitation, Master Horace. I felt like taking an evening ride."

"Ride, Your Excellence?"

He glanced around. Where could they possibly go up here? And what would they ri—?

Horace's tongue stuck to the roof of his mouth as a large oblong shape emerged from the shadow of the palace. It was long with curved sides, its wooden bottom extending to sharp wedges fore and aft. With majestic grace, it sailed down toward them.

No, it can't be possible.

The flying ship—and that's the only way he could describe it—floated down beside the terrace. Its upper deck had no masts or rigging, and nothing that resembled a wheelhouse. The gunwales were decorated with intertwining vines painted in gold leaf. This design continued to the forward section where it expanded into a bas relief display showing a row of ships sailing on a sea of clouds, all also done in gold. A purple canopy shaded the center deck.

Three men stood on the deck; one at the bow and two at the stern. As the ship got closer, Horace saw that each man clasped waist-high metal poles that rose from the planking.

"What do you think of my barge?" Byleth asked as she followed him to the balustrade.

Horace swallowed. "I would have never believed it if I wasn't seeing it for myself. A flying ship! A *real* flying ship just like in the legends. How does it work?"

She laid a hand on his wrist, sending feathery touches up his spine. "I'll explain during the trip."

"We're actually going aboard?"

"Of course. I want to show you something."

A voice hailed from behind them. "Good afternoon, Your Majesty. Master Horace."

Lord Mulcibar emerged onto the terrace, hobbling on his cane. He had changed since meeting with Horace into a soft cornflower robe with a black cape.

"Good afternoon, my lord." The queen drew nearer to Horace and shifted her hand to wrap around his upper arm. "Shall we?"

Lord Mulcibar nodded and waved them ahead. Horace, eager to see the flying ship up close, moved to the narrow gangplank that had been lowered. Byleth went across without pause, but Horace—despite his excitement—could not help from looking down. Empty space yawned on either side of the bridge, dropping hundreds of feet to the grounds below. His throat constricted at the sight and a momentary wave of vertigo took hold of him, but he forced his feet to carry him across.

He felt better when he stepped aboard the flying vessel and felt the buoyant spring of the deck. The wind blowing through his hair was dry and fragrant, but it was close enough to a sea breeze that he didn't mind. A faint vibration ran through the boards under his feet. It traveled up his legs and tickled his backbone, like he was standing on a vast beehive.

The deck was long but not very wide, and it felt crowded as the last bodyguard climbed aboard. The gangplank was pulled up, and the ship set off. It turned like a gigantic bird, with slow and gentle grace as it took a northwesterly course. The deck swayed gently from side to side, almost like the roll of a seagoing vessel.

"Where are we going?" Horace asked.

"We're taking a little tour," the queen said. "Come. Stand with me over here."

The others gave Horace and Byleth some room as she pulled him to the larboard side of the flying ship. He steeled himself to look over the polished railing that encircled the deck. The ship had risen even farther off the ground. The palace was already far behind and below them as they sailed over the city. The buildings and streets dwindled beneath them, the people shrinking to the size of fleas until he couldn't distinguish them anymore.

After a few minutes, his nervousness melted away. It felt good to be aboard a ship again, even one soaring hundreds of fathoms above the ground.

"Do you see there?" The queen pointed at a sprawling building with several wings and a large expanse of gardens inside a stone enclosure. "That is where I grew up. Except when my father sent me to the springs at Hikkak every winter."

"Winter?" Horace said. "Does it get cold here then?"

"Oh, yes. Sometimes we have to wear jackets or shawls outside and burn coals in our rooms at night." She pressed her breasts against his arm so that he could feel her small nipples through the silk. "Of course, there are more interesting ways to stay warm."

Not sure how to respond, especially in the company of Lord Mulcibar and the guards, Horace studied the city beneath them. They were passing over blackened areas that looked like they had engulfed entire neighborhoods. The destruction was complete, leaving not a single outbuilding untouched. "Are those the granaries?"

"No. Those were the barracks of my city guard. They were burned down on the night of the storm."

Horace looked to the queen, knowing he had to say something. "Your Excellence, I just want you to know I had nothing to do with the attack."

She reached up to run a fingernail along the underside of his jaw. "Of course not, Horace. I never suspected you for a moment. It was done by my enemies, who want to see me dead."

He held still, neither pulling back nor leaning into her. "People are trying to kill you?"

One of the soldiers shifted, making his armor creak. Horace glanced back. Everyone was watching them. Except Lord Mulcibar, who leaned against the starboard rail.

"Though I try to rule lightly," the queen said, "there are some who would stop at nothing to pull me down. Your countrymen, for instance. They used the cover of the storm to kill my guards and burn the granaries that feed my people. If they are not stopped, someday they may succeed in ending my life."

"I'm . . . I'm sorry. I hope they won't succeed."

"I believe that. Do you recall that you asked me about *Tammuris?*"

"Yes. That envoy, Lord Baphetor, mentioned it. You never told me why."

"The *Tammuris* comes in five days on the new moon. That evening I must wed my betrothed, Prince Tatannu. Lord Baphetor was so kind to remind me that my fate has been sealed."

"I don't understand."

"That is the pact I signed with the other cities when my father was killed." Byleth leaned over the rail, which made Horace's stomach want to crawl up into his throat. "In exchange for my life, I promised to wed the son of my father's archenemy. That day approaches, and when it comes the Sun Temple will rule Erugash in name as well as deed, and I will cease to be valuable. Do you know what happens to a queen once she no longer has any value?"

"In Arnos, the queen is the mother of our people. She always has value."

"In Akeshia, a woman has only what value her husband says she has, whether she is a queen or a shepherdess."

Horace cleared his throat and flailed for another subject, anything to take her mind off the situation. He decided on something that interested him very much. "So are you going to tell me how this ship works?"

She took him by the elbow. "Come along, Master Horace."

What followed was a detailed explanation of the flying ship, which, though extraordinary, was rather simple. The three men holding onto the metal poles were, of course, *zoanii*, and they powered the ship's engine—which was kept belowdecks—with their magic. The ship was steered by the helmsman at the fore instead of the aft like on a nautical vessel. The men at the stern controlled the amount of power that flowed to the engine.

"What if something happened to one of the men powering the ship?" Horace asked. "Would it fall?"

"Not at once," Byleth answered. "With two *zoanii* powering the engine, we could still fly, though at a far slower pace."

"And with only one?"

"I'm not sure. Shall I command them to let go and see what happens?"

"Ah, no, thank you, Excellence. Can I see the engine?"

Byleth huddled closer and squeezed his arm. "I don't know. It's quite cramped below, and I might not be able to restrain myself with you in such close quarters."

He leaned into her until their faces were almost touching. "Why don't we find out?"

She pulled back and looked into his eyes. "Are you more interested in me or how the engine works?"

He couldn't help from smiling. "Well, both, actually."

"Unfortunately, only those trained by the imperial school in Ceasa are allowed to view the inner workings. I'm sure you understand."

Of course I do. If Arnos had a vehicle like this, we'd keep it a secret, too.

Horace turned his attention to the land below. The sun was just a sliver of gold above the horizon. They had passed far beyond the city limits. The land hugging the river was divided into square sections of honey-brown fields, but everything beyond the riparian zone was a wasteland of cracked earth and dust. Ahead to the northwest, the wastes gave way to a vast golden sea. Even from a distance—and it had to be a score of leagues or more—the desert was impressive, beautiful and mysterious like the women of this strange land, and just as dangerous. The sun was setting before them, framing the world in a brilliant orange patina.

"Tell me more about your homeland," the queen said.

Horace studied the sky. It was crystal blue without a hint of clouds. From this high, he felt like he could see forever. "I miss the smells."

"The perfumes of your pale northern ladies?"

"No. The smells of leather and horse. The stink of the city streets, the middens and the fish smells of the docks. The smell of pitch and pinewood."

She wrinkled her tiny nose. "It sounds filthy."

"It is. But it's home."

He wanted to ask her if he could leave, just take a ship and go back to Arnos, but he was terrified of her answer. Why had she brought him along on this cruise? Somehow, he didn't think it was to woo him. Not in the romantic sense, at least.

"Our teachers say that the western countries are always making war," she said. "What do you say to that?"

"I guess I'd say they're right. We've had several wars just during my lifetime. And the Great War between the Nimean Empire and its outer states was only a century and a half ago. But we have peaceful times as well. Our trade depends on it."

"But you served on a ship of war."

"The *Bantu Ray* was merchantman originally. But when the crusade got underway, we were commandeered for the war effort. Our captain didn't have much choice in the matter."

Her fingers plucked at his sleeve. "So you are not a zealot, gripped by the furor of your one god? No, I think you are more like a piece of wood floating on the river, pushed wherever the water goes."

"Flotsam."

"What?"

Horace shook his head. "Nothing. You may be right. I signed on with the *Ray* because I wanted to belong to something real, something bigger than my life. I suppose that must be hard for a queen to understand."

"No, it's not." She traced the palm of his left hand, over the mottled whirls and dimples of the ruined flesh. "How did you get these scars? They are not immaculata."

Her eyes were so big and dark through the forest of lashes. He had the sudden urge to kiss her, but he tamped it down. "What do you want with me?"

He expected a rebuke for his forwardness or a disdainful look for failing to play her games, but instead the queen said, "I need to know more about your people. How far will they press their crusade against Akeshia? What would convince them to give up the fight?"

On some level, Horace knew she wanted him for something other than companionship, but it still stung to hear. "From what I saw, Your Excellence, nothing will deter them. The Church will not rest until your country has been defeated and converted to the True Faith, whether that takes a year or a century."

She said something under her breath that Horace didn't catch. They had entered the desert. The sands flowed beneath them like a golden blanket. Beautiful, but Horace could still remember their brutal heat. Thinking of the journey with Jirom and Gaz reminded him of the desert storm. That entire day was foggy in his memory. The only thing he remembered clearly was the moment the power—his *zoana*—left his body. It had been like drowning, only to break the surface of the water to find air once again.

He was lost in his thoughts, watching the dunes pass by, when he spotted a dark smudge on the horizon. Horace shaded his eyes against the dwindling daylight and made out some kind of settlement encircled by a long, low wall—at least it looked low from this distance. Square buildings and lean towers nestled inside the fortifications. The flying ship slowed its velocity and turned due west on a course that would take it close to the town. As they got closer, Horace could see a second dark smudge outside the wall. He squinted and leaned over the rail. It was too far away to count, but he guessed there had to be hundreds of tents staked out on the sands. Earthworks and defensive fortifications surrounded the walls. The town was under siege.

"Who's fighting?" he asked.

The queen pointed to the settlement. "That is Omikur, one of my most vital holdings in the desert. It had never fallen to an invading force, until two days ago when it was seized by an army from Etonia."

Crusaders. The soldiers aboard the Bantu Ray might have been in that army, if not for the storm that destroyed the ship.

"We suspect the invaders might have had an agent inside the town," she said. "However it was done, the capture was a bold move, especially since they are many leagues from the sea and the protection of your fleets."

Horace's anxiety returned, making him sweat despite the strong breeze that flowed across the deck. "And the camp is your army?"

"My Third Legion, under the command of Lord General Arishaka."

There must be five thousand men in that camp, with another three or four thousand strung out along the siegeworks.

"I'm afraid I won't be much use as a soldier, Your Excellence."

Her laughter rang over the winds. "Master Horace, really! You think I would ask you to fight your own people? No, we are here merely to observe."

A little relieved but still not sure how much to believe her, Horace focused his attention on the siege. With the daylight waning, he didn't expect much activity. Yet men scurried along the earthworks, and the town walls were filled with soldiers. Were any of the defenders from Arnos? It would be impossible to tell unless the ship flew close enough for him to make out their banners. Horace tried to imagine what the men on those walls were thinking, surrounded by a vast enemy, far from their own lines. The queen was right. Taking this town had been a bold move, and maybe a fatal one for the invaders.

Perhaps reinforcements are already on the march. If they can hold out for a few days, they might be rescued.

Horace glanced at the queen out of the corner of his eye, hoping she couldn't read his expression. He had a hard time swallowing, and not just from the dry desert air. Fortunately, a bodyguard came over with refreshments. Horace accepted a copper goblet and peered inside. It was a light red wine smelling slightly of cloves. He took a long drink despite its sharp aftertaste.

Horace almost spilled the cup as a horn sounded below. He hadn't noticed the ship descending; they were now only a couple bowshots above the dunes and sailing along at a slower pace. As he looked over the side, a forest of great wooden arms sprang up from the earthworks, sending dozens of fireballs sailing through the sundered twilight. The orbs of burning death burst, some upon the battlements where they spread viscous flames among the troops, and others inside the town, exploding in the streets. Yet the town was well designed against attack. The walls were protected by machicolations and hoardings with sloped roofs that repelled the burning missiles. Still, a few penetrated the defenses. Soldiers thrashed as they burned. The fortunate ones were put to the sword by their comrades, but too often those comrades also caught fire when they came too close to their burning fellows, and so the carnage spread. Horace had seen burning pitch demonstrated before, but the fires launched by these incendiaries stuck and burned for far longer than pitch or oil.

"My God," he muttered, unable to take his eyes from the devastation.

"Not your god," Byleth said, "nor any of mine. This is science and sorcery, the worst of both." She shook her head. "Do you see what monsters war makes of us all?"

Horace tried to watch the scene below with detachment, but it wasn't easy. Now seeing the town's walls up close, they were sturdier than he first thought. And although the firepots were deadly, the defenders were quick to douse them with sand, which worked much better than water. Gazing at the great catapults amid the earthworks cocking back for another volley, Horace was tempted to try his powers, to sever the pulley ropes that worked the siege weapons or to ignite the firepots in midair. He made no move to help the defenders, however. With the queen standing so close to him, she would sense if he tried anything.

His stomach dropped when a crackle of thunder raced across the sky above. The hull creaked as the vessel swung around on a northerly course, circling the town. Yet Horace was watching the sky.

Byleth said something, and the helmsman consulted a spherical device mounted beside his station before answering. The only word Horace caught was "hour." Then clouds appeared from nowhere, and the sky darkened.

He jerked upright when a powerful shock raced up his spine. Thunder crashed over the ship as a bolt of lurid green lightning shot from the sky. The clouds swirled with twisting winds, gathering into a maelstrom above the city. Horace's gaze was drawn to the center of the storm. There, behind the screen of thunderheads, he sensed a presence.

The hunger. An insatiable need to destroy and consume. It washed over him and entered him. He was powerless to resist its call, unable to stop the connection between him and the longing. And in that moment he sensed he was close to understanding something vital about the storm, or maybe himself.

The ship shuddered as a tongue of lightning slashed the sky off the starboard bow. Over the crackling after-rumbles, someone was laughing. Horace looked to the queen in shock. Her eyes were pits of utter darkness in the deepening twilight.

"What say you, Storm Lord?" she asked. "Shall we dance with the gods?"

CHAPTER TWENTY-TWO

Horace could only watch in horror as the chaos storm swept over the town. A fire had exploded within the urban center where the buildings were clustered closest together. Emerald brilliance stung his eyes again as another bolt lanced from the sky, and a tall tower collapsed. More fires leapt up inside the crumbling structure.

The urge to help almost overcame Horace, until cool fingers touched his hand. The queen leaned against him as the flying ship swung away from the town. The smell of the perfume in her hair drowned the bitterness lodged inside him. Squeezing his elbow, she smiled at him before she sauntered away.

Omikur drifted in their wake, now just a spot of yellow light in the darkness of the desert. The storm remained above the settlement, blasting the walls with occasional lightning. He felt drained and was tempted to lie down on the deck and close his eyes, etiquette be damned.

"She's testing you."

Lord Mulcibar came to stand beside him. Glass orbs had come alive at both ends of the flying ship, glowing like giant fireflies. Horace sighed as he looked into the impenetrable blackness below. "Then I wish she would find someone else to torment."

"Be wary of what you wish for, Master Horace."

"You mean it can get worse than this? I'm a prisoner to the people my country is at war with and I have to just watch as those crusaders down there are slaughtered. If this is a test, then I'm glad to fail it."

"You have to understand the delicacy of the situation." Mulcibar lifted his gaze to the west. "We are an old civilization. We watched your nations grow from tribes of fur-wearing savages, and some of us still have a hard time believing that your people have advanced all that much. Then there is our politics. All power in Akeshia flows from the *zoanii*. Yet the Temple of the Sun has clawed its way into dominance over all the other cults, largely due to the emperor's favor, and now it chafes under our rule. Akeshia has suffered through more civil wars than I can easily recall, and now we teeter on the edge of another, one which might change the face of the empire. Keeping you close is in Her Majesty's best interest. And yours."

"Oh? How is that?"

"You have the *zoana*, but you are not of the *zoanii*. You have no family here, no master, no liege."

"And no loyalties. Right?"

"Exactly. You are a weapon with no attachments. That makes you unique in Akeshia, and it makes you valuable."

"So the queen has to keep an eye on me to make sure no other faction scoops me up. I understand that much. But what's in it for me?"

"You can consider the alternative. We live in a time of violent upheaval. Without Her Majesty's aegis, you would be without allies."

Horace winked at him. "Not even you, Lord Mulcibar?"

"I'm an old man. You might be powerful—perhaps the strongest magician we've seen in generations—but you can't defeat the entire empire by yourself."

Soft footsteps crossed the deck. "What are you two whispering about?"

Lord Mulcibar bowed and retreated as Queen Byleth returned. She leaned against the railing beside Horace, and he couldn't help but think that with just one push . . . "Ah, nothing much. History, actually."

"Ack. My tutors bored me with history for years. None of it makes any difference. The past is gone. It's the future that concerns me."

"I don't know how you do it," he said. "You're the ruler of a city, but you're so young and a . . ."

"What?" She glanced at him out of the kohl-lined corners of her eyes. "A woman?"

"Well, I . . . uh, I just meant that . . ."

She laughed and put a hand on his forearm. "Don't worry. I've been called much worse than that. Ask Lord Mulcibar to take you on a tour of the river district in Erugash. There's some very inventive graffiti about me."

"I'm sorry, Your Excellence. It was ungrateful of me to refer to your sex."

"Master Horace, you are anything but ungrate—"

The queen's words were cut off by a terrific roar. The deck of the flying ship bucked as if the vessel had struck a reef. Horace grabbed the railing and threw out his hand as the queen tipped backward. He caught her by the wrist before she fell over the side. She opened her mouth as if to say something as he hauled her back from the brink, and then collapsed in his arms as limp as a clubbed fish. Horace tried to hold her upright, but the ship lurched again and rolled halfway over onto its starboard side. As the ship dropped out of the sky like a stone, turning Horace's stomach inside out, Byleth slumped to the floor. He was doing his best to keep her pinned in place with one arm when a second explosion occurred.

The wizard at the bow helm collapsed in a tangle of scorched flesh and smoldering robes. His body slid over the edge as the flying ship tipped forward. Several soldiers fell off, too, flailing at the air. Horace put his back to the railing and gathered the queen into his arms. He fought the urge to vomit as the flying ship continued to pitch, sucking in shallow breaths through gritted teeth to keep down the ball of nausea roiling in his gut. Lord Mulcibar lay flat against the deck next to him, somehow staying fixed in position. To Horace's right, only one wizard helmsman remained in the aft section, hanging from the metal pole. Gilgar held onto the railing with one arm. Horace craned his neck to look down and regretted it at once. The ground was coming up fast to meet them. He squeezed his eyes shut. In a few moments, they would all be dead.

Sari, I pray I'll be seeing you soon.

The queen stirred in his arms. Horace looked down to see her eyes opening. She appeared confused or perhaps just dazed. Then he felt the power thrumming in his chest. He reached for it and gasped as the white-hot energy surged through every fiber of his body. It roared in his ears, driving out all thoughts of dying. He wanted to live.

Horace hoisted the queen higher into his arms. He didn't have a plan, and there wasn't time to devise one. With only a handful of seconds to act, he embraced the first idea to cross his mind. His eyes sought out the helm pole at the bow of the ship, a dozen yards above him across the canted deck. If his powers could drive away a chaos storm, he reasoned that they should be able to manipulate something more solid. At least, he hoped so. With a tentative touch, he tried to reach out with the *zoana*. Nothing happened. The ship continued to plummet to the ground. The queen murmured something, but Horace couldn't hear her over the wind howling in his ears. He closed his eyes and blocked everything out. He reached for the metal pole again. This time he felt a chilling tingle like cool steel running across his brain. Horace didn't pause to appreciate the oddness of it all; he envisioned himself wrenching back on the handle. The deck rolled beneath his feet, slowly righting itself. Horace glanced over the side.

Too late!

The ground still raced toward them. He saw the river, so close he could make out the ripples of its current and the tops of several boulders sticking out of the water. Horace's heart thumped, and the energy pulsed with each beat. He tried pulling up on the helm pole, but the ship's trajectory remained fixed. Horace bit his tongue, not knowing what to do. Then firm hands slapped against either side of his head and forced him to look down. The queen's eyes were wide open. "Push against the ground!" she shouted.

And though her voice was torn away by the rushing wind, Horace heard it clearly. He almost laughed. Her demand was impossible. Insane! They were going to die. He reached out ahead of the falling ship, not expecting to find anything, but he did. A horizontal force beneath them, firm against his mental touch. With the queen's eyes locked on him, he pushed against it with everything he had.

The river wound like a sunbathing serpent, lush and brown amid the riparian grasses that grew along its flanks. Gazing at it from the shadow of a huge boulder on the riverbank, Horace could appreciate more it than he had from the air. In the desert, the river was life. Yet it had come close to being the site of their death.

Dawn had come, bringing with it the heat of the day. A line of sweat dribbled down his forehead as he thought back to those panicked final moments onboard the flying ship. At the queen's command, he had pushed against the ground. Or, to be more precise, against the powerful force he'd felt running along the ground. He could still feel it, under his feet, firm and unyielding, but also comfortable in a familiar way. At the time, he'd thought it would be impossible to stop a falling ship with just his mind, but the *zoana* had responded. The ship had bucked under him like an unbroken stallion, shaking so violently he almost lost his grip on the queen, but somehow he held on. Then the ship struck the ground hard enough to crack the hull in half and throw them over the side. He fell in the shallows of the river and got up without a scratch. His clothing, now caked in mud, took the worst of the damage.

Horace glanced back at their makeshift camp beside the river. The queen sat on a small rock, her arms wrapped about her knees, face resting on her forearms. Though she hadn't been injured as far as he could tell, she hadn't talked much since their landing either.

Lord Mulcibar sprawled on the ground beside the queen, a rolled cloak under his head. Horace had found him in the weeds, eyes open and staring up at the sky, but alive. With a little cajoling, Mulcibar had come around and managed to walk on his own, allowing Horace to focus his attention on the queen. One soldier had survived as well, although he'd suffered a broken leg. Horace had done his best to make the man comfortable under the tree. That was it. No sign of Gilgar or the helmsmen. Just four survivors out of a score, but it was a miracle any of them still lived. But what had caused the ship to crash? Horace recalled a loud sound like an explosion.

No, there were two explosions. The initial one that started the descent, and then another on the way down.

The ship now lay in pieces along the water's edge. Horace considered going over to take a look, but instead he went to check on the queen. She was looking a little better. Some of the color had returned to her face. She was talking when Horace got within earshot.

"—decide when we get back to Erugash."

Mulcibar struggled to sit up. "Your Majesty, it is not yet clear what caused this incident. We should consider all possibilities."

BLOOD AND IRON

They both glanced at Horace, and he resisted the urge to glower at them. Mulcibar was right. Until they knew what had happened, they had to suspect everyone. And he, as the only foreigner present, was a prime candidate. Then again, he was also the one who had saved their lives.

Byleth stood up, swaying a little as she regained her feet. Horace offered a hand, and she took it, leading him away. She steered him down to the river where they walked along the muddy banks. After a few minutes, he felt the need to break the silence. "What do we do now?"

"I summoned aid from the city. As we speak, another vessel is on its way."

Horace tried to calculate the distance between their position and Erugash based on the flying ship's speed. It had to be at least two days travel on foot. "How does that work? Can you call to anywhere?"

"No. Only to a location that has been specifically prepared to receive my call. There is such a spot in the palace, which is manned by my servants every hour of the day and night. It is a useful skill. One you should learn."

Watching the queen, Horace was struck by how normal she looked, just chatting and walking along the riverbank. If not for her fine clothing and jewels, she could almost be an ordinary woman out for a stroll. He felt an intense attraction to her, like hot steel poured into his veins, searing away his natural inclination for caution. But then Sari's face came to him and quenched the sudden ardor. Feeling the queen's gaze upon him, Horace tried to mask his awkwardness. "So now we wait?"

"Now we wait."

There were so many things Horace wanted to say, but he wasn't sure how far he could trust her apparent fondness for him. "Excellence, there is something I want to ask you."

"Anything. You saved my life and the lives of my servants. Ask anything of me, and it shall be yours."

A hundred possible answers stampeded through his head, but one pushed ahead of the rest. "Would you allow me to leave and go home?"

She studied him for a long moment that felt like hours. "Yes, if that is your wish." She held up a finger before he could thank her. "Within two turns of the moon's cycle. If I allowed you to leave now, there would be . . . repercussions. Give me some time to put my troubles to rest, and then I shall send you home. I swear this by the spirits of my ancestors, may they strike me dead if I do not."

Horace stood still, unable to speak for a moment. If he could believe her, he was as good as free. Then he realized something else, something that filled him with a bliss he hadn't known in a long time. For the first time in over a year, he was looking forward to seeing tomorrow. Then he thought of Alyra. "I would like something else as well, Excellence."

The queen gave him a look that was decidedly coy, and he realized what she might think he was going to demand. The idea of it sobered him. "My slave, Excellence. I would like her freed from bondage. Permanently."

The queen nodded, although her coquettish smile vanished. "As you wish, but I would urge caution. You would not be the first man of stature, nor the first woman for that matter, to seek affection in the arms of a slave. All too often, once freed of their bonds the object of desire is not so . . . agreeable as before."

Horace felt his neck grow warm. "Ah, no. That's not it. I'm just not comfortable being served by a slave. Call it a cultural difference."

Byleth leaned against his shoulder. "Are all westerners so gallant toward their servants?"

"You're teasing me, Excellence."

The smile returned. "Just a little. I try to deal fairly with my people, Master Horace, though it's not always easy. There are not many I can trust outside—"

Horace considered pressing his luck by asking for a third boon, that Jirom be freed, too. Yet before he could phrase the question, a stinging itch buzzed down the back of his neck. He reached for his power without realizing it and was mildly surprised at how quickly it came to him, rushing through his chest and out to his extremities. Byleth tensed as a sound like a swarm of hornets descended upon them. She shoved him, and they both tumbled to the ground as something blisteringly hot passed over them. The tops of several reed stalks evaporated in puffs of black smoke, delineating a horizontal line as if they had been sliced off with a saber. Horace started to sit up. "What in the hell—?"

BLOOD AND IRON

Byleth pressed a hand to his mouth, silencing him. Horace listened, but he didn't hear anything except the breeze through the weeds and the soft ripple of the river. He whispered through her fingers, "What are we listening for?"

Byleth removed her hand but did not speak. She froze as a person emerged from the tall grass beside them. His hair disheveled, he pointed something at the queen that looked like a baton, thin and black. It took Horace a moment to recognize the man as one of the aft-helmsmen of the flying ship.

The queen pushed out from her chest with both hands. A surge of wind picked up the helmsman, flipped him upside down, and flung him to the ground. This was the dominion of wind Lord Mulcibar had mentioned. Imuvar, he'd called it. The helmsman struggled against the currents of air pinning him down, but he couldn't break their hold. His jaws were stretched open like he was trying to shout, but no sounds emerged. Byleth stared at her servant with fierce concentration. After several seconds, the helmsman shuddered and then lay still.

Another figure emerged from the reeds. Horace moved in front of the queen and steeled himself for another violent encounter until he saw it was Lord Mulcibar.

Byleth stepped out from behind him. "How long do we have?"

Mulcibar's knees crackled as he knelt beside the dead helmsman. The nobleman found the baton and snapped it in half. "Not long."

"Why would—?" Horace started to ask, but then he noticed blood dripping from the queen's left hand. "You're hurt."

She opened her fingers to reveal blood welling from a deep gash in her palm. Horace stripped off his tunic and wrapped it around her hand. As soon as he had tied it tight, she grabbed him by the arm and pulled him along, away from the campsite. Mulcibar limped behind them.

"We have to move quickly," Byleth said. "They'll be here soon."

"They who?" Horace asked, and then put together the pieces of the puzzle. "Hold on. Do you mean the crash was an assassination attempt?"

"Her Majesty's entourage has been compromised," Mulcibar said. "As I feared."

"We don't know all the facts," Byleth said without looking back.

"I would know more if I could perform a death-reading on the bodies from the crash."

"It cannot be helped," the queen said. The reeds were thinning, revealing more of the desert beyond the river. They were heading east with the setting sun at their backs. "My soldier?" she asked, glancing over her shoulder.

"Dead," Mulcibar answered.

The queen nodded as if the news didn't bother her, but Horace caught a brief tightening of the skin around her eyes. Her words, spoken just minutes ago, came back to him. *I try to deal fairly with my people, Master Horace, though it's not always easy.*

Horace was about to ask where they were running to when a tingle ran up his neck, accompanied by a cold sweat across his brow. He whipped his head back and forth trying to determine where it was coming from. The queen or Mulcibar or someone else? Then he noticed that he was still holding onto his power. He hadn't let go after Mulcibar appeared. The feeling of the magic flowing through his body was a comfort.

A quiet hiss was the only warning he got that the next attack was upon them. Horace stopped, yanking his arm from the queen's grasp. Something urged him to get low, so he dropped to one knee and was a little surprised to see Byleth crouch down in front of him. Mulcibar did the same. As soon as Horace's knee touched the damp silt, a sharp crack like a snapping whip echoed past him. He blinked against a sudden bright light that flashed before his eyes. The queen whispered something, and the itch down his neck increased. More dazzling lights filled the air around them. Byleth and Mulcibar gestured in different directions. Everywhere they pointed, tiny explosions rocked the riverbank, followed by thin columns of black smoke. Horace had no idea what they were doing or how to help, so he kept low and waited.

After a handful of heartbeats, the dazzling display ended as Byleth and Mulcibar stopped whatever they had been doing, and all three of them listened. Horace's breath whistled between his teeth, his heart pounding. He started to hope that the danger was past, but then a horrible sensation welled up behind him as if a thunderstorm was about to crash down on his head. He turned and spotted something rising from the riverbank. It looked like

BLOOD AND IRON

a humpbacked creature covered in mud, but then it stood up straight and Horace's breath caught in his throat. It was a man-shaped thing more than ten feet tall with a wizened, wrinkled face. Brown water dripped from its body and limbs.

Mulcibar hissed something under his breath that sounded like a curse. A thin trickle of blood ran from a small immaculata on his forehead.

"Run!" Byleth shouted.

She and Mulcibar retreated from the thing, but Horace's legs were rooted to the ground. He didn't know what he was looking at, but some part of his brain recognized the dire threat it represented. The itch on his neck had spread down his back and across his shoulders like he was being stung by a troop of scorpions. A round shape sprouted from the mud-monster's chest. The protuberance rotated back and forth as the slime melted away from it. As Horace watched in terror, the bump formed into a second face, smaller and smoother than the one above. Both mouths opened wide and a somber moan filled the air.

Horace jumped as something grabbed him by the shoulder. Mulcibar tried to pull him along, but Horace still couldn't move. He just wanted to lie down and curl up into a ball until the horror passed. Yet as the thing started walking toward him with ponderous, earth-shaking steps, he realized it was going to destroy him if he didn't run. Mulcibar was hobbling south, away from the river. Horace took off to the east, thinking that splitting up would be the wiser course. He had no idea which way the queen had gone.

Reeds whipped past his face as he followed the river's course. The howl of the thing echoed in his ears. Horace didn't look back but focused all his attention on running faster. One of his sandals came off in the mud. He left it, sprinting with one sandal until it flew off, too. His bare feet dug deep into the wet earth with every step, but he felt faster barefoot. Then he passed through a thicket and plunged up to his shins in water before he could stop himself. The river had turned south in a long loop, cutting off his escape. He looked across its shimmering brown expanse to the far shore, too far away to swim before the monster reached him, and he was too tired to try. Swallowing his fear, Horace turned around.

The thing loomed before him, crushing reeds and tearing huge holes in the ground with every step. There was no sign of the queen or Mulcibar. The monster had followed *him*. Not sure what that signified, Horace tried to quiet his thumping heart as the juggernaut lumbered toward him. Its fists were larger than his head, and he could only imagine the terrible strength they possessed. The two faces cried out in unison, their snarling roars lifting the hairs on his head.

Horace tried to remember Mulcibar's lesson about how to control his *zoana*, but that sunny afternoon on the garden terrace seemed like years ago. All he wanted to do was smash the monster into a puddle of mud and end this terror.

He jumped back, deeper into the river. Droplets spattered his face as the massive hand missed him by inches. Cold water swirled around his knees, pulling at him. Horace tried to unleash his magic again, this time squeezing his eyes to tiny slits as he concentrated, but nothing came. His insides were twisted up in knots as he waited for the blow that would crush his skull. Fear constricted him, choked off his breath, but there was something else bubbling inside him. Hatred. The rawness of it shocked him, sending him down to a dark place that held no hope. His eyes closed, and everything fell away as a sense of peace settled over him. The water lapped around his thighs, rising higher even though he was standing still. A new sound rose above the growling roars. The hollow rumble of a gathering wave. Horace saw his second-heart in his mind's eye. It pulsed in time with his rapid heartbeat. Then it yawned wider, and a rush of energy surged through him.

Horace's eyes shot open as a wall of water washed over him from behind. The wave rushed past him to crash over the earthen creature. Horace remained still as the water pounded the shore with concussive blows that shook the ground. Then, the power inside him faded. The water level dropped as the wave retreated past his legs to rejoin the river.

Horace looked around. The riverbank was a swampy morass, the reeds battened down by the powerful flood, but the monster was gone. Where it had lain moments before, there was only a mound of slime that quickly melted away with the receding waters to reveal a pair of legs sticking out of the mud. And then an arm. The *zoana* humming in his chest, Horace approached as quietly as the clinging mud would allow.

BLOOD AND IRON

He made his way around the mud pile to find Gilgar's head. The sorcerer's eyes were closed as if in deep sleep. Trickles of brown water poured from his nostrils. Horace kicked him in the temple, but the wizard did not move. Then Horace staggered back as a wave of vertigo swept over him. His hands shook, and his stomach threatened violent rebellion.

Footsteps from behind made him jump. His power surged, ready to deal with a new threat. He sighed as Mulcibar emerged from the reeds. The old nobleman leaned on his cane with every step, both it and the hem of his robe encrusted with mud. "I am glad to see you, Master Horace. I must admit I feared the worst."

"I did, too."

The light-headedness was passing, but Horace still felt like he wanted to vomit. Mulcibar stood over the corpse. "Remarkable. He was one of my pupils, long ago. And he's served the queen for years. This is a black day for the court."

"I don't understand what he did."

Mulcibar pointed to the melting ooze around the corpse. "He transformed himself into a *kurgarru*, a creation of the Kishargal dominion. It is said that in ancient times, they were used as weapons of war, but their construction was banned over two hundred years ago by Emperor Otihakken after a series of disastrous wars. Few know the secret to fashioning such a thing today. Honestly, I did not suspect that Gilgar had it in him."

A shiver ran down Horace's spine as he tried to imagine what it must have been like to turn himself into a creature of earth and mud. And the thing had almost killed him. He noticed a silver medallion dangling around Mulcibar's neck. Peculiar shapes were etched into its flat square surface. "What's that?"

The nobleman tucked the talisman back inside his robe. "Nothing but an old superstition."

"Maybe I should get one, too. I could use a little luck."

Mulcibar knelt beside the corpse and rooted a hand inside Gilgar's clothing. "I would say you have more than a fair share of good fortune. No other *zoanii* alive can boast that they faced a *kurgarru* and lived to tell of it."

Horace shook his head. Drops of water pattered on his shoulders and chest. "I have no idea how I stopped it."

"Water is one of their few weaknesses." Byleth stepped out of the tall reeds. Even covered in sweat and mud, she looked stunning.

Mulcibar bowed. "Your Majesty. Are you all right?"

"None the worse, my lord." She had a long cut down the inside of her left arm, but it appeared shallow. To Horace, she said, "You were clever to use the river to fight it."

Horace glanced at Mulcibar and back to her. "So I've been told, but I had no idea what would happen. I was just trying to get away."

The queen took him by the arm. "Then your streak of good fortune continues."

"You may wish to see this, Majesty."

Mulcibar had left Gilgar's robe open. A symbol was branded over the dead wizard's heart of a circle around some wriggly lines.

The queen bent over the body. "The mark of a secret society?"

"I have only suppositions at this point," Mulcibar answered.

"I expect answers, my lord," Byleth said, the steel back in her voice once again.

"Yes, Majesty. I will unravel the truth."

Horace wanted to sit down. He was exhausted, both body and soul. "What do we do now?"

The queen shaded her eyes with a hand. "Now we go home."

Horace squinted against the rising sun as a flying ship descended from the sky. A lean man in a black robe stood at the bow railing. That was all Horace could tell until the vessel landed with a soft splash on the river. A gangplank extended from the deck, and the robed man disembarked.

"Lord Astaptah!" Byleth exclaimed as she went to meet him.

Horace found himself pulled along to meet a man who was taller than he had looked from a distance. His complexion was duskier than the typical Akeshian. A long, hawkish nose, bald scalp, and protruding cheekbones lent him a predatory appearance more suited to a bird of prey than a person, an appearance emphasized by his yellowish-brown eyes. They were flat like round pebbles, absorbing the daylight and giving nothing back.

The queen squeezed Horace's arm. "Astaptah, I want to introduce you to our guest from across the Great Sea. Horace, this is Lord Astaptah, my personal . . . counselor."

Horace put out his hand. "I've heard the name mentioned, but I don't think we've met."

Lord Astaptah gave Horace a measuring glance, and then he looked to the queen. "We should depart with haste. Events conspire at Erugash."

"Very well," Byleth said, and she boarded the ship with Lord Astaptah.

Mulcibar limped over. "Do you remember on the night of the storm when I warned you to be wary?"

"I remember you advised me to pick a side."

The nobleman nodded toward Lord Astaptah's departing figure. "Whichever side you choose, make sure you don't turn your back on that one."

CHAPTER TWENTY-THREE

An avalanche of gravel slid past Jirom's ankles as he lifted the heavy stone onto the pile. Then he stepped away to make room for the next man in line. Today's exercise was moving the Hill, in its entirety, from one side of the camp to the other. The companies took turns hauling rocks and rolling the larger boulders under the blaze of the midday sun.

The camp had been locked down tight since the rebel attack in the city. No accusations had been leveled, but everyone was tense. The guards were extra-vigilant in their duties, and the slaves attacked their training with renewed enthusiasm.

Jirom rubbed his sweaty head as he trudged back for another load. His back ached like a dozen tiny men with pickaxes were digging into his lower spine. He twisted from side to side as he walked, hoping to loosen the mass of knots back there, but it only made the pain worse. A man with an armload of small stones passed him going the other way. Their shoulders collided, and the other man rebounded, spilling some of his cargo. Jirom bent down, stifling a groan as his back protested, to help pick up the fallen rocks.

The other man didn't say a word. He had a wiry build and long bangs of black hair that hid his eyes. Jirom started to mumble an apology when the other man shot to his feet and hurried away, leaving the mess of rocks on the ground. A guard glanced over and shouted for the line to keep moving.

With a sigh, Jirom picked up the stones and started back toward the new Hill. He hadn't seen Emanon since morning roll call, which wasn't unusual—the rebel captain was somehow able to move about the camp without drawing attention—but Jirom had expected him to make an appearance at some point.

After depositing the stones onto the pile, Jirom headed back across the parade ground. It was another six hours until the evening meal break, and if the gods were merciful he would be able to spend the rest of the night in his bunk recovering from today's exertions.

A loud voice shouted behind him. "Make way!"

BLOOD AND IRON

Everyone scattered as a column of armored soldiers burst onto the field. *Kapikul* Hazael strode behind them. The camp commander wore a scarlet uniform jacket with wide shoulder cuffs over a white skirt. A round gold medallion hung on his chest, and a black skullcap shaded his head. The dog-soldiers waited as the commander's procession passed through their lines. The *kapikul* had almost reached the edge of the parade ground when he stopped before a gray-haired soldier. The old man was sturdy; perhaps he had once been a coppersmith or a quarry mason, but his arms trembled under the weight of a stone as large as a bread loaf. The *kapikul* stood before the soldier without speaking. Minutes passed by. Several of the men shifted as they tried to hold onto their burdens. The old dog-soldier looked straight ahead with sweat running down his weathered face. Finally, his arms gave out and he dropped the stone with a heavy thud. The *kapikul* gestured, and two guards seized the old man by the arms and dragged him toward the long path of the canyon wall, up to the hot boxes.

The commander looked around the grounds and then departed with a stiff walk. When the last of the *kapikul's* guards stepped off the field, the dog-soldiers returned to their task.

Jirom was going back for another load when a whistle blew two short bursts. Rest break. Most of the dog-soldiers slumped to the ground. One squad at a time, they were escorted to the camp well. Jirom's was the second group chosen to go. As he walked in line, he looked up to the cliffs above. Emanon was supposedly working on a plan to get them out of the camp for good, but tomorrow was choosing day when the first rank from every company would be taken out to join the army. Jirom was in the third rank now, and he didn't see any way to advance in just one day.

His squad gathered around the stone well and took turns drawing up the small pail on a rope and quenching their thirst. Jirom held back until everyone else had drunk. When it was his turn, the first pail went over his head in deluge of sweet relief. Then he tossed the container back into the well. The rest of the squad left as he hauled up the pail for his drink. He relished the moment of solitude. One of the things he didn't miss about camp life was the lack of privacy.

Footsteps announced the arrival of the next squad. Jirom set down the pail and turned, then stopped as six large dog-soldiers lined up in front of him. Three carried long sticks, and one swung a length of chain in a lazy circle. Algo, the giant, stood in the center of the line, glowering from under his thick brows. Jirom hadn't seen him since the day he tried to steal his victory meal.

"Don't hurry off," said the man swinging the chain. He had a gap between his front upper teeth. "We want to talk to you."

Jirom crossed his arms and inched his feet apart into a wider stance, but otherwise made no move.

The man with the chain looked to Algo. "You insulted our friend here, *meshi*. That was a mistake. Now you have to pay the price."

The six men rushed together in a group. Algo was the first to reach him, the big man lunging with his hands outstretched. Jirom backed up to put the well between him and them. Three of the men followed Algo in pursing him head-on while the other pair circled around the other side. Jirom pivoted and ran at the two. Both carried wooden rods. They halted when they saw him coming, but he lowered his head and threw himself at them. Their off-balance swings missed as his momentum took them to the ground in a tumble of flailing limbs. An errant knee struck Jirom in the nose, sending jolts of pain across his face. He punched the offender in the stomach hard enough to make the man double over and put him down with a punch to the mouth that split both lips and spurted blood across all three of them. The other man grabbed him around the throat, but Jirom threw him off with a violent shake and scrambled to his feet. As the second man got up on his knees, Jirom kicked him in the chest and sent the dog-soldier tumbling over the low wall and into the well. His shout was punctuated by a distant splash.

Jirom backed away as the other four men caught up to him. Two grabbed his arms while Algo stood in front of him. Jirom aimed a kick that glanced off the big man's thigh, and then lowered his chin as the first blows arrived. Algo's huge fists struck him on the forehead and the bridge of his nose, causing bright stars to flash before his eyes. Jirom shifted his weight and yanked hard, and he carried the men holding his arms down to the ground. The breath hissed from his mouth as the dog-soldiers fell on top of him. When Algo straddled him,

BLOOD AND IRON

Jirom caught one of the big man's wrists and wrenched it backward hoping to break it, but Algo simply lifted him off the ground with that arm and kept punching him with the other. Each blow made his head ring.

"Drop him!" the man with the chain called out.

Algo threw Jirom down on his back. The remaining men grabbed Jirom's arms and pinned him to the ground. The rusty chain slithered around his neck to hold him in place. The soldier with the split lips appeared over Jirom, a small knife in his hand. He slashed, and a line of pain cut across Jirom's stomach.

Jirom tensed as the knife lunged again, but it never made contact. A brown arm appeared around the knife-fighter's throat. Czachur grinned over the fighter's shoulder before he yanked the man backward. Jirom threw off the men holding his arms and grabbed the wrists of the fighter holding the chain around his throat. He flipped the chain-fighter over, climbed on top of him, and started punching without holding back, cutting his knuckles on the dog-soldier's teeth and cheekbones.

When he was through, Jirom stood up. A few yards away, Silfar and Partha were holding Algo down while Jerkul pounded the big man's skull with a wooden club. The last two dog-soldiers had run off. Jirom picked up the fallen knife and tossed it into the well where one of his attackers could still be heard splashing below. A cut about twelve inches long stretched across his stomach below his navel. It bled profusely but didn't look too deep.

Jerkul dropped the bloody club and came over. "You all right? Czachur saw them jump you and came to get us."

Jirom nodded to the young man. "My thanks."

The younger man smiled back.

He's handsome but so young. Damn me, I'm getting old.

Jerkul helped him up. "Come on. We'll get you patched up at the barracks."

The rebels strode away after delivering a few more kicks to the fallen dog-soldiers. As Jirom followed them, he spotted a face peering down from a window in the headquarters building. He stopped and stared back at *Kapikul* Hazael until the commander turned away from the window.

Jirom awoke to the sound of a light footstep. Before the last dregs of sleep had left his brain, he was reaching out to grasp the intruder. His hands encountered broad shoulders sheathed in muscle. Jirom sat up and suppressed a groan as his lower back protested.

"Bad dreams?" Emanon asked in a low voice.

The barracks was still asleep. Snores echoed off the rafters. Only a faint sheen of dawn's light shone through the slatted windows.

"Where have you been?" Jirom asked.

Emanon knelt beside his bunk. He wore a sleeveless homespun tunic with a sweat stain in the center of the chest. "I've been busy working on our way out. We need to be included in the next shipment of troops to the front."

"I don't know how you'll be able to do that." Jirom stretched to loosen the kinks in his shoulders and back. His entire body felt bruised. "Unless you convince the commander to send the entire company."

"That's beyond my abilities, but what I cooked up should do."

Jirom cocked his head to the side. "You sure come and go as you please around here. I wish you'd show me that trick."

"And spoil the mystery?" When Jirom glared, Emanon held up a hand in surrender. "All right. I have a hidden cache of silver. I use it to bribe the guards and other people I need to do me favors. I also keep my ears open for things I can use against our jailors."

"Blackmail and bribery."

Emanon gave him a wink. "They work every time."

Jirom was about to ask why they didn't just bribe the camp commander when whistles sounded from the yard. It was time for morning roll call. Emanon helped him up from the bed, and they walked out of the barracks house. Jirom took his place in the third rank as dog-soldiers fell in around him, rubbing their bleary eyes. Yet he noticed something strange as the company assembled. The two ranks in front of him were empty. He was tempted to look back to see if they were late in arriving, but the officers were already circulating through the formation, barking orders and passing out blows with their truncheons to those who didn't move fast enough. Jirom stood with his eyes trained forward.

"You ready to travel?"

Jirom stole a quick glance around. Emanon stood at attention to his left. Czachur, Jerkul, and a few other rebels he recognized stood to his right. Jirom wanted to ask what in the name of the gods was going on when the company officer called out, "Third rank! Advance two positions!"

Jirom's stomach was wrapped up in knots as he stepped forward along with Emanon and the others.

"First rank!" the officer shouted. "Report to the quartermaster's supply immediately and prepare to move out!"

The men of the first row from each company started jogging toward the south end of the camp. Jirom followed beside Emanon and asked in a low voice, "What just happened? Did you kill the men ahead of us?"

The rebel captain smirked. "Nah. That would've called too much attention. While we were in Erugash I got some *yergrub* root from my contact. I slipped it into their dinners last night. They'll survive, but they aren't going anywhere for a while."

"So what's next?"

"Telling you would spoil the fun." Emanon winked. "But be sure to pack an extra pair of boots."

They arrived at the quartermaster behind a crowd of dog-soldiers. Officers formed them into a queue, and each man stepped up to receive a large burlap sack. But no weapons, Jirom observed. When it was his turn, Jirom asked, "What's the load?" as he accepted his sack. It weighed at least four stone.

"Move on!" barked the burly man in the leather apron behind the window.

Jirom found a spot along the wall of the supply building where he could set down his satchel. He untied the hemp cord holding it shut and peered inside. Under several pieces of boiled leather strips with trailing thongs that appeared to be rudimentary armor, he found an iron helmet, a faded purple tunic, several bricklike packages that looked like trail rations, two stoppered bladders, a small digging spade, and a copper handpick. At the bottom was a pair of hobnailed boots.

The graduating dog-soldiers were soon herded toward the camp gates high atop the canyon wall. Now that freedom from this hellhole was close at hand, Jirom reflected back on his time here. A lot of men had died trying to get to where he stood now, but he felt no pride. This was not his army; he was just a slave forced to serve. Yet at least he was free of this place and its denizens.

Emanon came over, bringing with him a dozen rebel fighters. "Jirom, you're going to be commanding these men in the field."

Jirom frowned. That hadn't been discussed before. "I don't need a promotion. Let Jerkul lead them."

"He has his own squad," Emanon said. "I'm putting them in your hands."

Jirom squinted at the fighters. "Fine. But I run the squad my way. That means no interference."

Emanon slapped him on the shoulder. "Of course, Jirom. They're all yours."

Jirom ground his teeth together as the rebel captain walked away through the crowd. He didn't want this responsibility, but he had agreed to follow Emanon's orders.

"All right," Jirom said, pitching his voice to the men in front of him. "If everyone has their gear, get into formation with the others. We don't want to draw attention to ourselves."

As the squad started to comply, Jirom turned toward the sound of hoof beats. *Kapikul* Hazael rode up on a brown mare. The camp commander wore his usual uniform with a voluminous white cloak that flowed down past his steed's flanks. Several retainers followed him, also on horseback. The bad news was delivered by one of the officers.

"This unit will be honored by the presence of the *kapikul*, who rides with us to glory!"

Jirom's hands opened and closed as the commander rode to the forefront of the company. If he'd had a weapon, he might have tried to get close enough to use it, consequences be damned. Instead, he joined his squad and made sure the men were ready to march. He didn't know where they were going, but he could bide his time.

CHAPTER TWENTY-FOUR

The boots of the Queen's Guard pounded the floor as they marched down the hallway in the direction of the slave quarters.

Alyra counted to thirty and then slipped out of the vacant storeroom where she'd been hiding. She had almost walked straight into the patrol but was fortunate that she'd heard them before they spotted her. The corridor was now clear, yet she hesitated, wondering if this was a smart decision.

Go on. This is no time to let your nerves get the better of you.

After Horace had been summoned by the queen and Alyra learned that they would be going on Her Majesty's flying barge, she had stewed for a little while, imagining all the things a woman of power and hedonistic urges like Byleth could inflict on Horace. Then she received a note from her palace contact. It said simply, *Lord Astaptah has left the palace.*

Taking the coincidence as divine intervention, Alyra had shaken herself out of the pointless worrying and decided to take advantage of having the evening free at the exact time when Lord Astaptah was away. This might be her best opportunity to get inside the vizier's chambers.

She'd changed into a dove-gray tunic and covered it with a short, hooded cloak. Her only accessories were a small pouch, retrieved from under her bed, and a thin-bladed dagger she tucked into the back of her belt-sash and hoped to heaven she wouldn't have to use.

With her heart pounding in her chest, she made her way through the palace via seldom-used corridors and halls. After bypassing the kitchens, she entered into the forbidden hallways. Remembering her way from the last time she had followed Lord Astaptah, she found the dead-end corridor. Only she knew it wasn't a dead-end.

Alyra fumbled in the dark for her pouch, the contents of which had been smuggled to her through the network of agents in case she should ever get this far. She pulled out a small, thin rod and a square of rabbit fur. She rubbed the rod with the fur, praying for success. Since it could only be used once, she'd never had the chance to try it before. She breathed a sigh as the rod began to glow. Cool white light emanated from the tip, like a miniature lamp without the oil. Holding the light aloft, she hurried down the short passage to the stone wall at the terminus. The middle of the wall was hot to the touch, just like before. With the light, she was able to make out the outlines of a wide doorway but no opening mechanism.

Alyra opened the pouch again and took out the larger object inside, a black silk bag. It was soft and pliable in her hand. When she had described the stone door to her contacts, along with her suspicion that it might be triggered by *zoana*, they had given her this. The bag had come with two warnings. First, that its contents were unstable and should be kept away from open flames, sunlight, and her skin. And second, that its effects could not be guaranteed. She undid the laces holding it shut, and a pungent smell like burning brimstone leaked out.

She bent down and poured out the contents, careful to keep her face far back. A line of fine white sand filled the crease between the floor and the front of the door. Alyra stood back, tucking the empty bag back in her carrying pouch, and wondered how long the stuff would take to work, if it was going to work at all—

She jumped as a sharp sizzle burst from the sand. White smoke rose into the air as the sand popped and crackled like a campfire. Alyra snuck a glance over her shoulder, afraid the noise would attract unwanted attention, but the sounds died down quickly. When she looked back, the wall looked entirely different. The door's frame was outlined in silver lines. Twisting shapes covered its face, as well—curling lines, interconnected geometric designs, and some kind of writing. Alyra couldn't decipher the script. It didn't even look Akeshian.

Of course. Astaptah came from the south. It makes sense his notations would be foreign, too.

Alyra was looking for a way to open the illuminated portal when the stone door swung forward. She backed out of the way as a wave of hot air washed over her. Beyond the doorway yawned a dark tunnel with stone steps leading down. Standing at the top, she suddenly wondered what Horace was doing, if he was all right. The thought came out of nowhere, but it was accompanied by a simple and uncomfortable truth. She wished she could tell him about her true mission in Erugash.

He doesn't deserve to be lied to.

Alyra shook her head. Emotions were tools to be manipulated. The mission was the only thing that mattered. Focusing her attention, she rolled the empty pouch into a tube and used it to prop open the door behind her. Then, with the light-rod held high, she descended into the secret passage.

The steps were tall, making her descent even more jarring, but after about ten feet they stopped, and the tunnel continued downward at a steep slope. She tried not to think about the ramifications of what would happen if she was caught, but her life was meaningless compared to the oath she had sworn. She would gladly die for the chance to harm the empire. Akeshia needed to fall. Not just for Nemedia, but for the betterment of the whole world.

The passageway looked natural, its rounded walls resembling a winding tube. Every so often she passed under a glowing red symbol on the ceiling. Like the sigils on the door, she had no idea what they meant. The air was hot and dank, with a strange odor like the acrid smell after a thunderstorm. As she descended further, Alyra considered the massive weight of the temple above her head, and a twinge of anxiety stirred in her belly. After several minutes of walking, she arrived at an open archway. She approached with caution, shielding the light-rod inside her tunic as she peeked around the corner. Another passageway extended before her, its length broken by several openings. Alyra was considering whether she had time to investigate them all when a dull glimmer from straight ahead caught her attention. Orange light glowed at the end of the tunnel.

As she got closer, she heard a low rumbling noise that made her think of thunder. Slight tremors buzzed through the floor under her sandals. She slowed her pace as another sound came from ahead, a sharp hiss that raised the hairs on the back of her neck. Alyra eased up to the opening but stopped as a jet of blistering air shot past her face. Holding her breath, she peered inside and blinked as her eyes adjusted. The broad aperture overlooked a large chamber that appeared to be a natural formation, at least in part. The rough-hewn walls were craggy with whitish mineral deposits that reflected the orange glow. A series of metal catwalks connected by ramps clung to the cavern walls. Alyra couldn't see the source of the light until she edged out farther and her gaze traveled sixty paces down through a haze of smoke and wavering air. The floor far below was awash in yellow and orange flame. It was only after a moment of staring that she realized she was looking down at a pool of molten rock. Pieces of charred crust floated on the surface around a small island, upon which sat an odd framework of black metal and silver filigree. The metal construction was large, maybe three times the height of a person, and shaped somewhat like an inverted pyramid. Looking at the structure's lattice of beams, Alyra got the impression that it surrounded an empty space at its center. Was this the mysterious device Lord Astaptah and the queen had been discussing? Alyra craned her neck to see more, but she couldn't make out much from her vantage point.

You know what you need to do. You have to go down for a closer look.

Alyra put away the light-rod and wiped her damp palms on her cloak. She was inching out onto the catwalk to get a better view when a shadow leapt across the wall not far from her. She ducked back inside the cave mouth and froze, listening for any sign that she had been discovered. After a score of rapid heartbeats, she peered out again. The shadow came from higher up the cavern wall. Alyra's heart nearly jumped out of her chest as she peered up at the seven huge statues ringing the cavern ceiling. Carved from the rock walls, the dark watchers leaned over the cavern with hooded faces.

Taking a deep breath, Alyra put the imposing statues out of her mind and eyed the catwalk. There was no one else in sight, but the silence—punctuated by the hiss of the bubbling magma below—made Alyra nervous. Steeling herself, she started around the walkway. The metal platform shook a little with every step, and her footfalls sounded unusually loud to her own ears. She hoped no one was listening.

Just as she was about to step onto the ramp, a horrible scream erupted in the air. High and drawn-out, it echoed off the walls, sounding as if it came from all directions at once. Alyra wanted to turn around and run back up the tunnel, but instead she plunged down the curving ramp. The scream died off after a few seconds, but it echoed in her mind as she reached the catwalk's second tier and made her way to the next ramp, which she started down without hesitation. She swept her gaze across the bottom of the chamber. Now the heat from the molten rock below felt like it was scorching her skin. The ends of her hair curled up into crinkled knots. Even breathing became more difficult as if her lungs were rejecting the super-heated air. Yet she now had a better view of the structure on the center island. There was a narrow bridge connecting the island to a rock ledge that ran around the chamber's perimeter. Dark archways appeared in the walls, leading to parts unknown. Set in the rock between each archway was a glowing red rune as large as a dinner platter.

Alyra was astounded. She never would have guessed that the passages beneath the palace extended so far. Halfway down the second ramp, a new sound met her ears, a faint sizzle like meat thrown into a hot griddle. Something flickered inside the metal structure on the center island, looking like a cloud of white sparks swirling in a green mist. She paused to watch, and the mist became thicker, the sparks flashed brighter, as a new sound rumbled through the chamber. It was the unmistakable roll of thunder.

Alyra gasped as she brushed against the wall at her back. The rock was searing hot to the touch. Yet her eyes remained focused on the growing mist inside the metal construction, trying to discern what it could be. She didn't see any moving parts like pulleys or clockworks. Now the flashing sparks reminded her of nothing so much as tiny bolts of lightning zipping through the mist. Like a miniature thunderstorm.

Or a chaos storm.

What was Lord Astaptah trying to do down here in the bowels of the palace? Create his own chaos storms? The idea was both absurd and chilling at the same time. No one could create a storm, but if he could . . .

Alyra turned around. This wasn't something she could handle alone. She needed to get this information to her contacts so they could funnel it back to their controllers in Nemedia. She started back up the ramp, but froze as the metallic patter of footsteps rang out above her. Voices descended through the smoky haze. The catwalk was made of solid metal sheets connected by thin beams, but through the cracks she glimpsed a pair of shadows walking around the top level toward the ramp. The voices sounded male.

BLOOD AND IRON

The only other ways out of the chamber were the five archways around on the bottom level, but she had no idea where they went. For all she knew, they might delve deeper into the earth or wander endlessly beneath the palace with no exit at all.

Seeing no other choice, she hurried down the last few yards of the ramp. She stepped onto the shelf that ran around the edge of the chamber, and the heat of the stone penetrated her sandals. The magma, though several feet below, seemed frightfully close. One misstep, and she would be cooked in an instant.

Stop it and focus on the problem!

She pulled out her light-rod and moved to the nearest archway. The short tunnel ended in a stout iron door. With the footsteps above getting closer, Alyra made her choice. She ducked inside and went for the door. At the same time, she started devising explanations she might use if she were caught. That she was "lost" was too laughable to even contemplate. She could claim she'd been sent here by the queen to summon Lord Astaptah for a conference. That might get her out of immediate danger, but the queen would surely hear of it, and that would begin a line of questioning Alyra did not want to experience. Could she blame Horace? The thought stabbed her through the heart, even as she began to work out how she might make it work. She reached for the door's latch.

She yanked back her hand with a stifled yelp. The metal was as hot as a stovetop. Cradling her singed fingers, Alyra suppressed the string of vile curses that wanted to tumble off her lips. She wrapped her other hand in her cloak and tugged on the latch until the heat became uncomfortable through the barrier, but the door wouldn't budge. It was either locked or barred from the other side. Alyra ran back down the passage, hoping she had time to try another archway. Yet as she peeked out into the main chamber, the voices were descending the second ramp.

Alyra pressed against the passage wall and grimaced as the heat of the stone penetrated her sweat-dampened tunic. The voices approached, now close enough that she could make out their words, but they spoke in a tongue she didn't know. It was harsh and yet strangely lyrical, unlike anything she had ever heard before.

As she braced herself to be discovered, a powerful emotion sprung up inside her. She might be dead soon, or held captive in this awful place, and two things jostled for prominence in her mind—that her mission would go undone, and that she wouldn't see Horace again.

Her heart leapt into her throat as a loud squeal erupted behind her. She spun around as the metal door opened and a shrunken man in a gray robe stepped through. Alyra reached for her knife, but the man cringed from her as if she were a fearsome creature. No, he was flinching away from her light-rod. Without a second thought, she hit him in the forehead with the rod and ran past him, into the passageway beyond. After a dozen steps she came to a T-junction. She darted to the left, listening as she ran for sounds of pursuit. For a few seconds there was nothing, just silence, then the distant patter of sandaled feet behind her.

The corridor curved gradually to her left as she sprinted down its length. She passed another iron doorway on the right-hand side, but it was locked or otherwise secured. Worried that she might get lost down here, she continued her flight. When she came to a fork, she picked the left-hand branch again. Sweat ran down her face. Her lungs ached from breathing the noxious air of these catacombs. Then she noticed light coming from ahead, a steady orange glow. She ran faster, hoping it was a way out.

Relief poured through Alyra when she arrived at a tunnel mouth and saw that it opened into the main central chamber. A quick glance revealed that she was back on the top level. She poked her head out and spotted the exit tunnel on the other side of the catwalk. There was no one else on the metal walkway. Taking a deep breath, she ran for the exit. A voice shouted from below, and heavy footsteps rang on the ramps beneath her, but Alyra kept running without looking down. She darted into the tunnel and followed its winding upward curve as quickly as she dared. She didn't think any of the tunnel dwellers had seen her face. Her hood was down, and she had chosen this cloak because it was bulky enough to conceal her figure. She just hoped the outer door was still propped open. If not, she didn't have any more of the enchanted sand to open it again, and she didn't want to think about trying to survive alone in these tunnels.

BLOOD AND IRON

Fortunately, the big metal door remained wedged by her rolled-up pouch. As she slipped through and the cool air of the upper palace swept across her face, Alyra couldn't help but sigh in relief. She closed the heavy portal and put her back to it. She wanted to rest, but pursuit could be right behind her.

Ten minutes later, she stepped into the petitioners' hall on the ground floor of the palace, adjacent to the grand atrium. Because of the lateness of the hour, the hall was empty. She had hidden her cloak and light-rod in a supply room. Walking as if she belonged here, she crossed the hall toward the slave wing. If she could get back to the suite without being seen or stopped, she might be able to clean up and change her clothes before Horace returned.

Please, Mother of Heaven, let me get back undetected. There is so much I need to tell.

She was composing a message to her superiors in her head when a shadow detached from the darkness of the corridor in front of her. Alyra's sandals slid on the smooth marble as she stopped. Then she saw a familiar face and let out the breath she'd been holding. "Sefkahet! You nearly frightened me out of my skin."

The slim chambermaid drew near and spoke with a low voice. "Alyra, we've been worried about you. Did you . . . . do it?"

Alyra looked about to be sure they were alone. Sefkahet was one of her contacts within Erugash and a cautious woman by nature, but the queen's palace had many ears. "Yes. I was able to get inside. Sef, you would not believe what I saw there. I'm not sure I believe it."

"Later, Alyra. There is something you must know first. The queen's flying ship has crashed."

Alyra's relief at escaping Lord Astaptah's lair evaporated. "Where? Was anyone hurt?"

"Little is known except that they were returning when it happened. A ship has been dispatched to find the queen's party."

Alyra juggled the times in her head. "How long ago?"

"About one turn of a glass."

Alyra took a deep breath to calm herself. "Thank you, Sef. You'd better get back to your wing."

"What will you do?"

The question struck Alyra between the eyes as the knowledge sunk in that there was nothing she could do. "I'll be in Master Horace's chambers. Please get word to me if you hear anything else."

"Of course."

The women touched hands, and Alyra gave her friend, and sometimes lover, a quick kiss on the lips. Then Sefkahet hurried away down the dimly lit corridor, melding easily into the shadows. Alyra went to the stairs and hurried up the cold, stone steps, not caring now if she was seen by anyone. The queen might be dead at this very moment. Or Horace.

With a pounding heart, she climbed.

CHAPTER TWENTY-FIVE

Seven hundred and seven stairs ascended to the temple's summit. Arched windows set in the outer wall every fiftieth step showed glimpses of the city. From some of the views the city was highlighted by the rays of the setting sun, while from others the homes below lay swathed in twilight's growing shadows, as if Erugash were two cities occupying the same space. Out on the western terrace, the holy brothers were chanting the sunset vespers that ushered the sun to its nightly rest and praying for its swift return the next morning. Those same songs were being sung at every Temple of Amur across the empire. Normally that thought brought him comfort.

Rimesh paused at the top landing to catch his breath. He wanted to approach this meeting with a cool head, but his pulse was racing, and not only from the long climb. Before he arrived in Erugash, he'd heard rumors of the difficulties he might face in the pursuit of his mission, but he didn't lend them enough credence. Now he sensed deeper schemes at work. Between the queen's attitude and the mood of the court, the advent of the foreign abomination, and now this recent news, the city was spiraling out of control. He would include that in his report as well.

Surely the Council must see the danger. Erugash is the empire's first line of defense against the West. If it should crumble from the inside, it would be a disaster of the highest order.

Two acolytes, tall and sturdy youths, stood outside the high priest's door. One raised his hand, but Rimesh cut him off before he could speak. "You know my authority comes from the Great Temple. Be silent and stand aside."

The acolytes looked past Rimesh and then stepped away from the door. Rimesh didn't bother to knock.

The chambers of the high priest were as glorious as any king's bed-chamber. Pillars of golden marble supported a coffered ceiling. Huge open windows, trimmed with crimson silk curtains, gave entrance to the dwindling sunlight, which glimmered off the acres of gold leaf that encrusted almost every architectural detail and molding. The only furniture in the front room was a pair of wide chairs against the walls. All in all, despite its opulence, or perhaps because of it, the place felt more like a mausoleum than the private quarters of the temple's leader.

Now that he had entered, Rimesh hesitated, unsure of his next move. He had come to confront a dire threat to the faith, and yet here, on the threshold of another priest's personal space, he wondered if this was a mistake.

Soft footsteps whispered as a slave appeared through one of the far doorways, her slender frame wrapped in a sheer tunic with a short hem that suggested more of her body than he was comfortable viewing. Rimesh cleared his throat. "I've come to see the high priest. Summon him at once."

The slave scurried away, her tunic flaring up behind her and giving Rimesh another disconcerting view. He tore his gaze away and focused on one of the paintings on the wall, a fairly unimpressive rendering of a familiar scene from the holy texts: Amur appearing to Nidintu. The artist had given more attention to the young maiden than to the Sun Lord, and had also granted her with a more robust vivacity as she lay sprawled across a bed of grass than in other versions Rimesh had seen. There was also something in the way Amur was leering down at her that he found vulgar. He turned as more footsteps approached.

High Priest Kadamun wore a long robe of bright yellow, unbound by a belt. Its hem dragged along the floor, and the wide sleeves concealed his hands. He looked disheveled, as if he had been roused from a deep sleep, and something smudged his eyelids. It appeared to be red pigment like the makeup worn by some women of the court. Rimesh pressed his lips tight together.

"Yes?" said the high priest, his reedy voice echoing off the high ceiling. "What is the meaning of this, Menarch? My secretary informed me of no audience this evening."

Rimesh held up a slip of papyrus, now wrinkled and a little moist from his sweat. "What is the meaning of this?"

Kadamun peered at the message from under his crimson-stained lids. "I am not accustomed to being interrogated in my own chambers like a street criminal. What is that you hold?"

Rimesh ignored the high priest's icy tone and shook the document. "This message just arrived from the palace. The queen's entourage was attacked over the Iron Desert. Her ship crashed with unknown casualties."

"That is . . . unfortunate. But there was no need for you to bring the news in person. Any of the temple novices would have—"

"I'm not here to be your damned messenger!"

The high priest pursed his lips—which also had a faint ruby tinge—and Rimesh took a deep breath while he contained his anger. It was time for a different tact. "I apologize for the outburst, High Priest. But I am to ask you in person, as the representative of the Primarch and the Council of Hierarchs, if you had anything to do with this attack on the queen."

"I do not answer to envoys, Menarch. If the Council wishes to question me, they have the right to—"

"We require that the queen remain alive, at least until she has wed your Nisusi princeling. Her premature demise could destabilize our hold over this city at a time when we need to be most vigilant. The mood in the streets is not good. A spark like this might be enough to—"

"Bah." The high priest waved his hand like he was swatting at flies. "The streets of Erugash are never in a good mood. They breed resentment and false piety the way whores breed disease and fatherless whelps. You would do better to focus your attention on uncovering your suspected heretics than worrying about the city's politics."

Rimesh drew back as his suspicions crystalized before his eyes.

"Don't glare at me in that manner," the high priest said. "You would like Byleth removed from the throne as much as I. You need not deny it. She is a blight on this city, encouraging the people to seek out new ways, mocking the faith. And now she takes a savage to her bed. No, Menarch, do not reproach me. I know not what hand was at work, but while I must denounce the act in public, here in the sanctity of *my* temple I will applaud the effort."

Rimesh rolled back his shoulders. He had hoped it wouldn't come to this, but the high priest had given him no choice. "Kadamun et'Hittsura-Amur, by the authority of the Primarch, you are hereby stripped of your rank and power."

BLOOD AND IRON

"Save your threats for lesser men. I've been the leader of this temple since before you were inducted to the cloth. Now you *will* excuse me. I was in the middle of evening devotions when you interrupted."

As the high priest started to turn away, Rimesh snapped his fingers. The door of the chamber opened, and soft boots scuffed across the tiles as a quartet of Order men came to stand beside him.

"Leave your belongings," Rimesh said. "You will go at once to the seclusion cells to dwell upon your actions until I send for you."

He expected resistance, even a lengthy tirade about his abuse of the Primarch's authority, but Kadamun's shoulders slumped forward and his neck bent down in a long curve as if his head had suddenly become too heavy to hold up.

Two Brothers of the Order took the demoted high priest away to his new cell, and the others—at a gesture from Rimesh—went to remove Kadamun's painted slaves. The acolytes at the entrance peered inside and then ducked away when they spotted him. Rimesh gazed around the chamber with its gaudy decor.

I did not ask for this burden, but I accept it as the price of my duty.

When the servants were gone, Rimesh went to seek out a writing desk. He had much to report. And then he needed to revise his plans in the face of these new developments. If the queen was dead, that changed everything. He needed to position the Order and temple soldiers where they could respond to potential rioting. Also, the members of the royal court would need to be detained until the succession was decided. Speaking of which, perhaps they no longer required the prince of Nisus to control the city. Perhaps, finally, the temple could rule in word as well as deed. A return to the proper order of things. Of course, the kings of the other nine cities would expect some payment to ease their royal consciences, but the temple coffers were deep.

As he passed down a short hallway with several doors, Rimesh thought of the savage still in the queen's company. Horace Delrosa from Arnos. Best if the man was dead, too. An abomination such as him could not be suffered to walk free under the holy light of day.

CHAPTER TWENTY-SIX

The sun had set over Erugash. Although light from thousands of candles, torches, and lamps flickered across the city, all was quiet, as if everyone were holding their breath, afraid to break the fragile stillness. The news had flown from the palace that the queen was missing, and ill rumors lurked in every home and beer hall.

Alyra sat in the parlor of the suite, chewing her fingernails as she watched the door. She hadn't been able to sleep after hearing about the crash, so she bathed away the grime of the tunnels, put on a new fresh tunic, and cleaned every room of the suite. After that there had been nothing left to do but worry. She felt like a wash rag that had been wrung to shreds. She got up every time she thought she heard a noise, hoping it was Horace or news of his discovery, and each time it turned out to be just her imagination playing tricks. The same thoughts kept swimming around in her head. Was the queen dead? Was Horace? Were they lost in the desert or hurt?

She couldn't help wondering how this would affect her mission. If the queen was dead, the Temple of Amur would surely move to annex the city. The rulers of the other nine cities would protest, of course, but would they be willing to go to war over it? The initial chaos might benefit Nemedia, but her superiors would hardly be glad to hear that the Sun Cult had further improved its temporal power. Yet, if Byleth survived and Horace died, Alyra didn't see how the queen could possibly hold onto her throne. The wedding would go through as planned, and then the Sun Cult would gain control over the city through its Nisusi puppets.

But the Nemedians know this. All this time we've been undermining the power of the royals, and it's the cults—the Sun Cult especially—who have most benefited. And I never questioned it. Honestly, I didn't care as long as my mission hurt the empire. But why lift the priests to power? What do we gain from that?

Suddenly, she wasn't sure about the direction her life had taken. Everything had been so clear before. *Before Horace I believed in my mission, heart and soul.*

BLOOD AND IRON

Now I don't know what to think. The world doesn't make allowances for fools with love in their eyes. And yet part of me would like to put down this burden and run away with him, far away from this place and its endless perfidy.

Her heart almost burst from her chest when the front door opened. Alyra ran to the atrium and stopped, transfixed, as Horace walked in. His face was scratched, and his fine clothes were covered in mud, but otherwise he looked fine. She took two long steps and threw her arms around him. She was intensely aware of his smell, the way it drew her closer. With a slight cough, she released him and backed away. "I heard about the accident," she said. "Are you all right? I feared you might be hurt, or . . ."

"No, not at all. I'm fine, if you can believe it."

"Is the queen all right?"

"Yes. She got a couple bruises, but nothing serious. The royal physicians are hovering around her now."

"Thank the gods," Alyra breathed and was surprised to find that she meant it.

"Lord Mulcibar survived as well, although he's limping worse than before. There was an attack with magic and everything got very confusing."

"Tell me everything while I run your bath."

"That sounds divine." He brushed a hand down the front of his filthy tunic as she led him into the bathing room. "And we should probably just burn these."

"That's what I was thinking, too."

Alyra rang for hot water and then helped him out of the clothes. Mud streaked his legs and upper body, but she was relieved not to find any injuries worse than a few bruises. "So what happened? Where did she take you?"

"Out to the desert. She wanted to show me one of her towns that the crusaders had taken."

Omikur. What was she up to, taking him there? Did she think she could change his loyalties?

"We rode in a flying ship. It was amazing. Alyra, you wouldn't believe how far you could see from up in the sky. It felt . . . well, indescribable."

"What of the town?" she asked, and bit her lip. *Don't pry too hard.*

"It was under siege by her army when we got there. Then a storm appeared over the town and things got crazy." Horace let out a heavy sigh. "But that was nothing compared to the way back. I don't know what happened. One minute we were flying along with no problems, and the next minute there was an explosion and ship dropped out of the sky. People were falling over the side and the queen was unconscious. I thought we were all going to die. But then I . . ."

He got a distant look on his face.

"Yes? What did you do?" A knock on the door distracted her. "Wait here."

Alyra rushed out to the atrium and admitted a procession of slaves carrying buckets of steaming water. They filled the tub while Horace sat on a bench with a towel over his lap. Alyra let the slaves out and returned to find Horace already in the water, his head reclined against the side of the tub, eyes closed. She took a soft brush and a flask of bathing oil and knelt behind him. He seemed like he was on the verge of falling asleep. "Now tell me everything that happened after the explosion."

As she listened to his rendition, she was appalled by the brazen nature of the attack. Assassination attempts were nothing unusual in Akeshian politics, but they were usually done in private, with poison in the cup or venomous reptiles in one's bed, not with magical assaults in front of witnesses.

But they wouldn't have expected any witnesses to survive, would they?

The more she thought about it, the more an attack over the desert made sense. The conspirators could claim it was an unfortunate accident. Flying ships had crashed before. Never with such an important ensemble aboard, but still it was plausible. Then Horace described how Gilgar had tried to finish off the survivors with a magical mud-man construction. As he described their battle, Alyra's heart thumped at the base of her throat.

"Lord Mulcibar called it a *kurgarru*," he said at the conclusion of his tale.

Alyra swallowed her fear. Her handlers would want to know about this right away. "It sounds very frightening. Your bathwater is getting cold. I'll call for more."

She made to leave, intending to stop by her chamber and add a quick note to her report about what she'd found in Lord Astaptah's sanctum, but Horace got out of the tub. "That's all right," he said. "I'm about as clean as I'm going to get."

While he wrapped himself in a towel, Alyra moved toward the door. "Then let me fetch you a drink."

"Wait. I have something to tell you first."

She stopped at the doorway. The details of the shipwreck had destroyed her calm, scattering her thoughts in a hundred directions. Foremost among them was a deep-seated fear. Fear that this foe she had set herself against was too powerful for her to manage. Fear that Horace was in more danger than she had realized. And fear for herself. For the first time since she had set herself on this path, she was genuinely afraid. It took all of her resolve to stop and turn around.

Dripping water, Horace stepped closer to her. He reached up and touched her collar. It was shockingly intimate, and she felt a desire to pull away, but she stood her ground.

"Before the attack," he said, "I asked the queen to free you. And she said yes."

Alyra felt her eyebrows coming together in a frown. "You what?"

A slight tingle buzzed around her neck. Then Horace pulled his hand away, and her collar came with it. "You are a free woman, Alyra."

"Why would you do that?" Her voice creaked as the words escaped into the air. She knew it wasn't her place to question him, but she was too angry all of a sudden to maintain her composure. "How . . . why?"

He tossed the collar on a bench and smiled. "You're welcome."

With a growl that came from the pit of her stomach, she spun around and marched out of the chamber on stiff legs. She had wanted to see him so badly, and now all she wanted was to get away from him. The slam of her bedroom door was loud enough to drown out the thoughts in her head. Grinding her teeth back and forth, she retrieved a fresh piece of papyrus and a pen from under her bed and sat down at her small writing desk, but she kept her hands by her sides as she stared at the blank page. Her head felt like it was about to explode from the rush of emotions. She wanted to scream. She wanted to go back out there and shake him. After a few moments, the rage passed, and she recalled the look of confusion on his face right before she stomped away. He had been trying to do the right thing.

Yes, and his sense of decency just destroyed three years of work.

Tears formed in her eyes as she thought back to all the humiliations she had endured since she entered the queen's service, all the cruelties and horrors she'd been forced to witness. As a slave she'd been subjected to the worst of human nature, but the role had also granted her almost unrestricted access to her adversaries and the cover to act from the shadows to bring about their downfall. Now it was gone. He had freed her from slavery, but he had also condemned her to a life without meaning in the same stroke. But he didn't know what he had done, and that was the crux of her anger, because she couldn't even tell him.

She laid her head on the desk and cried.

Horace flinched as the door to Alyra's room slammed shut.

What the hell just happened?

He hadn't known exactly what to expect when he told her about her freedom. Happiness, certainly. A touch of gratitude, perhaps. But in his wildest dreams he hadn't anticipated this. He felt like he had insulted her but had no clue as to how or why.

With a sigh, he went to his bedchamber and searched the wardrobe for something light to wear. He just wanted to relax this evening, maybe go to bed early and sleep off the day's events. As he pulled out a maroon robe and laid it on the bed, a knock resounded from the front door. Horace listened, but it didn't sound like Alyra was going to answer it. Stifling a grumble, he threw the robe around his shoulders and went to the foyer. The door opened just before he reached it. "Chancellor?"

Unagon entered, bowing his shaven head. "Good evening, *Belzama*."

"Yes. How can I help you?"

"You have been summoned by Her Majesty, sire."

BLOOD AND IRON

"Now?"

The chancellor beckoned to the hallway, and two young servants entered.

Horace looked over his shoulder, hoping Alyra would appear, but she was evidently too angry at him to investigate. "All right," he said, trying not to frown and probably failing. "Wait here."

But the chancellor and the servants followed him to his bedchamber. Within seconds Horace had been stripped of his comfortable robe and stood naked in the middle of the floor while Unagon flipped through his wardrobe. A tunic of cornflower-blue silk with silver embroidery and a matching woolen skirt were selected, along with a clean pair of sandals. As he was helped into the clothes, Horace thought the ensemble looked too official for a casual audience. His throat tightened. He couldn't handle any more surprises tonight.

When he was dressed, Horace was ushered to a chair where he was shaved by an expert hand while Unagon supervised. After his hair was brushed and his teeth were cleaned, Horace was asked to stand for final inspection. He felt like a doll standing in front of the long mirror, but he had to admit he looked better. Even the skirt looked good on him. "Well, I guess I'm ready. Lead the way."

As he followed the chancellor and servants back to the suite's common area, Horace glanced at Alyra's door.

I should go say something before I leave. At least tell her where I'm going.

Why? So she can bite off my nose again? Give her time to cool down and I'll see her later.

Out in the hallway, Horace hardly noticed the squad of soldiers that awaited them. His thoughts were still back in his suite with the young woman he believed he had been getting to know, until tonight. Oil lamps on the walls gave off a sweet smell and filled the ceiling with a light haze. Chancellor Unagon led the party through narrow corridors and down spiral stairs for several floors. The soldiers' boots tromped on the stone tiles in unison, even on the steps.

After several minutes, they arrived outside the enormous doors of the throne chamber. Ten guards in purple uniforms stood before them, perfectly still. Chancellor Unagon bowed and announced Horace. The guards stepped away, and the doors opened.

A crowd of people in exquisite apparel turned to face him. Horace recognized many of the faces from the fete and knew them as members of the noble houses of Erugash—the queen's court, all dressed up as if for another gala. Horace swallowed as he started toward them. Lord Mulcibar stood at the foot of the throne dais. The queen's First Sword stood opposite the old lord in a suit of plate armor, with three gold knots emblazoned on his shoulder. Horace couldn't recall the man's name. He was a crusty veteran soldier, bald, about forty years old, with the stern bearing of a career officer. One hand rested on the pommel of the sword at his side.

From the doorway, Chancellor Unagon called out, "Horace Delrosa, loyal subject of the empire!"

Horace frowned at the introduction. Yet he strode ahead regardless. The dais did not remain empty. The door behind the throne opened, and half a dozen young women in silken robes entered to take places along the sides of the dais stairs. Then the queen came out and put all the other women to shame. A flowing turquoise silk gown accented her copper skin. Her hair hung straight down her back, adorned only with a golden headband.

Gilgar's brother, Xantu, followed the queen to her throne. Horace tensed at the sight of the sorcerer, envisioning the mud-monster standing in his place. He was shocked to see the man still guarding the queen after what his brother had done, but everyone else seemed at ease. Xantu watched the queen with his hands folded behind his back, appearing every inch the loyal servant.

Music began to play from somewhere beyond the walls. The sound of horns blended with plucked string tones to the slow, soft beat of a drum. Not sure what to do, Horace walked until he reached the bottom step of the dais and stopped. He tried to remain calm while everyone stared at him, even as his brain screamed that something horrible was about to happen.

Another woman came from behind the throne to stand beside the queen. Garbed in a bright white robe with silver trim, she was very old. Her silver hair flowed down around her shoulders. To Horace's amazement, Byleth bowed her head and descended a step in deference to this old woman.

The crowd fell silent as the woman in white lifted her hands and addressed them in a rich contralto voice. "This night we gather before the gods of heaven and earth to welcome a new light into the celestial realm. In the name of Lady Sippa, She Who Lights the Darkness, who presents this man?"

Mulcibar stepped forward. "I do."

A murmur passed through the crowd, but Horace was concentrating on the old woman's words, which had the ring of a religious ritual. He was torn between two desires. On one hand he didn't want to take part in any heathen rite, but he also didn't want to jeopardize his progress with these people. He was just starting to feel accepted, at least by some of them, such as the queen. Byleth watched the proceedings with a serene smile.

"Master Horace," the old woman said. "You have been found in possession of the holy *zoana*, which has been passed down to us from the stars. As the first *zoanii* did in ancient times, this court welcomes you into their sacred family."

Someone gasped, and another person grumbled something Horace couldn't make out.

The old woman turned and nodded, and one of the ladies-in-waiting, or whatever they were, carried a small box to the queen. Byleth opened it and lifted out a golden medallion on a long chain. "By the authority bestowed upon me as queen of Erugash, and in the name of the emperor, may he reign forever unto eternity . . ."

Did her voice stumble on those last words? Lord Mulcibar's lips moved as if he wanted to smirk.

". . . I, Byleth et'Urdrammor, hereby elevate you to the rank of *ne'jun* with all the customary rights and privileges."

More than a little uncomfortable from all this attention, Horace ducked his head to accept the necklace and get it over with. Yet the queen continued to speak.

"In addition, you are named our new Commander of the Queen's Guard. Lord Hunzuu?"

As Horace stepped back with his medallion, the First Sword drew his weapon. He held the sword in both hands as if about to offer the weapon to Horace, but then reversed it and set the point against the seam between his breastplate and scaled skirt. Horace froze in fear as his brain registered what was about to happen. Then Lord Hunzuu lunged forward, falling on the hilt, and the blade pierced through his stomach. Horace stumbled backward, his gorge rising. Everyone else in the chamber watched the soldier's suicide without expression.

When it was over, and the body lay still on the floor in a widening pool of blood, Byleth climbed back to her throne and sat down. "Lord Horace, our personal safety is now in your capable hands. Please come to our chambers at the seventh hour to discuss your new responsibilities."

Mulcibar bowed, and Horace did likewise. His legs felt like they were going to buckle as he and the nobleman backed away from the dais together, bowing every tenth step. Then they were outside the hall, and the doors closed in front of them. Horace glimpsed the queen walking behind the throne with Xantu and her ladies in tow, while the old woman in white stood over Lord Hunzuu's corpse.

"What the hell—?" Horace said, on the verge of shouting.

Mulcibar held up a hand and glanced at the guards positioned outside the doors. With a curled finger, he beckoned Horace to follow him down the wide hallway.

CHAPTER TWENTY-SEVEN

After the ceremony, Lord Mulcibar took Horace to an outdoor eatery where they sat on a rooftop overlooking the city and drank fiery concoctions under the stars. Mulcibar gave several congratulatory toasts, but otherwise they spoke little.

While he nursed his sixth cup of spirits laced with lime juice, Horace played back the crash in his mind. Something had been bothering him. "Why would Gilgar betray the queen? I don't understand what could possess someone like him, who had everything, to do that."

Mulcibar looked over, bleary-eyed in the candlelight. "We rarely know what people are thinking in the privacy of their own thoughts. Some *zoanii* use mental sifting on their servants and vassals, but Her Majesty has seldom done so. Perhaps that will change now, though I hope not. The queen enjoys the support of her people, more than any king I've ever seen, because while she is a stern mistress, she is not cruel."

Horace started to nod in agreement when another thought sizzled through his brain. "Why did the power react like that? At the riverbank. I wasn't trying to summon the water. I was . . . I don't know what I was trying to do, but hitting that thing with a big wave was the furthest thing from my mind."

Mulcibar reached for his cup but found it empty and pushed it away with a sigh. "The *zoana* is more than a source of power. It guides us through our intentions."

"It controls us?"

"Not exactly. Many *zoanii* spend their entire lives trying to understand the power. There are tomes in the royal archives you should study, going back centuries."

It had never occurred to Horace that he could visit the archives. Perhaps Alyra would help him translate. "This sounds strange, but it felt like the river came alive somehow. Like it was fighting for me, or through me."

"That is curious, but not altogether implausible." When Horace frowned,

BLOOD AND IRON

Mulcibar continued, "The Typhon River *is* Akeshia. Even our name, the Land of the Black Earth, comes from its rich soils that sustain us. But the river is more than that. It is the embodiment of our entire culture. The old stories say that during the Annunciation when the gods came down to earth to see what they had wrought, Temmu, queen of the waters, claimed Akeshia for herself. She created the Typhon to protect this land and its people. In fact, the first people to settle here were called the Temmurites. They were conquered by a tribe called the Kuldeans more than a thousand years ago and vanished from the earth. And then my ancestors, the Akeshii, conquered the Kuldeans around six centuries ago."

"And you consider my people warlike? Sure, we knock each other around some, but we don't slaughter entire nations."

Mulcibar smiled as a servant girl placed a new cup before him. "We have a violent history, and some of that continues to this day. But you can still see signs of the Kuldeans among us. We borrowed their architecture and their letters. We even adopted their gods!"

The old nobleman slapped his knee as if he'd just told the funniest joke in the world. They finished their drinks and rode back to the palace. Gazing out the curtains of the palanquin, Horace admitted to himself that Erugash was a beautiful city, especially at night when the moon shone down on the pale rooftops. Mulcibar imparted another tidbit of information as he dropped Horace off at the palace gates. Prince Zazil had gone missing.

"Is the queen all right?" Horace asked. "She must be worried out of her mind."

"She appears to have taken it in stride."

One of the gate wardens had to help Horace navigate the palace's maze of stairs and corridors. By the time he arrived back to his rooms, he was so tired and inebriated he could barely walk. The guardsman got him inside and onto one of the divans in the sitting chamber before leaving.

Horace leaned back against the sumptuous cushions. Beams of moonlight slanted through the room's darkness and formed pools of silver on the floor.

All hail the queen's new chief bodyguard. Until I mess up, and then I get the honor of killing myself for Her Excellence's amusement.

Soft footsteps sounded across the room. "Horace?"

Alyra stood at the door to her room. Her hair was mussed as if she'd been tossing and turning in her sleep. "First Sword Horace, present!" he answered, and for some reason that made him chuckle.

"Are you . . . ?" She came closer. When the moonlight caught her, Horace froze. She was beautiful, perhaps the most beautiful woman he'd ever seen since his wife.

"What?"

"I'm sorry about before," she said.

He waved a hand in the air. "It's all right."

"No. You were being kind, kinder than I had any right to expect. I was caught by surprise and reacted badly. Please forgive me."

"Sure. Come sit with me."

She came over to the divan. Her scent penetrated the miasma of spirits swirling around in his head. He touched her hair where it lay on her shoulders. Then Sari's image appeared to him, the way she had looked the last time he saw her. There was something in Alyra's eyes, too. A note of curiosity. Horace let his hand drop to the cushion.

"They made the old guard commander kill himself," he said. "Did you know that? He just put his sword against his belly and . . ." He rammed both hands against his stomach. "Done."

She tucked one leg under the other as she leaned back beside him. "I know. It's their custom. When a soldier fails, there's only one way he can make amends."

"It's fucking insane."

"Because you're not Akeshian. If the queen hadn't asked for his life, the shame would have been greater. This way, his family can keep their honor."

Horace snorted. "Honor and shame. What good are they if you're dead?"

"Don't you believe in a life after this one?"

"Sure, but we're talking about the here and now."

"You have to learn how the Akeshians think. For them, the next life isn't an abstract idea. It's the cornerstone of their entire lives, from birth to death."

"That's . . ."

"Crazy? Not to them. You're an important man now, Horace. You have rank and authority, not to mention your magic."

"Yes, let's not mention that."

Alyra sat up and pushed her hair back over her ear. Horace watched the gesture, so natural she probably didn't notice she did it, but he was entranced. Sari did the same thing when she was trying to convince him of something. He found himself drifting into thoughts of the past until Alyra's voice jerked him back to the present. "I'm sorry. What?"

She was watching him closely, her eyes big and dark. "Horace, you won't be able to hide anymore."

He laughed, struck by the concern in her tone. "Is that what I've been doing all this time? I was taken captive, beaten, marched across a desert, and attacked at every turn."

"Yes. Those things were horrible, but they are nothing compared to what you face now. You are a foreigner, and yet you possess the *zoana*, which is as close to divinity for the Akeshians as the Prophet is to you. And being *zoanii* is about more than religion. It's also political, and the Akeshians play politics like other people wage war. They will not sit idle while you get your bearings. They'll come for you."

The breeze from the open window caressed the back of Horace's neck. "Then what should I do?"

"Stay one step ahead of them and don't be afraid to meet their hostility with force. Trying to negotiate will only make you look weak in their eyes. And stay near the queen. She seeks to use you, obviously."

Horace fought back a smirk. Was that jealousy in her voice? "Obviously."

"But that doesn't mean you cannot use her, too. Erugash is one of the most powerful cities in the empire. As the queen's fortunes rise, so, too, can yours."

Listening to her, Horace realized that Alyra cared about what happened to him. She was probably the only one who did in the entire country. "I . . . ," he started to say, but then trailed off as his tongue became tangled in the powerful emotions swelling inside him.

"What?"

"I was just going to ask what I've done to deserve such compassion. You're a slave and—"

"Not any longer."

He sat up, not sure if she was starting a fight, but then he saw the smile turning up the corners of her mouth. "I should have asked you before I approached the queen about that."

"No, it was a noble gesture. I'm sure the queen was surprised."

"She was . . . uncertain of the results."

"Did Her Majesty suggest that I would be more attentive after I was freed? Or less?"

Horace was glad for the dark, to hide his embarrassment. "She, ah, wasn't specific."

Alyra ran her fingers along his jaw. His heart started beating faster and louder. His throat, though amply lubricated with many drinks, was suddenly dry. "Well," she said, "I hope you didn't think that taking off my collar would obligate me to do anything . . . special . . . for you. Or to you."

"No!" He lowered his voice. "Not at all. It just seemed like the right thing to do."

"Good. Because I'd hate for you to misinterpret this."

She leaned forward and put her mouth to his. Her kiss was tender but insistent at the same time. Her tongue dipped between his lips. Despite his inebriated condition and the conflicting thoughts in his head, he found himself responding to her. Eventually, she pulled back.

Horace took a moment to catch his breath. "That was unexpected."

"Good."

Alyra got up and walked back to her room. Horace didn't know whether or not she wanted him to follow, not until she closed the door firmly behind her. He sighed.

God in Heaven, you certainly made women to test us, didn't you?

Eventually he tottered to his own room. Still in his clothes, he collapsed on the bed. He thought he should drink some water, but he was too tired and the pitcher was on the other side of the room. With a yawn, he closed his eyes.

BLOOD AND IRON

Horace lifted his head from the pillow and listened as fragments of the dream spun around in his mind like jagged puzzle pieces. He could still feel the fierce heat of Sari's grip on his hand, making his old scars tingle.

He thought he'd heard a noise, but everything was quiet. It must have been the dream. Trying to clear his mind, he closed his eyes again.

A faint creak reached his ears.

Horace sat up. As he looked across the dark room, he wondered if it was Alyra. He wasn't sure how he felt about that. He couldn't help but feel he was betraying Sari. Yet he also couldn't deny his attraction to Alyra. She was beautiful and intelligent, the kind of woman that men fought wars over. The door creaked as if someone was pushing against it. Was the latch stuck?

Horace wished he had gotten that drink before he went to bed. His mouth tasted of spirits and beer. He could see the door, but it wasn't opening. The creaking continued louder than before. A sense of enormous power swept over him, and he felt an irrational urge to pull the sheets over his head like he'd done when he was a child and something frightened him. Instead, he swung his legs over the side of the bed to check it out. As his feet touched the cool floor, a sudden pain penetrated his chest, and a horrible smell like raw sewage swept through the room. Horace tried to stand up, but the agony boring through his breastbone made breathing difficult. Through the pain, he saw an inky shadow play across his bedroom door. It looked like a black rope or a serpent crawling through the crack between the door and jamb. A second identical shadow joined it, and then a third. Before Horace could take a full step, wood crackled and the door was ripped out of its frame. He stopped, fear seizing his insides as something heavy pounded on the floor hard enough to send vibrations up his legs. Then something hard struck him in the chest. The air left his lungs as he was catapulted over the mattress and onto the floor on the other side. He never saw what hit him.

Gasping for breath, Horace barely had time to clamber to his knees before a powerful grip seized him by the back of the neck. A hot wind blew in his face and choked him with its horrid stench. He reached up behind his head in an effort to break free. His blood turned cold as his fingers closed around a huge, hairy wrist as big around as his thigh, iron-hard with corded sinew under leathery flesh. Sharp nails dug into his neck as the massive arm threw him across the room.

Horace struck the wardrobe, shoulder first. Wood exploded as he burst through the door panel and fell, half inside and half out of the cabinet. Heavy footsteps slapped on the floor behind him. Pulling himself out of the wardrobe, Horace felt a sharp pain jabbing him under the ribs. Looking down, he saw a piece of wood sticking out of his right side. Blood soaked into his clothes. He pulled on the end of the giant splinter and hissed as it came free. He swayed back against the frame of the wardrobe just as a line of raw agony ripped across his abdomen. More blood dripped from a set of three parallel cuts that ran across his stomach from hip to hip like he'd been attacked by some wild beast.

With memories of the *kurgarru* fresh in his mind, Horace twisted away and flung himself toward the door. Something thin and ropelike caught his ankle, and he sprawled headlong onto the floor. His blood was everywhere, coating his hands and making it difficult to find traction on the slick tiles. He clawed his way to one of the bed's foot posts. He was hauling himself up it when a scream rang out from elsewhere in the suite.

Alyra.

His fear vanished. Fingertips tingling, Horace opened himself to the power. The pain of his injuries was shoved away. All he could feel was the *zoana*, urging him to lash out. He turned around. A huge shape rose before him, the top of its head almost brushing the ten-foot-high ceiling. Although he couldn't make out many details in the dark, Horace knew at once it was nothing human. And nothing like any animal he'd ever seen either. Rubbery appendages hung from its head, wriggling like a nest of serpents, and hornlike projections rose from the backs of its long arms. The awful stench rolled off of it.

Clenching his teeth to keep from vomiting, Horace thrust out his right hand. The power inside him hesitated for an instant, like a hiccup, and then erupted, not from his outstretched hand, but from his chest. The pain flared inside him, so powerful that his vision dimmed and his muscles locked up in an agonizing rictus.

Strangest of all, he didn't see anything happen. No ray of fire shot across the room, no orb of ice or stone, no gust of wind. Nothing at all like the elemental dominions he'd been taught about. And yet the creature staggered back as if it had been struck by a battering ram. A titanic roar resounded off the walls. Horace winced as he poured out more of his power, concentrating through the rising pain. Starlight filtered through a cloud of dust forming behind the creature where his power was chewing a hole in the wall. The monster tried to resist the invisible force, growling and swiping at the air with its hooked talons. Tile crackled as its horned toes dug into the floor. Yet it could not reach him. Horace looked around. He could hold the creature at bay, it seemed, but it would be on him the moment he let up. He didn't see how he could get to Alyra without releasing it.

A large shape loomed in Horace's peripheral vision. He ducked, but too late as the chair crashed into him, heaved by his attacker. The heavy furniture struck him on the side of the shoulder and spun him completely around. Horace grasped the bedpost to keep from falling. His right arm felt like it had been torn from the socket.

He shoved away from the post as the beast's shadow towered over him. With no time to think, he just reacted. His power flared again, and again there was no visible effect, but he sensed a sudden and dreadful connection to the creature, throbbing in his hand as if he held the creature's beating heart. He could feel the blood pumping through that mighty muscle, strong and fierce. Horace wasn't sure what he was doing, but in that instant he didn't care. He squeezed his fingers.

The creature halted, grasping its chest with both hands. Horace tightened his fist, and the creature teetered back, tearing its own flesh away in bloody strips to dig inside. Spurred on by this behavior, Horace twisted his fist sideways and yanked. A hollow gurgle issued from the creature's mouth as it fell on its side with an impact that shook the floor. A crystal candleholder rolled off the sideboard table and broke. The creature didn't move.

Horace ran for the door. The sitting parlor was dark, but enough starlight came through the large window for him to navigate between the divans. He kicked open Alyra's door. Candlelight flickered against the walls and cast deep shadows in the corners of the small room. Alyra stood against the far wall, her white tunic drenched in blood from long scratches across her upper chest. She waved a long knife back and forth as if fending off something she could not see.

Horace reached for his powers again. He found it more difficult this time, like trying to exercise a fatigued muscle. The magic came back slowly instead of the instant rush he'd felt before. Once it came, though, his view of the room changed. A horrible, squat shape appeared in front of Alyra. It hissed from a dog-like snout as it pawed the air, trying to get past her weapon.

Ignoring his throbbing shoulder, Horace snatched up the chair beside Alyra's desk and approached the creature from behind. Alyra glanced up, and her eyes grew wide as she looked over his head. "Behind you!"

A heavy weight dropped on his back. Claws dug into his shoulders as he was knocked to the floor. The chair clattered out of his grip, and Horace found himself pinned face-down by what felt like a small pony perched on his lower back. He tried to push up, but his right arm was useless, and his left lacked the strength to move both him and his assailant. Alyra yelled as deep scratches opened across her knee and slashed with her knife, but the creature stayed beyond her reach. Then Horace's vision was wrenched away as the thing on top of him yanked his head back by the hair. Thin claws grasped for the front of his throat.

Horace struggled to buck the creature off his back, but he was held fast. Blood dribbled down his neck as the claws dug deeper. Then the grasp holding him went limp, and the weight slid off his back. Horace scrambled away. Another small demon lay on the floor with a knife hilt protruding from its throat. Alyra had jumped up on her bed as the other creature swiped at her ankles. Horace lunged and grabbed it by the bony leg. A fierce heat erupted inside him, filling him with tremendous strength. He jerked his arm and flung the creature across the room. Its impact dented the stone wall and knocked mortar loose from the ceiling. The dog-faced thing dropped beside its brother and did not move again. Yellow ichor dripped from its head, which was caved in down to the bridge of its snout.

BLOOD AND IRON

Horace rolled over onto his back. The fire inside him was dwindling, leaving him wrung out and exhausted. Alyra sat on her bed, her chin drooping to her lacerated chest. He crawled over to her and touched her leg, careful not to aggravate her wounds. "Are you all right?"

She nodded, looking as tired as he felt. "I think so. What about y— oh, your arm!"

His right arm hung slack, leaking blood from several cuts and a deep tear where it joined to his shoulder. Oddly, it didn't hurt too badly. Then his sense of balance abandoned him without warning. Alyra caught him by his good arm as he fell back against the wall with a minimal amount of jarring.

Horace took a deep breath. His chest ached behind the breastbone. "I'm okay. Just give me a moment."

Alyra grabbed a sheet from her bed and tied it around his injured arm. "I've heard about your powers, but I never believed . . . I mean, to see the *zoana* in action. . . . It's amazing."

Horace sighed as the pressure dug into his wound. "I'm still trying to wrap my head around it. One day I'm a normal guy, and the next I'm a . . . I don't know. A freak."

"You're not a freak!" She brushed a hand through his sweaty hair. "We would be dead if not for what you did. I was so scared. I couldn't control it."

"You didn't look scared to me. You looked brave, like an angel of vengeance. All you needed was a flaming sword."

Her laughter was a good sound. One he wanted to hear again. Horace started to close his eyes when a loud crash echoed from outside the room. The front door had been forced open. He stood up, grimacing as the room tilted around him. "I'll take care of it," he said through gritted teeth. "Barricade the door behind me."

But Alyra had already retrieved her knife from the dead demon. "No. We're both going out there together."

"Alyra—"

She opened the door, and Horace had no choice but to go with her. He felt shaky, and the fire of the *zoana* no longer tingled in his veins. He clenched his fists, willing it to return as he stepped into the sitting area. Bright light shone from the foyer. With Alyra beside him, Horace lifted his good hand, intent on unleashing whatever power he had left on the first thing that walked through the archway. They both sighed in relief when a pair of the Queen's Guard shouldered their way into the room with swords bared.

While the soldiers searched the bedchambers, Horace sat on the arm of a divan. Alyra curled up beside him. "They say people heard horrible noises throughout the palace," she said.

"Those things made enough racket to wake the dead. What in the Almighty's name were they?"

"I don't know. When they appeared, all I could think of was . . ."

"Demons," Horace finished for her.

"Yes. Just like the stories my mother told me when I was little."

"I've seen the images carved on the walls of the basilica at Arnos. They don't look anything like those creatures."

She shivered as she pressed against him. More soldiers entered the suite, until the rooms were filled with men in armor. All of them held a weapon ready as if another attack was imminent. Eventually, a flock of royal physicians entered. Horace reclined on the divan and closed his eyes while the doctors worked on him. After a few minutes, the sounds of their voices faded away, and he drifted back to sleep.

CHAPTER TWENTY-EIGHT

"**O**Sippa, lady of the moon, watch over your city, for we are beset by darkness in the night and need your light to guide our footsteps. Protect us from the evils of the world until we return to the safety and comfort of your breast."

The alabaster statue of the goddess towered over Byleth as she whispered the supplication in the inner sanctum of the Moon Temple, where only royalty and the high priestess were allowed to enter. Though not as grandiose as the Temple of Amur on the other side of the Street of Gods, this shrine was larger than most palaces. It had been the spiritual heart of the city since its founding, whatever the Sun Cult might choose to believe.

When she was a girl, she hadn't paid much attention to the priestesses or their teachings, which had seemed out of touch with the real world. Yet as she grew older, the gods seemed nearer to her every day, especially the patroness of her city.

Lady goddess, tell me what to do. What advice would you have given my father?

She had been thinking about her father more and more in recent days. After years of hating him for throwing his life away, she finally felt she had begun to understand him. The throne was not as comfortable as it appeared from afar. Almost all the noble Houses had abandoned her over the past few weeks as her wedding day approached. Oh, they replied to her overtures for assistance with polite words, but she could read the truth behind the pretty phrases. They had been seduced by the Sun Temple. She was alone except for a handful of viziers and court functionaries.

With a sigh, Byleth bowed to the goddess and turned away. Mother Iltani stood in the doorway. Her bright white robe gleamed like polished alabaster. Though her face was lined with deep wrinkles, her smile was warm and vibrant. "Someone is waiting for you, Majesty," she said. "In the nave."

Byleth had known the high priestess of Sippa for most of her life. "Thank you. I'm done here."

BLOOD AND IRON

The priestess joined her at the center of the room and took her hands. Mother Iltani's fingers were thin and bony with paper-fine skin, but their grip was still firm. She looked up, and Byleth followed her gaze through the round hole in the ceiling. The three-quarters-full moon shone down on them.

"I've been praying for you, Majesty," Mother Iltani said. "Right here every night, a prayer to the Silver Lady to deliver you from the forces that threaten our city."

"I appreciate that. I hope the Lady answers, and soon."

"She will or she will not. As I told your father many times in this very chamber, it is not for us to command the gods, but to listen and bend to their wishes. That goes for kings and queens as well as for the farmers in their fields and the cooks in the kitchen."

"And what would you have advised my father if he was in my position?"

Mother Iltani patted Byleth's hands. "That even the tallest tree must bend before the storm, or be broken by its fury."

But I'm not fighting a storm. I'm battling schemers and plotters who want to steal my throne.

Byleth kissed the priestess's cheek and left the chamber. She found Lord Mulcibar in the temple's main chamber, standing before a marble frieze. "I didn't think I would see you again this night, my lord."

Mulcibar bowed to her and straightened up slowly. "Forgive me for intruding on Your Majesty's devotions."

"I was finished anyway. I'm not much for kneeling and praying, even though I could use the divine assistance. What of our new First Sword?"

"I saw him back to his rooms at the palace. He may have celebrated his good fortune a bit too much."

Byleth caught the evasive sideward glance. "You still don't approve of his promotion."

"It is not for me to—"

"Forget decorum, Mulcibar. Speak plainly."

He cleared his throat. "No, I don't believe it was in the best interests."

"Whose best interest? Horace's or my own?"

"Both. Lord Horace is very powerful, but he's not in full control of his *zoana*. Furthermore, he doesn't possess the knowledge or political acumen to act as a proper First Sword. Lord Hunzuu—"

"Lord Hunzuu failed to protect his queen." She lowered her voice as it echoed through the large stone chamber. There was no one else here, but you could never be too careful. "He was given a warrior's death, which was more than he rightfully deserved after the catastrophe in the desert."

"That much is true. Yet Lord Horace isn't prepared to handle this responsibility. He has no allies and no protection outside of Your Majesty's favor."

"What about you? I was under the impression that you thought highly of our visitor from across the sea."

"I do. He is intelligent, thoughtful, and not at all what I imagined a man from the West would be like. However . . . forgive me, Majesty, but elevating Lord Horace to the *zoanii* caste will not solve your impending troubles."

She sighed and rubbed her fingers together. "Am I that obvious, my lord?"

"Only to someone who has known you since birth. Forgive my candor, but your court will never accept Lord Horace as your royal consort, much less their new king. And, if I may, it would only make your situation more untenable." He bowed his head. "If I have spoken too freely, please accept my sincere apology. But you are my primary concern, Majesty. Your protection and the continuation of your line."

"Yes, yes. No one is questioning your loyalty, Lord Mulcibar." She didn't look down at his lame leg, which would have shamed his pride, but she allowed the tilt of her head to convey that she was aware of it. "You've given more than anyone has a right to ask. Have you found out anything new about the crash?"

When they had returned to the city, Byleth charged Lord Mulcibar with discovering the author of the attack. No one knew the city's politics better than her father's trusted vizier.

"Nothing of note, Majesty," he replied. "I've placed Lord Gilgar's family and acquaintances under surveillance, including his brother. I don't expect to find anything. House Mamaunothos had nothing to gain by Your Majesty's demise and everything to lose."

She agreed privately. When they had returned from the crash, her first action—after bathing away the stink of sweat and river mud—had been to summon Xantu and force him to submit to a thorough mind-sifting. She'd found no hint of disloyalty in him, nothing that tied him to Gilgar's treachery. In fact, when she had informed him of the events on the riverbank, he had been genuinely enraged that his twin could do such a thing. But she was no closer to understanding why Gilgar would betray her. She had known both brothers since they were children. The treachery was a bitter knife in her breast.

"What about the other nobles?" she asked.

"They are restless, Majesty."

"A result of naming a savage as my First Sword, without a doubt."

"Quite possible. But I would have heard if any of the city's major Houses were planning an attempt on this scale."

She turned to face the frieze. It showed a huge, round moon hanging over the city's skyline. She assumed it was intended to be soothing, but it made her feel lonely. "Forgive me, my lord. We both know who was behind both attacks."

"You mean the Cult of Amur."

"Of course. Who else has the means and the audacity to strike at the crown? I'd wager that slug Rimesh was behind it."

"That is a bold accusation. One that should not be voiced in court without some form of proof. There have already been demonstrations in the public squares, Your Majesty."

"Riots?" she asked.

"Not as yet, but the temple soldiers do nothing to quell the civil unrest. And so it grows. If you'll heed my counsel, now is not the time for a confrontation."

"Then what? Shall I ignore that the menarch tried to have me killed?"

"I'm only suggesting that we proceed with care. Allow me to make more inquiries, gather evidence. If the Sun Temple was behind these attacks, I'll find out."

"Fine." Byleth wanted to pull out her hair, but instead she placed a gentle hand on his shoulder. "We'll do as you suggest, for now. But time is running short."

He bowed nearly to his waist. "I will do everything in my power."

"I know you will. Come to me the moment you learn anything."

"Of course. And there is one other matter I wished to discuss." He took a breath. "This is a matter I am loathe to discuss with Your Majesty, but I feel I must."

She didn't like how this sounded, but she nodded for him to continue. "Go on, my lord."

"It concerns Lord Astaptah, Majesty."

Byleth lifted her right eyebrow to let him know he was treading on dangerous ground.

Mulcibar cleared his throat, which turned into a choking cough. When he recovered, he said in a reedy voice, "Majesty, I fear you might have entered into an unsafe arrangement with his lordship. Please forgive an old man, but I swore a sacred oath to your father, to watch over you and protect you in all matters. I clearly failed in regard to Lord Gilgar, but I do not wish to fail again."

Byleth studied her oldest counselor. How much did he know? Or was this all based on suspicion? What would he do if he learned the truth about her pact with Astaptah? "I appreciate your concern, my lord, but my dealings with Lord Astaptah do not fall under your purview."

"As you say, Majesty."

As the old nobleman started to leave, two soldiers in royal uniform entered the temple. They knelt when they spotted her. "Majesty!" one said.

Byleth opened a pathway to her *zoana* as she strode toward them. Since the crash, she had lost much of her trust in her servants, seeing a potential assassin in every face. "What is it?"

"The palace," the soldier said. He was sweating profusely. "There's been an attack."

"On the royal residence?" Lord Mulcibar asked. Byleth noticed that the old man had nonchalantly stepped between her and the soldiers. The gesture was touching.

"No, my lord," the soldier answered. "In the First Sword's rooms."

CHAPTER TWENTY-NINE

The Iron Desert surrounded them, an ocean of sand and scattered stones with a few clumps of scrub brush clinging to life. The sun's blazing rays reflected off the white dunes. The company marched through the wastes in a loose line, double file for the most part, but the officers showed little inclination to enforce formation discipline.

Jirom wiped his brow with the back of his forearm.

I thought I was done with soldiering when I was captured. The gods must be laughing their asses off.

Irritated and thirsty, he called for his platoon to tighten into a diamond formation. The dog-soldiers squinted at him as if gauging his seriousness, but they moved. Czachur hustled to take the point position. Jirom watched them with a critical eye, ready with a verbal tongue-lashing.

"Attention! Make way!"

A cavalry regiment rode up from the rear of the column. *Kapikul* Hazael rode in their midst, his dark eyes scanning the troops. A junior officer stood up in his stirrups. "Who leads this squad?"

Jirom lifted his chin. "I do."

"The *kapikul* wants to know why these soldiers are in assault formation." The officer kept talking before Jirom could answer. "Assemble them in double file at once!"

Jirom's troopers looked to him, and he considered the price of disobeying, but then changed his mind. "Double file!" he called out.

The men rushed into the new formation with practiced ease. The *kapikul* said something to his officer and then rode ahead up the line with his bodyguards.

"Half rations for two days!" the officer shouted before kicking his steed to catch up with the others.

Jirom bit down on his tongue to keep from saying something he and his squad would regret, but that didn't stop him from fantasizing about putting a spear through the officer's back. Or Hazael's, for that matter.

"Looking good, lads!"

Heads turned as Emanon appeared among them. The rebel captain was all smiles as if this were a pleasant stroll instead of a brutal march into the heart of the most dangerous desert north of the Zaral. But everyone perked up at his arrival. One of the troopers started to step out of formation to greet the captain, but Jirom stopped him with a shout.

"Back in line!"

The soldier, Partha, glared at Jirom from under the cloth wrapped around his head but resumed his position. Emanon went over to clap him on the shoulder and share a word. Then he came to Jirom. "The men look good. They're responding well to you."

"Is that so?"

Emanon scratched the whiskers under his chin. He was growing out his beard in a scruff of black with some gray poking through. "Well, perhaps you're a bit hard on them. We're revolutionaries. We aren't used to military discipline, eh?"

"Didn't you tell me I could run this platoon how I saw fit?"

"Aye. I did."

"Then let me run it."

Emanon held up his hands and laughed. "So be it. I just came to tell you to be ready."

Jirom looked around at the leagues of desert all around them. "What? Escape? Are you insane?"

"Not now, but everyone needs to be ready. We'll be arriving soon."

That caught Jirom's attention. They had set out from Erugash three days ago, a convoy of four hundred troopers, sixty-some officers, twenty-one supply wagons, and a complement of cooks, armorers, and drovers. They spent the first day on the river, sailing west in a convoy of barges, and disembarked at a small hamlet with no name. Then they marched northwest. The soldiers hadn't been given a destination, only a general heading, but Emanon's contacts had ferreted out these details within an hour on the road. They were going to a town called Omikur. According to the rumors, that was where the invader army was holed up. Jirom hadn't welcomed the news that they were marching for a fight so soon, but there wasn't much he could do about it.

He shaded his eyes to peer over the heads of the soldiers marching ahead of him. It took him a minute, but he finally spotted a dark smudge against the horizon. That had to be Omikur, unless it was another mirage. "We won't reach it before nightfall."

"Word is that we'll stop an hour before sunset to make camp and approach the town in the morning."

"Understood. What about getting us extra water rations?"

Emanon pointed over his shoulder. A wagon loaded with clay jars rolled up from the rear of the column. "Already taken care of. And I have something else for you. A piece of information from Erugash. Your friend, Horace, has joined the queen's court."

A knot formed in the center of Jirom's chest. "What are you talking about?"

"That's what my sources are saying. He's the new First Sword of Her Majesty's Guard. I don't have to tell you that's a sensitive post. She must trust him an awful lot."

Jirom shook his head, only half-listening now. What did this mean? Had Horace gone over to the Akeshians?

"All right," Emanon said. "I have other people to see. Keep your eyes open and remember: Be—"

"Ready. Yes."

Emanon clapped a hand on his shoulder. "Right. See you later."

The rebel captain jogged ahead, sliding through the ranks as easily as an eel through a murky riverbed.

Jirom watched him go, wondering how much he could trust Emanon's information. He couldn't believe that Horace would embrace a people who had put a collar around his neck. Then Jirom thought back to the sandstorm and how Horace had faced it. After that, the pale Westerner had been a different man. Had he changed so much he would follow a tyrant like the queen of Erugash?

The sun glared down as the army marched onward.

BLOOD AND IRON

The call to halt came down an hour before sundown, just as Emanon had predicted. Troops dropped their packs and fell out of formation at once, most of them dropping to the ground where they stood.

"Get up!" Jirom shouted at his unit before they could fall asleep.

Heads lifted, but no one moved. Jirom leaned over, his back crying out in agony after the long march, and picked up the man closest to him. Silfar's eyes opened wide as he was hauled to his feet. Jirom growled in the soldier's face, "Get out your spade and start digging."

Every night on the march, no matter where they were or how long they'd traveled, Jirom forced his platoon to dig a trench around their campsite before they bedded down. Six feet deep and six across. He would have had them install stakes, too, but he couldn't get his hands on enough disposable wood. His men had refused the first night, until he put three of them on their backs with bloody lips and busted noses. The second night they'd tried to go over his head to Emanon, but the captain shrugged and left. Part of him didn't blame them. Twelve hours on the road in this terrain was enough to kill a man, but if he let up discipline for even one night, he'd lose them for good.

"Up!" he shouted. "On your feet and get this camp squared away!"

With groans and curses, they obeyed. Despite the pain shooting down the backs of his legs, Jirom got in the trench with them as he did every night and came out as sweaty and fatigued as everyone else. Then he got them fed and let them sleep in peace, taking the first watch for himself.

The sun was setting behind Omikur's ramparts. Lights twinkled in the towers studding the long curtain wall. Jirom wondered about the people inside. He'd heard that the crusaders had allowed the town's inhabitants to leave in peace when they occupied the town. About half had taken the offer, leaving with as much food and water as they could carry, but the rest—as many as a thousand people—had chosen to stay. Why?

Jirom knew Akeshian tactics, having fought against them enough times in the past. He had seen it firsthand. The people inside, the civilians, had to know they would receive no mercy when the legions took back the town. Many would die. Savagely, painfully. The soldiers would sate themselves with rape and looting, and the survivors would be sold into slavery. It was madness to resist.

"Hail!" a voice called from across the trench. "Do I need to know a password before I can cross?"

Jirom scowled at Emanon. "Yes. It's 'asshole.'"

The rebel captain scrambled across the ditch. Brushing off his hands, he surveyed the sleeping soldiers. "I'm amazed you didn't have to kill anyone tonight."

"Me too. How many did we lose today?"

Two men had fallen down dead on the first day of the forced march, and six more on the second day. Jirom's platoon hadn't lost anyone yet, mainly because he made sure they got plenty of water throughout the day.

"Thirteen," Emanon replied.

Jirom let out a sigh, too tired to make more of a comment. What could be said? Nothing. The dead were dead, and the living had to keep on going. "Well, we're here. Now what?"

"We've been attached to the Third Legion, the Queen's Silver Demons," Emanon said.

"Charming name."

"They're charming lads, I'm sure. They've had the town under siege for almost a fortnight now. Earthworks and siege weapons. Your kind of stuff."

Jirom grunted. "Any luck with the gates?"

"Not from what I've heard. Omikur's a tough nut to crack. The walls are thirty feet high in most places and at least ten paces thick. The gates are sheathed in iron."

"How many defenders?"

"The command is guessing about two thousand."

"That means three thousand, at least."

"More. My friends tell me there are freed slaves on those walls."

"That's why they didn't leave when they had the chance. The foreigners offered the slaves their freedom." A thought occurred to Jirom. "You aren't planning to sneak inside and join the defense, are you?"

BLOOD AND IRON

Emanon laughed and shook his head. "No, I'm not *that* crazy. I feel for those poor bastards inside, but I'm not suicidal."

"So what are we going to do?"

"Just follow orders for now. And be—"

"—ready," Jirom finished for him. "Don't you ever get tired of saying that?"

Emanon grinned in response. Jirom was about to ask for more details on the secret plan when a boom exploded above their heads and bright green light illuminated the sky. Black clouds formed over the town, despite the fact that the sky had been clear all day. A powerful wind sprung up out of nowhere, showering the camp in sand and the unsettling stench he had come to associate with sorcery.

Lightning struck several times in succession, most of the jagged green bolts landing inside the city. Horns blared in the gathering night as fires sprung up within the walls. The wind continued to whip over the camp, tugging on blankets and cloaks. Jirom's unit was awake now, every man standing and staring at the pyrotechnic barrage. Jirom thought he should say something, but there were no words for it, only a sense of dread in the pit of his stomach. The storm lasted for the better part of an hour, and then slowly died down, the lightning coming less frequently until it ended altogether. The clouds dissipated to reveal a firmament of twinkling stars. The wind was the last thing to go, taking with it with the reek of black magic.

Jirom looked around his camp. His men were mumbling to each other, their faces shadowed with worry. He cleared his throat. "Czachur, get a fire going! Minach, you're on watch!"

The commands snapped some life into the soldiers, and before long most of them were settled on the ground around a growing fire. Jirom wished he had some way to take their minds off what they'd just seen, but he didn't have the heart to assign them any more camp chores.

Emanon touched his elbow. "Get some sleep. We'll be up early tomorrow."

Jirom nodded, though sleep seemed leagues away. He watched the rebel captain leave the same way he had come, over the trench and off into the night. Jirom found his gear and unrolled his trail blanket. Lying on the rough material cushioned by the sand, he gazed up at the night sky. All the constellations were out. If he blocked out the camp sounds, he could almost believe he was somewhere else, perhaps even back home. But then the afterimages of the storm flashed through his head and destroyed the pleasant illusion.

With a sigh, he closed his eyes and tried to ignore the pain chewing into his lower back.

CHAPTER THIRTY

Horace shifted to find a better position, but the ache in his shoulder made returning to sleep impossible. With a groan, he kicked off his sheets. He had been dreaming again, something he had come to fear of late. From the bits he remembered, he and Sari had been picnicking at one of their favorite spots, a grassy hill outside Tines overlooking the bay. In the dream, they ate pastries and drank *oloi*. Neither said anything, but Horace couldn't stop staring at her. Even now, with the dream fading from his mind, her beauty struck him as unearthly. His yearning for her overshadowed the soreness in his arm.

He sat up as the door opened and bit back a yelp as he wrenched his shoulder in the process. A young serving man entered with a bowl and a tall clay pitcher in hand.

"*Sobhe'tid, Belzama*," the man said. *Good morning, Storm Lord.*

Horace plucked at the sling binding his arm to his chest. "*Sobhe'tid, Teukomen.*"

The servant opened the shutters, letting in a deluge of morning. Horace declined his offer to assist him in dressing. Once he was alone again, he swung his legs over the side of the low bed. He flexed the fingers of his right hand to get the blood moving and was rewarded with painful tingles under the layers of bandages. The past few days had been a whirlwind. After the attack of the demon-creatures, he had been given alternate accommodations, which Horace didn't mind in the least. He didn't know if he would have ever been comfortable sleeping in that suite again. The queen gifted him with a new home, one of the estates that surrounded the palace. The house was gorgeous, more angular and blocky than an Arnossi manor, but still possessing the clean, solid lines of Eastern architecture. Built entirely of salmon-colored marble, the manor gleamed like mother-of-pearl in the sunlight. He couldn't believe that it now belonged to him. He'd grown up with a small degree of affluence, but his father could never have afforded a manor estate such as this.

BLOOD AND IRON

He went to use the water closet outside his new bedroom. Through the small window over the latrine hole, he saw the enclosed garden below. Like many Akeshian homes, this one was built around a central courtyard. Broad green fronds shaded the pavestones around a spraying fountain carved to resemble a great, long-nosed beast he had been told was an elephant. He had a magnificent view of the city over the stone walls. The palace rose above everything only a short distance away. All this luxury—he didn't know how to react to it. Only weeks ago he had been a captive with a collar around his neck. Now, he congregated with lords and a queen.

It's all because of the magic. Without it, I'd be back in irons before lunchtime.

The jingle of metal reminded Horace of another gift that had come with the house, one that thrilled him quite a bit less. A soldier in scale armor strode across the courtyard, his head moving from side to side as he patrolled the grounds. Her Majesty had sent him a squad of ten soldiers handpicked from her own bodyguard. They were supposed to belong to him now, along with twenty house slaves including a cook and a horse-master. Horace had wanted to return the slaves and bodyguards until Alyra convinced him it would be a grave insult to the queen. So, he had freed the slaves instead and offered them gainful employment, paid for by the generous stipend he received as First Sword. Alyra seemed to approve.

As the sentry disappeared into an archway toward the kitchen, Horace finished his business in the water closet. He had not seen the queen in the last two days since taking ownership of the estate, though he'd sought an audience each morning since the attack. Her staff kept him at the estate, and he was still too banged up to protest. But he wanted answers.

The pitcher on the sideboard held cool water. He poured a measure into the bowl and washed up one-handed. The face that peered back at him from the polished glass mirror over the basin was still bruised, with small cuts around his eyes and across his cheekbones, but otherwise was little the worse for wear. Going to his wardrobe, he settled for a loose robe tied with a sash and a pair of slippers rather than attempting to put on a proper outfit with all the ties and toggles.

As Horace exited his personal chamber, two soldiers flanking his doorway saluted with a fist over their chests. The taller of them was Pomuthus, the captain of his guard. They followed Horace down the winding staircase to the garden. It was a gorgeous morning. He spent a few minutes enjoying the flowers, which reminded him of the tiny herb garden Sari had planted behind their old townhouse in Tines. It was a good memory, one of many that came to him at the oddest moments. He was able to take pleasure in it without guilt or biting melancholy rushing over him.

Humming a seaman's chantey, Horace walked past a tree with pendulous orange globes hanging from its branches. He'd never seen such a fruit before coming to Akeshia, but he had come to love the tart juice and meat inside. Using his power, he extended a ribbon of the Imuvar dominion to summon a zephyr. The breeze tugged at one of the low-hanging fruit and pulled it off the branch. He tried to use the power to catch the fruit, but the wind slipped from his mental grasp and the orange orb splattered on the pavestones. With a sigh, he plucked another fruit with his good hand and stopped by the flower beds to pick a long-stemmed lily before going inside.

In the kitchen, the cook was working over an array of pots and ovens. Horace procured a tray and a tall cup to hold the flower. He placed the orange fruit on the tray, along with a paring knife and a carafe of juice. The cook brought over a plate of fresh-baked rolls with a shy smile. Beads clacked, and the gardener, Shulgi, entered the kitchen. The man was quite old and stout with a crooked back. Hideous red boils covered his round face. He usually hid under the brim of a wide straw hat, as he did this morning.

"*Sobhe'tid,*" Horace said, wanting to put the man at ease.

The gardener bowed low and rose painfully. "*Sobhe'tid, Belzama.*"

As the man shuffled over to the oven for his breakfast, Horace balanced the tray in his good arm and went to find Alyra. Her suite was on the upper floor in what was called "the mistress chamber." The term had been almost enough to make him blush until Alyra explained that "mistress" didn't carry the same connotation in Akeshia as it did back home. Any female relative was given the title if she was unmarried and living under the same roof as a male.

A female servant was exiting Alyra's room as Horace reached the landing. She bowed and scurried off but left the door open. He was trying to figure out how he could knock without a free hand when Pomuthus rapped on the doorframe with a firm staccato. Horace nodded his thanks to the man and waited. After a few seconds, her voice carried out to him. *"Mannu hi?"*

"It's me," Horace said. "May I come in?"

The door opened all the way, and Alyra stood there in a nightgown of peach-colored silk. "Good morning, Horace."

"Sobhe'tid, boleta," he said in greeting.

"Beleti," she corrected and stepped aside to allow him to enter.

"Beleti," he repeated. "Damn. I thought I had it perfect."

"Don't fret. You're getting much better, if one can overlook your accent."

He set down the tray on a small mahogany table. "That bad?"

Alyra scrunched up her face like she's bitten into a sour tart. "Dreadful."

"I'll keep working on it. How did you sleep?"

"Good." She picked up the pastry. "Thank you for this."

But Horace hardly heard her. The sight of her biting into the roll reminded him of his dream. For a moment he sat on a hillside above the bay at Tines again, staring at his wife.

"Horace?"

He forced himself to smile. "Sorry. I was just . . . in another place."

"It's all right. As long as you're back now."

"I'm all yours. Say, I was wondering if you'd like to take a walk. It's a beautiful day."

"Whatever you w—," Alyra started to say. "I mean, I wish I could, but I was going to see a friend today."

"Oh. In that case, perhaps we could—"

A throat cleared behind him, and Pomuthus poked his head in the door. "Pardon for the interruption. Lord Mulcibar is here to see you."

Before Horace could answer, Alyra told the captain to admit Mulcibar and make him comfortable. Horace shook his head. "You planned this."

Alyra opened the door of a tall armoire. "What?"

"Lord Mulcibar's arrival. It's rather convenient that he shows up unannounced right as you're going out. Who is this friend anyway?"

A slight furrow creased Alyra's forehead. She closed the armoire door and faced him. "Am I free?"

Now it was his turn to frown. "What? Of course you are."

"If I am no longer your property, then I may come and go as I please. True?"

Horace sighed, resigned to being in the wrong. "Forgive me, my lady. It's not my place to question you. I was just . . . concerned."

"Well, then, perhaps I will tell you." She winked. "When I return. Now go see Lord Mulcibar and be nice. You don't have enough friends in Erugash that you can afford to lose this one."

Isn't that the truth? "Yes, my lady. Have a good time. Oh, and take the soldiers with you when you go."

"No, thank you."

Horace paused halfway to the door. "Pardon?"

She peered around the armoire door, holding a plain white tunic. "If you must know, I'm going to see some of my friends at the palace, and they won't enjoy being surrounded by men with swords."

"Tell the guards to wait outside. I'd just feel better if they escorted you."

"Horace, I've been making my way through this city for a long time now. *Years* longer than you have. I can take care of myself."

"I know, but those things tried to kill both of us. If there are more of them, I don't think they'll think twice about trying again on an open street. Please, just take the guards."

Horace braced himself for another argument, but Alyra nodded. "All right. I'll take two men, but no more."

"Thank you. Now I suppose I have to go entertain our guest while you're out gallivanting."

She gave him a withering glare, and Horace held up his good hand in a gesture of surrender. "I'm going, I'm going."

Closing the door behind him, Horace considered going back to his chamber to change into something more suitable, but his feet carried him toward the main stairs. The guards clinked in their mail behind him. He was glad Alyra had accepted his offer to take some men with her. The attack in the palace had rattled them both, but she seemed to have recovered faster.

Father always said women were the stronger sex where it counted. I never understood that when I was younger, but the Almighty smite me if he wasn't right.

BLOOD AND IRON

Horace pondered what his father would make of his current circumstances as he entered the parlor off the front vestibule. He hadn't had a chance to change the decor of the house since they'd moved in, and this was the room he hated the most. The light-brown plaster of the walls was textured like dried baby shit. The chairs and divan were upholstered with a gaudy floral pattern out of a pastoral nightmare. Bronze ladles and old farm tools hung on the walls; on the east wall were four alcoves containing small statues. These, he'd been told, were the gods of the household. The clay representations with their beady lapis lazuli eyes made him uncomfortable, like he was an intruder in his own home.

He put on a good face as he greeted Lord Mulcibar, who stood looking at a painting hung on the wall. The piece was called *Beast in Repose*, but it featured a trio of nymphs bathing at the feet of a matron reclining on a bench. Horace didn't like the image, especially the old woman's eyes, which were black and penetrating. He tried to ignore them.

"My lord."

Horace made a bow, but Mulcibar waved a hand at him. "None of that, if you please. I get enough scraping and ass-kissing at the palace."

Horace took a seat on the divan. "Please sit. Would you like something to break your fast?"

"No, I've already eaten." The nobleman sat in a chair facing the center of the room. He had brought a long, thin bundle wrapped in purple cloth, which he set beside his chair. "I wanted to check in on you. The commander of the Queen's Guard is an important post."

"I don't feel very important," Horace replied. "Then again, I suppose not everyone has demons trying to kill him."

"Yes, quite. Since you broach the subject, I have been to your old suite. To peruse the wreckage, shall we say?"

Horace winced. He'd been forced to use every ounce of his power to fend off the creatures, and it nearly hadn't been enough. "How bad was it?"

"I am glad to say the palace will remain standing, although between the damage from the storm and your encounter, the royal engineers have their hands full. Judging by the evidence, the magnitude of energies you unleashed that night was impressive. Yet it was also quite evident that you lack precision."

"I'm still working on that. Do you know what it was that attacked us?"

"I do."

Mulcibar reached into his impeccable gray robe and withdrew a glass bottle sealed with a cork, which he handed to Horace. A pile of teeth filled the bottom third of the bottle, each sharply pointed and much larger than human teeth. They looked like the fangs of a bear. A really big bear.

"We call them *idimmu*," Mulcibar said. "Our myths are filled with them. Evil spirits that eat human flesh."

"Lord of Light," Horace breathed, not sure whether he could believe it or not. He'd seen the creatures himself, fought them, bled from the injuries they'd inflicted on him. Yet it still felt unreal, like a nightmare left over from childhood. "Do you know why they attacked us?"

"Not for certain, but part of the reason I've come today, besides congratulating you on your new home, is to warn you that you are now swimming in very dangerous waters."

Horace fought back a snort, but failed. "More dangerous than washing up alone and helpless on the shore of your sworn enemies? More dangerous than being put in chains and collared like a dog?" He shook the bottle. "More dangerous than this?"

Lord Mulcibar met his gaze without blinking. "Yes. As a captive and a slave, you enjoyed certain protections. Lord Isiratu, for instance, might have had to pay recompense if he'd killed you and later found out that another *zoanii*, such as the queen, had claim to you. That's why he handed you over without protest. Once you passed into the queen's possession, she was responsible for your welfare."

"No offense, but she put me in a fucking dungeon cell, my lord. She didn't seem too concerned about my welfare then."

"On the contrary, you were well-treated, given food and water, and— most importantly—you were safe."

Horace started to curse in Arnossi but stopped himself. "Are you saying I'm not anymore? Safe, that is."

"Precisely. The court plays by a different set of rules. Status is everything. Sons will betray fathers to gain it. Wives will plot against their husbands and lovers. Nothing is beyond the pale."

BLOOD AND IRON

"What about the queen? Why doesn't she stop it?"

"Whatever for? Her Majesty was born into this environment. She thrives on the unending conflict and retains much of her political power by playing the factions against each other."

Horace leaned forward with his elbows resting on his knees. "I remember you gave me the same warning on the night of the queen's party. So I'll ask you again. What do I do?"

"Obviously, you must tread carefully. Under normal circumstances, a new member of the inner circle is tested rigorously by the others. Yet your elevation to this position is unprecedented. The court will watch and wait, seeking to know your strength before they make a move. You must use this time to your advantage."

"What about the *idimmu*?"

"I suspect they were a blunder."

"That's one hell of a blunder," Horace said.

"Yes. They dwell beyond our world and must be summoned with sorcery. Not an easy feat, and one which only the darkest sorcerer would attempt."

One person came to mind. "Gilgar's brother."

"Lord Xantu was my first suspect. However, he is innocent as far as I can determine. If anything, he appears more upset by his late brother's treason than anyone."

"He would appear that way," Horace said, "if he were engaged in the same conspiracy."

Mulcibar smiled, which deepened the lines around his eyes. "Lord Horace, I'd say you are adapting well to Akeshian society. In any case, discovering the identity of the culprit is now your duty as First Sword."

"Lucky me," Horace muttered.

"Yes. In the meantime, we need to work on your self-control."

"I've been trying those exercises you taught me."

Just thinking about them made Horace's head ache. Lord Mulcibar had instructed him in a series of mental puzzles such as studying an object, like a painting or a glass vase, then closing his eyes and trying to keep that object in his mind for a duration of several minutes. Or the opposite, emptying his mind of all images or thoughts and remaining that way, completely blank, for a similar period of time. He'd found these exercises to be much harder than they sounded. The point, Mulcibar had said, was to focus his mind on specific tasks, and thereby strengthen his connection to the *zoana*. "But they don't seem to be working. At least, not consistently."

The old nobleman smiled like a patient grandfather. "*Zoanii* train from the time they are children. You cannot expect to master the five arts in a single moon."

"Five? I thought you said there were only four."

"Each dominion comprises an art of *zoana*. The fifth art is Shinar, the study of the void."

"What is the void?"

Mulcibar picked up his bundle and gestured to the door leading to the garden. They went outside where the bright, cloudless sky promised a fine day.

Mulcibar stopped beside the orange-fruit tree. "Now, even your learned men understand that the heavens are a distant bowl inverted above the earth. The sun and the stars travel along this celestial dish above the sky, but there is a space between the heavens and the sky. An emptiness. This is the void."

Horace looked up. Above the roof of his house he could see the edge of the sun surrounded by blue. "I don't see anything above the sky. It's all just air."

"Shinar cannot be seen," Mulcibar said. "It cannot be touched or smelled either. Yet the universe is connected by emptiness. The sky above our heads, the ground beneath our feet, the space between our breaths. The void exists in all these things. Understand the nothingness, and you will understand everything."

"It sounds . . . I'm sorry, but it sound like pagan nonsense. If it can't be seen or felt, what use is it?"

"When the *idimmu* attacked in your bedchamber," Mulcibar said, "which dominion did you employ to drive them away?"

"It was . . ." Horace thought back to that night, something he'd been trying to avoid these past couple days. The battle with the demons was still fresh in his mind. "I don't know. I couldn't see anything happening, but the demon—whatever you call it—felt it."

BLOOD AND IRON

"Creatures from the Outside, as many *zoanii* have discovered to their detriment, are resistant to the four traditional dominions. They can only be destroyed, as far as we know, by the power of Shinar."

Horace sighed, trying to take this all in. "All right. So I used the fifth dominion. Is that a problem? Like I said, I've been practicing the techniques you taught me."

"You aren't understanding. Let me make this plain. There are no practitioners of Shinar in all of Akeshia. The last *zoanii* rumored to control the void died more than two centuries ago. To say it is a rare talent would be a gross understatement."

A cool breeze rustled the leaves of the garden trees. Horace looked down at his chest, remembering the invisible power that had erupted from him. He recalled the pain and the ecstasy of it, the feeling of unbridled freedom.

"This also explains your affinity with the chaos storms," Mulcibar said. "And perhaps your lack of immaculata as well. We have precious little information about the fifth dominion. There's no record of the techniques required to control it or the risks involved."

That last part caught Horace's attention. "Risks?"

"Shinar is more than an element of the world." Mulcibar touched his chest and then his head. "When we *zoanii* meditate to hone our precision with the power, it is the void we seek to comprehend. All of us fall short, yet it is the search for that perfect nothingness that compels us to master our *zoana*. But you apply the Shinar as easily as I am breathing this air."

"I wouldn't say it's been easy," Horace muttered.

"Horace, I have been contemplating the void every day since I was seven years old. And you already know it more fully and more deeply than I ever will. It staggers me to imagine what you will discover in the time to come, the wonders you will weave. If you survive."

"There you go again with the risks and my survival. What's the danger? Am I going to explode or something?"

The nobleman uncovered his bundle and rolled out a square rug on the pavestones. It was about four feet on each side and stitched with an intricate design of geometric shapes inside and around a wide golden circle. The interior designs included a series of concentric squares around another circle in black, which was divided into four quadrants surrounding an innermost circle of white. The rug's pattern was beautiful, but it was so elaborate that Horace found it difficult to focus on any single design.

"This is a *ganzir* mat," Mulcibar said. "There are many variations. In fact, each family has its own unique version. This is the *ganzir* of my house."

"It's very nice."

"Please, sit down."

As they both got comfortable on the ground, the nobleman said, "Your lack of control stems from an absence of inner harmony. The *ganzir* is used to focus the mind, much like the hand positions I taught you. These designs impress upon the mind that everything is one. As above, so below."

Mulcibar indicated the center circle. "Here you see the wheel of the arts, with the four dominions surrounding the circle of the void. He who controls the emptiness also masters the other four dominions in conjunction."

Horace leaned over the mat for a closer look. There was a tiny design inside the innermost circle. It resembled a man sitting cross-legged, stitched in platinum thread. "So what do I do with it?"

"The key to your power is balance and harmony. Gaze upon the patterns and allow them to merge with your thoughts. The goal is to reach a state of heightened consciousness wherein you observe the entire universe at once."

Horace considered the nobleman's words. It was preposterous to think that looking at a carpet would help him control his powers, but he was willing to try for the old man's sake. Horace stared at the jumble of shapes and colors, letting his eyes roam across it without focusing on anything specific. Yet, as the minutes passed by, he found his gaze drawn again and again to the tiny figure sitting in the center circle. There was something odd about the figure, but he couldn't pinpoint what it was.

"Now try to access your *zoana*," Mulcibar said. "Allow it to flow naturally out of you."

Horace was surprised to find the magic already coursing through him at a low level. He tried to follow Mulcibar's instructions and let it out, but the power evaded his mental grasp. It was like trying to grab a greased eel, and every time he reached for it, a jolt of pain ran through his chest. After about a dozen attempts, he gave up with a grunt. "I can't. It won't come."

"Try again."

"I did, all right!" Horace stood up and dusted the seat of his robe. "Maybe your carpet doesn't work for me. I'm a savage, after all."

Mulcibar used his stick to lever himself to his feet, looking for that instant like an old, broken man. "Perhaps you are right."

Horace reached out to help him, but the nobleman waved him away. "I'm sorry," Horace said. "That was churlish of me. Thank you for everything."

"No need to apologize. I hated my teachers in the art. Black-hearted bastards, every one of them. Of course, I was not the most attentive pupil. I lost count of how many sticks they broke across my back."

"Do you think that would help me learn? I'm sure I could find some switches around here somewhere."

They were both laughing when a soft voice called from the parlor door. Horace turned to see a servant girl waiting. He struggled to remember her name. "Dharma, right? What do you need?"

"A messenger came to the door, sire. He left a package."

The girl moved aside, and one of Horace's guards carried a long box about the size of a map case past her. The man held it gingerly, as if afraid to break its contents. Horace bid him to set it on a bench.

After the guard left, Horace started to reach for the box, but Mulcibar stopped him with a word. "Wait. Please, allow me to inspect it first."

"You don't need to do that," Horace said. "I can get it."

"What if the box has been enspelled? Can you spot a *rek-plag* curse without touching the outer surface? Do you know the thirteen anti-bindings that can be used to corrode a sorcerer's connection to the *zoana* and cause his own power to rebound against him? Do you know what the toxin from a *tsi-tsi* adder smells like?"

The case looked innocent enough, made of dark wood with a rich varnish and brass fittings. Yet Horace stayed where he was. "Ah, why don't you look it over first?"

"An excellent idea, my lord."

Mulcibar leaned over the case without touching it, mumbling something under his breath. An itch prickled the back of Horace's neck. After a few minutes, Mulcibar stepped back. "I do not find any tampering or enchantment on the package."

Horace reached out. The lid opened smoothly. Inside, a knife lay on a bed of white silk. The weapon was exquisite, with an ivory hilt inlaid with silver, but the blade was smeared with a reddish-brown substance. Horace peered closer but did not touch it. "Is that . . . ?"

"Blood," Mulcibar said. "Yes. It has started earlier than I imagined."

"What's started?"

"A knife dipped in blood is a traditional challenge between rivals."

"A challenge to what? A duel?"

Mulcibar stepped past Horace and pulled a slip of blood-encrusted papyrus from beneath the knife's blade. He unrolled it and started to read, "I, Varazzar, Lord of Perosus and Assam, do challenge thee, Horace of Tines, the Queen's Protector, to fight me at the setting of the Holy Sun on the Third Day of Hekkar before the Gods and Our City."

Horace peered at the message. The bottom was bordered by a long strip of printed wedge-shaped characters that formed the lord's signature. Alyra had shown him how they were formed with clay cylinders dipped in ink and rolled across parchment. Each was unique to an individual. "It sounds serious."

"A duel between *zoanii* is to the death."

Mulcibar held out the sheet of papyrus, but Horace kept his hands by his sides. "What if I refuse?"

"It will weaken your standing in court. Also, your name will be mocked in public."

"Fine. I've dealt with worse. I refuse." He took the piece of papyrus and tore it in half, and then in half again before dropping them back in the box. "Let them talk."

Mulcibar watched him with pensive eyes but said nothing more on the subject.

CHAPTER THIRTY-ONE

Alyra held her cloak shut with one hand and her hood pulled low with the other as she hustled through the dim avenue. The last thing she wanted was to be recognized. Sefkahet, also concealed within a long cloak, glanced about as she accompanied Alyra through the narrow streets.

This was an awful risk, but what choice did we have?

No choice, and that was the truth. Yesterday evening Alyra had found a message on her dressing table saying merely, "Night has fallen." It was code, of course. A code she never thought she'd see. "Night" was the code name for the head of the Nemedian spy service, a person so cloaked in mystery that neither Alyra nor any of the operatives she'd known could say if Night was male or female. The message meant simply that Night was here. In the city. Then this morning, another message arrived on the edge of her bathtub. It gave only a time and a place. She'd been summoned.

She had left her bodyguards at the palace with orders that they be plied with cool drinks and plenty of female companionship to occupy their time. Sefkahet met her at one of the palace's side gates, and together they left the compound. They entered a part of the city known as the Dredge, a warren of narrow streets and mud-brick tenements abutting the river district. Shadowed alleyways, like cave tunnels, twisted between rows of beer-shops and drug dens where sleepy-eyed people smoked the pollens of exotic flowers to escape their daily lives. The houses were stacked atop each other, their edges jutting out over the dirty street to block out most of the sky.

A dark place for dark dealings.

The funny thing was, lying to Horace had been the most nerve-wracking part of it. He'd been good to her and more honorable than she had any right to expect considering that she had been a slave under his control. And his fear for her safety was genuine. Yet there was more to it than that. More to him. He had a sadness that she couldn't penetrate. It was almost as if . . .

Alyra stopped in the middle of the street as people brushed past her.

BLOOD AND IRON

Sefkahet kept walking for a few steps and then paused to look back with a pained expression. Alyra ignored the woman as she sifted through her last conversation with Horace. He'd said something along the lines of "For a moment I was somewhere else."

Alyra didn't know what had triggered it, but in that instant when Horace was remembering some past event, a look of such sorrow had crossed his face that she thought he might break down.

He's lost someone and he's holding it in.

Suddenly, things about Horace made more sense. His gentleness, the awkward way he tried not to stare at her when she was undressed, his insistence on setting her free. They all stemmed from this traumatic loss. As Alyra put the pieces together, a cold realization came over her.

The court is going to tear him to pieces. Those jackals can smell fear, and he's emotionally defenseless.

"Alyra!" Sefkahet hissed above the noise of the street. "We must go."

Alyra hurried onward, her thoughts divided between Horace and the interview before her. They took several turns, careful out of habit to be sure they weren't being followed, until they arrived at a small blue door set below street level between two potted *messhagan* trees. This was where she often came to report and receive new instructions. While Sefkahet waited in a shadowed alcove across the street, Alyra descended a short flight of steps and rapped on the door. The wait seemed interminable, but finally the peek-hole opened and a jaundiced eye surrounded in black kohl peered out.

"Peace be on your home and your hearth until the end of days," Alyra whispered.

The door opened, and Alyra hurried inside. The old woman who let her in, whose name she'd never learned and never asked, secured the door with three bolts and a heavy chain before ushering her down the dark hallway to the rear of the house. Among those who served the spy ring, names were usually left unknown unless there was a reason. Alyra supposed the old woman might be the house's owner. She was a native of Erugash; that much Alyra knew from the few words they had exchanged over the years. Each of Akeshia's city-states had a distinct way of speaking if one had an ear for accents.

The backroom was dark except for a candle in a tin dish sitting in the center of a plain wooden table. The windows were draped in thick brocade that blocked out exterior light. Alyra's stomach fluttered when the door shut behind her with a solid click. She cleared her throat and heard a slight echo return to her. Then a male voice spoke in the darkness beyond the candlelight. "Alyra du'Braose."

She stood up straighter. "Yes."

"Do you know who I am?"

Alyra couldn't see anyone, just a vague shape in the darkness. "I believe you might be Night."

"That is correct. Do you know why you're here?"

Alyra was tempted to ask if the voice meant here in this room or here in Akeshia, but she assumed he was talking about the former. "There are several possibilities, such as the recent attack on the palace or the incident with the queen's ship."

"We are aware of these events. No, it was your report on this apparatus you claim that the Akeshians have built under this city. I wanted to hear it from you directly."

"Which part exactly?"

"All of it. Start at the beginning, when you first entered the underground tunnels."

Alyra took a moment to compose her thoughts and then began a lengthy narrative of the hour she'd spent in Lord Astaptah's lair. She spared no detail, even telling about her near-discovery and escape into the labyrinth of tunnels. As she finished, she heard voices whispering in the dark. Trying not to fidget with nervous energy, Alyra clasped her hands in front of her and waited.

The whispering stopped, and Night addressed her again. "You say that you suspect this machine may be intended to affect the chaos storms. On what do you base this idea?"

"It's just a hunch," she replied. "The energy inside the wire cage had the look of a storm, only much smaller."

"But you admit you only got a brief look at it."

"That's right."

BLOOD AND IRON

A man emerged from the darkness. The stark light shone on one side of his face, while the opposite side lay in deep shadow. He was older than she imagined, with silver-gray hair cut short almost down to the scalp and a network of wrinkles across his cheek and mouth. His one visible eye, though, was clear and crystal-blue. "You have our gratitude," he said. "You've done more in Erugash than I ever imagined you could when I first approved your assignment here."

"That . . . that sounds final," she said.

The visible side of his mouth turned up in a tight smile. "It's time to come home, Alyra."

Her stomach lurched as if she'd been kicked. After all these years, she had stopped even dreaming about the day she would hear those words. Now it felt odd, like this was happening to someone else. Yet Nemedia had never truly been her home, only another stop in a long string of temporary homes. "I appreciate that, sir. I do. But I feel that there's more to do here. The mission isn't complete."

"It is for you," he said. "You've earned a rest. I know it can be difficult leaving an assignment, but you've completed—"

"What are you going to do about Lord Astaptah and the construction?"

His face tightened, the smile dropping away. "That decision will be made in due time. You're a fine field operative, Alyra, but policy matters are not your responsibility."

She knew she should accept the rebuke, but she pressed forward anyway, not knowing if she'd ever have this access again. "Forgive me, but I think the people on the forefront of the operation—those serving here in the palace— are the ones in the best position to influence those decisions."

The smile returned, though a bit more rueful than before. "I remember thinking the same thing when I was a lot younger, and in the same position you're in now. But I learned, sometimes the hard way, that things must be done a certain way. Our country rests in a delicate position. I don't expect you to understand, but I have to weigh the interests of many against the desires of any one person." He nodded as he watched her. "Yes, I thought as much."

"Thought what?"

"Do you love him?"

She felt a touch of heat bloom in her cheeks but kept a straight face. Night received reports from every spy in the network. Someone must have tipped him off about her closeness to Horace. "Of course not."

"Good. Few things will ruin a good operative like falling for an asset."

"I know my duty. I know why I'm here."

Night stepped forward, and the darkness swallowed his face again. "And I know why you're here, too. Revenge for your father, killed by the Akeshians. For your mother, left a widow and forced to beg to feed her child. For yourself, stripped of your past and your homeland by circumstances you couldn't control. Revenge is what you truly want, isn't it?"

"Yes," she whispered. Her hands shook within the clenched folds of her skirt.

"Then you must sever your feelings for this Storm Lord. Use him, make love to him, tell him whatever you must to keep his trust, but never forget why you're here. Do you understand?"

"Then . . . I'm staying?"

Several heartbeats passed before he said, "Yes. Everything will change with the queen's wedding. If we fail in our mission, Akeshian power may grow beyond anyone's ability to overcome. Can I count on you?"

Alyra nodded with all the conviction she could muster. Her stomach still hurt, but she felt more in control. "What should I do next?"

"Your asset has become quite popular of late. Use this to our advantage. If he becomes a big enough distraction, it could give us some play in other areas. Encourage him to take some chances, to utilize the powers of his new position."

"What if he could be turned to our side?" she asked.

"Focus on the task at hand, Alyra. Lord Horace is a convenient thorn in the Sun Cult's side at a time when we need the Akeshians distracted. Keep him on that path."

"I understand."

"Good. You are dismissed."

Alyra had more questions, but she kept quiet and left before she said something out of line. Her insides were all twisted up, worse than usual. For the first time in years, she didn't know what she was going to do.

Sefkahet waited in the street. She flashed a smile when Alyra emerged from the house, but it couldn't erase the worry lines etched around her pretty eyes and mouth. Alyra could see she wanted to ask how it went but held back. "It's all right," Alyra said. "Just a debriefing about my mission."

"So you're staying in Erugash?"

"For now. I need to get back . . . ," Alyra almost said "home" but caught herself, "back to the First Sword's manor."

Sefkahet put her arm around Alyra's waist as they left. "I hope the savage is not a cruel man. I'll be glad when you can return to the palace."

Alyra leaned into the other woman. "Yes. We all have our trials to endure."

CHAPTER THIRTY-TWO

The sun was setting behind the city's skyline as Horace walked into his new home with four bodyguards in tow. Sweat covered his face and dampened his clothes. He had spent most of the day in a meeting of the queen's war council where he'd been forced to endure hostile stares from the other nobles while they droned on and on about some treaty, much of which he missed because they only spoke in Akeshian. It might have been more bearable if Alyra had been able to attend with him. Or even Lord Mulcibar. Anyone to help him make sense of this office he was supposed to be filling. When he'd received the summons, Horace assumed the queen would be attending—the invitation had certainly made it sound so—but he was informed soon after arriving by one of the lords that "Her Majesty seldom attends these meetings."

The man had added, "My lord," after such a long pause that no one could have failed to notice it. Judging by the glances exchanged around the table, no one had. Horace suffered the insult in silence and left the meeting feeling like a fraud and a pariah, not to mention a target. Now he was feeling the several cups of wine he'd drunk to while away the time and was starving for something to eat.

Yet he had learned some things. For instance, he found out that the city owed a great deal of money to the emperor, a debt that no one believed the queen meant to pay. After all, she would be married soon, and the problem would fall into the lap of her husband, the new king. Among the gossip about possible changes coming after the nuptials, Horace had also learned that the crusaders still held out in Omikur, which was almost too implausible to believe. Yet the council expected the town to fall within the next few days. Horace would have liked to help the defenders, but he wasn't in the position to help anyone.

He stopped on his way to the kitchen. A table in the vestibule was piled with flat scrolls bound in ribbon and sealed with wax. There were no servants in sight, so he inspected them himself. Each seal with impressed with a different signature roll, some of them quite ornate with animals and strange symbols. Horace picked up one at random and broke the seal. His injured arm was getting better.

He read the characters written on the papyrus. With Alyra's help, his reading comprehension was actually better than his spoken Akeshian. The greeting was addressed to him.

To the Queen's First Sword, Horace of Arnos,

In accordance with all the laws of Akeshia and the strictures of the Heavenly Spheres,

I do hereby challenge you to a duel of—honor?—on the fortieth day of . . .

Horace scanned the rest of the document, which just went on with flowery language to thrust home the point that he was duty-bound to answer this challenge or be "deemed unworthy in the eyes of Man and the Gods."

He dropped the scroll in the pile and opened another. The words were a bit different, but they amounted to the same thing. Another challenge. He counted the scrolls and arrived at thirteen. Thirteen challenges to fight to the death. He gathered them up and went to the kitchen, which was empty. He fed the scrolls into the brick oven and lifted the lid of the firebox in the corner, but the coals inside had gone cold. With a scowl, he pointed at the oven and envisioned a tongue of yellow flame consuming the parchments. Nothing happened. He clenched his fists in frustration.

"God damn you all! You sons of whor—!"

He stopped in mid-curse as a rush of heat exploded in his chest, like a door to the hottest furnace imaginable had opened inside him. He flinched back as bright green flames erupted from the oven, rising almost to the ceiling.

Squeezing his eyes shut, Horace focused on closing the flow of energy. After a few heartbeats, the fire died down. Horace leaned against the nearest wall. He was bathed in sweat.

Control! I have to learn better control or Lord Mulcibar is right. I'm going to hurt someone.

With that thought in mind, he went to the armoire in his bedchamber and retrieved the *ganzir* mat. He unrolled it on the floor and sat down. As before, the intricate designs drew his eyes in several different directions. It was so chaotic he couldn't concentrate on any one part. Then, leaning closer, he noticed there was a specific distance at which the patterns on the mat coalesced into a harmonious pattern. Though he allowed his gaze to wander freely, he found himself always coming back to the platinum man sitting in the center of the *ganzir*. His breathing slowed and his shoulders relaxed as he felt the tension leaving his body. He attempted to open his *qa*.

A tickle fluttered in the pit of his stomach. He felt a pulling in the muscles of his midsection as his body seemed to get heavier, and a grounded sensation came over him. He had opened himself to the dominion of earth. Kishargal, Mulcibar had called it. It felt good, like he was more in control of the power. He looked beyond the mat to the slate tiles that made up the floor of his room. Wondering if he could break one free, he lifted his hand. A sense of strain gathered in the back of his head.

"Horace."

Alyra's voice shattered his concentration. Letting out a deep breath, Horace closed his connection to the *zoana*. The heaviness left him as he climbed to his feet.

Alyra waited in the atrium. She had changed into a light-blue tunic and sandals with calf-high bindings. "Horace, I need to talk to you."

He had things he wanted to say to her as well, about how his feelings for her were changing, becoming stronger, but her expression was so serious he pushed those thoughts to the back of his mind. "Of course."

She took him by the arm and led him out to the garden courtyard. Once they were outside, she pulled him to a bench secluded among a cluster of tall frond bushes, and they sat.

"This is a bit clandestine," he said, hoping a little teasing would ease the dire expression she wore.

"Horace, there's something I have to tell you."

"I'm not going to accept them," he said. "The challenges. They can rot for all I care."

Alyra nodded but did not lose her earnest appearance. "That's good, but that's not it. I came to Akeshia for a reason."

"Came? I thought you were captured and enslaved. That's what you told me."

BLOOD AND IRON

She glanced down at her hands, clasped together in her lap. "That's what everyone believes. I've been telling that story for so long that sometimes even I believe it, but the truth is that I chose to come here."

He batted away a frond that was tickling the top of his head. "You're Arnossi, the same as me. Why would you choose to come here? Didn't you know what they would do to you?"

"I was counting on it."

"I don't understand. You wanted to be a slave?"

"I know that must sound crazy to you."

"Crazy isn't the word. More like baying-at-the-moon mad. Why would you do that?"

Alyra looked him in the eye. "Because I had a mission. I was sent here by the government of Nemedia to spy on the Akeshians and disrupt their plans—if they had any—for attack. So that's what I've been doing for the past few years, spying on the queen as her handmaiden."

Horace opened his mouth, but nothing came out. His voice was paralyzed by her revelation. Finally, he croaked, "So all this . . . being a slave, it was just an act?"

"Yes and no. I was truly a slave, but few people knew my real purpose."

Horace took a deep breath as he tried to make sense of this news. "And all this time I thought I was really getting to know you, to understand you. I thought . . ."

"You *do* know me, Horace." She touched his hand, but gently, as if afraid to spook him. "What I told you about my family is true for the most part. My father was the governor at Marico. He died when the Akeshians attacked, but my mother and I escaped. We found safety in Nemedia, and that's where I found a way to strike back at our oppressors."

"So you became a spy and a slave."

"We were counting on the fact that slaves have a lot of freedom to move around and be places where free people would be questioned."

"That's why you were angry when I freed you. I took away your invisible hat."

She frowned. "My what?"

"It's from a children's story about a magic hat that made a little boy invisible so he could get past his enemies unseen. That's what slavery was to you, a way to move around the royal court undetected. I . . . I had no idea."

"I know. I forgave you."

"You did?"

"Yes, but not until afterward."

He tried to smile, but he was still reeling. This changed everything.

Am I part of her scheme now, too? What if the queen finds out? She'll lock us both away forever or make us fall on our swords.

Alyra stared into his eyes. "Horace, I've never trusted anyone with this before. You could have me arrested if you wanted. No one could blame you for not knowing."

"I'd never do that," he said and realized the words were true as they left his mouth. He wanted to kiss her again, wanted to feel that love from another person. It had been so long. He found himself babbling, trying to take his mind off his feelings. "I don't know much about Nemedia, but I've learned enough about Akeshia that I can see why someone would want a spy in their court. When we were flying over Omikur, Byleth unleashed a storm against the defenders. It was horrible. Entire buildings collapsed as the lightning—"

"Did you say she unleashed a storm?"

"Yes. Just like the storm that appeared over Erugash, but worse, if you can imagine that."

He could see Alyra wasn't listening anymore. Her face was turned down, staring at the patio flagstones. "What is it?"

She didn't answer for several heartbeats, though her face scrunched up like she was arguing with herself. "While you were away, I went down into the tunnels under the palace and entered the abode of Lord Astaptah."

A chill ran through Horace, driving away the heat of the day. "Alyra! That was a huge risk. I don't think I'd want to cross him."

"And you don't know half the story about him. But I had to know what he does down there. I found tunnels filled with strange servants."

"Strange how?" he asked.

"They wore thick robes even though it was hot as blazes down there, and there was something about their skin. Their complexion was too . . . gray, almost like corpses. Anyway, that's not the important part. I also saw a metal contraption down there. I don't know what to call it, but it was big. Bigger than the statue of King Daalak in Yeznudin Square."

Horace had never heard of King Daalak and had no idea how big his statue was, but he got the point. "Go on. What was it?"

"I don't know. It looked like a combination of metal and sorcery, and I think I saw . . . this is going to sound insane, but I think I saw a tiny storm brewing inside it."

Horace sat back in the bench. From what little he knew about the chaos storms, they were wild, unpredictable aspects of nature. Yet if Astaptah had the ability to create them . . .

Was that what I witnessed over Omikur? A man-made storm?

"So what are you going to do?" he asked. "Tell your people about it?"

"I already did."

Alyra told him about a meeting with her superior—a fellow named Night. "He didn't seem very interested in the device," she said. "But I don't know. I feel like there was a lot he wasn't telling me, which isn't surprising. He has a mysterious reputation."

Horace didn't like him already. "Did he give you any advice on how to proceed?"

"Yes, unfortunately. He told me to focus on my mission."

"That's it? That's all he said."

Alyra bit her lower lip. "He's not a man of many words. But no matter what he said, I know what I have to do. I have to destroy that thing. If there's even a chance that Lord Astaptah and the queen can control the chaos storms, I have to make sure they can't use that power. It would change everything. No army would be able to stand against them."

Horace thought of the crusaders inside the town. Power over the storms would change the entire nature of warfare. On the other hand, he understood why the queen would pursue such a weapon. She was trapped by her enemies, soon to be locked into a marriage she didn't want and possibly killed as soon as her new husband took control of her city. Didn't she have a right to defend herself by any means possible? "You're right. A weapon like that is too powerful for anyone to control. What I can do to help?"

She stared at him for a long moment and then launched herself at him. He sat rigid as her arms tightened around his neck, feeling the softness of her bosom against his chest, and then he returned the embrace.

She murmured into his shoulder, "Thank you, Horace. That means a lot to me."

He inhaled the scent of her hair and tried not to think about the past, about anything except this moment, which felt like it could last forever. Too soon for him, Alyra backed away and composed herself. Then he heard the footsteps approaching.

Captain Pomuthus arrived with a narrow wooden case about four feet long. He stopped at military attention and presented the case. "This just arrived. From the palace."

At a look from Alyra, Horace flipped open the lid. Inside was a long, curved sword. The weapon was a gorgeous piece of art with intricate gold inlay along the scabbard and hilt, all polished to a high shine. Horace was running his fingers over the cross guard when he realized where he'd seen the blade before. It was Lord Hunzuu's sword.

He yanked his hand back as an image of the former First Sword lying in a pool of his own blood burst in his brain. "Get this out of here."

Alyra placed a hand on his arm. "This is tradition."

"I don't care what it—" Horace bit off his words as Pomuthus produced a scroll tied with a scarlet ribbon. He thought it was another challenge until he noticed the seal stamped into the blood-red wax. A crown over a full moon flanked by two men with dogs' heads. The royal seal.

Horace took the scroll and broke it open. He read the message feeling this wasn't going to be good news—a summons to another war council or a late-night meeting with the queen—but it was worse than he imagined.

"What is it?" Alyra asked.

"It's Lord Mulcibar." Horace lowered the scroll to his lap. "He's missing."

BLOOD AND IRON

Horace slowed his pace as he tried to make out the lettering written on the side of the building. He sounded out the words under his breath.

Vashidom. No, that's the gymnasium.

Motioning to the others, he kept walking. The sword—the First Sword's weapon of office—felt strange on his hip. He would have left it at home except Alyra insisted he wear it in public. "You have to look the part," she said as he dressed to go out, "if you want others to see you as the First Sword."

Not exactly feeling like a First anything, he walked the streets of Erugash in search of Lord Mulcibar. He had already been to the vizier's home where he discovered from the chief steward that Mulcibar had gone to visit the city archives yesterday afternoon but never returned. Now Horace was heading to the archives to see what he could find out. He had brought four of his body-guards along, leaving the rest home with Alyra, although she protested long and loud that he needed the protection more than she did. She had a point, but he insisted anyway. He worried about her safety, even when she didn't.

That woman thinks she's immortal, but I'm not going to let happen to her what happened to—

Horace bit down on his tongue and renewed his focus on the buildings around him. Alyra was fine.

Until what? Until you run back to Arnos and leave her here to face the queen and the court alone?

He considered Pomuthus, who walked beside him. The veteran with the jagged scar down his face rarely said anything outside his official duties, and Horace realized he knew next to nothing about this man who was sworn to defend his life. "How long were you with the Queen's Guard, Captain?"

"Seven years, my lord. The last two as watch commander."

"And before that?"

"I served in the Sixth Royal Legion."

Horace nodded as he scanned the nearest buildings. "See any action?"

"We were part of an excursion into Etonia about ten years ago. After that I was offered a post at the palace."

"And now you're here with me. Tell me, Pomuthus. Does the idea of pro-tecting a foreigner bother you?"

"From my experience, outlanders are the same as anyone else. They eat, shit, fuck, and die. My lord." The captain pointed to a broad building at the end of the street. "I think that's it."

They strode to the structure. Flambeaux flickered on either side of a tall bronze door, its surface tarnished with verdigris. Pomuthus rapped with a heavy fist. The sound of his knocking echoed down the street. Horace looked over his shoulder. He could see the palace above the rooftops. He and Alyra had talked about the message as he dressed to go out. It was his impression that the queen wanted him to turn out her personal guard and scour the city, but Alyra had argued for a subtler approach. "If he was killed, his body is likely floating down the Typhon," she'd said.

"We shouldn't think that way," he had responded as he belted on a crimson surcoat emblazoned with the golden sigil of his rank.

"No, we *have* to think that way, Horace. After the attack on you, and now Lord Mulcibar's disappearance, it's clear that someone is trying to eliminate the queen's allies."

So he'd begun the search without involving the Queen's Guard. Alyra's suggestion that he begin at Mulcibar's home had been a good one. Now he hoped to pin down the time of the nobleman's disappearance. The door opened, and a slight man in a loose tunic and woolen skirt looked out. His face was wrinkled like old leather, his eyebrows and the halo of hair around the edge of his scalp just the merest puffs of white. "The archives are closed," he said in a wispy voice.

Horace made a small bow. "I am Horace, First Sword of the Queen."

The old man glanced at the guards surrounding Horace before he bent his head a few inches. "What do you want, my lord?"

When Horace asked if Lord Mulcibar had been there, the old man frowned. "These are the royal archives, not a social club."

The archivist actually looked as if he was going to close the door. Horace put out his hand, just wanting to ask another question, but Pomuthus shoved his shoulder against the bronze valve. The door yawned wider, and the old man staggered back as if he'd been kicked by a mule. Horace grimaced. "I'm sorry, sir!"

BLOOD AND IRON

The archivist retreated another step, but there was no fear in his gaze, only anger. Horace held out both hands. "Forgive me. The queen sent us to determine the whereabouts of Lord Mulcibar. He has gone missing, and this is the last place his servants knew him to be. Please, did you see the vizier yesterday?"

He got all that out in broken Akeshian while the old man glared, but when he finished, the archivist gave a terse nod. His reply was long and detailed, and more than once Horace had to ask him to repeat himself. Finally, Horace bowed his head and gestured for his guards to follow him out. Once back on the street, Horace took a minute to consider what he'd learned. Lord Mulcibar had indeed been to the archives yesterday. In fact, he was a regular visitor. The archivist estimated that Mulcibar arrived an hour after midday and stayed until evening vespers. He himself had seen the nobleman and his manservant to the door.

Standing on the cooling pavestones, Horace eyed the homes lining the avenue, all of them elegant manses of stone and brick with their own walled enclosures. Had anyone seen anything out of the ordinary?

Horace pointed to a pair of his guardsmen. "You two go door to door and ask if anyone saw something strange last night around sunset."

The two guards saluted before jogging to the nearest gate. Horace took Pomuthus and the remaining guard on a slow walk down the center of the street in the direction of Mulcibar's home. He felt like he should be looking for something, like a shepherd tracking a lost sheep, but he was no tracker and he had nothing to go on.

If he left in the evening, the sun would be going down. The light would be dim and the street almost empty, like it is now. Where would he have gone?

Horace tried to imagine he was in danger. What would he do? Approach one of these fine houses for help? Not likely. Calling for the watch also wasn't an option. The idea of a militia that patrolled the streets, keeping the peace, wasn't embraced in Erugash. Instead, those who could afford it hired their own guards. Everyone else remained behind locked doors until morning or took their chances.

Horace paused at an intersection of two avenues. The old bookkeeper also told him what Lord Mulcibar had been reading yesterday. The reply had surprised him. The tomes dealt with the Annunciation, the era of ancient history when—according to Akeshian legend—the gods came down from the stars to rule directly over the world. *Zoanii* meant, literally, "children of the stars," and *zoana*, their term for sorcery, could be translated as "starlight." Yet, though the terms "star child" and "starlight" had a poetic ring, what little Horace knew suggested that this mythical time had been marked with strife and terror. It seemed that the people of this land had not enjoyed the reign of their pagan deities. What had possessed Mulcibar to take up studying those old myths?

After a few minutes, his guardsmen returned with a negative report. No one had seen or heard anything out of the ordinary. Horace cursed under his breath. This was getting him nowhere. He ordered the two guards to walk the route back to Mulcibar's home, look for anything amiss, and then report back to his manor to check on Alyra.

"Where are we going, my lord?" Pomuthus asked.

Horace was about to say back to the archives to see if they could discover anything else that might help the search, but then a gleam of pale light flashed from the gutter. He went over to the deep stone trench and bent down. Something was stuck in the channel, half-submerged in the dirty water and night soil. Holding his breath against the odors rising to meet him, he fished it out.

The silver square hung on a chain. By the moonlight Horace could make out the design of an eight-sided star surrounded by squiggly lines engraved on the obverse side. He didn't know what it meant, but he recognized the medallion at once. Mulcibar had worn it on the day of the flying ship crash.

Horace wiped the medallion on the hem of his robe and stuck it in a pocket. Then he turned to his guard captain. "To the palace. Right now."

They walked quickly through the vacant streets as the shadows lengthened and the cover of night fell over the city. Horace glanced over his shoulder every few strides as a feeling came over him, the feeling that he was being watched. He needed to converse with the queen about how she wanted to proceed.

BLOOD AND IRON

God be good. Let her dismiss me from this whole affair.

As the thought crossed his mind, Horace was stabbed with guilt. Lord Mulcibar had been kind while all the other nobles shunned him. The old man deserved his best effort. Gritting his teeth, Horace hurried his steps.

They ran into a patrol of temple soldiers as they crossed an empty plaza. Horace's stomach dropped at the sight of twenty yellow uniforms, but he straightened his shoulders and placed a hand on the pommel of his sword as he walked forward with purpose. The officer at the head of the platoon raised a hand. "A moment, my lord."

Horace was made to show his papers indicating his rank and authority to be in this part of the city. As the temple man examined his documents by torchlight, Horace became more and more exasperated. "Is everything in order?" he asked after several minutes of waiting.

The officer handed back the papers. "It seems to be. My lord. I wasn't aware that Byleth had promoted a new First Sword."

Horace blinked at the soldier's casual use of the queen's name. The *zoanii*, especially royalty, were treated as living deities by the people of this land. "Yes. Now if you have no further questions, I'll be about my business."

He tried to use the imperious inflection he'd often heard from other *zoanii*, but it sounded bizarre coming from his own mouth. The officer's lips bent downward in a stern frown, but he waved them along. Horace strode away before he said something he would regret.

The palace gates were a welcome sight. Horace and his guards were questioned briefly and their persons searched before being admitted, and then were stopped again at an inner gate for a repeat of the procedure. The palace grounds swarmed with soldiers. Horace looked around, wondering if there had been a problem, but Pomuthus bent close and said, "They've been on alert since the night you and Lady Alyra were attacked. All who come in or come out are handled like this. Even the lords."

At last, they were admitted into the palace proper. Horace ordered his guards to wait outside as he entered the atrium alone. He hadn't gotten farther than a few steps into the huge chamber when a servant in a long, white robe approached him. Horace asked to see the queen, adding that it was very important. The servant bowed and bid him to wait, and then disappeared through a side door. Several other people stood around in small groups. By their clothing and bearing, they were clearly of the upper class, possibly minor *zoanii* or persons with political connections. He was still uncertain about the strata of Akeshian society and how it all fit together.

After a few minutes, Chancellor Unagon appeared. His bald pate shone in the light of the many oil lamps hanging from the ceiling as he hastened across the wide chamber. "Pardon me, my lord," he said when he arrived before Horace and made a short bow. "I was not made aware of your arrival until just now. How may I be of service?"

"I need to speak with the queen."

"I understand, my lord. Please pardon me." The chancellor made another bow, a little lower this time. "But Her Majesty is not able to receive visitors at the moment. May I suggest that you make an appointment for tomorrow?"

Horace looked around to make sure no one else could overhear. The nearest person was fifty feet away, but still he lowered his voice. "Please, if you could inquire. This is very important."

The chancellor had the good grace, or the proper training, to appear embarrassed as he shook his head. "I must beg your pardon, my lord, but I have explicit instructions. Her Majesty is not to be disturbed at this time." He leaned a little closer. "She is in conference with an official from the Temple of the Sun. I should fear for my head if I were to interrupt."

Horace rubbed his eyes. He wasn't getting anywhere. "All right. But I need to see her as early as possible."

"Thank you, my lord. I will send a messenger in the morning with the arrangements."

Horace turned back toward the front entrance. He was suddenly exhausted, but he couldn't shake the feeling that Mulcibar needed his help. He started toward the front entrance when a party of four men intercepted him. The men were as different as any he could imagine. Two of them had skin like beaten copper, one with a thick beard and the other sporting only a well-trimmed mustache that curled down at the ends. The third man was taller than the others, with broad shoulders and an ample belly. His skin was burnished ebony, even darker than Jirom's. The fourth man was so pale he might have passed for an Arnossi, except for his hair, which clung to his head in oily black curls. Shoulder to shoulder, they stood between him and the exit.

Horace's hands tightened into fists. He didn't see any weapons on them, but after the events of the last few days he wasn't taking any chances. He reached for his power. It awakened instantly, slipping through his veins like a shot of fine whiskey. He held onto it, ready for anything.

The light-skinned man spoke first. *"Su shoma'akekalata hisu."*

The language of the phrase was so formalized, it made translation difficult. Yet the man's tone dripped with hostility.

"I don't understand," Horace replied.

The large man with the round stomach responded in a deep baritone. "He makes you a challenge here in the queen's hall, under the eyes of the gods."

Horace frowned as he looked at each of the men in turn. "All of you want to fight me?"

The light-skinned man stepped forward and jabbed himself in the chest with a thumb. "Only me. Do you accept?"

Horace studied the man more closely. His tunic was made of fine linen and cut to the current Akeshian style with wide sleeves and a narrow collar. "You seem to know who I am, but who are you?"

While the others looked on with hard stares, the big man responded if as by rote. "He is Puzummu of the House Arkhandun, lord of Ghirune, defender of—"

Horace threw up his hand to cut the man off and noticed that three of the four men—including this Lord Puzummu—drew back as if afraid he might lash out at them. Only the big man had not moved, though the hint of a smile creased his lips.

Horace took a deep breath. He was tired of being pushed around, tired of being afraid, and the disappearance of Mulcibar had grated on his already-frayed nerves. "Fine," he said. "I accept. Name the time and place."

"The day after tomorrow at sunrise," the big man intoned. "In the Canathenaic."

"Why wait?" Horace asked, his anger flaring even as a part of his mind urged him to reconsider. "Why not tomorrow?"

The three smaller men looked back and forth in confusion. The big man smiled at Horace with his teeth showing. "That is agreeable."

"Tomorrow at dawn. Do I need a second?"

Their looks of bewilderment increased, and even the big man had difficulty with the concept at first. "No," he answered finally. "Here in Akeshia, all duels are fought only by the challenger and the challenged. A duel between *zoanii* is a sacred thing, and to interfere means death."

The more Horace heard, the less he liked it.

I've already accepted. There's no backing out now, not that I would give these bastards the satisfaction.

"I understand," he said. "Now get out of my way."

Horace started walking straight ahead, and the men hurried to step out of his way. By the time he reached his guards, he had made up his mind to go home. As much as he wanted to find Mulcibar tonight, he had no leads and no help from the palace, and now he had the specter of a duel hanging over his head.

As he exited the palace grounds, the haunting feeling of being watched returned. He glanced around, but there was no one there. Even the rising sickle of the horned moon seemed to mock him.

CHAPTER THIRTY-THREE

Byleth played with the rings on her fingers as she paced across her parlor. At the end of each circuit she stopped and looked to the water clock dripping on the shelf between the bronze nudes of the Earth Mother and Ishara, the Lady of Love. The hour was getting late, and still there was no word on Lord Mulcibar. She started to chew on a fingernail. Her world was crumbling around her. In two days it would be *Tammuris*. Two days until she lost her freedom, unless she did something to stop it.

She had tried everything she could think of to put off the wedding. She had dithered and stalled, claimed poor omens and improper astrological alignments, and even outright refused, but the priests remained adamant. And so her desperation grew by the day. She stopped praying that Astaptah would come through with a solution in time. Every time she sent for an update, the same message would return: *Patience. I am making progress.*

Yesterday, she had ordered the messenger flogged and sent back to show his bloody back to the vizier, but the answer hadn't changed.

A chime rang from the ceiling. Byleth stood up straight and smoothed the folds of her damask gown, which was more demure than her usual attire but she was trying to make an impression. She signaled to Aisa to admit her visitor, and then changed her mind about standing and reclined on a plush divan as footsteps echoed in the admitting chamber. The slave-girl returned with Menarch Rimesh. The priest looked extremely warm in his long robe of yellow, but no sign of perspiration glistened on his smooth head. His priestly tattoos glowed crimson and gold in the light slanting in through the large windows behind her.

"Majesty," he said with a slight bow.

"Menarch, please sit down. I thank you for answering my request. Can I offer you refreshment?"

She gestured to the side table where wine bottles were displayed alongside bowls of fresh fruit.

"No thank you." He sat on the edge of a cushioned chair. "I would rather get directly to the reason for this meeting."

He could have been a stone for all his face revealed. Byleth accepted a piece of dew melon from Aisa and took a small bite. She considered allowing a drop of juice to trickle down her chin but dismissed the idea. The priest would not be swayed by her sex appeal. "I called you here to discuss the upcoming event."

"The feast of *Tammuris*," he said.

"Exactly."

"The temple has been working on the details of the event with your court officials. If you require an itinerary—"

"I require it not to happen at all."

Rimesh smiled. It was a tepid smile, the kind reserved for the very old and the very young. "No one can stop the turning of the days. Not even a queen."

I would love to summon a few of my less-savory guards and show you exactly what a queen can do, you swine.

She put on her most charming smile. It had seduced men of great station and wealth since she was a girl. "Let the feast come and go, dear Menarch, but remove the demand that I marry. Just for this year, and I will pour so much gold into the coffers of your temple that you'll be able to gild Amur's holy image from head to toe."

His eyes narrowed a trifle. "The priesthood of the Sun Lord does not want for treasure or prestige, Majesty. The emperor's gifts are both frequent and ample, certainly dwarfing whatever largesse Erugash could manage."

She swallowed the fruit to give herself time to consider her next words. "Perhaps. It is known far and near that your sect enjoys the emperor's favor and the status that comes with it, but surely it must chafe."

He started to shake his head but stopped himself. "How do you mean?"

Byleth shrugged, allowing the front of her gown to gape open just a sliver. "Being at the behest of the imperial whim. The gods did not intend for men, even the mightiest of rulers, to reign over the houses of the holy. But if you were to grant my humble request, your order would find a most welcome home here in my city, free from burdensome laws and edicts."

"Majesty, allow me to be blunt?"

"By all means."

"We already control your city. The devotees of the Order of the Crimson Flame here in Erugash outnumber your court, and the temple soldiers are better armed and more experienced than any levies you have currently inside the city. Furthermore, on the eve of the *Tammuris* you *will* wed Prince Tatannu, and then we shall have everything we desire, a return to the old ways when your kind knew their place in the natural order—as servants of the empire, not its masters."

She felt the blush of heat running across her cheeks but refused to acknowledge the shame his words had inflicted. "And you would place yourself at the head of this new order, Menarch?"

"Our Lord Amur presides at the head, and all must serve *His* divine word or perish."

"All you say well may be true, but as a queen and the daughter of Rathammon et'Urdrammor, I can tell you that things change. Your well-laid plans may turn to ash before they bear fruit. Accept my offer and have the surety of a lasting bond between my House and your temple. Who knows? Perhaps someday Erugash will be the heart of Amur's worship, the envy of all other cities in the world."

Rimesh stood up. "Of that, Majesty, I have no doubt. We know the iniquity that lurks in the dark places of this city."

Byleth's heart nearly stopped at his words. Did the Sun Cult know about Astaptah and the storm engine? How could they? Unless they had a spy in her inner circle . . .

"And we know that if you are not the architect of the evil dwelling within Erugash, you surely have done nothing to root it out, and for that you will someday face Lord Amur's judgment. But until that time, the Temple of the Sun will seek out the wicked wherever they hide and deliver the proper justice."

Byleth stood up slowly, reaching out with her *zoana* as she got to her feet. Just a trickle. If her words could not convince him, then she would change his mind another way. She sent the power to burrow into the menarch's subconscious but frowned as she encountered resistance. She pushed harder, but her effort crumpled against what felt like an iron shield around his thoughts.

Rimesh reached up and pulled a chain out of his collar. The metal circle dangling from his fingers was covered in a spiral of dense runes. Byleth could feel her power ebbing away.

Zoahadin.

"A wise man takes every precaution," he said.

As she released her *zoana*, she was struck by his physical presence. Not since she was a small girl had she been intimidated by a man because of his size. He could probably kill her with his bare hands. He took a step toward her and then turned toward the door. "Good night, Byleth."

After he was gone, she broke into silent tears. The order to have him seized and executed on the spot hovered on the tip of her tongue, but they went unspoken as she collapsed on the divan. It wouldn't do any good. He had won. Her fate was sealed.

She looked up to the bust of her father set in a niche beside her household gods.

I've failed you, and soon our line will be extinguished by the priests you labored your entire life to bring down.

Idle thoughts entered her mind, of ending her life tonight to rob her foes of the pleasure of watching her brought to heel—a subtle venom mixed into her favorite vintage, and then never-ending slumber. She envisioned herself entombed beside her father's mastaba as the tears slid down her cheeks. *Is this my fate? To claw and fight my way to this point, and then have it all taken away? Is this what you foresaw, Father?*

She wiped her face with a pillow and called for her protector.

Lord Xantu entered the chamber from a side door. "You heard?" she asked as he stood before her.

"Yes, Majesty. I wanted to rip the pig's heart out of his chest."

"If only it was that simple."

"He could disappear. No one could prove I had anything to do with it."

Byleth smiled, wanting to laugh but too troubled to do so as she considered her shrinking list of options. "Barring some miracle, I must marry the Nisusi prince."

Xantu dropped to one knee at her feet. "Majesty, I beg you. Flee the city and travel to one of your remote holdings. Or take refuge in Haran. I will follow you anywhere, in this world or the next."

Overcome by his display, she touched his shoulder and bid him to rise. "You know I cannot. This is my fate. I accept that, and so must you."

"I will not!" he growled as he stood up. His face was contorted into a purple mask. "I will not stand by and watch this charade. You are a queen and—"

She shushed him with a smile. "You must. That is my command and my wish. You will make your peace with your new king. Go to him now and swear your everlasting fealty. Do this for me."

He stared at her for a long moment and then bowed low. Turning so fast his cloak billowed behind him, he strode out of her chamber, leaving her alone once again.

CHAPTER THIRTY-FOUR

The clamor sounded like thunder rolling out in one long, continuous boom. Horace looked up at the wooden ceiling and tried to imagine the hundreds of stomping feet above his head, but he was too lost in his thoughts to focus on anything external.

He stood alone in a long underground chamber where the gladiators prepared for their bouts. Wooden benches lined the walls. The floor was strewn with sawdust. Faint beams of morning light filtered through the cracks in the gate at the top of the ramp before him. In a few minutes, that gate would open, and then he would fight another man to the death.

He hadn't been nervous on his way over, but now that he was here a layer of sweat was forming across his forehead and under his arms. The words of the Prophet came to him. *Whoever takes a life shall forever more be tainted. All hands will be turned against him and all doors will be shut to him, and he will know the meaning of despair.*

He rocked his head from side to side to loosen the tight muscles in his neck. The cool weight of Lord Mulcibar's medallion bumped against his chest under his clothes. He'd decided to wear it for luck, even if it hadn't been particularly lucky for Mulcibar. He had returned to the nobleman's manor in the hours before dawn, only to find it locked up tight and no one answering the gate bell.

Wood creaked on old hinges as the gate opened, spilling daylight into the dank chamber. The roar of the crowd surged, drowning out everything else. Horace took a deep breath and started walking. Sand crunched under his sandals as he got to the top of the ramp. The pit of the arena was a vast oval, open to the morning sky. Tiered bleachers rose behind a stone wall.

Horace's stomach tightened when he saw the crowd of people, shouting and screaming and stamping their feet. He thought this would be a private duel, but evidently word had gotten out.

I suppose I shouldn't be surprised. It's not every day people get to see the queen's favorite pet fight for his life.

BLOOD AND IRON

He looked for Alyra and found her on the lowest row of seats. Surrounded by a sea of clapping, stomping citizens, she looked like she was about to cry. She hadn't reacted well to the news. In fact, he'd been shocked when she announced she was coming to the duel, despite his protestations.

Seeing her in the stands only made him realize how stupid he'd been. What was he fighting for? His honor? It didn't exist, not here and not back home anymore either. For the queen? Horace looked over Alyra's head to the covered box where Byleth sat with half a dozen of her court. The queen was leaning against a younger man in a bright-green tunic, smiling at whatever he was saying into her ear and not paying any attention to the spectacle below her. Horace released the breath he'd been holding without realizing it. What did he owe her? His life? His freedom? No, she might have the power to have him imprisoned or killed, but she didn't own him. If he was going to fight, he would have to do it for himself and by himself. Then Byleth glanced down and a look of sorrow flashed across her eyes. She blinked and it was gone, replaced once more by a mask of cool confidence.

A high-pitched creak cut through the cacophony. Across the pit, another gate rolled open. At first, the gaping tunnel beyond appeared empty, but then a lean figure strode into the light. Horace swallowed to moisten a throat suddenly gone dry. Lord Puzummu strutted into the arena in a tight-fitting suit of jet-black silk. The fabric rippled with every movement, making it look like he was wearing a slick second skin. A short cape hung from his shoulders, flapping gently as he turned in a slow circle, both arms raised to the crowd. The shouting and cheering elevated to a new level that made Horace want to crawl back down the tunnel. Yet a loud clang announced that the gate had closed behind him. "Once those gates shut," Pomuthus had told him on their way to the stadium, "they don't open again until someone is dead."

Let's get this over with.

A chorus of trumpets blasted. The people in the seats rose as one, and all eyes turned to the queen. Byleth stood up with a smile and lifted her arms. Her voice echoed through the stadium with the power of a hurricane. "People of Erugash, a challenge has been issued and answered. This day, Lord Puzummu of Ghirune—"

Cheers broke out amid the clapping of a thousand hands.

"—meets Lord Horace of Arnos—"

The applause turned to boos and jeers from the stands. A portly man in wine-colored robes flung insults about Horace's parentage from behind the retaining wall.

"—in sacred combat." The queen looked down and met Horace's gaze. "Only one of them shall leave this place alive. The other will rise to the heavens to take his place among the stars."

A procession of bald priests in robes of yellow and gold emerged from the far gate. Swinging incense burners and droning prayers, they made a slow circuit around the pit and left clouds of sweet smoke in their wake. By the time the procession walked all the way around the stadium floor and exited via the same gate, the sky had turned bright blue.

The trumpeters blew a shrill salute, and Byleth shouted, "Begin!"

Horace had been paying so much attention to the pageantry that he didn't notice the prickling along the back of his neck until a gust of wind slammed into him. Sand scoured his face and got in his mouth. Coughing as the grit entered his windpipe, he turned away. Something hard smashed into his lower back, sending a lance of pain shooting up his spine. Before he could right himself, another heavy force punched him in the shoulder, and he collapsed to the soft ground with the wind howling in his ears. With eyes closed tight against the flying sand, he fought to stand up, and a powerful grip seized him from behind and hurled him upward. His stomach turned somersaults as his feet left the ground. He flipped over and crashed back down in the sand, twisting his left ankle on impact. Something hit the ground beside him, showering him in more grit.

In a burst of anger, Horace ignored his throbbing ankle and rolled to his feet. It took him a moment to locate his opponent in the center of the pit, just outside the cloud of flying grit. Lines of blood dripped down the nobleman's hands from a pair of shallow immaculata. His face showed the strain of using his *zoana*, but there was also ecstasy in the nobleman's eyes, a cruel type of bliss that made Horace want to run. Instead, he opened the gateway of his *qa* as he'd been taught. Power rushed into him, as hot as molten steel. He unleashed it, and a section of ground on the other side of the arena exploded, raining sand across the pit. It hadn't been what he was trying for, but the explosion distracted Puzummu. The winds died down enough for Horace to draw a full breath. He reached out with his power with the idea of using it like a lasso to restrain his opponent, but before he could create it, a blade of red flames appeared in mid-air and slashed at him. Hot pain sizzled down the front of Horace's chest and knocked him to his knees.

Ripping the smoldering scraps of his shirt away, Horace focused on Puzummu. He tried to unleash the same energy he had used against the demons at the palace, but he couldn't seem to differentiate the sensations churning inside him. Dodging another sweep of the flaming sword, he just seized the power and lashed out. In an instant, the fiery weapon and the last of the winds vanished.

Horace scrambled to his feet. Puzummu stood a dozen paces away, glowering as he swayed back and forth, his arms pulled tightly to his body as if he were struggling against invisible bonds. Ribbons of blood ran down from gashes at his temples.

Horace's *qa* pulsated inside him, brimming with energy, but the power was elusive. It thwarted his efforts to seize hold of it. Lord Mulcibar had said the Shinar dominion was unpredictable, that no one living understood how to tame it, but right now he could have used some instructions. He tried to reach deeper into his *qa*, hoping to find some enlightenment, but let off when Puzummu howled. The sound wasn't anything Horace had ever heard from a human voice. The nobleman strained harder, the tendons in his neck bulging as he bellowed and pulled against the invisible cords. Horace tried to put more of his strength into the bindings, but he wasn't sure how. Just thinking about it didn't seem to do anything.

A terrific roar filled the arena as the winds picked up again. Puzummu's cape fluttered behind him as the sand at his feet began to stir. Knee-high ridges rotated around him in a circular pattern like a pinwheel. Horace braced himself as the winds swirled around him. They pulled him forward toward the churning sands, which were growing wider by the second. A hole had appeared under Puzummu's feet, dropping down into the ground beneath the *zoanii* while he levitated above it. The blood ran more freely down the nobleman's head, down his neck and into his shirt, but he didn't seem to notice. His eyes glowed with a faint yellow light as he continued to howl, and the moan of the wind rose in harmony with his voice.

Horace glanced up and saw the horror written on Alyra's face, and she wasn't alone. The crowd had stopped cheering. People on the lower tiers were moving back from the wall.

A boom like thunder crackled in the air. Horace staggered back and lost his concentration. He felt the bindings on his opponent slip away. Puzummu rose higher into the air, raising his arms as if welcoming the crowd. The ground beneath him had transformed into a spinning whirlpool, sucking sand into its maw. The wind swirled in the same direction, yanking Horace sideways. A cloud of sand showered over him. He screwed his eyes shut and tried to come up with a counterattack. The skin on the back of his neck writhed to the point where he wanted to reach back and claw it off.

He threw both hands out in front of him and poured out everything he had in one big push. He envisioned something like lightning bolts or a stream of fire, but all he saw was a mass of blurry lines like heat waves coming off a hot street. Puzummu convulsed as if he had been dunked in ice-water and fell to earth, barely missing the wide hole he'd created.

Horace gulped for air as the wind died down. He was feeling light-headed, and his stomach roiled like he'd swallowed a barrel of eels. He watched Puzummu crawl to his knees. A thin trickle of blood ran down the nobleman's chin from the corner of his mouth. With a muted growl, he raised a hand and curled his fingers into a fist. A gust of air buffeted Horace to his knees. Another sudden gust knocked him flat on his belly. The sand continued its swift descent into the whirlpool, sucking him along. Horace tried to push up onto his hands and knees, but he couldn't find any purchase. Taking a deep breath, he projected his power again and winced as a strange twinge erupted behind his forehead. He ignored the sensation, just wanting to end this nightmare, but his *zoana* didn't feel right. Instead of the energy flowing out of him, it felt like it was being yanked from his mental grasp.

The second-heart in his mind's eye thumped in a frantic rhythm, beating faster and faster. All the while, the wind battered him like iron fists, but he hardly felt it as terror seized hold of his brain. Echoes of his fights with the demons and the mud-monster flashed across his mind. Part of him was screaming to get up and continue the fight, but the rest just wanted it to be over. He was outmatched.

Horace fought through the fear and reached for his powers again. It was like trying to draw water from a nearly empty well. He pictured the magic seizing his opponent, but a blast of solid air clouted him in the nose, shooting pain through his skull. With blood running down the back of his throat, he made one last effort, raising his hand in the direction where he'd last seen his enemy. The *zoana* answered his call, running along his arm and out through his open palm.

The wind ceased and the sky reappeared, azure blue above the walls of the arena. Was it over?

A furious yell answered him, and Horace found himself back on his feet. He touched his nose. It was broken, but he wouldn't bleed to death. Puzummu stood just a few yards away. His face was remarkably pale and he appeared to be trembling, shaking so hard Horace expected to hear his teeth chatter. The nobleman raised his hand as if to—

Horace threw himself to the side as a bolt of blue-white lightning shot across the distance between them. The electricity sizzled along Horace's back and shoulder as the bolt missed him by inches. He almost tripped in the sand but caught himself, whirling around to keep sight of his enemy. Smoke rose from Lord Puzummu's blackened fingers as they followed his movement, like a hunting dog trailing its prey. Horace didn't know what to do. He was tired—physically and emotionally—and he just wanted this battle to be done. Puzummu had shaken off everything he had thrown at him, but he had enough strength left for one more attack. Horace took in a deep breath through his nostrils, feeling the power trickle inside him. He needed to get close. He needed a knockout punch. So he did the last thing he ever thought he would do. He charged.

Lord Puzummu smiled, revealing the hollows of his cheeks. The ends of his burnt fingers began to twitch. Sprinting at full speed, Horace delved into his *qa* for the Shinar as best he could, but it was like trying to catch the wind. He got a tiny hold on it, but there was no time for anything complicated. He shaped it like a spear, thin and sharp, and let it go.

At first, he didn't think the attack had any effect. A nimbus of crackling energy surrounded Puzummu's hand. Lightning flared like a second sunrise, its incandescence filling the arena pit. At the same moment, an intense cold burned against Horace's chest, but he barely noticed as he twisted out of the way of the blast. He landed face-first in the sand, arms extended to cushion his fall. He looked up, prepared to be cooked alive. Lord Puzummu stared back at him. Then a gout of bright blood spurted from the nobleman's shoulder as his right arm sheared away. He fell onto his side, blood pumping from the severed stump. His mouth opened and closed, but only a shallow groan emerged.

Horace wanted to throw up. Legs shaking, heart pounding, he teetered away from the fallen noble. Mulcibar's medallion was cool against his flesh.

The crowd stared down at him with barely a sound. Gone were the jeers and the catcalls, gone the cheers for his opponent. Alyra stood alone at the edge of the retaining wall, her face wet with tears.

Horace started the trudge toward the gate by which he had entered, but he hadn't gone ten steps before the queen's voice filled the stadium. "None shall leave," she said, "until one of the two combatants is dead."

He stopped and looked back. Lord Puzummu was lying on his side, somehow still alive and conscious even as blood soaked into the sand under him in a growing pool of crimson. Horace glanced up at the queen. Her eyes watched him as if she were desperately hungry. Like they wanted to reach down and pick him up.

"Then kill him yourself," he said. "Majesty."

Horace reached out with one hand, and the gate flew off its hinges with a loud snap. The dozen paces to the tunnel seemed to take him hours, but by the time he reached the shadowed ramp, the crowd had found its voice again. There were many boos, to be sure, but in the background he heard something else, a chorus of *"Belzama! Belzama!"*

The back of his neck tickled for a moment and then subsided as the trumpets blared.

CHAPTER THIRTY-FIVE

Birds trilled outside his window, announcing the beginning of a new day. Horace sat up and grimaced as a host of aches announced themselves. His chest was wrapped in bandages, as were several places on his arms and legs, and every inch of his skin felt like it had been scoured with a wire brush.

Alyra entered, carrying a covered tray. "*Sobhe'tid*, Horace."

He stifled a yawn. "What time is it?"

"Past time you were up and about." She lifted the cover to reveal a plate of sliced oranges with clotted cream, two cups, and a silver teapot.

As she poured the tea, a knock came from the door. Horace sat up as a servant woman named Murtha peeked inside. She fell to one knee at once. "Master Horace, men are here for you."

Horace stood up carefully to avoid taxing his sore muscles and reached for a robe hanging on the wall. "Is it news of Lord Mulcibar?"

Before the woman could reply, loud footsteps echoed in the hallway. The door opened farther to admit Pomuthus. "Priests have come, sire. From the Temple of Amur."

Horace pulled on the robe, wincing as the wounds across his chest flared up. Alyra helped him. Within minutes she had brushed out his hair, washed his face, and cleaned his teeth. Then she and Murtha took off his bedside robe and dressed him in fresh underclothes and a new robe of olive-green silk stitched with tiny gold birds.

"What do you think they want?" he asked as the women finished with him.

"I'm not sure," Alyra answered. "But be mindful of what you say."

"What's that supposed to mean?"

"You publically embarrassed the queen at the grand arena. It's an unforgivable offense among the *zoanii*. She could have you executed for less."

"I don't care. I'm not an assassin and no one is going to force me to kill a beaten man. Anyway, you keep telling me how valuable I am."

Alyra sighed. "Yes, well, today is *Tammuris*. Tensions will be high. Remember that you are a member of the court, which means you are due a certain amount of respect, but the cult of the Sun God is very powerful. The wrong word could put you in a great deal of trouble. And Her Majesty may not be as forgiving the next time."

"Thanks for putting me at ease."

Horace left, following Pomuthus down to the ground floor of the house. Two of his bodyguards stood at attention outside the parlor. Inside the room, men in yellow robes could be seen, standing quietly. Horace took a deep breath and went inside. Five men in priestly garments stood along the opposite side of the room. Their bald heads shone in the light coming through the glass doors that led out into the garden. One of the priests looked familiar, and Horace realized it was Rimesh, the official who had interrupted his first audience with the queen. It seemed like ages since he'd seen the man, but he was certain this was the same priest. He generated an aura of command like some ship captains Horace had known. He was holding one of the house's deity figurines.

"*Mina'ce shomana?*" Horace asked. *How can I help you?*

Rimesh put the idol back and replied in perfect Arnossi, "We can speak in your home tongue if it makes you more comfortable."

"Ah, thank you." Horace indicated the cushioned seats. "Please, sit."

Rimesh sat in a chair, but the rest of the priests remained standing. Horace eased himself down on a loveseat. "Would your comrades like to—?"

"No, thank you. We haven't met properly. I am Rimesh, envoy from the Temple of the Greatest Sun in Ceasa."

"The Greatest Sun?"

The priest apologized, though there was nothing deferential in his eyes or tone. "I forget you are a foreigner. That's a term we use to connote the rank of the various temples. The temple in Ceasa is the highest rank, the font from which all knowledge and authority flows."

It reminded Horace of everything else about Akeshian culture: the castes, the ranks of the *zoanii*. Everything was tightly regimented. "So what brings you to my home this morning?"

Rimesh smiled. It was thin-lipped with no teeth showing. "I have heard much about you and so decided I must meet you in person. It's rare for someone to rise so quickly to the heights of the royal court."

"Especially for a savage," Horace said, unable to help himself. There was something about this man, a conceit that oozed from his pores like a strong musk. The priests Horace had known back in Arnos were sometimes pompous in their station, but none had such an overpowering personality as this man.

"You misunderstand me. I have not come to preach but to learn from you."

Horace's stomach grumbled and he was thirsty enough to drink a river, but he had already decided he would starve before inviting these men to breakfast. "I've already told the queen everything I know about the plans of my countrymen, which wasn't much. I was just a—"

"A common sailor," Rimesh finished for him. "Yes, I've read the transcripts. I've read everything I could obtain about you, which is more than you might realize."

Horace wasn't sure what that was supposed to mean, but he was getting tired of this uninvited interview. "Sir, if you'll excuse me. I have much to—"

"Radiance."

"Pardon?"

"The correct term for an envoy of the temple is 'Your Radiance.'"

Horace cleared his throat and climbed to his feet to signal that the conversation was over. "I'll remember that."

He was about to call Pomuthus to show the priests out when the glass doors opened and his gardener entered. "Shulgi," Horace said, "this is not the right . . ."

Horace's voice trailed off as Shulgi took off his wide hat. Underneath was not the boil-covered countenance Horace expected. Instead it was a face he recognized at once, despite the missing mustache and beard. "Lord Isiratu? What in the hell . . . ?"

"Is it done?" Rimesh asked.

Isiratu nodded. Though he still wore the dirty clothes of a gardener, he stood tall with the haughty bearing Horace remembered so well. "*Manzazu leku'ima, Imaru.*"

355

BLOOD AND IRON

Horace froze, caught between panic and anger. The anger took precedence as he addressed the envoy. "I want an explanation. What is this man doing in my home?"

His throat went dry as the four attendant priests behind Rimesh dropped their outer vestments to reveal crimson robes underneath, and he realized there were now four priests of the Order of the Crimson Flame standing in his parlor. As Horace reached for his *qa*, a gust of wind knocked him on his back, and two arms of living stone burst through the carpet and clamped around his middle, holding him in place. As Horace struggled, there was a commotion behind him. Captain Pomuthus ran past. A sharp snap like a cracking whip split the air, and warm blood spattered Horace's face. Pomuthus fell to the floor beside him, the soldier's body cleanly separated in half at the waist as if by a colossal razor.

Horace felt his gorge rising as he struggled against the stone arms. They refused to budge, but he still had his *zoana*. He focused on Rimesh and lashed out, hoping that by taking out their leader the other priests would relent. Yet his power struck something in the way, a barrier that surrounded the envoy like a bubble. Horace threw all his strength against the unseen bulwark, but it resisted. Too late, he thought of trying to free himself with the power. Before he could even make the attempt, something unseen struck him behind his right ear.

Points of light swam before his eyes. He must have blacked out for a moment. His face hurt and blood leaked from his nose. The stone arms still gripped him, so tight he could hardly draw breath. Isiratu stood beside Rimesh, both of them watching him. Horace heard a muffled yelp and craned his neck as Alyra was dragged into the room by two Order sorcerers. A strip of green cloth gagged her mouth. Their gazes met, and his heart crawled up into his throat.

"I apologize for this indignity," Rimesh said. "Yet it has become necessary."

Horace strained to sit up, but he couldn't move an inch. "Let her go. I'll go quietly."

"We'll leave no witnesses today. Soon, the city will have forgotten about you. That will be for the best."

"What are you going to do with us?"

"You will be taken to—"

As Rimesh answered, Horace grabbed for the nothingness inside him and focused it into one mighty push. Not at the envoy, but toward the two sorcerers holding Alyra. Both red-robed men flew backward and slammed against the far wall. Freed, Alyra looked to Horace, but he yelled, "Run!" before an invisible gag filled his mouth. She fled, not toward the foyer as Horace had expected, but out the glass doors.

"Bind him!" Rimesh shouted.

A sorcerer knelt beside Horace and produced a pair of shackles. Horace's heart beat faster at the sight of the *zoahadin* cuffs. The Order priest reached for his arms, but Horace unleashed his power again. The sorcerer staggered back as if he had been kicked in the chest. As Horace started to form another attack, a powerful clout clipped him above the left temple. His vision dimmed for a moment, and he felt the cool touch of the shackles around his wrists before it cleared. Horace sagged against the floor as the *zoana* poured out of his veins, leaving him empty and weak.

"That was a foolish gesture that only delays the inevitable," Rimesh said. "And her end will be the crueler for it."

The envoy gestured, and one of the sorcerers went after Alyra. The stony arms released Horace, but before he could get up, the carpet rolled itself around him so tight he couldn't move anything except for his toes.

"Take him to the temple," Rimesh said. "And make sure the woman is eliminated."

The rolled carpet rose into the air and then started moving. Tucked inside, Horace could see only the circle of daylight above him.

As Horace was carried out the front door, he caught a glimpse of his bodyguards lying on the foyer floor, their armor shredded like bloody paper. Their sightless eyes followed him out into the morning light.

BLOOD AND IRON

Alyra held her breath as the Ordained Brother followed the garden path just a handful of paces past her hiding spot behind an origanum bush. She didn't know much about the Order's magicians, except that they were a secretive lot, trained by the cult of the Sun God to be utterly loyal and without fear. And they were extremely dangerous. As the Brother passed by, she wanted so badly to part the fronds of the bush and watch to be sure he wasn't coming back, but she didn't trust her hands not to shake and cause some noise.

Horace, thank you for giving me this chance to escape, but damn you to all the gods. I warned you time and again to be careful.

She gave a silent sigh.

You're as much to blame as he is. You got lax, Alyra. Now Horace is dead or soon will be, and you are hunted by magicians who won't hesitate to kill you on sight. So what's your plan?

A muted squeak came from the west end of the garden. When she fled the house, she had opened the wrought iron gate and slipped back inside, hoping to throw off any pursuit. She strained to listen, but the garden was quiet. Alyra counted to thirty and then counted it again. She had gotten to twenty-seven when she spotted the top of the Brother's bald head hurrying back in the direction of the house. She allowed herself a small sigh of relief.

She waited another couple minutes to be sure, but when no one emerged from the manor, Alyra slipped away through the garden. She had been happy for the short time she lived here, but that was over now. She exited the garden gate, looking both ways down the narrow avenue to be sure she wasn't being watched, but the only person she saw was a tiny old man in a broad hat shoveling offal into a wheelbarrow. She darted past him, heading deeper into the city.

It was almost midmorning, and she was able to slip into the crowd once she reached a main avenue. Her mind whirled as she tried to foment a plan to help Horace. She tried not to think of what she would do if he died.

Don't even consider it. He's alive! He has to be.

Her feet led her away from the storied manors of the palace district to the alleys of the Dredge and the house with the blue door between the *messhagan* trees. The old woman answered at once, as if she had been expecting a visitor.

CHAPTER THIRTY-SIX

The clacking of the winch echoed against the chamber's circular walls. Horace winced as he was lifted off the floor, the *zoahadin* cuffs digging into his wrists. The Order sorcerers who had been holding him upright stepped back and watched him hanging there. Horace stared back at them.

After being taken from his home, he had been placed in the back of a wagon and transported through the city. He wasn't able to see or hear much, still rolled up inside the carpet, but eventually the wagon stopped and he was carried into a building with a dry, musty smell. His bearers took him down several flights of steps, through heavy doors that boomed when they closed behind him, and along a dark corridor. The carpet was unrolled in a large, round chamber without windows, illuminated only by torches set on the stone walls.

Horace flexed his fingers, which were growing numb. He considered begging for his life, but he didn't think they would be receptive. Whatever they were going to do to him, there wasn't much he could do to stop it, not with these shackles blocking his access to the *zoana*. He just hoped that Alyra got away. She must have.

Horace looked around the chamber. They were clearly underground, and he had a good idea where. This had to be the Temple of the Sun, in the catacombs Queen Byleth had mentioned. There was a single door, a slab of dark iron that looked like it could stop a charging buffalo. Then he noticed a flat circle of bronze set in the floor beneath his feet. It was about three feet across and etched with some kind of markings. They were difficult to make out in the flickering torchlight, but he thought the designs might be some kind of script. Yet it wasn't Akeshian or any other language he knew.

The door opened, and a stocky man in a crimson robe entered the chamber. Horace took a deep breath as the former Lord Isiratu approached. With an imperious gesture, he motioned for the other sorcerers to leave, and they did, shutting the door behind them.

BLOOD AND IRON

Horace braced himself for anything—for torture, for a slow death, even for a tirade of accusations about how he was a savage and therefore unworthy to breathe the same air and so forth. Instead, Isiratu spoke in a low tone, almost a whisper. "The temple contacted me after I was stripped of my title. I had planned on returning to my ancestors' home to end my life, the last dignity afforded to me. However, the menarch convinced me that I might still have a place of honor in this world, if only I would assist them in eliminating you. I was pleased to accept."

Isiratu started to pace around the chamber. "Life is amusing, yes? Just a short time ago, I had you in my power. I could have put you to death anytime I wished. You escaped me for a time and rose to great heights. Yet now you are here, once again in my power, and I will have the privilege of sealing your doom. Thus, we will close the circle together."

Horace turned his head around to follow the fallen noble. Part of him wanted to shout, *Then get on with it, you miserable fuck!* But he wasn't so in love with the idea of dying that he was willing to throw away a chance to cling to life for a little while longer. He licked his dry lips. "So this is all about revenge? The queen took you down a few pegs, so now you use me to get back at her?"

Isiratu walked around to stand in front of Horace again. His brows came together in a dark line across his craggy forehead. "You wear the robes of a *zoanii* and have rank in the royal court, but you know nothing of our ways. Revenge is immaterial. The universe knows your crimes, whatever they are, and it will punish you according to your path. What I do now, I do to restore the balance between our lives."

Horace's brain was spinning as he tried to make sense of Isiratu's words. There must have been a problem in translation because he still didn't understand why this was happening.

Yes, you do. You always knew it had to end like this. You're a foreigner, a savage, at war with their country. What would Good King Fervold have done if an Akeshian soldier washed up in Wyr Bay? Give him a big house and a pat on the head? No, he would've had the man marched to Truficant Square and chopped his head off while the city cheered.

Isiratu raised his hand, and the bronze circle on the floor lifted away to reveal a black hole underneath. A cold draft rose from the pit, stinking of death and decaying things. Horace strained with his eyes, but he couldn't see what lay below. The darkness just kept going down and down. The winch began to unwind again, lowering him inch by inch.

"There are many things you do not know about our ways," Isiratu repeated. "How we deal with rogue *zoanii*, for instance. Now and again one of our rank decides to break away from his liege lord, to plant the seed of rebellion or seize by force what he has not earned. Such persons usually die violent deaths, as you can imagine, but when one is caught alive a problem is created. A *zoanii* cannot be executed like a common peasant. They can be stripped of rank." He touched his crimson chest. "And dismissed like an unwelcome guest, but public execution would send the wrong message to the people. The Temple of the Sun has a better way of dealing with undesirables."

The nobleman stepped to the edge of the pit. "This prison has been imbued to keep you alive without sustenance. I've been told that there are prisoners down here in the abattoirs that are almost as old as the temple itself, dwelling in darkness for centuries. They never perish, but they will live forever in solitude. I wonder, Lord Horace, how long will your mind survive before it snaps under the weight of an eternity spent alone?"

Horace's lower half was submerged in the pit. He looked up, trying to devise a clever insult that would haunt Isiratu for a long time to come, but all he managed was "You'll see me again."

Isiratu watched without comment or expression as Horace continued to drop.

The descent seemed to take forever as the chain clattered and the circle of light above Horace's head grew smaller. He tried pulling himself up with some half-formed notion of climbing the chain back to the surface, but his arms were too numb and his shoulders not strong enough to lift him that high. In the darkness he couldn't tell how far he was dropping, but it felt like miles before his toes touched something solid. He let out a deep breath as the strain on his aching wrists lessened. The chain stopped. Then something made a metallic clicking noise above him, and Horace's arms were released. He tried to reach up and grab the hook, but his shoulders were too tired and numb to react. By the time he could lift his arms above his head again, his fingers found nothing to grab. The chain rattled as it was swiftly drawn back up, taking the last of his hope with it. A few minutes later, the spot of light above him winked out as the pit was covered again.

He wanted to yell. Instead he collapsed on the hard ground, which turned out to be cold, slick stone. He sat cross-legged and let his head droop. Thoughts of Alyra and Sari and Josef, and even Jirom for some reason, floated through his mind, but mostly he thought about Isiratu's words. *I wonder how long will your mind survive before it snaps under the weight of an eternity spent alone?*

He didn't want to believe the man, but there hadn't been any malice in Isiratu's voice. Just cold, hard certainty. His stomach growled, reminding him that he hadn't eaten today.

Not today and not ever again. Will I just get hungrier and hungrier as the days pass by?

It was a horrible thought, and he couldn't help but imagine himself as an emaciated, pale beast slavering at the bottom of this pit. He was trying to put that image out of his head, too, when something moved behind him.

Horace turned to a faint sound like dry paper scraping across a brick. Then something heavy landed on his back, bearing him to the floor. Horace barely had time to cover his head before sharp points dug into his shoulders. The low growls in his ear sounded like a bobcat. Horace rolled sideways to throw the creature off and kicked out with both feet. His heels struck something solid, and the attacks let up, but only for a moment before the creature was on him again, clawing at his legs. Horace kicked again and missed, and then a heavy lump fell on his chest. Smooth hands, not furry paws, grabbing at him with long, clawed digits. A sharp point gouged his left cheek.

Horace yelled at the top of his lungs as he punched up with both shackled fists together. The thing grunted and slid off him. Caught up in his fear and frustration, Horace clambered after the creature, rolling on top of it. His hands found a scrawny neck and squeezed down. The creature thrashed about, but it could not dislodge him. As the seconds passed, its struggling became weaker. Hard nails clawed at his wrists, but the shackles protected him somewhat. The cables of the neck under his grasp vibrated and then went slack. Horace held on for several more minutes before releasing his grip. Then he fell back on the floor. He lay there, bathed in a cold sweat, and listened to the pounding of his heart. A morose curiosity compelled him to crawl back to the thing in the pit with him. It only took a few moments to confirm that the creature had been a person, small and wiry, and very definitely male. It was, or had been, roughly his height, though much thinner. In fact, it was extremely bony as if it hadn't eaten in . . .

This prison has been imbued to keep you alive without sustenance. I've been told that there are prisoners down here in the abattoirs that are almost as old as the temple itself, dwelling in darkness for centuries. They never perish, but they will live forever in solitude.

Horace scuttled away from the corpse. A scream rattled in his throat, but he clamped his lips together and refused to let it out, afraid that someone might hear.

No, I'll just stay quiet. Down here with the corpse of a magician they threw down here who-the-fuck-knows how long ago. That's what I'll become, a crazed, starving beast of a man. Then, someday they'll throw someone else down here, and I'll . . .

Horace cut off the thought and huddled against the wall with his face pressed to the hard bricks, as far away from the corpse as his prison would allow.

CHAPTER THIRTY-SEVEN

"**I**ncoming!"

Jirom ducked as a mule-sized boulder struck the ground not far from him, scattering sand and shrapnel in every direction. A blast of warm air washed over his position.

His unit had only been at Omikur for a day and a night, but it already felt like weeks. They arrived at first light and were marched directly to the trenches on the southern side of the town. An hour later, they were launched at the walls. That first attack was still vivid in Jirom's mind. They had been sent at the battlements in a screaming wave. Chariots pulled by swift onagers swept ahead of the infantry, the archers in their compartments firing on the wall's defenders before retreating. All the while, flaming missiles rained on the battlements.

Jirom got his squad to the base of the wall intact, only to be met by boiling pitch and rocks from the defenders. They tried to set up scaling ladders, but each attempt was beaten back. Eventually, they retreated under heavy fire, and an hour later they were sent to try again. By the midday meal break, the dead under the walls were piled as tall as a man. And so it had gone all day, until Jirom lost count of the number of attacks they'd been called upon to make. Yet he remembered exactly how many men he'd lost. He spoke their names in his head.

Herstunef. Appan. Enusat. Udar the Younger.

Only four men, but each one felt like a personal failure. Throughout the fighting, Jirom had struggled to keep a cool head, even as his body shook at times with the desire to lash out. He held his rage in check for the good of his men and cursed Emanon with every second breath for putting him in charge.

As the sun set, the soldiers found what rest they could amid the trenches. Jirom had been about to visit the wounded when the first boom of thunder struck. It was just like the night before. Storm clouds appeared out of a clear sky to cover the town. The winds whipped up, and within minutes the lightning began. The display had been disturbing from several miles away; this close to the target, it was terrifying. Soldiers shouted with their hands pressed over their ears as bolts of green lightning shot down from the heavens.

Jirom kept his head down. The past couple days had reminded him of the worst parts of his soldiering days, of the senseless slaughter that filled his brain with bloody images that refused to leave. He didn't notice that Emanon had joined them until he was tapped on the shoulder.

"Where have you been?" Jirom hadn't meant to bark, but his voice was raw from shouting all day and his patience had expired.

"Taking care of business. How's it going here?"

"How do you think? We're getting butchered." Jirom watched the electrical storm wreak its destruction over the town. "Is this every night?"

"Aye. The lads from the Third say it's been going on for over a week now. The storm arrives every night at sunset, lasts for about a turn of an hourglass, and then—poof—vanishes."

Jirom grit his teeth as a bolt of lightning flashed outside the walls, only a spear's throw from the trench where he sat. The thunder was immediate and deafening. "I've never seen such a thing. How can they survive in there?"

He hadn't meant for the question to be heard, but Emanon answered. "Those western lads are half-crazy to begin with, coming all this way to fight over a desert. But they won't crack."

They must be men of iron, with molten steel in their veins.

Jirom shot a glance back through the lines to the sea of tents where a large portion of the legion was camped, safely out of range of the town's defenses. It hadn't taken the dog-soldiers long to realize they were being fed to the invaders in droves while the "real" soldiers were kept out of the fray. He couldn't help himself from adding, "Is this all part of the plan?"

"Not exactly." Emanon looked up at the opaque sky. "I was hoping they would—"

Thunder crashed above them as a barrage of lightning strikes illuminated the town.

"I was hoping they would wait a little longer before throwing us at the walls," the rebel captain finished. "This is too soon."

"Too soon for what?" When Emanon didn't reply, Jirom leaned closer until their noses were almost touching. "What have you got planned?"

Emanon's lupine grin faltered. "All right, but keep this to yourself. It was all part of the scheme—to convince Queen Byleth to send as many of her legions as possible out here in the open desert." The smile returned. "And now we can crush them."

Jirom's mouth fell open. He couldn't believe what he had just heard. This man, whom he had chosen to follow, was obviously insane. "Crush them?! Didn't you hear me? We're getting massacred out here. We won't last another day! And the queen's army must number in the—"

Emanon put a hand on his shoulder and squeezed gently. "Calm down, Jirom. Trust me. I'm working on it. Just stay put for now. And remember to be—"

"Go play nursemaid to somebody else," Jirom said without looking at the captain.

Emanon left as quietly as he had arrived. The storm continued for an hour before it departed. Jirom watched the disappearing clouds, wondering what could be causing this occurrence. He had lived in Akeshia long enough to know that such storms were unpredictable, striking anywhere at any time. He had never heard of a storm that reappeared night after night at the same location.

It must be the gods of this land, trying to drive out the foreigners.

Czachur appeared above the trench. Jirom grabbed him by the arm and hauled him down behind the wall of wood-reinforced sand. "Keep your head down."

Czachur plopped down on the ground and removed his iron helmet. Jirom opened his canteen, and they both had a drink of tepid water. Jirom was tempted to upend what little was left over his head to wash away the grime and sweat, but he capped the container and put it away.

"It's damned hard to find you guys out here, especially in the dark," Czachur said. "I wish they would've given me a torch."

"If you had a torch, someone would've put an arrow through you by now."

The rebel laughed. "Huh, yeah. I didn't think of that."

BLOOD AND IRON

"What's the news?"

"You won't like it. The Lord High-And-Mighty General has ordered another assault."

Jirom didn't need to look at his men to know their expressions. They were beyond exhausted and almost beyond caring at this point. He had been in too many sieges, on both sides, to hold much hope. They were fodder, meant only for wearing down the enemy. They would be flung at the walls again and again until they were all dead. Then the real assault would take place.

"How long do we have?"

"There will be a signal. They wouldn't tell me what it was, but they said to watch the sky. When it comes, we're supposed to charge with everything we have."

Back into the maw of death.

Jirom looked to the ramparts again. They looked as unassailable as before, an impossible mountain to climb without proper siege equipment and a few months to invest in more extensive siegeworks. A nighttime charge would be suicide. "All right," he said. "Head back to the command tent."

The youth looked over, his feathery eyebrows raised in a steeple. "What? I just got here."

"So turn your ass around and go back."

"No! My place is here with the platoon."

Jirom gave him points for loyalty, but he didn't care. He glanced away so he didn't have to see the kid's eyes, like moons of polished onyx. "Fuck your place. One of us is going to survive this battle, you hear?"

"What if I won't? What if I stay here no matter what you say?"

Jirom drew the long dagger sheathed at his belt and slammed it into the ground between them. "Then I'll kill you myself for refusing to follow an order."

Czachur took a deep breath like he wanted to continue the argument, but he held his tongue. Jirom let him say good-bye to the others, most of whom just nodded without saying anything, before chasing him off. He felt better seeing the youth's willowy frame disappear into the gloom.

A party of horsemen rode up, their riding tack jingling as they stopped behind the trenches. *Kapikul* Hazael peered at the city through the gathering gloom and then turned to his officers. Not wanting to look at the commander, Jirom focused on the walls. They were four hundred yards away—not a long walk, but it felt like miles when enemy fire was whistling past your ears. On the last assault, a firepot had exploded on the battlements right above where Jirom and his unit had been trying to set their ladders. The liquid fire that rained down had enveloped two of his men, burning them alive. Jirom could still smell their roasted flesh. Oddly, though, he couldn't remember if they had screamed before they finally died. They must have, but he had no memory of it.

Partha crawled over to him. His eyes rose to the officers behind them. "Looks like bad news."

"Watch the sky. We're supposed to see a—"

Jirom nearly bit off the tip of his tongue as a titanic crash boomed over their heads. A fresh bolt of vomit-green lightning split the darkness. Stone burst asunder and men fell from the battlements where a hole as big as a wagon gaped in the town's curtain wall directly across from them.

"Holy god of fucking and shitting," Partha whispered and touched his forehead.

Whistles blew down the line. Jirom picked up his shield and stood, trying not to wince as the pain in his lower back flared up from sitting too long. "That's our signal! On your feet!"

Jirom shouted to be heard over the cacophony of thunder that boomed overhead as more lightning struck in and around the town. His men, to their credit, stood ready. Clutching their spears, they looked to him. Hazael and his officers made no move to join the attack. They watched from atop their steeds as the infantry troopers poured out of the trenches.

Despite his doubts, Jirom's training took over. Part of him wanted to dive for any bit of shelter until the storm departed, but his men were counting on him. He might not give a damn about the higher-ups and their war, but he wasn't about to let his soldiers down. "Leave the ladders! Stay on my ass and stick together!"

Jirom's boots kicked up clods of sand as he climbed out of the trench. Every sense came into sharper focus as he ran toward the objective. The smell of woodsmoke and sweat, the brush of warm air across the back of his neck, the sound of his heartbeat in his ears. The town swelled before him, its skyline framed by banks of black clouds, but he concentrated his sight on the breach. If he and his men could reach it, they'd have a fighting chance. Or so he told himself.

He hadn't gone fifty paces before the first arrow buried itself in the sand at his feet. Jirom kept moving, breathing in short huffs through his mouth. Something buzzed past his face, too fast to make out in the dark. He lifted the shield above his head. It would have helped to have decent armor instead of the thin leather cuirass he'd been given. Neither it nor the padded leather strapped to his calves would stop an arrow, but the shield was sturdy bronze over a rectangular wooden frame.

Jirom's heartbeat quickened as he approached the midway point between the trenches and the town. Sweat ran down his chest and back, making the leather shirt slick again his skin. More arrows flew overhead. He started to look back to make sure his crew was still following when a flash of green light blasted his eyes. He was lifted up by an irresistible force and hurled forward. Gravel dug into his knees and elbows as he landed. Blinking away the swarm of tiny lights dancing in his vision, Jirom rolled onto his side. Everything had become deathly quiet. Then he realized he was deaf. Shaking his head, he used his spear like a staff to climb to one knee. His hearing returned after a couple moments with the faint roll of thunder above. Jirom raised his spear to wave his crew onward and looked back to find them scattered around a smoking crater, their armor split open and blackened from the lightning strike. Jirom staggered back. He knelt on the blasted sand and checked them over for signs of life. A pain went through his chest when he rolled Czachur over. The flesh hung from the young man's face in bloody ribbons, his eyelids torn off and his eyes scoured to red patches.

I knew you wouldn't listen, and now you're dead. All of you, dead.

Rage bubbled up inside him like an old friend, threatening to wash away the last shreds of his self-control. The palms of his hands itched. Then a movement caught his attention. An arm twitched on the other side of Czachur's body. It was Partha, half-buried in the sand. Jirom dropped his shield and helped the man sit up.

"What the hell was that?" Partha asked in a hoarse voice.

Thunder bellowed above them as Jirom pulled the rebel fighter to his feet and started to lead him back toward the trenches. "The storm isn't playing favorites."

"Where are we going?"

"The field hospital."

Partha dug in his heels, or tried to. Jirom held tight to keep him from falling. "Stand up, dammit!"

Partha twisted back around. Another burst of thunder swallowed his words, but Jirom could see the angry refusal written across his face. "—to the walls."

Jirom heaved the soldier over his shoulder. "We've done enough today!"

He started to carry Partha back to the trenches but halted in mid-stride when he saw a roiling disturbance rip through the ranks of legionnaires lined up to assault the town. At first, it looked like a riot had broken out, and he wondered if the soldiers were refusing to march into the fight. Then he spotted a soldier collapsing as if his legs had turned to water. Behind the fallen legionnaire stood a man in sand-colored garb—a long-sleeved coat over breeches tucked into his tall boots. The killer held up a sickle-bladed knife, slick with blood, and leapt to attack another soldier.

Jirom didn't know what to do. The fighting among the ranks was fierce, but he wasn't sure which side to support. Loyalty to his fellow soldier had been drummed into him for decades, but he had no love for the Akeshii. He almost heaved a sigh of relief when he sighted Emanon ducking through the mob.

"You still alive?" Emanon asked. Jerkul and a few other rebel soldiers followed the captain, pulling a handcart.

"You sound surprised. Where have you been?"

"Getting things ready." Emanon examined Partha for a moment and then shook his head. "Is he the only one from your unit still alive?"

"Yes." The admission was bitter.

"We're making our move. Several members of the royal court are in camp to observe the assault. We're going to take them out."

"Now?"

BLOOD AND IRON

The rattle of massive chains filled the air as the town's nearest gate opened, and a river of armored men rushed out, their banners whipping in the wind.

Emanon grunted a quick laugh as he studied the emerging crusaders. "I didn't know if my message got through, but it looks like someone inside was ready."

Jirom's head was spinning. Between the sudden appearance of the desert fighters and the sallying defenders, he didn't know what to say. He looked at Emanon with new admiration, even as a part of him wondered if the rebel captain had a heart of coal. "You did all of this?"

"I had a little help. Now we need to move."

At a nod from their leader, the rebels lifted Partha into the cart along with a couple of other injured soldiers. "We'll haul them over to the infirmary tent."

The storm continued to rain down its violent assault, raking over both the town and the battling armies on the field. Emanon's crew skirted the fighting, gathering up more wounded men into the cart as part of their act as they trundled through the camp. When they reached the infirmary, which as yet had not been targeted by the desert warriors, Jirom helped unload their cargo. Injured soldiers were laid out on the ground outside the hospital tent. Many were badly burned; others bled from arrow wounds and smashed limbs. Their moans filled the night with a gloomy lament, but the screams coming from inside the tent, raw and filled with agony, sounded even worse.

Emanon gathered his men behind the cart. Weapons emerged from the vehicle. Bows and quivers of arrows, javelins and lances. Emanon handed Jirom a demi-lance with a bright-silver head. "Here. Try this."

Jirom dropped his army-issue weapon and accepted the replacement. Its shining tip caught the distant fires and sparkled in the dark. When everyone was armed, Emanon led them away between rows of canvas tents. Unlike the makeshift shelters built by the slave-soldiers in the trenches, this part of the encampment was neat and orderly. Jirom followed at the rear. He still couldn't believe what he had seen. What else had Emanon been keeping from him? How far could he really trust this man?

The rebels stopped at the end of the row. The command pavilion stood a stone's throw from their position, surrounded by a cordon of sentries. Flames licked the gusty air from torches staked outside the door flap.

Jirom stalked up beside Emanon. "Do you know how many are inside?" he whispered.

"The Lord General and his three captains. Plus four *zoanii* from Erugash."

Mention of the city made Jirom think of Horace. Something must have flashed across his face, because Emanon leaned closer. "Don't worry. Your friend isn't among them."

Jirom nodded. Eight men inside, four of them sorcerers. Add to that the ten or so sentinels outside the tent. He counted twenty-two rebels in the group, including him and Emanon. Slim odds. "We need more men for this. The risk is too great."

Emanon's teeth gleamed in the night. "That's not plain steel on the end of that pig-sticker."

The rebel fighters with bows were bending them, aiming silver-headed arrows at the pavilion. The rest of the rebels gathered into a knot, their weapons likewise glowing in the intermittent light. Emanon drew a sword from the scabbard on his hip. Jirom half-expected the blade of the weapon to be *zoahadin*, but it appeared to be ordinary steel. Jirom held out his lance to the rebel captain, but Emanon shook his head.

The signal was a low whistle. The archers let fly, sending their arrows through the thin material of the pavilion. The bowmen reloaded and continued shooting even as shouts rose from inside the great tent. Emanon waved, and the rest of the rebels charged forward.

Jirom hesitated. Was this the right path? He couldn't be sure. Yet, when the first death-scream pierced the night air, he lowered his weapon and ran forward to join his comrades, for better or worse.

The sentries fanned out to meet the attack. A soldier charged at Jirom with a drawn sword held in both hands. Jirom dropped into a low stance and thrust. The lance's brilliant point snapped iron scales as it drove into the soldier's stomach. His attacker fell back, screaming like an exotic bird with both hands clutching the new hole in his belly. The demi-lance came free like it was eager for more, but Jirom stepped away as more shapes appeared around him.

He batted aside a bronze-headed mace aimed at his face and responded with the butt of his weapon to the soldier's temple, which didn't drop the man but slowed him down long enough for Jirom to reset and lunge. He struck the soldier in the chest, but the man's armor held, and only the tip of the lance penetrated. Before Jirom could make a second thrust, a bearded axe swung at his head. He caught the blow on the shaft of his weapon and wrenched its wielder off-balance. He skewered the axe-wielder through the throat one-handed and was pulling back for another thrust when a hard blow hit him in the back. The lance fell from his hand.

With painful tingles running up his spine, Jirom pulled the axe from the dying soldier's hand, spun it around, and buried the head in the shoulder of the man behind him. Warm blood splashed across Jirom's face and neck as he wrenched the axe free and whirled around to find a new foe, but the soldiers surrounding the pavilion were all down, along with two rebel fighters. Emanon slashed open the tent wall and leapt inside. Jirom followed on his heels.

A lamp had fallen over on a large bronzewood table at the center of the pavilion, leaking burning oil across a parchment map. Light also came from flaming braziers in the corners of the single room, one of which had been knocked over. An older man with short, gray hair lay beside the toppled brazier, both hands around the shaft of the arrow protruding from his stomach. Three other men were scattered on the floor around the table, but four were still on their feet, including a middle-aged man with receding hair in gold scale armor and a pair of courtiers in silken raiment. Emanon jumped over the table, swinging his sword at the general.

Jirom's entire body tingled as he ran up to assist, and a gush of water wrapped around his middle like a great constrictor snake. The air rushed out of his lungs as his insides were crushed under the sudden pressure. While his legs shook under the tremendous weight, he spotted one of the courtiers staring at him with fierce concentration. Wishing he had brought the lance instead, Jirom shuffled toward the sorcerer. The other courtier started to raise his hands, but then an arrow sprouted from his chest and he went down with a pitiful groan. Jirom strained to take another step. The watery appendage was dragging him down as it squeezed. With a grunt, he twisted his shoulders and threw. The axe flew from his hands to split the face of the sorcerer attacking him. The water fell away, and Jirom dropped to one knee on the drenched carpet, his breath coming in labored gulps. His hands shook as he forced himself to stand up.

Emanon pulled his sword from the Akeshian general's chest. Moving around the burning table, Jirom stooped to pick up a fallen tulwar. It was heavy but well-balanced with a keen edge. He looked around, but none of the dead were Hazael. "The *kapikul's* not here."

Emanon frowned as he kicked over a fallen courtier. "He was supposed to be. I won't feel right until that snake is dealt—"

A blur sliced through the tent wall. One of the rebel soldiers, Eiger, collapsed.

"Down!" Jirom shouted as he dropped to his stomach.

Crossbow bolts whizzed through the air. Emanon lay beside him, their noses inches apart. The rebel captain's face was grim.

"I'm guessing this wasn't part of your plan?"

Emanon answered with a grunt. Jirom tried to estimate how many shooters were firing from outside. It had to be at least half a dozen. Their ambush had been ambushed. "We need to get out of here."

The crossbow fire hesitated, replaced by the sounds of clashing steel from outside the pavilion. With a roar, Emanon jumped up and raced for the tear in the cloth wall. With an uneasy feeling in his stomach, Jirom ran after him. They plunged into a chaotic brawl. Emanon's remaining men were locked into combat with a score of soldiers. Near the rows of tents, a squad of arbalesters was reloading furiously. A familiar figure sat above the fray on his brown mare, *assurana* sword flashing in the lightning barrage that continued over the town.

Jirom followed Emanon toward the crossbowmen, but a heavyset Akeshian soldier leapt in his way. Jirom lashed out with a horizontal slash. Blood spurted from the severed stump of the soldier's wrist, but Jirom was already moving past him. Emanon had cut down a pair of arbalesters before he joined him. A bolt shot between Jirom's legs, almost hitting his left kneecap, and he cut down the shooter with an overhead strike. The tulwar clove through the soldier's shoulder and got struck in the links of armor as he fell. As Jirom used both hands to wrench it loose, a wooden stock connected with his chin, knocking him back a step. A red veil dropped over his vision as he returned a vicious thrust. The tulwar's point pierced armor and flesh to spill his attacker's entrails to the bloody ground.

Jirom's lungs heaved as he turned around. Emanon stood a few steps away, his sword dripping with fresh blood. Just past the rebel captain, *Kapikul* Hazael leaned low in his saddle as he rode toward them. An intense heat flared up inside Jirom's chest like he had downed a bottle of Haranian fire spirits, searing his lungs with every breath. It was the old rage, the inner demon that had plagued him all his life. It pressed against his skin, clawing to get out. Jirom clenched the tulwar's hilt tight in both hands as Hazael's *assurana* sword swept down in a smooth arc, and he flinched when blood sprayed. But then he saw Emanon diving away from the horse's churning hooves. A young rebel fighter from Jerkul's squad collapsed behind him without a head.

Jirom felt a rumbling in his chest that drowned out the fury of the storm in his ears. His sight dimmed, and his hands went numb. All his fear vanished, melting away like morning mist, as he started to run.

CHAPTER THIRTY-EIGHT

Cracks riddled the walls of the pit. Droplets of condensation collected in these crevices. Horace wriggled his tongue inside those he could reach. It was maddeningly slow work drawing out the water drop by drop, but he didn't have much else to do.

Darkness defined his existence. He had spent a long time huddled on the floor of the pit, battered by thoughts of what would become of him. But after an hour, or five hours—time was impossible to track down here—he forced himself to move around. He avoided the center of the floor where the former occupant had tried to kill him, instead pacing around the circular wall on stiff legs, his right hand keeping contact with the rough brickwork.

The pit wasn't very large, perhaps twenty feet across. He didn't expect to find any handholds in the wall, but he couldn't resist searching for some anyway. He discovered a couple spots where the exterior brick had crumbled away to make rectangular holes, but they were down at knee-height. Reaching into one of them, he found a handful of spiky pebbles. He was putting them back when he realized he was handling teeth. Human teeth. He dropped them and wiped his hands on his shirt, and thereafter he avoided sticking his hands into the small holes. That is, until he found a crack running down the wall. It was too narrow to use for climbing, but his fingers felt the dampness within.

At times he slept and suffered dreams in which he was blind or crazed or both, dreams in which he was the last person in the world, alone in a vast nothingness. He woke from one of these dreams thinking he'd heard a familiar voice. The words were too soft to make out, but he thought it might have been Lord Mulcibar talking. Sitting in the dark, his arms wrapped around his knees, he wondered if Lord Mulcibar was languishing down in one of these abattoirs as well. The nobleman might even be nearby, separated by as little as a few yards of earth and stone, yet so unreachable he might as well have been on the far side of the world. Horace strained to hear the voice again, but the pit was silent except for the sound of his own breathing. He pushed his forehead against the brick wall.

BLOOD AND IRON

God, why are you doing this to me? Wasn't taking my wife and my son enough? What else do you want? Will you make me suffer until I grovel like a worm? Is that what you need?

Horace shook his head back and forth as a wave of bile rose up inside him, driven by an anger so hot he couldn't contain it.

No! Fuck you and all your saints. I gave you my heart and my soul, and you've never given me back anything except pain. You took Sari and Josef from me, and then you cast me to my enemies.

The words echoed off the walls, and Horace realized he had been muttering out loud. He squinted, trying to see anything in the darkness, but everything was black. He might as well have been blind. The cold was beginning to sink into his bones, making his teeth chatter. The understanding that this was how he would spend the rest of his life, however long or short, motivated him to keep looking for a way out. He shook his wrists, making the shackles chatter. The first step was getting rid of these chains.

He searched for something to help him get the shackles off, but all he could find on the pit floor were slivers of broken brick that were too small and crumbly to be useful. In fact, the more he examined the cuffs, he more he came to realize that he would need a hammer and chisel to break them. The metal was strong, and the chain links joining the cuffs were too thick to break with anything less. He felt the keyholes that locked the cuffs. If only he had a key.

Horace lifted his shirt and felt for his waist. He was still wearing his belt, the length of supple leather joined with a bronze buckle. Taking it off, he sat on the floor and inserted the buckle's thin prong into the keyhole of his left cuff. He twisted it around for several minutes, trying to trip the lock, until his fingers and wrists were sore. Frustrated, he jimmied it harder and dug the prong deeper into the lock with each thrust, until a tiny sound made him freeze. He felt the buckle, and his heart sank into his stomach. The post had broken off.

Horace threw the belt down and covered his face with his hands. It was hopeless. He wasn't a burglar. He was just a—

A simple shipbuilder, right? You've been telling everyone that, but you know it's not the truth. Once, you were a husband and a father, but you let them go and now you're nothing but a failure. Death is all you deserve, so just lie down and close your eyes until it takes you. Or better yet, bash your head against these walls and end it.

He jumped to his feet, ready to give in to his conscience. He raised his head and froze. A light had appeared above him, a tiny circle of yellow. He held still, not even daring to breathe, as a distant sound reached his ears. The jangling of a chain.

A dozen scenarios played through his mind as he listened to the noises. Had Isiratu returned to torment him some more, or was this some new torture? The lowering of the chain seemed to take forever, and every second Horace feared the priests would stop and pull it back up. By the time he could see the links swinging above him, his hands were clenched into hard, shaking fists. Then the jangling stopped. The hook at the end was three feet above his head.

You rotten sons of—

"Grab onto it!" a voice cried from above.

Horace's breath exploded from his lungs as the woman's voice touched his ears. For a moment, he thought it was Sari calling for him, even though he knew that was impossible. Tears came to his eyes as his sorrow was swallowed by a burst of joy. "Alyra?"

"Horace! Grab the chain and we'll pull you up!"

"I can't! I can't reach it yet!"

Moments passed, and then the chain was lowered to within his grasp. He pulled himself up until he could put a foot in the hook. "Got it!"

A giddy sensation filled Horace as he was lifted up the dark shaft of the pit. His fears of spending an eternity in solitude evaporated, replaced by concerns for his immediate future. As soon as he reached the top, he clambered out and pulled Alyra into a tight embrace. She went rigid in his arms, but only for a moment, and then she melted against him. He was content to bury his face in her hair.

Thank you, thank you, thank you.

He wasn't sure who he was thanking—God or the pagan idols that ruled this murky land, or some other power entirely—but he let his gratefulness fill him up. "How did you get down here?"

"I had to bring someone."

BLOOD AND IRON

Dread washed over Horace as a tall man in black robes stepped out of the shadows by the door. "There are many secrets under Erugash," a deep voice intoned. "And the adherents of the Sun God do not know them all."

Horace forced himself to meet his savior's gaze. "Lord Astaptah. You might be the last person I expected to see here."

"He was the only one I could find who was willing to help," Alyra said.

Horace held out his hand. "You have my thanks, my lord. But I must ask why you would put yourself at such risk for someone you barely know."

Lord Astaptah glanced at the proffered hand but did not move to take it. Although they were almost the same height, the vizier seemed to loom taller. His eyes gleamed like discs of electrum in their deep-set sockets. "Today the queen is to wed and lose her status as ruler of this city," the vizier said. "A circumstance I much desire to prevent. This one convinced me that you would assist my efforts to prevent that from happening."

Horace looked to Alyra, who was biting her bottom lip. "I see. You were informed correctly. I would help the queen if I can. What do you propose?"

Astaptah reached out and seized Horace's hands. With quick movements, he opened the shackles with a brass key and tossed them into the pit. Horace rubbed his wrists. The skin was broken and raw, but as soon as the cuffs were removed he felt his power return in a surge that made him light-headed.

"The ceremony has already begun," Lord Astaptah said. "And the priests will not willingly allow it to be stopped. Therefore, force is in order."

"You mean fighting them. The priests."

Lord Astaptah drew his hands up into the long sleeves of his robe. "If you would save the queen, yes."

Horace resisted the urge to look down into the pit. Unless they did something, he would be sent back down there and Byleth would die at the hands of her husband, the new king of Erugash. He looked to Alyra. "Is this what you would have me do?"

"I don't know," she answered. "The queen has shown little love for the common people of her realm, but the Sun Cult won't stop here. With Ceasa and Nisus and now Erugash under their control, their power throughout the empire will become absolute. I fear what that may mean for all our futures."

Horace considered it. Arnos and the other western nations had enough trouble fighting a divided Akeshia. How would they fare against an empire united under the banner of a pagan religion? He thought back to the destruction of Omikur. "Fine. I'll do it, but first we must find Lord Mulcibar. I think he's being kept in one of these pits."

Astaptah's dark brows came together in a fierce line, making him look even more menacing in the dim light. "That was not the bargain. The lady insisted that, once liberated, you would assist me in disrupting the nuptials. To do that, we must go now. Once the vows are spoken, nothing we do will change the fate of this city."

Astaptah strode out of the chamber before he could answer. Horace ground his teeth together. He had just been saved from a fate possibly worse than death, and now he was being asked to let a friend suffer that same doom without doing anything to help him. But what choice did he have? If Byleth married and control of Erugash passed to her cult-puppet husband, everything was over.

Telling himself that it was what Mulcibar would have wanted, Horace started to follow the vizier out, but Alyra grabbed his arm. "Wait. I need to tell you something. I'm sorry for lying to you. It hasn't been easy these past few years. I didn't know if I could trust you. And I didn't want to put you at risk."

Horace placed his hand over hers. "You did what you thought was right, and I don't blame you. When I was down in that hole, the thing I regretted most was that I wouldn't see you again. This feels like a second chance at life. A chance to do things better."

"Horace, I—"

He cut her off. "That's why I need you to do something for me. I want you to get out of here and find a place to hide. Just lay low until this is over, and it wouldn't hurt to be ready to flee the city if things go badly."

"No, I'm not leaving without you."

He wanted to shake her but instead placed his hands lightly on her shoulders. "I can't do this—go up there and fight—unless I know you're safe. Please, do it for me."

"This was my fight before you set foot on Akeshian soil, Horace. I won't leave now."

Seeing the intensity in her eyes, he relented. "All right. But you'll stay close to me, right?"

"There's one more thing. Your friend Jirom. I met him."

"You did? Where is he? Is he all right?"

"He's a soldier in the queen's legions. The last I heard, he was marching northwest."

"Omikur," Horace whispered to himself. Then, louder, "All right. We'll worry about that later. Right now, we need to help the queen, or all this is for nothing."

They left the chamber together, out the door and down a dark corridor. Alyra had brought a small lantern. She clutched his arm with her other hand as they walked together, and he was grateful for the contact.

They arrived at a flight of steps. Alyra started up, but Horace hesitated, suddenly not feeling well. He put a hand on his chest. His heart was pounding. He looked to Alyra, so beautiful in the ethereal light. Now he had something to lose again, and it scared him to death.

"Horace?" she asked. "Are you all right?"

"Fine." He cleared his throat. "I'm fine. Let's go."

They caught up with Lord Astaptah at the top of the stairs. The vizier stood at the entry to a broad hallway with his head cocked slightly to one side, as if he were listening intently. Horace and Alyra stepped up beside him without saying anything. Horace looked about, trying to determine their position inside the temple. Colorful frescoes decorated the walls and arched ceiling, illuminated by glowing orbs on bronze sconces. They were probably on the ground floor of the main temple structure, but the place was huge. Then he heard something. The distant beat of a drum. He held his breath and strained to hear more. High-pitched notes danced in the air. Pipes, perhaps, but it was definitely music.

They passed a side corridor, down which Horace saw a high oriel window. By the hazy orange cast of the light coming in, it was almost sunset. Astaptah stopped on the threshold of a large chamber. They had reached the temple's grand atrium. A cluster of temple guards stood beside a gushing marble fountain in the center of the chamber, with two red-robed priests in their midst.

Astaptah held up a black cube about the size of a chicken egg. Its sides gleamed with a mirror finish. Horace felt something emanating from it, like a front of cold air, but for some reason it made him sweat. He wanted to ask what it was, but Astaptah threw the black cube into the chamber before he got the chance. It landed at the feet of the soldiers and exploded in a cloud of inky smoke. Tendrils of black shadow slithered out of the cloud to wrap around the legs of the temple guards. Their yells of surprise echoed off the high ceiling as they were pulled into the smoke, where much thrashing and an eerie, sibilant hissing was heard.

Horace started to take a step inside the chamber, but he froze when the nearest Order sorcerer launched twin orbs of orange flame toward him. At the same time, the other sorcerer jabbed the air with a finger, and a line of pure white frost shot across the chamber. Acting out of instinct, Horace summoned his power and formed the emptiness of the Shinar into a hasty barrier in front of them. The fires and the icy ray struck at the same time, battering against the invisible bulwark. Smoke seeped around the edges, and spots of frost formed on the outer shell, but the barrier held.

"Push through!" Astaptah shouted. He held something else in his fist, but Horace couldn't see what it was.

Not sure what the vizier meant, Horace thrust out with both hands. To his surprise, the barrier scuttled a few inches farther into the room. The black smoke remained, cloaking the majority of the atrium.

Alyra reached around his shoulder to point out one of the Red Robes sprinting toward the eastern end of the atrium. "Over there!"

Horace ground his teeth together and attempted to separate the power maintaining his shield into two flows. It was something he had practiced with Mulcibar, though not with much success. Expecting another failure, he was amazed when the *zoana* divided into two channels. The barrier shook but held together while Horace shaped the second flow into the first thing he thought of—a rope. A lasso of flames lashed across the chamber from his open hand like a striking serpent. The sorcerer, now almost to the wide doorway leading to the sanctum, turned and put up both hands, palms facing outward. Horace saw the counterspell before it landed and turned his left hand in a small circle. The fiery rope slipped past the sorcerer's outstretched hands and wrapped around his neck.

How did I do that?

He was amazed that he was performing miracles that had been impossible for him just weeks ago. On the other hand, a growing unease lodged in his chest every time he tapped into these strange powers. His father had drummed into him from birth the concept that nothing was free, that a man could only truly rely upon those things he sweated and bled over. The sense that there was a terrible doom poised over his head was stronger than ever.

Just let me get Alyra and the queen to safety. Then I'll accept whatever I have coming without complaint.

Working by instinct, Horace tugged on the blazing cord. The sorcerer stumbled forward, smoke rising from around his neck and both hands as he tried to pull the magical rope away. Horace jerked again, and the sorcerer fell on his face hard enough to knock himself out.

Horace let the fiery cord evaporate with a sigh, and panic seized him when the barrier fell as well. But Astaptah pushed past him into the chamber, waving away the lingering smoke. Some of the soldiers were groaning and shaking their heads where they lay; a couple weren't moving at all. The other sorcerer knelt on the floor, groaning as his hands hovered over something small protruding from his stomach. Alyra ran up and kicked him in the head, and the sorcerer slumped over.

Horace hurried over. "You promised you would stay behind—"

He paused when she plucked the small object from the fallen magician and held it up. It was a long dart of silver metal. "It's *zoahadin*," she said. "I had some friends make me a few of these."

Horace kept his distance from the potent throwing dart as he looked around the chamber. Four large doorways exited the atrium in the cardinal directions.

"The ceremony will be on the west terrace," Astaptah said.

Alyra looked to the ceiling. "That's three stories above us."

"Yes. And every approach will be guarded by members of the Order. The ceremony has begun. Do what needs to be done."

"What about you?" Horace asked.

"I will stop anyone else from interfering. Go now if you wish to save the queen."

The vizier left them, heading across the atrium with long strides. Horace rubbed his hands on his tunic. His palms were tacky with sweat. He had assumed they would be confronting the priests together. The thought of going alone was much less palatable.

I could walk out of here, maybe even escape the city and have a chance at getting my life back. Or I can roll the bones.

He looked to the soldiers scattered across the marble floor. More would die because of him, because of his decision. Their blood would be on his hands, and in the end it might all turn out to be meaningless anyway.

Alyra asked, "Are you ready?"

He knew the answer as he faced the massive doorway to the west. He'd spent the last couple years running away—from his pain, his responsibilities, his future. If he was going to die today, he wanted it to be while he was running *toward* something. He clasped Alyra's hand, a little harder than he intended, but she squeezed back. They left the chamber together.

CHAPTER THIRTY-NINE

More than a hundred aristocrats arrayed in silk and glittering diadems crowded the western terrace of the Sun Temple. Emissaries from every city stood with the members of her court. They all turned to witness her entrance as the orchestra began to play. Queen Byleth allowed herself a small sigh.

Yes, look upon me, you vermin. I am Byleth, the last queen of the et'Urdrammor dynasty, delivered into the hands of my enemies.

She had spent the entire day being bathed, dressed, and made up. She wore the traditional bridal gown in gold silk and damask. Her hair was pinned up and festooned with a fortune in jewels. She might look like a goddess, but inside she felt like the biggest fool in the empire. She should have heeded Astaptah's advice. She should have removed the Sun Cult from the city long ago when she had the chance, but she had chosen the path of patience, hoping to wait them out. Tomorrow, Erugash would belong to the priests in all but name. She had failed herself and her people.

She almost wished Lord Astaptah were here now. A smile spread across her lips as she imagined the scene he would create, with the priests struggling between their opposing desires to see her wed off as soon as possible and putting her apostate vizier to a gruesome death. However, she had met with him this morning before the sun rose. He hadn't said much as she gave her final instructions. Whatever happened to her, she would not allow the storm engine to fall into the priesthood's hands. With much regret, she had commanded Astaptah to dismantle his life's work and destroy all records of its existence. He had taken the news in silence and then departed her chambers for the last time. Theirs had been an odd relationship, tempestuous at times, but at the end she had to concede that he had been one of her most loyal servants. She did not envy his chances for survival once her new husband sat on the throne.

As custom demanded, she arrived first to the altar with her train of atten-

BLOOD AND IRON

dants. Xantu stood beside her in the place of her ceremonial father, wearing a stern expression, but she knew him well enough to see the anxiety in the way he stood, the way he looked about, as if searching for an assassin.

There will be no need for assassins after this night, my protector. After tonight, I am merely the wife of a king.

Thousands of citizens filled the temple grounds beneath the terrace. Their voices rose like a wave of sound as she arrived. Byleth smiled back at them despite her fears. They were still her people for this moment, and she had loved them all her life. It had been a day much like today fifteen years ago when her father had introduced her to the city at her official "arrival" ceremony. Her throat tightened as she recalled walking out on the lower balcony of the unfinished palace for the first time, and the sea of faces staring up at her.

I was overwhelmed that day, and today my people remind me that I love them still, more than ever. Please forgive me.

Four priests of the Sun Lord entered behind her, led by Kadamun. The high priest looked like he had aged ten years since the last time she'd seen him. His back bent almost into a shepherd's crook, the skin of his bald head wrinkled and pale, tattoos faded. Menarch Rimesh followed him with two acolytes. Byleth glared at the envoy with every ounce of loathing inside her, which was substantial. His face was perfectly neutral, but she could imagine his smugness. He had beaten her. This wasn't her special day; it was his. The day he would make a queen of the blood grovel before the entire world. The *zoana* bubbled up inside her, wanting an outlet, and she was sorely tempted to unleash it. It wouldn't do her a bit of good, not with a dozen hounds of the Order seeded among the honored guests, ready to pounce at a moment's notice.

Everyone turned as Tatannu stepped onto the terrace. The prince of Nisus was resplendent in a coat of silver scales that shimmered like snakeskin in the failing daylight. Gold adorned the sword at his side, his fingers, and the large sunburst medallion hanging from his neck.

How touching that he wears the favor of his true love over his heart. I wonder if he will pray before he attempts to consummate our union. Or perhaps during?

Behind her groom marched an honor guard of famed Nisusi White Sphinxes, soldiers of fearsome reputation for both their skill at arms and unwavering loyalty. Statuettes of their mythological namesake perched on the crests of their tall helms.

The last members of the entourage were more priests, one from every faith as was also traditional in a marriage of such high status. The final members, votaries of Nabu the Keeper of Ancient Knowledge, closed the doors behind them as they entered. With deep voices chanting in unison, they pronounced the portals sealed. No one would be allowed to enter or leave until the ceremony was complete.

While Byleth eyed the doors with a powerful desire to be on the other side, the prince came to stand beside her wearing a small smile, and her heart sunk. His wasn't a smile of happiness or even of anticipated post-nuptial bliss; it was the self-satisfied smirk of a cat about to swallow the bird it had caught. The absurdity of the situation weighed down on her. She was standing in her own city, facing a man so much weaker in the *zoana* that she could kill him without much difficulty if she tried, but once their lives were joined in marriage, he would become her lord and master. She would be trapped for the rest of her life, which she presumed would be cut short unless she came up with some scheme. Pregnancy was the first thing to come to mind. Few men, especially those of the *zoanii* class, would willingly give up the chance to have a legitimate son. If she conceived right away, that could buy her nine months. And by the time she delivered—Kishar, make it a son—she was confident she could have the prince wrapped around her finger. She had ensnared far more willful men into her web.

Although the savage proved immune to your charms, didn't he?

Thinking of Horace evoked a warm rush of feelings. She'd thought he would be her salvation, but he had disappeared along with Lord Mulcibar, just like every other man in her life.

Father, why did it have to be this way?

Rimesh cleared his throat. High Priest Kadamun lifted a hand slowly to the height of his chest. His fingers shook a little as he intoned the blessing of the Sun Lord, which Byleth automatically repeated as she had at so many rites before.

"Homage to thee, O Lord of Light. He who sails across the sky, blessing all the world with His warmth. Watch over us, Great Lord . . ."

BLOOD AND IRON

Even as the words fell listlessly from her lips, Byleth felt her spirit—her *qa*—shrivel up. Her legs began to tremble as she saw a glimpse of her future extending before her, an endless landscape of scheming and deceit punctuated by moments of mortal terror until the day she was quietly dispatched. Her chest began to ache as she had to fight for each breath. She blinked and caught herself before she tumbled against the altar. She glanced up, ashamed at this sudden weakness, but no one else seemed to have noticed. Tatannu was piously reciting the prayers in response to the high priest's droning. Rimesh watched the crowd, oblivious to her.

I'm just a prop. I could collapse on the floor and I doubt old Kadamun would even break cadence.

Byleth put out a hand to steady herself and found herself thrown against the hard granite altar block. The air rushed from her lungs in a painful gasp as a burning heat saturated her back through the thin material of her gown. She tapped into her *zoana* and raised a ward of hardened air around herself as she twisted around. Where the doors to the temple had stood, now only an empty space remained. Their smoldering remains sagged on broken hinges amid a cloud of smoke. The stench of sorcery laced the air. Those witnesses who had not been knocked flat by the blast were quickly hurrying away from the sundered entry.

Shouts rang through the chamber as something flew through the smoke and landed on the terrace floor. It was a person wrapped in black rags. Byleth steadied herself as she peered closer. No, not black rags. Deep crimson robes like those worn by the men of the Order, seared nearly to charcoal.

Her heart almost stopped as a tall figure stepped through the broken doorway, wisps of smoke curling around his shoulders.

CHAPTER FORTY

S omber music filled the broad corridor. Deep drum rhythms echoed off the walls in time to a chorus of pipes and horns, all warning him that this was a bad idea.

Horace wiped his upper lip as he contemplated what they were about to do—interrupt a royal wedding and accuse the groom of colluding with the most powerful priesthood in the empire in a plot to kill off the bride before the ink on the marriage contract was dry. He tried to swallow, but his mouth was parched.

At the end of the hallway loomed double doors of varnished wood reinforced with iron bands. The back of Horace's neck itched as he approached the exit. "Are you sure this is the way?"

Alyra nodded toward the doors. She appeared calm. "That leads to the western terrace."

He took a deep breath and released it. When they got to within a dozen paces of the doors, a figure appeared from the shadows of the archway. Horace's stomach knotted at the sight of the man's shaved head and blood-red robes. He was quite short, no taller than Alyra, and built like a scarecrow, but an aura of power surrounded him. Horace started to lift his hand when bands of solidified air clamped around his torso, crushing his arms against his sides. He wove a net of fire, working off the idea of the lasso he'd used before, and sent it spinning down the corridor. The sorcerer deflected it with a wave of air that wrapped the net into a ball and shunted it into a wall where the flames burst harmlessly against the stone.

Horace erected another barrier right before a blob of what looked like red-hot lava landed on him. Instead, it spattered against the shield in front of his face. Trying not to think about what would have happened if the stuff had hit him, Horace visualized himself holding two huge boulders and brought his hands together in a sharp slap. The sorcerer's eyes bulged as invisible fists of air crushed him from both sides. His face dripped blood from a series of widening immaculata on both cheeks.

BLOOD AND IRON

A light touch fell on Horace's shoulder, but he didn't turn. He wanted this over. He thrust both his hands at the sorcerer. A stream of livid orange flame jetted down the corridor and caught the sorcerer, hurling him back into the doors, which smashed open with a thunderous boom. Horace shook his head to clear away an annoying ring that echoed through his skull. The doors were gone. Not just burst open, but completely ripped away from the frame. A cloud of smoke billowed in the entryway. A metallic, almost chemical odor wafted from the ruined doorway. It reminded him of a foundry, but more exotic. There was no sign of the sorcerer either. A tremor of unease rippled through his stomach at the sight of the destruction he had caused.

Horace relaxed his powers and glanced back at Alyra. Her face was ashen, but she took his hand with cool fingers. "Ready?" he asked.

"No. But let's get on with it."

Trying to project a confidence he didn't feel, he led her through the smoke. A susurrus of voices rose before them. Horace squinted as he stepped across the threshold. The rays of the fading sun shone upon a grand platform. The queen leaned against a stone altar beside her fiancé at the center of the terrace. The prince appeared aghast at the intrusion, while Byleth wore a look of bemused astonishment. Four priests, including Menarch Rimesh, stood behind the altar with pained expressions, perhaps because of the smoking body of the Order sorcerer at their feet.

Horace was about to shout for everyone to stand clear when the two younger priests by the altar stepped forward. Horace only had an instant to process the itching down his spine before twin attacks of jagged stones and freezing cold rushed at him. He braced himself for pain. Yet the sorcerer on the left threw back his head to reveal a thin shard of metal protruding from his neck, and his partner on the right jerked away with a similar dart through the meat of his hand. Both their magics dissipated into the air. Before either man could recover, Horace harnessed his *zoana*, and a mighty gust of wind poured out of him, hurtling both sorcerers over the side of the terrace.

The two older priests had already retreated behind the altar. As the pall lifted, soldiers with white figurines perched on their silver helmets pushed through the throng, and Horace got a glimpse of how many people were in attendance. More than a hundred, to be sure. Then he looked below and saw an ocean of faces filling the temple courtyard. Taking a deep breath, he raised his right hand, open palm held out.

The soldiers stopped at the front of the crowd, fingering their weapons as they watched him, but none advanced any closer. The *zoanii* watched him as well with various expressions. Most appeared shocked, but some whispered to each other, their eyes never leaving him. Horace started to beckon to the queen, his plan no more complicated than escorting her out of the temple. He cursed as a sheet of brilliant white spray cascaded from the south end of the terrace where another Red Robe pushed through the crowd. The nobles and soldiers in the path of the sparkling cone fell to the floor covered in hoarfrost.

Horace grabbed Alyra and conjured a barrier just as the whiteness crashed over them. Spiderwebs of rime formed across the surface of the bulwark. Horace visualized a ray of fire shooting from his palm. Instead, three blazing spheres the size of apples zipped across the space. Two impacted on a frosty buckler shield conjured by the Red Robe with dull thumps, but the third sphere curved around the shield to strike the sorcerer in the forehead, dropping him to the floor. Horace prepared to fashion some kind of magical cage to hold the man down, but before he could act, a massive stone spike erupted from the terrace floor, impaling the fallen sorcerer through the back as it lifted him off the ground.

Horace looked for the person responsible for the killing. At the altar, the venerable priest slumped on the floor with his eyes closed. There was no sign of Rimesh. The queen and her betrothed glared at each other but otherwise hadn't moved. Standing beside Byleth, Xantu glared at the bridegroom like he wanted to roast the prince over a slow fire. Then the bodyguard winked at Horace out of the corner of his eye, and Horace swallowed his annoyance.

It was over. The rest of the attendees and their soldiers didn't seem inclined to get involved. The queen was safe, and now they could get out of here.

He was about to release the protective shield when Alyra pointed upward, and Horace noticed for the first time the balcony above the terrace. Men stared down from the gallery; at least twenty of them, their crimson robes glowing darkly in the sun's dying light.

BLOOD AND IRON

Horace dragged Alyra down to the floor and poured all his strength into the barrier. His knees had barely touched the floor stones when a powerful force smashed against the shield. A sharp pain ripped down the center of his head as screams reverberated through the terrace. Horace didn't want to look, but he forced himself to as Alyra stiffened against him. Wedding guests lay all about him, their limbs and torsos contorted in sickening positions. With an ache in his stomach, he realized they had been crushed. He held Alyra close as his barrier was pummeled as if by a thousand invisible sledgehammers. The din of the pounding blocked out any other sounds. They were trapped. Eventually his mystic barrier would fail, and then they would both die.

A stream of blood ran from under the pile of crushed bodies. Horace squeezed his eyes shut, but the darkness brought no reprieve from the images cascading through his mind. He stood once again on the deck of the *Sea Spray*. His family was safe from the plague consuming Tines. As Sari chased Josef through the crowd of sailors, Horace shaded his eyes and viewed his dying town.

The crackle of splitting wood made him whirl around. The burning schooner in the next berth lurched as its foremast broke loose from its moorings. The tall pole fell like an axed tree. Sari screamed, Josef still squirming in her arms.

An anguished yell erupted from Horace as his family disappeared under a mountain of flaming wood and rigging. He leapt toward the inferno, digging at the fiery debris with his bare hands until strong grips dragged him away. He struggled against the sailors holding him back, his gaze on the spot where Sari and Josef had been standing only moments before. A trickle of blood ran along the deck.

"Sari," Horace croaked, hunched on the terrace floor. A bitter taste flooded his mouth. "Josef!"

"Horace!" Alyra gasped.

He shuddered against the painful memories. If he hadn't taken his family aboard that ship, they might still be alive today. It was his fault they had died. If he was any kind of man, he would have thrown himself into the flames after them. Better to die that day that live with this shame.

Warm wetness touched his fingers. He looked down to see the rivulet of blood had touched his hand. He watched it pool around his fingers, running against his old burn scars. He could still remember being on his hands and knees on the deck of the *Sea Spray*, digging through the burning sailcloth and rigging while his wife and son screamed. Those wails echoed inside his head now just like they had on that cursed day. If he closed his eyes again, he would see their faces, melting before his eyes, calling out for him . . .

A ragged scream erupted from his mouth as he hauled himself to his knees, the agonies of his past and the icy fire of the *zoana* fusing together in the blazing furnace behind his breastbone. A tracery of tiny cracks ran through the barrier as he delved into the gray space inside him, gathering up every bit of magic he could summon. Tears ran down his face like beads of molten lead. His bones ached with the intensity of the power running through him. With a deep gasp, he lashed out.

Crackling forks of green lightning flashed from his hands. The Shinar dominion pulsed within him while the energy poured out, seemingly without end.

Skin blistered and blackened as the emerald bolts raked across the gallery. Crimson robes burst into flames. The enemy sorcerers fell in droves, their shrieks echoing off the temple's inner walls.

Horace kept a tight rein on his thoughts, knowing that if he dwelt for even a moment on the fact that he was killing people—human beings with families and dreams of the future—his control over the *zoana* would evaporate. He focused on the task at hand. Ignore the cries of agony. Incinerate each enemy in turn and move on.

The soldiers on the terrace rushed toward him, but a gust of frosty wind sent them tumbling back in a clatter of metal. The queen and Xantu pushed them back with alternating blasts of wind and multicolored flames.

As the last sorcerer fell from the balcony, Horace released the power and gasped as a stinging jolt, like ripping off a fresh scab, passed through him. His insides trembled and he felt like he might be sick, but the feeling passed after a couple deep breaths. In the hazy smoke rolling across the terrace he saw the faces of his wife and son, and the pain of losing them ran through him like a spear. He held onto that agony, cherished it, knowing it was the only thing keeping him together. Without it, he would shatter into a thousand pieces. And yet, holding onto the memories was killing him. Slowly, day by day, eating him from the inside, denying him the chance to truly live again.

Sari, Josef, forgive me. I can't do it anymore.

Then Alyra stood beside him. Spots of soot smudged her face, but she had never looked more beautiful. In that moment, he realized he could let go of his past. The pain remained, but it was now a dull ache that was fading with each breath he took. He was free, though an empty hole remained inside him. He was about to reach out to Alyra when a cool voice spoke behind him.

"You astound me yet again, Lord Horace."

Byleth strode toward them. She sounded pleased for the most part, but there was something else in her tone. Wariness, perhaps. Despite some smeared makeup and a little perspiration beading on her forehead, the queen's magnificence shone like a bonfire.

Yet Horace wasn't as swayed by her looks as he had been before, and he found his gaze wandering back to Alyra. "I was merely repaying a debt owed, Your Excellence."

"Just remember." Byleth stepped closer to him and placed a hand over his heart. "You are *my* champion."

Horace started to stammer a reply when he caught a glimpse of movement from over his shoulder. He turned in time to see a man in a yellow robe dart out the ruined doorway.

Rimesh.

Horace reached out with his power, intending to seize the priest in a grasp of solid air, but the power slid off without slowing him.

Horace grasped Alyra's hand. "Accompany the queen back to the palace."

He couldn't tell which of the two women was more taken aback by his command, Alyra or Byleth. Both stared at him with odd expressions. "Please," he added. Then he took off after the menarch.

The women called after him in a bizarre chorus, "Where are you going?"

Horace kept running.

CHAPTER FORTY-ONE

*T*his *is a mistake.*

Horace squinted as he ducked through the ruined doorway after Menarch Rimesh. Getting the queen to safety should have been his primary concern, but the sight of the priest escaping this death-trap of his own making had infuriated Horace. He had to be brought to justice. However, a little voice nagged in the back of Horace's head that he was only doing this because he wanted revenge for being locked down in that pit. He ignored it.

Several doors opened along the corridor. Horace started trying them all, but as he moved down the passageway, an impulse tugged at him. It drew him toward a small door farther down. Horace pushed it open. Inside, glowing orbs on the walls illuminated a narrow corridor of dressed stone. Hearing footfalls ahead, he sprinted down the hallway. He passed several doors but didn't check them. The footsteps came from ahead, or so he thought. The close walls played tricks on his hearing.

As he followed the corridor around a corner, Horace tried to ignore his shaking hands. The *zoana* lent him strength and clarity, but it also put his nerves on edge. He kept expecting the menarch or another Red Robe to leap at him from every shadow. Yet it was more than that. Over the past weeks all of his old assumptions had been challenged in ways he could have never anticipated. It was apparent that the Akeshians believed in their heathen gods every bit as fervently as the men and women who packed the churches of Arnos every Godsday. They were different, but they weren't evil. At least, not all of them.

Horace stopped in his tracks as he entered a large chamber with a very high ceiling. A massive golden effigy, twenty feet tall, dominated the room. The statue was of a muscular man on a throne holding a spear in one hand and a fiery ball in the other. Golden flames radiated from his high crown. This could be none other than the Sun God of the Akeshians. The thing looked like

BLOOD AND IRON

it was made of solid gold, but he couldn't believe that. The cost would have been beyond imagining.

On the other side of the chamber he found a stout wooden door, but it was locked. There was no keyhole, and he didn't have a key anyway so it didn't matter. The door felt solid enough to withstand anything less than a battle-axe. He didn't have one of those either.

Reaching out with his power to the door's stone frame, Horace winced as the effort became slightly painful. Not a sharp pain like he had injured himself, but the dull ache of an overused muscle. Gritting his teeth, he tried harder until he was rewarded with the familiar rush of energy. Cracks appeared as the stone frame flexed. A hard kick swung the door open with pieces of the lock mechanism flying off.

The chamber beyond was smallish, about ten feet on each side, with tall cabinets against the far wall. Horace took a step inside and felt a slight tickle down the back of his neck. He halted in mid-step and then stumbled back when something slammed into the other side of the door. He caught his balance against a wall and stared through the gloom, looking for the threat. A hole the size of a dinner platter had been ripped through the center of the door. Horace looked himself over but didn't find any new injuries. With a grunt, he summoned the Imuvar dominion and projected a gust of wind ahead of him. It ripped the door off its hinges and tossed it across the room. He heard foot-steps rising above him to the left. A quick look revealed a case of ascending stone steps. Horace charged up them two at a time. Just as he reached the first landing, the familiar tickle itched down his spine. He jumped back just before the wall in front of him exploded in a rain of shrapnel. Horace looked up in time to see a heavyset man in red robes escaping around the next turn of the stairs. Fists clenched, Horace ran after him.

He rounded the next turn a little more cautiously and wasn't surprised when a rock the size of his head flew just inches in front of his face. It hit the wall beside him and caromed down the stairs. Horace erected a barrier of solid air in front of him as he edged around the corner. Isiratu stood on the landing above, breathing heavily. Blood dripped from a deep gash down the side of his neck, but the former nobleman didn't seem to mind it as he raised his hands.

Horace glimpsed something falling from the ceiling a heartbeat before a huge piece of stone crashed down on him. His shield collapsed, holding just long enough to deflect the stone so that it missed his head by a few inches. Startled, Horace opened himself to the Mordab dominion and tried to fashion a ball of ice, hoping to distract or at least slow down the former *zoanii*, but instead a cold mist filled the stairway. He threw himself against the wall as Isiratu made another gesture. Another large stone dropped from the ceiling to shatter on the steps between them.

Time to fight fire with fire.

Lord Mulcibar had said that a master of the Shinar dominion was a master of all the dominions. It was time to test that theory. Horace opened his *qa* to the Kishargal dominion. His earlier exhaustion faded as a new strength seeped into his veins. He was suddenly aware of the stone around him—the walls, floor, and ceiling, as well as the many chips of stone scattered on the stairs. With a thought he lifted the small pieces of rock and sent them flying up at his foe. Isiratu raised his arms to protect his face, the sleeves and front of his robe shredding from the onslaught, and Horace pressed his attack. Isiratu motioned with one hand, and chunks of stone tore loose from the stairway walls, but Horace shattered them with his thoughts, one by one, as he climbed the steps.

Isiratu's face had turned purple. Blood streamed down the front of his robe from the immaculata on his neck, but he continued to fight. More rocks flew at Horace from every direction as he kept climbing toward his foe, but not a one touched him as he discovered he didn't have to shatter them all. Just by altering their paths by a couple inches, he could force them to swerve around him. Isiratu gasped as he lifted both arms to the ceiling. Larger blocks of stone rained down, but they curved away from Horace to strike the steps behind him.

"Why did you have to stay in Erugash?" Horace asked, mostly to himself. "Why couldn't you leave me alone?"

He reached out with his *zoana* and exploded a slab of stone as it fell. Bits of shattered rock showered over Isiratu. Horace launched a blast of air and shoved the former lord back across the landing. Isiratu struck the far wall, pressed there by the powerful wind, but still sustained his attacks, even as new immaculata spread across his face.

"I would have let you go!" Horace shouted at him. The *zoana* coursed through him like a mighty river. Its taste was intoxicating. "Even after the pit, I would have let you live. But you won't stop until one of us is dead!"

Isiratu made a growling sound in the back of his throat. He reached for the ceiling, and a tremor raced through the steps under Horace's feet. Cracks sprouted in the walls, spewing dust into the air. Horace braced himself for a knockout punch. Then the rain of stones ceased. Isiratu stood rigid, his eyes wide and bloodshot. Blood from his immaculata gushed from his neck and poured down the front of his robe. Then he slumped against the bands of air holding him upright, his life extinguished. Horace looked upon the man who had delivered him over to the temple, now dead by his hand, and wondered if this ending had been destined to happen from the first moment they met. He severed his connection to the magic and stepped over Isiratu's body. He wasn't finished yet.

The stairs took him up several more stories. His knees ached by the time he arrived in a large, open-sided chamber at the apex of the temple. Cyclopean stone pillars at each corner held up the domed roof, the interior of which was painted in a breathtaking mural of the Akeshian pantheon amid a starry sky. Horace peered around for the menarch. There was nowhere else he could have gone. Then he heard the soft whisper of leather scuffing across stone.

Rimesh stepped out from behind the southeastern pillar holding a long dagger. Its bare blade shone in the starlight. "I thought my mission was to purge this city of its sins and bring it under the protective aegis of Amur. But then I learned of you and I realized the corruption went deeper. You are no mere savage. You are a cancer lodged in the city's breast, spreading your destructive influence to everyone and everything you touch." He pointed the dagger at Horace. "And the only way to stop your menace is to cut you out."

Horace wanted to strike the priest down where he stood but suppressed the temptation. He had spilled enough blood this night. "It's over. The queen is returning to the palace, unwed and still in power."

"For today." Rimesh advanced, moving with the measured tread of an experienced warrior. His face betrayed no fear or apprehension. "But tomorrow or the day after, or next week, my Order will have its way. The gods have spoken."

"The gods? You mean a sect of old men who want to rule the empire."

"And you? You are an abomination conceived in chaos. It would have been better for the world if your mother had strangled you the day you were born."

"I never asked for this! But now that I've—"

A scraping sound met his ears. Horace turned and fell on his side as a blast of freezing wind threw him to the floor. Two Red Robes came out from behind other pillars, flinging sorcery ahead of them. Horace rolled away from a jet of blue flame and back to his feet. Rimesh had vanished.

Horace sent a barrage of fiery embers at the sorcerers. The gusting wind scattered the embers, and more tongues of flame lapped at him. Horace reached for the Kishargal dominion again and imagined his hands grasping the stones of the floor. With a mental yank, he pulled up a dozen flagstones and threw them at the Red Robes. One sorcerer pushed out with his hands, but the stones tore through his wind shield and slammed into him. Bones crunched and blood spurted as the sorcerer fell on his back, sharp edges of stone protruding from his body. The other Red Robe flung himself away in time to avoid the deadly missiles. Horace sent a bolt of hardened air after him, but the sorcerer ducked behind a pillar before it found him.

Horace approached the southeastern pillar looking for the menarch, but the space behind it was vacant. A stone balustrade bordered the edge of the terrace overlooking the city. Horace was turning around when a vise of air seized him around the middle and lifted him off the ground. All of a sudden he became very aware of the great fall that waited over the side of the balcony. Across the chamber, two more Red Robes were coming up the stairs. One held out a clenched fist like he was squeezing an orange. Unable to draw breath, Horace delved inside himself for a solution, but his grasp on the dominions seemed to fray. Only his connection to the void held steady. He grabbed onto it like a lifeline. An inclination passed through his mind, cutting through his desperate struggle to survive. If he would just do *this*, then . . .

Visualizing a huge sword, Horace invoked the emptiness welling inside him. The power sliced down through the space between him and the approaching sorcerers. Suddenly, the force holding him evaporated, and he fell almost a full body-length to the floor. He landed hard with both feet and staggered a step before catching himself on the balustrade.

New attacks rained down on Horace, pelting him with fire and ice, with battering winds that stank of brimstone and showers of stone, but nothing got through the invisible barrier of Shinar energy he had erected. With a thought, he bent the barrier until it enclosed him on all sides. A sense of security enveloped him as his enemies continued to batter his sanctuary without success. He took a deep breath, and then he stepped away from the guardrail.

He conserved his strength and didn't counterattack as he advanced toward his enemies. Then two more Order sorcerers appeared from the stairway and joined their brethren. Their robes were fresh and pristine, not yet marked by signs of battle.

The addition of the new sorcerers halted Horace's advance. His barrier thudded from a series of heavy blows. Their magical bombardment resounded in his ears. He didn't want to contemplate what would happen if the shield collapsed. He opened a pathway to the Mordab dominion and targeted one of the new arrivals. A cloud of water vapor appeared around the sorcerer and quickly froze, encasing him in ice. As he turned his attention to another assailant, Horace felt a twinge of pain in his chest. He shunted it aside as he launched a flurry of icy orbs at his next target. He managed to keep the Order sorcerers on the defensive with quick counterattacks, but there were too many for him to defeat by himself. His connections to the dominions were shrinking as exhaustion set in, his *qa* growing weaker with every passing heartbeat.

"Who are you to defy the empire?" Rimesh's voice echoed off the domed ceiling from his hiding spot. "No one will mourn your death. You are an insect before the power of Amur. Insignificant. Meaningless."

Horace flinched from the words, because he'd said them to himself in the dark of night when he was alone. Since Sari and Josef died, he'd had no purpose, no guiding star. Perhaps death would be a blessing.

A beam of moonlight shone into his eyes, making him blink. The full moon hung over the city. Its heavenly beauty stirred a memory in the back of his mind. It took him a moment to realize what it was—the innermost circle of Mulcibar's *ganzir* mat. The din of hostile sorcery receded from his ears as the rest of the design came to him. He could see it now, a picture of perfection with all of creation contained within its many-hued borders. Everything that existed was represented in the *ganzir*, from the sky and stars to the earth below and every creature under heaven. Everything was connected. He existed everywhere in the universe, and all the universe existed within him. His family was still with him, too. As long as he breathed, his love for them would never die.

As above, so below.

He opened the gates of his *qa*. Warm tremors radiated through his body, not the hot flashes that the *zoana* usually sent into his veins, but a deeper, more powerful sensation. The designs throughout the *ganzir* in his mind danced in ten thousand colors, each etched in argent moonlight, merging and separating as if they moved to some music he couldn't hear. Sweat trickled down his face as he poured his energy into the effort.

Something exploded against his barrier with the brightness of the sun. Sharp pain ripped through his chest. His eyes shot open. The moon was gone, replaced by a bank of thunderheads flickering with emerald-green light.

A roar filled the lightning-charged air as Jirom ran. It sprang from his own lips, originating from deep down in his bones. The rage had broken free of its cage and taken hold of him. Everything around him was stained with a red patina, every face twisted into an evil visage he longed to smash. He swung the tulwar over his head, reveling in the feel of the steel in his hands, the sweet song as it tore through the gusty air.

His gaze was focused on Hazael, who galloped through the rebel force, reaping death with every swing of his red-steel blade. Jirom ran to intercept him, but the *kapikul* wheeled his steed around and sped away into the lightning-etched darkness. With a curse, Jirom turned toward an Akeshian officer watching the battle on horseback. The lieutenant appeared startled when he ran up to him and swung his cavalry sword, but Jirom caught the stroke on the guard of his tulwar. Grabbing the officer's wrist, Jirom threw him to the ground.

Leaping onto the back of the tall dun stallion, Jirom grabbed hold of its chestnut-red mane and kicked his heels. The horse took off like a javelin, tearing past the rows of tents. He spotted the *kapikul*, galloping a dozen yards ahead of him. Jirom coaxed every ounce of speed out of his animal, slowly closing the gap. As he caught up, he leaned forward, ready to unleash the anger brewing in his heart.

Side by side they raced through the camp. Jirom swung his tulwar like an axe with heavy blows meant to crush the *kapikul's* defense, but the *assurana* sword met each strike and turned it aside. Jirom growled as a return thrust sliced across his back, but he hardly felt it. His entire being was focused on killing this foe. He leaned in for another attack, but his horse stumbled, and the swing fell short. Hazael responded with a quick slash that cut up his side, shearing away part of his leather armor and slicing into his ribs. Jirom hissed through gritted teeth as his steed righted itself. A quick glance down revealed a deep gash through the meat of the muscle. Blood poured down his side.

Hazael reined up to a sudden halt. Jirom's horse thundered past before he could get it turned around. The *kapikul* waited, his sword extended straight ahead in something that looked like a dueling position. Jirom kicked his heels and leaned forward as his horse accelerated. The tulwar's grip was slick in his hand. He tightened his fingers in anticipation.

Shock vibrated through his body as the two steeds collided, chest to chest, hooves flailing. Jirom tried to bat the *kapikul's* blade out of the way, but Hazael made a circular motion with his wrist and disengaged their weapons. Jirom found himself on the receiving end of another upward slash that he barely parried before it slit open his belly. He lashed out, and again his attack was deflected. His shoulder was getting tired, even through the fog of his rage. He could feel his attacks growing weaker. The *kapikul*, however, seemed as strong as ever.

When the *assurana* sword swung inward on a horizontal arc at chest height, Jirom dropped the tulwar and leapt from his horse. A sharp pain shot through his lower back as he crashed into Hazael. They both fell to the ground, with Jirom landing on top of the commander. The *assurana* sword flashed downward, but Jirom caught the wrist and wrenched it aside, and then the air exploded from his lungs as the *kapikul's* knee came up hard into his groin. Hazael shoved him over on his back. Jirom started to push himself to his hands and knees but toppled over with a grunt as the *kapikul* kicked him in his injured side. Painful jolts pierced the fog of rage clouding Jirom's mind. Hazael stumbled to his feet, grasping at the ground for something. His sword. Jirom lunged and caught the *kapikul* around the waist, wrestling him to the ground. Jirom's side screamed in agony as they grappled, but he held on, slowly pinning Hazael to the ground. Inch by inch he forced his foe's face down into the sand. The commander strained and kicked, but Jirom kept up the pressure, shoving his foe's nose and mouth into the loose soil until, eventually, he stopped fighting.

Releasing the limp body, Jirom rolled away. The rage curled around his brain, invading every thought. He tried to let it go, but fragments of old pains flashed before him. He saw himself as a young boy, exiled from his family, chased away with stones and spears. He recalled wandering the plains of the Zaral alone, weak and hungry and filled with shame. All the years spent fighting and killing only added to the loneliness. But then he remembered meeting Horace, and how the dark cloud that had followed him all his life had melted away, replaced by a glimmering hope that his future could be better if only he had the strength to seize it. He still wanted to believe that. It was the reason he had joined the rebel slaves and also the reason he needed to help Horace, even though those two desires seemed to be pulling him in different directions.

He slowly got to his feet. His back was cramped up, making every movement a new experience in agony. He started to look for his fallen tulwar, but then he spotted the red-gold blade sticking up out of the sand. Jirom leaned over and picked up the *assurana* sword. The hilt was bound in cord instead of leather, making for a softer feel, but the biggest difference was the heft. Although the blade was slightly longer than the tulwar, it weighed half as much, and he could attest to its strength.

As he stripped Hazael's body of the sword belt and scabbard, Jirom considered leaving the camp on his own. With a tired sigh, he tracked down the stallion, which had wandered among the tents, and rode back to the command pavilion.

He found Emanon leaning against a post, his sword dangling loose in his hand. The melee had ended. A dozen rebels remained standing, and a few more lay on the ground with injuries.

"You all right?" Jirom asked as he rode up.

"I'm still breathing," the rebel captain answered with a tight smile. "What about you?"

"I'll live."

Jirom surveyed the camp, half-expecting to see reinforcements heading their way, but the battle had moved to the east, where distant screams and the clash of arms resounded in the pauses between thunderclaps. Fires burned amid the tents where countless bodies sprawled. The storm was focused over the town, which now sported a flickering golden corona. Omikur was burning, too. He didn't wish to dwell on what the morrow would bring, no matter which side won. Death, disease, looting, and rape—the spoils of war.

Jirom dismounted. He had expected to see a congregation of the desert fighters, but the only people moving around the command tent were Emanon's rebels. He did a quick tally of the night's cost. Six dead, and a couple hurt badly enough that they would have to be carried—more than a third of their force. Yet Emanon didn't appear perturbed as he waded among the men, supervising the treatment of wounds and redistribution of gear. Jirom had the urge to go over and say something, but he held his tongue. He didn't have the words to express the turmoil brewing inside him. He was tired, right down to his bones.

When the captain gave the call to move out, Jirom followed the rebel fighters through the quiet camp, heading west.

Horace winced when the first bolt of lightning struck the temple. The second bolt hit the dome overhead with a deep boom like the ringing of a gong as large as the world. One of the stone ribs holding up the ceiling broke loose, and two sorcerers disappeared under an avalanche of rock and broken mortar. The entire floor of the chamber shook, but Horace kept his attention focused on the image in his mind. His exhaustion had fallen away, and the dark fog that had clouded his thoughts for so long was gone.

"Bring him down!" Rimesh shouted above the rumble of falling masonry.

More lightning lanced down into the city. The thunder shook more stones loose from the ceiling. The dome was fracturing, its support pillars creaking as the massive weight shifted. Rain blew in sideways and pattered on the smooth tiles. Horace concentrated and noticed that the white circle in the center of his mental *ganzir* was throbbing—not in a regular rhythm but sporadically. He looked out to the roiling storm clouds. The connection he always felt with the chaos storms remained, just beneath the surface of his consciousness. Was that the key? The storms and his power, they were linked somehow. He stared into the white circle, intent on discovering its secret. The way it remained steady while the other designs danced around it almost reminded him of . . .

The eye of a storm.

Horace did the first thing that came to mind. He flung open his pathway to the Shinar dominion and pulled with all of his will. Ravenous hunger filled him, seared his flesh down to the bones, and threatened to turn his mind inside out.

Dazzling light filled the open chamber, followed at once by a titanic crash. To Horace, it appeared as if the entire world had frozen in a tableau of green and black. Power, beyond anything he had handled before, poured into him. His lungs were paralyzed; he was unable to draw breath as the storm's energy shot through him. Every nerve in his body was on fire, but he could not scream, and the moment seemed to last forever as he soaked in more and more energy. His *qa* yawned open like a bottomless pit. Then it was over.

Horace gasped for air as his legs gave out. He fell to his knees on the wet flagstones. The energy hummed in his chest. Then he realized his mystic barrier was gone, and panic washed over him. He looked up, ready to continue the fight, but the sorcerers were all down on the floor. Scorch marks covered their bodies, their robes burned to ash.

BLOOD AND IRON

Horace tried to stand. His entire body felt numb, like someone else was moving his arms and legs. Then a shout rang in his ears. Rimesh, his robes soaked and streaked with black soot, appeared from behind a pillar. The dagger gleamed in his raised fist as he charged. Horace reached for the Girru dominion and froze in shock as the power exploded inside him, surging through his body with intense heat. He launched what he intended to be a bolt of fire at Rimesh, but instead an inferno burst from his open palm. He expected to see the menarch drop to the floor as a charred corpse, but the flames curved around Rimesh without touching him. Horace accessed the Imuvar. A gale-force wind swept across the chamber, but it merely fluttered the priest's sodden robe without slowing him as if he had an invisible shield.

How in the Hell . . . ? He's no sorcerer. Is he?

The dagger flashed. Horace fell backward. He blocked the menarch's wrist with his forearm, and the blade sliced across his upper arm instead of his throat. Horace kicked upward and was rewarded with a strained grunt as his instep connected with Rimesh's groin. He tried to shove the priest away, but Rimesh was stronger than he looked. The dagger came down again, and Horace shouted as the sharp point plunged into his left shoulder joint. The pain was fierce and immediate, shattering his concentration.

As Rimesh pulled free the blade for another strike, Horace delved into his connection to the Shinar dominion and threw everything he had at the priest, but the power couldn't find anything to latch onto. Then he noticed a chain dangling from the menarch's neck. On the end of it swayed a metal circle with twisting symbols engraved into its surface. He recognized the silvery alloy at once and knew why his magic had failed him.

The dagger came down with startling swiftness. Horace made a grab for it, but his wounded shoulder couldn't react in time. He shouted in pain as the tip of the blade struck his collarbone. Warm blood spurted across his neck and chest. He grabbed Rimesh's wrist as the dagger was turned under the bone and driven deeper, but he didn't have the strength to resist. The menarch leaned over him, white spittle dripping from his lips. Horace braced himself for the final thrust.

A fresh splash of blood showered down on him. Blinking it away, Horace looked up. Rimesh glared down at him, his face a rigid mask with the hilt of a knife protruding from his neck. Then the priest toppled over.

Alyra's mouth was a grim line as she pulled her knife free, but her lips turned up in a faint smile as she reached down her other hand to him. "I had a feeling you might need some help."

Horace let out the breath he had been holding. He felt wrung out like a ratty old handkerchief. He grunted as Alyra shoved her shoulder under his good armpit and heaved. With her help, he managed to get back on his feet. His shoulder was killing him, and a sharp pain ripped through the center of his chest every time lightning flashed over the city.

"What are you doing here?" he asked. "I told you to see the queen out of the temple."

"Her Majesty is on her way back to the palace. Oh, Horace, this is really deep." She pressed on the wound in his shoulder. "Can you feel that?"

He swayed on his feet as the urge to pass out came and went. "Don't do that again. Listen to me. The ceiling is—"

A piece of masonry as large as a horse cart hit the floor on the north side of the chamber, shattering tiles and sending a shockwave through Horace's legs. "Get out of here!" he yelled.

Alyra steered him back to the staircase. "Not without you!"

The groan of shifting stone chased them down the steps. An ear-splitting crash resounded from the chamber they'd left behind, and Horace knew the dome supports were collapsing. He erected an umbrella of solid air over them as they rushed down the steps. The tumult of crashing stone followed them down. Mortar dust dropped from the ceiling.

By the time they reached the grand atrium, the entire temple sounded like it was coming down. Alyra pulled him out the tall doors. The sky was pitch-black. Stinging rain pelted their faces as they ran toward the main gate of the complex. Stones fell all around them, massive chunks of masonry that smashed through the pavestones and lodged deep in the earth. Horace's eyes had just started to adjust to the gloom when a bolt of vivid green lightning traced a jagged path across the sky. Thunder boomed right behind it, almost knocking them over. Horace hunched as a jolt shot through his body. It took him a moment to realize the ground was trembling. Alyra stumbled against him, and they held onto each other for balance as fist-sized stones whistled past their heads. He looked upward and wished he hadn't. The upper stories of the temple were tilted askew. Pieces of the architecture sheared away as the entire structure swayed. Biting down on his tongue, Horace moved as fast as Alyra and his legs could carry him.

We're not going to make it. We're not going to—

Horace exhaled a prayer as they reached the gate, which had been left ajar. They staggered out onto the street and turned to look behind them. The temple's upper half had sloughed away, spilling across the courtyard in a long pile of rubble that reached to the outer boundary walls of the complex. He couldn't believe his eyes, nor the fact that he had been responsible for such destruction. He thought of the pits beneath the temple's foundation and wondered how many unfortunate souls were trapped down there, but there was nothing he could do for them.

"We should go," Alyra said.

With a nod, Horace started toward the palace with her. Lightning crackled above the city, showing with every illuminating flash that they were the only ones insane enough to be out in the storm.

CHAPTER FORTY-TWO

The white expanse of the desert undulated in an endless sea, shimmering silver and gold with the first rays of dawn. It reminded Jirom of the grass fields of the Zaral, which also seemed to run without end, framed only by the bowl of the boundless sky. He sat atop a pile of boulders, holding the *kapikul's* sword across his lap.

The rebels had marched most of the night to reach this place, which Emanon called "a safe harbor." A small cave mouth led down to a hollow den beneath the boulders. Jirom had tried to lie down inside, but it had been too much like a tomb, and so he came out for some air while the grateful sentry left on guard duty retired inside.

As he watched the sun come up, Jirom wondered about the things beyond his sight. He wondered about the men he'd lost at Omikur, whether they'd be buried with funeral rites or be left to the jackals. He wondered about the defenders and how many of them had died in that hellhole. Mostly he wondered about a man still back in the queen's city.

I swore I would get him out, but now I'm farther away than ever and getting farther with every step I take.

He heard the footsteps before he saw Emanon's head pop up from the cave. The captain climbed up beside him on the rocks. Jirom could feel the warmth of the man's arm against his own. Emanon smelled of sweat and leather, and the new beard accentuated his devilish good looks. Jirom was tempted to speak first, to say something witty or ironic, but he held his peace. Silence had always worked best for him when it came to men.

"I thought I'd find you out here." Emanon gestured to the rising sun. "It's pretty, eh?"

Jirom gazed at the sky. He'd spent the past couple hours thinking about what to say to this man, but now he was unsure how to begin.

Emanon gestured to the *assurana* sword. "That's blood-steel, a mixture of *zoahadin* and red gold. There's only a handful of smiths in all the empire who know that recipe. That blade is worth a small kingdom."

Jirom looked him in the eye. "So what happened to your secret army?"

"They're out there." Emanon turned to survey the barren landscape. "Waiting for the next phase."

"And what's that? Or is that a secret?"

Emanon turned to face him. "I think you already know."

"I suspect I do. The queen's legions were bloodied, but not crushed. Isn't that right? And there will be more dog-soldiers to replace us. So what's left but to hide out here?"

"You think we're running," Emanon said.

"Aren't you?"

"There's more than sand and scorpions out here, Jirom. The desert is freedom. The desert is shelter from our enemies."

"A lot of men die in the desert."

"Aye. That they do, but others grow stronger. Like a certain former gladiator I know. We'll stay here and gather our strength, and then go out to find some friends."

"Why not just go?" Jirom pointed to the far horizon. "Leave Akeshia for good. You're free."

"Because Omikur wasn't the end, Jirom. It was the beginning. All across the empire, slaves are gathering in secret. Waiting for a sign. We will be that beacon, calling them to throw off their iron chains and reclaim their liberty."

Jirom looked out over the rolling sands and imagined how many graves were hidden under the shimmering facade. "I have to go back to Erugash."

Emanon spat over the side of the boulder and shifted his sheathed sword. "You really want to die that badly? You may as well dig yourself a hole right here and let the desert swallow you up. It'd be a lot less painful."

"I can't abandon Horace. From what little we've heard . . ."

"Aye. It sounds like Her Fucking Majesty has her claws sunk into him deep. You know, he's probably already dead, too."

"Mayhap. But I couldn't live with myself if I didn't try to help him."

"Jirom, why is this man so important to you? Is he . . . ? Dammit!"

Before Jirom could react, Emanon's lips were pressed against his mouth. He remained still at first, not trusting his feelings after a lifetime of pain and disappointment. Now they rushed back to him like an ocean of longing, all the fiercer for having been denied for so long. He opened his mouth and wrapped his arms around Emanon's broad shoulders.

When they parted, the breath rushed from Jirom's lips like a sigh. He braced himself for another rejection, but there was only softness in Emanon's eyes and something else he had rarely seen. Understanding.

"I'm sorry if that was sudden," Emanon said. "But I couldn't let you leave without telling you . . . or showing you . . . how I felt. Do you love him?"

Jirom almost laughed to hear the jealousy in his voice. "No. We went through a lot together. You understand what that does."

"Stay with us. We'll get your friend out. I haven't forgotten my promise."

"When?"

"The time will come, and we'll be there to make it happen. But going back alone is crazy. I don't care how good-looking you are, our former masters don't have a sense of humor when it comes to escaped slaves."

"I have to try."

"All right." Emanon started to get up. "Then I'm going with you."

Jirom put a hand on the captain's forearm. "No. You have an army to lead. These people are relying on you."

"And I need your help for that to succeed. I didn't get these men out by myself. You're a big part of this operation, Jirom. I can't do it without you."

Jirom sighed. He didn't want to leave, especially now with the way Emanon was looking at him. "You promise you'll make every effort to free Horace?"

Emanon tapped his chest over his heart. "I swear it."

Jirom held out his hand, and they shook. The captain's grip was firm and comforting. "Then if I'm staying," Jirom said, "I have a few ideas."

Emanon's smile faded. "Ideas? Like what?"

"Like some changes that need to be made around here. Starting with unit discipline. These men are too soft."

"Too soft? They survived the training camp, didn't they?"

"Surviving isn't enough." Jirom held Emanon's gaze for a moment, and then they both laughed.

"Come inside," the captain said. "I'll show you what I'm planning. There's an old spice road that runs through the desert. If we follow that to . . ."

Jirom half-listened as he followed Emanon down to the cave entrance. He looked again to the east. The rising sun burned like a ball of fire over the desert. Was this the right choice? He didn't know, but it felt right.

Swallowing his apprehension, he ducked into the dark confines of the hideout.

CHAPTER FORTY-THREE

The sun rose through a crystal-blue sky, searing away all traces of the rain from the previous night. Horace stood on the balcony of his bedchamber and gazed across the cityscape. Reminders of the storm remained in the burned-out homes and devastated gardens, some of them littered with stony debris from collapsed retaining walls and fallen buildings. Yet the streets were already bustling with people—merchants and workers, silk-curtained palanquins and servants in fine livery.

When they had reached the palace last night, a contingent of soldiers escorted him and Alyra to the queen's chambers where he received effusive thanks from Byleth and even begrudged nods from Xantu, who refused to leave her side. There was no sign of Lord Astaptah, and no one mentioned him either. As the royal physicians looked Horace over, the queen had made him an offer.

"Nothing can convey the depths of my gratitude, Lord Horace," she said while perched beside him on a fur-covered settee. "But there is one thing in my power that means as much to you. Your freedom. You can leave Erugash at any time and take with you a document in my own hand giving you permission to travel wherever you want. There is an invader stronghold on the Etonian border. You could be there in a couple weeks."

Horace hadn't known what to say, so he'd said nothing at all. After the doctors finished stitching him up, he and Alyra went back to his manor house. The servants and guards who had survived the attack welcomed them home with broad smiles. After sleeping like a dead man, he awoke in the early morning hours to feelings of emptiness. He wandered out to the terrace to think. If the queen could be believed, he could go back to Arnos or rejoin the crusade. With what he had learned over the past couple months, he could give his people a fighting chance.

But a chance to do what? Conquer these lands? Sack Erugash? And then what? People will die, a few rich men will become richer, and the Akeshians will have to rebuild. Is that what these powers were meant for?

In the past he might have turned to prayer when wrestling with a weighty problem, but the idea of going down on his knees right now seemed . . . wrong. Had the Almighty saved him from the sea and the wrath of the Akeshians, or had he saved himself? Was this magic a gift or a curse? And where did he really want to be? Who did he want to be with?

The bedroom door opened, and soft footsteps crossed the carpet. Alyra joined him with a covered tray in her hands. "Hungry?"

"Let's eat out here," he suggested.

Alyra brought out chairs and placed the tray on a table between them. The dish was a blend of eggs and goat cheese cooked into a funnel shape and stuffed with vegetables from the garden. Despite being hampered by an injured shoulder, Horace surprised himself by eating his half in three big bites, and then took a bit of her portion when she insisted.

"Do you want to talk about last night?" she asked.

"I feel a hundred years older this morning. I'm exhausted, but I can't sleep another wink. There's so much spinning around in my head."

"Like what?"

He looked over the city as he considered his words. "I had a dream that we left Mulcibar entombed down in those pits under the temple."

"You did what you could, Horace."

Did I? I brought down an entire temple on top of him. He was a good man, and now he's buried under a mountain of stone.

Alyra touched his hand. "Horace, Lord Mulcibar played a very dangerous game. He knew the risks, but he followed his conscience. You are not to blame for what happened. You didn't start this war, but you did as much as anyone could do to end it."

He didn't want to be mollified, but her words seeped into his mind, soothing away the sharp edges of his guilt.

"What else?" Alyra asked.

"What?"

"You said you had a lot of things on your mind. What else?"

"Well." He hesitated, not sure how to broach the subject that had plagued his mind since he woke up without her. He decided to plunge forward and take his lumps. "Us. You and I. Do we have a future together?"

"Is that what you want?"

"Yes. There's nothing for me back in Arnos. This is my home now. I'm still the queen's First Sword. A man with ambition could go far."

"Or end up in an early grave."

"A man might be willing to risk that, if he had the right woman by his side."

She blinked, looking back down at her lap. "Horace, I don't—"

"I lost my wife and son in a fire."

The words came out in a rush. Horace closed his eyes as the pain rose up inside him. He had to let it out. "Tines had been hit with the plague. Everyone was panicking. I got us passage out on a boat, but there was fighting and a fire broke out and I saw them die right in front of me. I saw them . . ."

A cool touch lifted his hands and pressed against the scars on his palms. "That's where you got these," she whispered.

He opened his eyes and found her watching him. Her eyebrows had come together in a frown as tears rolled down her cheeks. Horace wanted to pull her close and crush her against his chest. "I've been lost, Alyra. For so long. It's like I've been sailing across an ocean with no land in sight."

"I know how that feels. I was lost, too. Then I became an agent and things seemed to get better. But that fear never really went away. I can still feel it. Maybe we could . . ."

A soft knock rapped at the door. Before Horace could yell for them to go away, Alyra hurried to the door, wiping her eyes with the backs of her hands.

One of his guards, Gurita, stood in the doorway. "There is a message, my lord."

The guard held out a wooden tube, both ends capped with wax plugs. "It came by courier. No name was given."

Alyra brought the tube to Horace. He broke off one of the endcaps and slid out a rolled tube of papyrus. It was crisp as if freshly pressed. He glanced at Alyra as he unrolled it.

Horace's heart beat harder as he read the fine, precise script in Arnossi.

My friend Horace,

I hope you will permit me to think of you as a friend, for I have few these days and I think that you and I have much in common. We are both men out of our natural element, thrust into positions of power we never desired. You, I think, adapted better than I have. Certainly better than anyone expected.

This message will reach you sometime after my death or disappearance, and I'm afraid it contains few words of hope. By now you must have some sense of the troubled waters you are navigating. I fear that an old enemy has come prowling at the empire's gates. The queen will need your strength, for though she is a goddess in the flesh, she is not infallible—may the gods not punish an old man too harshly for writing such blasphemy.

But as your influence grows, so too will the list of powerful people who wish for your downfall. The ear of the queen comes with a high cost. Guard yourself always and learn whom you can trust. Be faithful and steadfast and never fear to tell her the truth. I will pray for your longevity and your success.

Your friend, Mulcibar Pharitoun et'Alulu

And forgive Lady Alyra. Despite her mixed loyalties, she has always been the very model of grace and constancy.

Alyra gasped as she read over his shoulder. "That . . . that . . . faker! All this time, he knew!"

Horace considered the message. If he was really staying in Erugash, then things were going to get more dangerous, not less.

Thank you for everything, old man. I wish we'd had more time together, and I hope you find contentment in whatever heaven your gods have made for you.

"So," he said. "You were saying something about the two of us."

"I was?"

Horace let out a deep breath, exhaling all his anxieties for the moment. "I'm just going to say this. You can stay here as long as you like, but I won't hold you back if you want to leave."

She smiled over the top of the papyrus. "I'd like that."

"Well, it's decided then."

"All right."

Horace went back out to the balcony and leaned against the railing, taking in the sights and smells of the city. It was his home now. Alyra came up beside him, and they looked out over the rooftops together, watching the shadows vanish as the sun rose higher in the bright Akeshian sky. Horace knew what he needed to do now. Taking a deep breath, he began.

"My father was a shipwright for the crown. After I graduated from the University at Altiva, I followed in his footsteps, working first at the company of Lagford and Sons, and later forming my own shipbuilding business. I met Sari and we married within a year, and Josef came along soon after that . . ."

She leaned on his shoulder and listened.

EPILOGUE

The glowing orb in the center of the ceiling flickered with a pale light, giving off just enough illumination to show the four walls of the small cell. He lay naked on a stone slab except for a breechclout, strapped down with *zoahadin* bands and unable to move. He reached for his *zoana* for the hundredth time since he'd awakened here—a little more than a day ago by his best reckoning—and felt nothing.

No, that wasn't completely true. Although he was cut off from his power, there was something above him, beyond in the ceiling. A raw, throbbing sensation that made his neck skin crawl like a hundred *zoanii* were embracing their power at the same time.

He tried to swallow, but his throat was too dry to form any moisture. He'd seen no one else since he woke up bound in this manner, but he anticipated that would soon change. If his captors had wanted him dead, he would already be so.

The creak of the cell's door announced a visitor. He craned his neck and fought to keep his expression from showing the cold ropes of dread uncoiling in his stomach.

"Greetings, Lord Mulcibar," the vizier said as he entered and closed the door behind him. Mulcibar got a glimpse of a rough stone corridor outside, but nothing else.

"Is the queen alive?" he asked. The rasp in his voice was almost a croak.

"Indeed, Her Majesty is in fine health, thanks to myself and your apprentice."

Apprentice? Does he mean Lord Horace?

"So the menarch's plot failed?"

"Was there ever any doubt?" Astaptah went to a metal shelf beside the head of the stone table and fiddled with something. "It is not yet time for the lovely Byleth to leave the throne. But don't fret."

Astaptah came over to the slab with a long, metal hose in his hand. It was segmented like an earthworm and flexible. Three steel prongs jutted from the open end. The vizier leaned over him. "I will keep the queen safe until it is her time to experience my creation in a more personal way."

"If you—!"

Mulcibar's words were cut off as Astaptah placed the pronged end of the hose against his forehead. A gurgling scream started in his chest and raced up to burst from his mouth. The pain was excruciating, as if the hose was sucking out his brain matter. No, not his brains. His *zoana*. He felt the power flowing out of him into the mouth of the hose. It was obscene. At the same time, the throbbing sensation from above grew stronger, so strong he couldn't believe it.

His eyes darted to Astaptah as another scream was wrung from his throat, but the vizier was leaving. "No! Come . . . back!"

Astaptah turned. "I have other clients to attend to, my lord. You are part of a glorious enterprise. One that will elevate a humble soul—" he placed a hand on his chest "—to such heights of power that even the gods will watch on with envy."

Mulcibar shouted as the vizier went out and closed the door behind him once again. His shouts went on for a long time before his voice gave out, but the machine never stopped.

HERE ENDS THE FIRST PART OF THE BOOK OF THE BLACK EARTH.

ACKNOWLEDGMENTS

As with any work of this size and scope, there are many people besides the author who made it happen. I would like to thank the following people: the staff of Pyr Books and Prometheus Books for all their hard work; Lou Anders, who continues to make dreams come true; Eddie Schneider for his friendship and his faith in me; Jeff, Fred, Channon, and Justin for their expertise; my family for their never-ending support; and all my readers, who inspire me on a daily basis. I am truly not worthy. Up the Irons!

ABOUT THE AUTHOR

Author photo by Jenny Sprunk

Jon Sprunk is the author of the Shadow Saga—*Shadow's Son*, *Shadow's Lure*, and *Shadow's Master*—which has been published in seven languages worldwide. An avid adventurer in his spare time, he lives in central Pennsylvania with his family. Visit him online at http://www.jonsprunk.com or at http://www.facebook.com/JonSprunkAuthor. Follow Jon's Twitter feed @jsprunk70.